THE DIFFERENCE
A DAY MAKES

THE DIFFERENCE A DAY MAKES

Barbara Longley

Montlake
Romance

Published by Montlake Romance
P.O. Box 400818
Las Vegas, NV 89140

ISBN-13: 9781611099379
ISBN-10: 1611099374

To all the storytellers who have touched my life,
may you never run out of words.

CHAPTER ONE

"HI, HONEY. I'M HOME." RYAN'S voice reverberated through the stillness, bounced off the bare walls, and came back to mock him. He set his lunchbox on the kitchen counter and leaned over to retrieve his supper from under the sink—a brand-new bottle of Johnnie Walker Red.

Gripping the bottle by the neck, he moved to the living room and set it on the coffee table next to his vintage .357 revolver, the letter he'd written to his folks, and the picture of his platoon— Task Force Iron, First Armored Division, Fourth Brigade. One more item, and he could begin his nightly ritual. He retrieved the snapshot of Theresa from his billfold, laid it down, and took his place on the couch.

Letter. Pictures. Gun. Bottle.

Theresa. Reaching out, he traced the laminated photo with his finger. His throat tightened. God, he missed her. How different his life would be if he hadn't insisted they go riding that morning five years ago. He'd be coming home every evening from some swank advertising agency job. They'd have a couple of kids by now. A family. His family. He'd be surrounded by love instead of this soul-sucking loneliness.

Ah, but he wasn't entirely alone, not if the hollow-eyed ghosts plaguing him counted. He closed his eyes, and images from the suicide bombing near Mosul played across his shattered mind.

"Jackson, radio ahead and have Staff Sergeant Reilly pick up the pace," Lieutenant Langford ordered. "If the civilian truck gets too close, we'll fire a few rounds into the ground to warn them off.

"You hear that, Gunny?" the lieutenant called to him over his shoulder.

"Yes, sir," Ryan shouted from his place in the artillery turret.

Yeah, he'd heard, all right. He should've aimed the M240B machine gun straight into the payload before the truck got anywhere near their platoon. If he had, the IEDs would've detonated in the desert instead of in the middle of their convoy. Five soldiers died. Soldiers whose backs he'd sworn to protect.

Familiar sensations gripped him. Sweat beaded his brow, and dread banded his chest until he couldn't draw breath. Powerless to stop it, he rode the wave of internal chaos, helpless to keep from being pulled under.

"Blow the suckers out of the sand! Shoot to kill. Shoot to kill," Lieutenant Langford shouted.

Ryan opened fire, sending a flurry of metal casings raining down on their Humvee. Too damned little too damned late. The truck detonated, plunging them into the fires of hell, turning the insurgents into pink mist.

Their Humvee lifted and flipped. Jettisoned out of the turret, Ryan flew through the air amid the flaming debris and superheated particles of sand. Bones snapped and cracked on impact. Fire burned through his uniform. He rolled in the sand to put it out and tried to curl in on himself to protect his head. Unimaginable pain assaulted every inch of his broken body.

Seconds passed. Pain-filled, life-altering seconds of mayhem followed by the moans and screams of the injured and dying. Choking on the smell of burning plastic and the acrid stench of singed hair and flesh—was it his?—he opened his eyes to survey the damage.

Bad decision.

His best buddy lay in pieces not three feet from him. The back of his skull had been blown away, along with most of his left side. Jackson's eyes were open, empty and lifeless—an expression of shock permanently etched on what remained of his face.

Ryan forced himself onto his side to vomit. Another mistake. Grit thrown by the desert wind peppered his raw, exposed burns. The edges of his vision darkened. The blackness spread, and the nightmare around him faded.

Pressing his fists into his eye sockets, he tried to dislodge the memories eroding his psyche. Jackson had a wife and kid to get home to. His best friend had not deserved to die like that. *No one* deserved to die like that. The familiar viselike guilt squeezed the air from his lungs, and rage roiled through him. *Why did I survive?*

He glanced at the table, drawn by the picture of his platoon. There he was, wearing his desert fatigues, all his gear, and a stupid grin. Jackson stood beside him, his arm slung around Ryan's shoulders. *He should've lived, not me.*

Sweaty and shaking, Ryan sucked in a breath through his clenched teeth, lifted the pistol, and checked to see that it still held a single bullet. He undid the safety and spun the chamber. Carefully, he set the gun back in its proper place and hoisted the bottle. Up till now he hadn't had the balls to end his miserable nonexistence. Not once had he even come close to pulling the trigger.

"Cheers." He unscrewed the cap, lifted the bottle in a toast to the fallen, to Theresa, and took a long pull. Leaning back on the couch, he stared at the ceiling. A few more drinks, and he'd do it. Tonight he'd end the pain once and for all. He took another drink and lifted the gun. The cold metallic weight promised instant, irrevocable relief.

The handle resting in his palm warmed. Taking another swig, Ryan savored the heat going down his throat and waited for J.W. to do his part. It didn't take long before the alcohol dulled the screaming in his brain to a manageable decibel. He brought the gun to his mouth—so close he could smell the tang of gun oil on steel. It took several long seconds before he managed to get his lips apart to place the barrel against his palate. It needed to be positioned just right, or with his luck, he'd live. Not acceptable.

Ryan took a deep, slow breath and held it. Ever so slowly, he cocked the hammer with his thumb and curled his finger around the trigger. He blinked against the tears running down his face. When had he started crying? Hell, this was a new twist. It had to mean something, right? *Yes.* An uncharacteristic calm and determination steadied his trembling hand. It meant tonight was the night he'd find peace at last. He put pressure on the trigger.

The wall-mounted phone next to the kitchenette started to ring.

Pulling the gun out of his mouth, he closed his eyes and willed the interruption away. His heart pounded, and his breathing came in short gasps that did little to fill his lungs. The phone kept ringing and ringing. He took another drink.

If it was his mom, he didn't want to talk to her—or his dad, brothers, or sister, for that matter. He hadn't had much contact with his family since Theresa's accident. The ringing stopped. Finally. But his momentum had been disturbed, and he had to start over. He reached for liquid courage. One, two, three swallows.

Once again, he brought the gun up to the roof of his mouth and wrapped his finger around the trigger. Closing his eyes, he tried to picture Theresa and started the slow pull toward oblivion.

The phone rang again.

"Son of a bitch!" Ryan slammed the gun down on the table and leaped up from the couch on unsteady legs. He was tempted to rip the thing off the wall, but when he reached for it, something inside, some spark of morbid curiosity, had him lifting the receiver instead. He never got calls. Bringing the handpiece to his ear, Ryan struggled to get his breathing under control. "Hello."

"Gunny Malloy? Is that you?"

Adrenaline surged through his bloodstream. The room began to spin, and he had to lean against the wall to stay upright. "Lieutenant Langford?" Ryan's eyes shot to the photo on his coffee table. *No fucking way.*

"Yeah. Yeah, it's me. You were a hard man to track down, buddy. I thought you moved back home to Oklahoma once we got out of the VA hospital."

"Naw, nothing for me there." He had to swallow hard a few times before trusting his voice to sound normal. "I...I need to..." His eyes darted around his apartment in a frantic search for something that would buy him time to pull himself together. "Can you hold on for just a minute? I have something on the stove."

"Sure, I'll hold."

Ryan placed the receiver on the counter and made some noise with his lunchbox. Why not? It was metal. He gripped the edge of the counter, closed his eyes tight, and leaned over. *You can do this, soldier. Front. Come across like everything is all right.* Isn't that what he did every day of his miserable life? He fronted at work and while shopping at the grocery store. He even pretended he wasn't *really* checking out all the rooftops in town for insurgents. Pretending had become his normal.

Ryan gritted his teeth, straightened, and picked up the phone. "Hey, Lieutenant, it's good to hear your voice." He ran a shaky hand through his too-long hair. "Where'd you end up, anyway? Last I heard, you were on a mission to find your stepbrother's kid. How'd that work out?"

Laughter filled Ryan's ear, and an unidentifiable emotion ricocheted through him. Jealousy? Hope?

No. Not hope.

"It worked out really well." Noah chuckled again. "I adopted my stepbrother's daughter and married her mother. We have a little boy now too, but I want to hear about you. What are you up to?"

"I'm back at the same place in Texas I worked before I enlisted."

"Cabinetmaking?"

"Yep, prefab." *Dead-end boring.* "I go by Ryan now. Gunny is…it reminds me of…"

"I understand. Listen, are you happy working for that cabinet place?"

"No, but I'm not *happy* in general." He swallowed hard. "Man, it's been a while, hasn't it, Lieutenant?" He had a white-knuckled grip on the phone, as if holding on that hard might save him somehow.

"Yeah…Yeah, it has…I don't go by Lieutenant anymore either. How about we start all over as a couple of civilians? Ryan for you. Noah for me."

"Deal." Ryan had to blink hard against the emotions swirling through him. Hearing the lieutenant's voice brought it all back—the good times, the bad, the worst. "Where're you living now? What are you up to? I know you never went back to Philly, because I tried to find you a year or so back."

"That's why I called. I live in Perfect, Indiana, not too far from Evansville. A couple of years ago, my wife's cousin and I started a custom furniture company. We sell mostly over the Internet. The business has been growing faster than we anticipated."

"OK. That's good, right?" Where was Noah going with this, and what did it have to do with him?

"We recently took over a building in town. It used to be a general store or something. There are two stories above the storefront. We have a showroom, production space, and offices."

"Sounds like you're doing great."

"We are, and we need help."

Ryan frowned. "Shouldn't be hard to come by in this economy."

"Probably not, but I have a new mission."

"Well, of course you do. You haven't changed much." Rusty laughter grated its way out of Ryan's throat. He remembered every time he'd heard those same words come from his commanding officer's mouth. Sometimes his missions involved getting his hands on some kind of hooch so they could all get plowed. "I'll bite. What's your new mission?"

"I'm only going to hire veterans."

"To do what?"

"Right now, I need someone with a graphic arts and design background, and preferably someone who has experience working with wood. I need help with the website, advertising, processing orders—that kind of stuff. Someone who can jump into production when needed would be nice. Naturally, you came to mind. I remember you saying you have a BFA or something to do with graphic design. I also remembered you worked as a cabinetmaker."

"MFA. I have a master's." Ryan rubbed his forehead and tried hard to wrap his head around where the conversation had taken them. "So...Let me get this straight. Are you offering me a job?"

"I am. We can't pay you a huge amount of money right now, but there's room to expand. You can make something out of this, Ryan. It's an opportunity to grow with Langford & Lovejoy Heritage Furniture."

Ryan's heart thundered so hard his ears rang, and his legs gave out. He slid down the wall until his ass hit the floor, and the phone cord stretched to its limit. "No shit?"

"No shit. You interested?"

"Hell yes." He hadn't done anything creative since Theresa died, hadn't even wanted to. Back then, he'd just wanted to blow things up, aim a gun at something and shoot away the pain eating away at him from the inside out. Did he even have it in him to be creative anymore? He didn't know.

"Like I said, we can't pay much. We've put most of our profit into this recent expansion. But my wife and I have a carriage house on our property. I can offer it to you dirt cheap. It's completely furnished."

"I don't care about the money. As long as I have a roof over my head, I'll be fine." Ryan ran his free hand over his beard. "It's been...It's been hell. At least working with you I'll be with someone who gets it...someone who was *there*." He harbored no illusions. It would be great to work with the lieutenant again, but it wouldn't make a difference. He'd strayed way too far into *unfixable* territory to expect miracles.

"Exactly. You get the mission. If we hire only vets, we can help each other through the tight spots. How soon can you start?"

"Give me a couple of weeks to settle things here."

"Great. You have an e-mail address? I'll send you the details and directions to Perfect."

He rattled off his information, and the lieutenant hung up. Still sitting on the floor, Ryan stretched his legs out and leaned his head back against the wall. He started to laugh, cry, and shake, all at once. One minute he'd been pulling the trigger, and the next he'd accepted a new job in a different state. The emotional shift left him weak and wobbly as a newborn foal.

It took about twenty minutes before any semblance of control returned to his limbs. Ryan pushed himself up to standing, put the phone's receiver back, and turned to face the coffee table.

Letter. Pictures. Gun. Bottle.

Curious, he moved toward the table and hefted the gun. What would've happened? Would he have hit an empty chamber, or...? He aimed the pistol at his couch and pulled the trigger. The single bullet exploded through the barrel, burning a black hole through the cushion. A tidal wave of shock slammed into his gut. The gun fell from his hand, thudding to the carpet a full two seconds before he lost his legs again and landed on his knees right next to the discharged .357.

"Damn."

❧   ❧   ❧

Paige hit the lock button on her Mini Cooper, lifted her briefcase strap over her shoulder, and headed into work with a wide smile on her face. Life was good. Her mind drifted back to the fantastic sex she'd had with Anthony the night before.

She really shouldn't be dating a coworker, and it was wise of Anthony to insist they keep it a secret. That way they could avoid any awkwardness at the office. Once she proved to her father that she could make it in a male-dominated industry, she'd leave Ramsey & Weil Construction Equipment and take over the family empire—Langford Plumbing Supplies. Then she and Anthony could go public with their relationship. A thrill tingled its way through her at the thought. *Maybe he's the one.*

Pulling her black wool coat tighter against the chilly March wind, she crossed the parking lot to the steps leading inside. The glass entry doors opened with a quiet rush of warm air, and the tap of her high-heeled leather boots echoed pleasantly through the granite-floored foyer.

"Good morning, George," she called out to the security officer manning the desk in front of the elevators. She slid her ID card across the sensor on the turnstile and walked through.

"Hey, Miss Langford. You're looking lovely today."

"Why, thank you." She beamed. Of course she looked lovely. How could she not, with the best of everything at her disposal? She'd been born lucky—born with her dad's brains and her mom's good looks.

Shifting her briefcase, Paige hit the up button and waited for the sleek stainless-steel elevator to come back to the first floor. Maybe she'd surprise Anthony today and have lunch delivered for both of them.

The elevator opened, and she pressed the button for the fifth floor while mentally going over the calls she'd have to make right away. The metal doors parted to a carpeted reception area with a wall-length desk paneled in mahogany. Paige headed to her mailbox to the right of the desk.

"Miss Langford, Mr. Weil wants to see you right away this morning," the receptionist informed her. "I'm to send you right up."

"OK. I'm on my way." Paige smiled at the young woman. Her boss probably wanted to congratulate her on the way she'd handled Meyer Construction's latest deal. She'd been pleased and gratified to be assigned one of Ramsey & Weil's largest accounts, especially considering she'd only been with the company a little over two months.

She checked her watch. Ten minutes early. Good. Better drop her things off in her office before heading to the boss's suite on the seventh floor. Sliding her coat off as she went, Paige walked down the hall to her tiny office. Tiny, yes, but she had a window.

Anthony's office at the end of the hall was windowless. It bothered him, but at least he had an office, unlike the assistant account reps, who worked in cheerless little cubicles. She hung her coat on the hook behind the door, dropped her briefcase under the desk, and locked her purse in the bottom drawer. Straightening her burgundy gabardine skirt and brushing off a few specks of lint from the jacket, she headed back out for her meeting with Mr. Weil.

His secretary glanced at her over the rims of her reading glasses. "Miss Langford, Mr. Weil is waiting for you."

"Thank you." Mrs. Hadley's expression was as dour as ever. Paige had heard she'd worked for Ramsey & Weil from the beginning. She had to be close to seventy. Throwing her shoulders back, Paige knocked on Mr. Weil's door.

"Come in," he barked from inside.

Smoothing her face into a professional mien, she opened the door and strode in. One look at his expression, and she faltered. He looked serious. Seriously unhappy. What the hell?

"Have a seat, Langford." He moved a pile of folders aside.

She took one of the chairs in front of his huge, imposing desk. "You wanted to see me?"

"Hmmm." He scowled her way. "Meyer Construction needed our bid five business days ago. They never got it. They've gone with another supplier."

An adrenaline shock hit her system, and her heart leaped to her throat. She gripped the arms of the chair. "That's impossible! I sent that bid with a same-day courier two days before it was due."

"Like I said—they never got it." He leaned back in his expensive leather chair and fixed her with a baleful scowl. "I've also had two other accounts you handled complain that their bids were late, holding them up and delaying their contractors. If it weren't for Anthony Rutger's intervention, we would've lost those accounts as well."

"Anthony's...intervention?" Her mind spun with the implications. *Anthony?*

Her mind flew back to the day the courier had come to the lobby for the Meyer bid. She'd been in the middle of a phone call, and Anthony had offered to take the envelope down to the lobby for her. At the time, she'd thought it was sweet. Come to think of it, he'd also offered to put a few of her bids into the office's outgoing mail bin for her. No, he wouldn't purposefully sabotage her. Would he? They were a couple.

Heat filled her face. "I'm sorry. It won't happen again."

"Damn straight it won't. You're fired."

"Oh, no. There's been a mistake. I had somebody else put the bids in the mail for me. They must've forgotten, or..." *Shit. Shit. Shit.* She glanced around the office as the reality of Anthony's betrayal sank in. "I won't let it happen again, Mr. Weil. I'll get the

Meyer account back somehow." She sucked in a breath. "From now on, I will personally put things in the out bin myself, and—"

"Miss Langford, you're done here."

The expression in his eyes was pitying, and she got it. Mr. Weil knew exactly what had happened, and ultimately, she was responsible. She'd been so naive, so trusting...*Oh my God! I've been sleeping with the enemy.* No wonder Anthony had insisted they keep their relationship a secret. Who would believe her if she claimed he was responsible for losing the Meyer account? Paige couldn't get enough air into her lungs. Black dots danced in front of her eyes. This couldn't be happening, not to her.

"Paige"—Mr. Weil's tone softened—"learn from this, and you'll know better next time."

She tried to swallow, but her mouth felt like the wool her expensive designer coat had been cut from. "Give me another chance. I can't be *fired,*" she croaked out. Harvard graduates don't get *fired.*

"It's already done. Security is here to escort you to your office. Take only your personal belongings." Mr. Weil stood up and moved to the door. He swung it open, and George the security guard waited for her in the hall. He wouldn't meet her eyes.

Humiliation. Shame. Mortification. A maelstrom of ugly emotions overtook her, and white-hot anger followed. *Anthony.* He'd done this to her. Why? She blinked away the sudden sting of tears. No time to deal with that now. She rose on shaky legs, lifted her chin, and walked out of the office without looking at Mr. Weil or George. Aware of the security guard's presence behind her, she made her way back to the elevator with as much dignity as possible. Was that a smug look on Mrs. Hadley's prune-like face? Paige lifted her chin a bit higher.

"I'm sorry about this, Miss Langford," George murmured once they were alone on the elevator.

"Thank you, George." She swiped at the single tear escaping down her cheek. "Do me a favor, would you?"

"Sure."

"If you ever get the chance, hawk a loogie into Anthony Rutger's coffee for me."

"What?" He gave her a confused look for a moment and then laughed. "That's the spirit. You'll come out of this all right."

Harvard grad fired from her first real job. She doubted she'd come out of it all right. With this on her record, who would hire her now? *Shit. Shit. Shit.* She wanted to stomp her feet and scream like a two-year-old. Her father had just been proved right. How had he put it? Oh, yeah. *"Plumbing and construction are still predominantly male. Paige is brilliant, but she's also naive and mostly fluff. She's led a sheltered, pampered life..."*

At the time she'd overheard those words, she'd tossed it off as another example of what a sexist he was, but now? Maybe she was nothing but fluff. Fluff with a very expensive, impressive degree. A degree that meant her daddy had deep pockets. Nothing more.

Somehow, they'd reached her office without running into anyone who mattered. George stood in the doorway while she emptied her briefcase of anything having to do with Ramsey & Weil. She tossed her things, including her purse, into her brand-new, butter-soft leather briefcase. It had been a present from her mom to celebrate her new job. She choked back the sob rising in her throat. How could she face her parents?

They'd spent a ton of money on her education, had supported and nurtured her all along. How could she tell them what a failure and a fool she'd turned out to be? She grabbed her coat from behind the door and followed George down the hall and onto

THE DIFFERENCE A DAY MAKES

the elevator to the front lobby. He took her ID card from her and stood by as the glass doors whooshed open once more.

"Bye, George. Thanks for being decent about this."

"You take care, Miss Langford. Something better is going to come along. Give it some time, and you'll see."

"Sure." *Not eff-ing likely.*

The worst part? Anthony's betrayal and the cold, cruel way he'd used her. It was all so calculated, so detestable and deceitful. What had she done to deserve that kind of abuse? What had she ever done to him? She'd been so flattered by his attention from the first day she started working with him. He'd literally swept her off her feet, and now she knew why. *Oh my God, what an idiot!* Not only had she handed him the means, she'd invited him into her bed while he destroyed her career.

Shame stole her breath. A short half hour ago she'd been thinking he was "the one." Nausea roiled through her, and a cold, clammy sheen of perspiration dampened her forehead. She covered her mouth with one hand and hurried to the sanctuary of her car. Once inside, she gripped the steering wheel and rested her forehead against the backs of her hands. Sucking air in through her nose, she let it out through her mouth until the nausea receded. She had to get out of here. She fished her keys out of her pocket, started her car, and sat up.

That's when she saw him. Anthony stood watching her from the top step of the front entrance with a nasty smirk on his face. He lifted a hand, saluted her, and turned to walk inside. She gave him the finger, not that it did any good. He didn't even see it. Paige pulled out of her parking spot and headed for her condo.

Once she was behind closed doors, safely inside her own space, the tears came. She dropped her things on the floor, including her coat, and moved to the living room to collapse on the sectional in a defeated heap. What was she going to do now? Unlike her stepbrother Noah, whose maternal grandparents had set up a trust fund for him, the deal she'd had with her parents was that they'd pay for her education, give her a great start debt-free, and the rest was up to her. A few months out of the chute, and she'd already screwed up royally.

Thank God the condo she lived in belonged to her mom. She paid rent, but not a lot, and she'd already paid for March. That gave her almost the entire month to figure something out. She'd have to keep paying, or her folks would know something was up. Good thing she had a little bit tucked away in savings. She also had credit cards. Those she'd use only for emergencies. Maybe she could ask one of her uncles for a loan—or a job.

No. Word would get back to her dad, and she didn't want that to happen. She had to find her own way out of this mess if she still wanted to convince him she was worthy of his trust when it came to LPS. Was that even a remote possibility anymore?

A fresh spate of tears tracked down her cheeks as another insidious thought wormed its way into her consciousness. How could she face her friends? All the brilliant people she knew were already climbing their chosen corporate ladders, leaving her in the dust—more like in the mud. The urge to run away and hole up somewhere overwhelmed her.

Noah. She could visit her brother. "Yes!" Her mind raced, and she sat up straight. She'd have a safe place to hide out until she could figure out the rest of her life, and nobody would have to know what had happened until she got back on her feet.

She swiped the tears from her cheeks. No use calling now, not like this, all weepy and stuffed up. Better get a grip first, or he'd hear the misery in her voice. She unzipped her boots, kicked them off, and rose from the couch. *Act like everything is normal.* She slipped out of her suit coat and let it drop to the couch before heading to the kitchen.

She leaned against the counter and stared out the balcony doors at the Philadelphia skyline. Could she manage to sneak away before news of her demise hit the grapevine? Anthony might put the word out himself to crow about the deed to his buddies. Her face grew hot, and anger stiffened her spine. She headed for her cell phone and hit speed dial. Noah answered on the third ring. "Hey, big brother. How're things in Perfect?"

"Good. Things are good. What's up, Paige?"

"I was wondering if I could come down for a visit. I have some time on my hands, and I want to see my favorite niece and nephew."

"Of course. You know you're always welcome, and we'd love to see you." He paused. "Are you sure you can take the time off? Didn't you just start that new job a couple of months ago?"

Her chest tightened, and she had to swallow a few times before she could speak. "I have the time, Noah." She bit her lip to keep from bursting into tears. "I wouldn't ask if I didn't."

"Come on down. We'd love to have you."

"I'm going to drive. I have a few things to wrap up here, and I'll leave tomorrow sometime. I'll see you when I get there. Don't wait up for me."

"Great. Looking forward to it." Someone in the background said something, and she heard Noah cover his cell to answer. "I gotta go. We'll talk when you get here."

"See you soon. Love you." Paige hit End Call and sank back down to the couch. At least she had somewhere to go while she licked her wounds and figured out the rest of her life. Funny. She was more pissed than heartbroken about Anthony. Proof that she knew nothing about life, love, or the pursuit of happiness.

🐏   🐏   🐏

Paige glanced at her dashboard clock as she turned into Ceejay and Noah's driveway. It was almost midnight, and she didn't want to wake them or their children. They'd given her a key to the carriage house when she'd come down for Toby's baptism, and she still had it. Noah wouldn't mind if she crashed there tonight. It would be far better than waking up the entire household at this hour.

She parked next to an old Chevy pickup—could it belong to Ceejay's cousin?—then grabbed her stuff and headed out back toward the carriage house. Praying their dog Sweet Pea wouldn't sense her presence and start barking, she tiptoed along the path from the gate to the door. All she had to go by was the scant light of the new moon.

So far, so good. Sweet Pea remained blissfully quiet. She dropped her bag on the concrete and rifled through the pockets of her purse for the key she'd stashed there. "Aha. Got you." She fumbled a few times in the darkness, trying to insert it into the lock. Finally, she got the key in the right way, turned it, reached for the knob, and pushed, just as light flooded the interior. The door was yanked from her grasp so suddenly she fell inside, right into a naked man—a naked man wielding a gun.

"Aaah!" She squealed and scrambled back to regain her footing, staring in shock at the wild man before her. Shaggy blond hair hung down to his shoulders, and an untrimmed, tangled mess of a beard hid most of his face. Panic-filled brilliant blue eyes were riveted on her with a haunted look that stole her breath.

"What the hell?" he stammered, dropping the hand holding the gun to his side. He snatched something from the inside wall and covered his interesting bits.

A cowboy hat? She blinked. He stood five or six inches taller than her five-foot-five frame, and there was nothing to him but wiry muscle and bone. He had a nasty scar that extended from his right hip all the way down the front of his leg almost to his knee. Plus, he was bare-assed-like-the-day-he-was-born naked. Her brother wouldn't allow anyone dangerous near his family, but still…She lifted her chin and looked down her nose at him, going for imperious. "Put that thing away."

"If you insist." He tossed the cowboy hat to the recliner.

"The *gun*!" She slapped a hand over her eyes. "I meant the gun."

"Well, that's not where you were looking."

CHAPTER TWO

THE LAST THING RYAN EXPECTED to find when he yanked that door open was the hot little number standing before him. She wore an expensive black leather jacket, snug jeans, and high-heeled leather boots—also high quality. Diamond stud earrings and a matching pendant twinkled at him in the fluorescent light.

Lord have mercy, she was a looker—tawny-blonde hair, perfect skin, curves everywhere, and the face of an angel. Her eyes had been all over his naked self a second ago. Now she was blushing like a virgin.

What did she expect? After the eye-raking perusal she'd subjected him to, how could he resist giving her an eyeful? Besides, he'd been half in the nightmare that woke him when he reached for the door. His brain still hadn't come completely up to speed.

"Hold on." He put his .357 on the coffee table, grabbed the jeans draped over the arm of the couch, and shoved his legs into them. "All right. I'm decent."

"Who are you, and what are you doing in Noah and Ceejay's carriage house?" She tipped her face up in challenge, keeping her gaze above his shoulders.

Ryan stared down into the lovely pair of green eyes glaring at him. Glaring? Wait just a doggone minute. *She* was the one breaking into his apartment, and now she had the nuts to look down her very fine nose at him? Ryan could see the judgment and the dismissal in her expression. She looked at him like he was some kind of crazy homeless guy.

Granted, that might have something to do with the smart-ass hat toss. Still, it bothered the thinking part of him, but the nonthinking part? If the instant hard-on he'd gotten was anything to go by, that part didn't give a frog's fart what she thought. It just wanted in.

"What the hell am *I* doing here?" Ryan's eyes narrowed. He'd play along with her obvious assumptions. Exaggerating his Oklahoma twang and donning his hillbilly hat, he let her have it with both barrels. "I think y'all have that question backward, darlin'. This here's my apartment. The question is, what are y'all doing with a key to my place?" He held out a hand for the key.

Her mouth tightened into a straight line, but she didn't give him the key. "I thought this was Langford & Lovejoy's office." Her lovely brow creased with confusion mixed with a touch of suspicion.

Ryan raised an eyebrow and performed his own down-the-nose look. "Not anymore, and even if it were, this ain't exactly what you'd call normal business hours, now is it?" He winked. "Please tell me you're Perfect's idea of a welcome-to-town gift, because I'm definitely in the mood to accept."

Her eyes threw embers hot enough to set him aflame. "Ass," she hissed.

"Hey, now. I see no reason to call names. You're the one breaking and entering here. Not me."

Barking started from up at the big house. The back door light came on, and the lovely little perp leaned over, picked up her suitcase, and gave him her back. Ryan grinned as she disappeared around the corner. He shut the door and paced around the living room.

The exchange had been exhilarating, and the buzz thrumming through his veins made him restless and edgy. He needed to do something. No way could he fall back to sleep now. Not that he wanted to anyway. He'd made the mistake of going to bed too close to sober, and the nightmares had begun almost the moment he'd closed his eyes.

Should he drink himself into passing out? Naw. He had a better idea. Ryan strode back to the bedroom and tugged his duffel bag out from under the bed. He unzipped it and fished around inside for the sketch pad and charcoal pencils he'd bought on a whim. Coming back to the living room, he tossed them on the coffee table, the only piece of furniture he'd brought with him from Texas, and headed for the kitchen to start a pot of coffee.

Settled on the couch with a steaming mug in his hands, Ryan conjured his midnight visitor's image. Her face, a perfect oval with wide-set green eyes, a fine straight nose, and full lips, had captivated him. And if that hadn't done it, her generous curves would've. Thinking about the way that leather jacket and tight jeans hugged her figure sent blood rushing to his groin again. And what about those high-heeled black leather boots? He groaned. How long had it been since he'd had sex? Too damn long.

He opened the sketchbook, traded the mug for a pencil, and tried to capture her snooty expression. Adorable. He smiled. What must she think of him? More than likely, she believed the Langfords had taken in a stray from the street.

He couldn't blame her. He'd stopped with the haircuts and shaving more than a year ago. What was the point? He didn't work for corporate America, and it wasn't likely that he would any time soon.

As her image took shape beneath his hand, he wondered who she might be. A friend of Ceejay's, maybe, or another Lovejoy cousin. Probably. There were hundreds of them. Hell, it didn't matter who she was. Life in Perfect had just gotten a whole lot more interesting.

❦   ❦   ❦

Showered and dressed for work, Ryan headed to the veranda to wait for Noah so they could ride in to work together. He reached the corner of the house and heard voices. Noah's daughter Lucinda and his midnight visitor. He stopped to listen.

"Be still, Luce, so I can tie your shoes."

"I can tie them by myself."

"I know you can, honey, but your hands are full with your backpack and lunchbox. I'll do it this time."

"Auntie Paige, you know what?"

"What?"

"We got Johnny Appleseed living in our backyard."

Paige. Her name soaked into him like summer rain after a long drought, and her throaty laugh ignited a slew of erotic thoughts. It took a few seconds for things to register. *Aw, shit. Noah's kid sister.* He wanted to kick something. She might as well have OFF-LIMITS tattooed across her chest. Never a good idea to get involved with the boss's sister. And even if Noah weren't his boss, he wouldn't want his sister mixed up with a screwed-up, going-nowhere head case like him.

"Why do you think Johnny Appleseed is living in your back-yard, Lucinda?"

"'Cause my teacher is reading his story to us, and he looks just like the man in the carriage house. Only, he wears shoes *here*, and in the book, he *doesn't*."

Ryan's jaw tightened at the sound of more of that sexy laugh of hers. Damn his bad luck.

"You know what else, Auntie Paige?"

"What else?"

Ryan could hear the smile in Paige's voice. He wanted to see her smile, even if she was off-limits.

"I can read the whole book all by myself. My teacher says I'm hyper-lex-ick."

Ryan lifted his cowboy hat, pushed his unruly hair into submission, and set the Stetson back on his head before walking around the corner. "You're hypercute is what you are." He grinned at Noah's six-year-old daughter. Sweet Pea, their mastiff-wolfhound mutt, sat on the top step doing his best gargoyle impression. "Hey there, tubba-ugly." He reached down with both hands and scratched the monster dog behind the ears. Sweet Pea's tail thumped away on the wooden slats.

"Sweet Pea's not ugly." Lucinda reached for her aunt's hand and gave it a tug. "See? Told you."

"You must be Noah's sister." Ryan straightened and tipped the brim of his hat. "I can see the resemblance now."

"And you must be Mr. Appleseed." She grinned. "Or are you Noah's newest ranch hand?" She raised an eyebrow and looked pointedly at his hat.

"Langford & Lovejoy employee," he corrected while his heart thumped away against his sternum. He tamped his unruly libido right back down to the pit of his stomach where it belonged. "Just plain old Ryan Malloy, I'm afraid. No relation to Johnny."

"This is my auntie Paige. She's going to wait for the school bus with me." Lucinda hopped down the steps. "Come on. Mrs. Hebert doesn't like it when I make her wait."

"Where's that little cowpoke brother of yours?" Ryan didn't want them to leave just yet. Maybe it wouldn't seem too weird if he walked with them down the driveway. Yeah. It would.

"Mommy's feeding Toby breakfast. He makes a big mess. That's what she says. I never made a mess when I was a baby."

"I'm sure you didn't, sweetheart." He couldn't help grinning. Lucinda was going to break a few hearts when she grew up. Sweet Pea ambled down the steps after the two as they walked down the gravel drive. Paige glanced back at him over her shoulder. The half smile she turned his way stole his breath. Ryan sat down on the top step. *Damn.* How long was she going to be in Perfect? Not long, he hoped. His poor heart couldn't take the hit.

The door behind him opened, and Noah came out with two thermal cups. "Coffee?" He handed one to Ryan.

"Sure. Thanks." He took it. "I just met your sister."

"I heard you met her last night." Noah shot him a wicked grin. "She said she saw a lot more of you than she wanted."

Heat crept up his neck. "No names were exchanged, and in my defense, she woke me out of a dead sleep. Freaked me out to hear someone messing with the door at midnight."

"My fault. I should've told her you were living in the carriage house before she arrived. I expected her to come to the house, not head straight for your place. I forgot we gave her a key." He walked down the steps. "She's coming into town with us today to tour the new facility and take a look at what we've got going on."

Ryan tried to swallow, but his mouth lacked the spit to get the job done. He pushed himself up from the stairs, and his gaze strayed down the gravel drive. "Great." There she was, walking that enticing walk, all curves and feminine sexiness. Time to cowboy up. He couldn't have her.

Besides, even if he could make a move on her, what did he have to offer? He was a broken man, barely functional. Heading in to work and heading home to the bottle were about all he could handle. The realization brought him low. He'd been reduced to self-medicating, careful to keep the drinking to a strictly night-time activity, and then it was only to shut out the voices and the dreams so he could get some rest.

"What's with the hat?"

"Huh?" He jerked back to the present. She stood looking up at him with an amused expression. Too close, but he wasn't going to be the one to back up.

"And the accent. Where are you from, anyway?"

"Southwestern Oklahoma. I grew up on a ranch."

She smirked. "You're not on a ranch now, cowboy."

"You don't like my hat? You don't have to wear it." He didn't like the sting her words caused. "There you go, looking down your nose again. You don't know anything about me, but I can sure tell a few things about you."

"I doubt that." She turned to her brother. "Are we taking the minivan?"

"No. Ryan's driving today. I can't leave Ceejay without a vehicle."

She regarded his beat-up Chevy with a frown. "Where's your pickup, Noah?"

"In town for service. I'll have it back later today."

Wonderful. His cab had no backseat. That meant Paige would be sitting in the middle between him and her brother. Ryan slid behind the wheel. Paige scooted over so her brother could climb in. Her thigh touched his, and her scent—soft, sweet, with a hint of musk—went straight to his head, sending all the blood from his brain to his lap. He leaned back to peer down at her. "I may be a hick in a cowboy hat, but I know a spoiled little rich girl when I see one."

She sucked in an audible breath and tensed.

He grinned. "Score one for the cowboy hat."

"Ass."

"Ass in a *Stetson*, ma'am." Ryan chuckled and started the truck.

"What's with you two?" Noah frowned at them.

"Nothing." Paige crossed her arms, screwed her face on tight, and stared straight ahead.

A twinge of guilt tugged at Ryan. He'd caught the flash of hurt in those pretty eyes before they turned to the double-barreled ember shooters he'd glimpsed last night. He'd hit a nerve, and it puzzled him.

If she truly were a spoiled little rich girl, she'd wear the badge proudly. He'd been around enough society types to know that much. Something was up with Noah's little sister, and Ryan wanted to know what that something was. Sure, it was none of his business, but he could use the distraction. Getting into her shit would sure beat wallowing in his own for a change.

He pulled around back to the parking spots behind Langford & Lovejoy and cut the engine.

"Ryan is designing a sign for us," Noah said as he climbed out and moved to the side so Paige could follow. "You'll have to take a look at what he's come up with so far."

She made a noncommittal noise and took off for the doors.

Ryan watched her go, climbed out of his truck, and turned back to wait for Noah. Once again, he was amazed at how well his friend got around with that state-of-the-art prosthetic. Noah had told him all about how it had been designed by a marathon runner who'd lost a leg in a car accident. They'd even gone jogging along the river together so Noah could demonstrate how the flexible carbon-fiber blade performed. Ryan hadn't lasted more than a mile. Noah had gone on for five.

He should have felt ashamed of how out of shape he'd gotten, but he'd let that go about the same time he stopped having haircuts. He didn't feel good. Why try to look good?

"What's going on with you two?"

"Huh?" Ryan's brow rose. "Between me and your sister?"

"Yep. I'm sensing some tension."

"She saw me naked, man. There's gonna be tension."

Noah laughed. "You have a point."

"How long is she going to be here, anyway?" He sounded like a whiny kid, and embarrassment burned his face. Good thing his facial hair hid it.

"She really got to you, huh?"

"Naw. Just startled the hell out of me, is all. I'll get over it." He shoved one hand into the front pocket of his jeans, gripped his thermal cup with the other, and headed for the loading dock. Ted must be at work already, because the double doors were propped open to let in the fresh air.

Noah followed. "Paige is good people. She can't help that she was born into the Langford fold. She's fought against the image of the spoiled little rich girl her entire life. Cut her some slack. Plus, she's whip-smart."

Ryan nodded. What else could he do? Being good people hadn't prevented her from looking down her nose at him. That bothered him. It shouldn't, but it did. He walked into their production area to find Ted giving Paige a bear hug greeting. She was all sweetness and happy smiles for the kid. That shouldn't bother him either, but it did.

Ryan made a beeline for his workbench, booted up his Mac, plopped onto his stool, and brought up the file for the sign. Later today he'd have to photograph a few of the new pieces Noah had created and post them on the website. He tried to lose himself in his work. Instead, all he could focus on was the conversation going on between Ted and Paige.

Sure, it was all about business, but he saw the way Ted looked at her. Another thing not to like. He blew out a long breath. He wasn't going to get much done with her around. Hyperawareness of her presence had exerted a magnetic pull, and he couldn't break free. Frustrated, he grabbed his thermal cup and gulped a mouthful of coffee.

"Hey, Paige," Noah called. "I want to give you the grand tour. This is production, obviously." He gestured to the table saws, jigsaws, lathes, and shelves full of a variety of tools, stains, varnish, acrylics, and scads of sandpaper and shop cloths.

She turned in a circle to take everything in. "The space is wonderful."

Ryan watched from the corner of his eye until the two disappeared into the freight elevator. Relieved, he let out the breath he'd been holding and turned back to his work, able to concentrate at last. If she stuck around, he'd move his computer to the third floor, even though he preferred to be here in the open space with the noise and the other men. Something about being with them calmed him.

He watched Ted go over a new cradle with fine-grade sandpaper. Cradles and nursery furniture were still Langford &

Lovejoy's primary focus, and he knew they'd been the beginning of their enterprise. They needed to branch out, and when he had the chance, he'd suggest it to Noah and Ted. Dining rooms, living rooms, bedrooms—they should be doing it all. He turned back to his computer, grabbed his earbuds, clicked on iTunes, and settled in for the morning.

"That's the sign?"

Ryan pulled out one of the earbuds. Paige stood right behind him, close enough to peer over his shoulder. He gulped. "So far."

"I like it." She tilted her head to take it in from another angle.

He tried to see it through her eyes: an oak oval with LANG-FORD & LOVEJOY curving along the top rounded edge and CUS-TOM-MADE HERITAGE FURNITURE straight across the center. The web url, street address, and phone number curved along the bottom. The larger letters he'd fashioned to resemble woodworking tools. The overall effect was old-fashioned and craft-oriented. "I wanted something that would fit in with Perfect's post–Civil War historic provenance, with an image conveying the company's commitment to quality artisanship."

One side of her mouth quirked up. "Provenance? Commitment to artisanship? Hmm, y'all talk real different at work."

"Come on, now. You know you deserved it, darlin'." He grinned back.

She chuckled. "I was as surprised as you were last night, maybe even more so. I'm sorry for barging into your place. I didn't know Ceejay and Noah had a tenant, or that they'd moved the business. Can we forget it ever happened?"

"Sure thing." Last night had been indelibly etched into his memory. Forget that first impact, her sweet body plastered up against his? Not gonna happen. "I plan to use the sign as the banner for our website."

"Oh. You're messing with my work?" She frowned. "I designed the website. Didn't Noah tell you?"

"He did, and it's great." He watched the frown disappear. "I'm sticking with a lot of what you did, but we need distinctive branding, since I&I, has been in business for a while now."

"Sure. That makes sense."

"Hey, come see the storefront," Noah called. "We have it set up so that if someone wants to come in to browse through the prototypes, they ring a doorbell. Then one of us has to act like a store clerk for a while."

"Usually me," Ted retorted, "since Noah and Ryan aren't real comfortable with strangers. After we photograph them, all the samples go into retail."

Paige laid her hand on Ryan's shoulder for an instant, and his lungs seized.

"I'm glad we're starting over, Mr. Appleseed." She patted him and followed Noah to the front.

Ryan struggled to get his lungs working again. Memories of Theresa's touch, her affection, swamped him. Guilt tore him apart. He shouldn't be attracted to another woman, shouldn't be flirting and teasing the way he had. Besides the fact that she was Noah's sister, she'd be better off not having anything to do with him. It was bound to end badly. Everything else had.

More coffee, that's what he needed. To be more specific, he wanted to look at Noah's sister some more. Not wise given the circumstances, but he couldn't help himself. Grabbing the coffee mug, he headed for the kitchen. *Damn.* He couldn't see her from around the bare brick wall separating the staff area from the showroom. He could hear them, though, and something about

Noah's tone had him honing in. He filled his cup and listened, all the while kicking himself in the ass. Since when had he turned into an eavesdropping freak?

"OK, Paige," Noah said. "What's going on?"

"What do you mean? Can't I spend a little time with family without there being something going on?"

"As driven as you are? I doubt it. Plus, how much time off could you have accumulated in two and a half months?"

"I'm just not sure if Ramsey & Weil is where I want to be. I needed to get away and give my future some serious thought."

Here there was a long pause, and he could imagine Noah giving his sister the commander stare. Nobody did that stare better than Lieutenant Langford. The pause went on, and he could practically see her squirming. Hell, it made him squirm, and Noah's stare wasn't even directed at him.

"All right, Noah. There was this guy—"

"Ah, now it all makes sense. You had your heart broken."

"Not really. Dented a little, maybe."

"I'm sorry, Paige, but that doesn't explain how you managed to get time off from work."

"I managed."

He could hear the hedge in her voice. No doubt Noah caught it too. She was hiding something, and Ryan wanted to know why, not to mention what. Something about Paige piqued his curiosity in a way that made him feel more alive than he had in…forever. He wasn't an idiot. Part of the allure was her being off-limits. That made her all the more irresistible. *Fight it, soldier. You don't want to mess up what you have here.* Noah's voice brought him back to the conversation.

Noah grunted. "How long do you plan to stay?"

"Not long. A week or two."

Their voices grew closer, and Ryan started to make noise like he'd just gotten there. He put the carafe back on the burner and opened a cabinet for powdered creamer so that his back was to them. "Hey"—he glanced over his shoulder—"what do you think of the showroom?"

"Very nice." Paige glanced at him.

Ryan didn't miss the rabbit-in-a-trap expression on her face. He wanted to put his arms around her and tell her it would all be all right—after he pried what was going on in her world out of her. So much for fighting *it*. Wait. If he managed to piss her off enough, he wouldn't have to fight the attraction. She'd stomp all over him with those fancy high-heeled leather boots of hers.

"I have to make a call about my truck. Do you want to stick around down here?" Noah asked.

"What's on the top floor?" she asked.

"It used to be the apartment where the family who owned the place lived. We have a couple of rooms set up for photos so the images we put on the website give customers an idea how our stuff might look in their homes." Noah nodded his way. "Ryan's brilliant idea."

"Do you mind if I poke around?"

"Be my guest."

The two of them veered off toward the elevator, and Ryan went back to work, mulling over the conversation he'd overheard. Spoiled Little Rich Girl had a secret. He should leave her alone, but he wasn't going to. Torn between curiosity, attraction, and self-preservation, he walked back to his workbench with fresh coffee he didn't want.

An hour slid by before Paige reappeared. She gravitated his way, dragged a stool over, and plopped down to watch him update the website. Occasionally, she'd make a suggestion or point out something. He understood her sense of ownership since she'd created the site, and he welcomed her suggestions. She knew her stuff—that much was clear.

"Paige, how about I take you to Jenny's diner for lunch?" Ted put his sandpaper down and stood up to stretch. "I know she and Harlen would love to see you."

"Oh, I'd love to see them too." She moved away from Ryan. "How is your aunt doing?"

"Still cancer-free, knock on wood." Ted rapped his knuckles against the workbench. "Let's go." He grabbed her leather jacket from the hook by the door and tossed it to her.

Ryan had to fight the urge to snatch her back to his side. The thought of Ted taking her anywhere didn't sit well. Something ugly coiled in his gut and sprang free before he could check himself. "Don't you think Paige is a bit out of your league, pup?"

"My *league*?" Ted glared. "I suppose you see yourself as being *in* her league? Man, you're not even on the same planet."

Probably true. No. Absolutely true. What planet was he on, anyway? "Maybe I'll join you for lunch." Ryan rose from his stool. "I could eat."

Ted moved closer to Paige. "I don't recall asking you to join us."

"And don't think I didn't notice that lapse in manners, kid."

Paige gasped and glared his way. "What is wrong with you?"

"Post-traumatic stress disorder. Irritability. Hostility. Aggression. All part of the package."

She'd moved to stand toe-to-toe with him. "That's no excuse. Noah has PTSD, and he doesn't act like a prick."

This close, there was no mistaking the anger he'd caused. He was no stranger to shame, but this was different. He'd acted like a jerk toward Ted for no good reason, and she'd called him on it. That laid him low. A painful lump formed in his throat. "Your brother is a far better man than I'll ever be." His voice came out a hoarse rasp, and her mouth formed an O. All the anger he'd glimpsed turned to pity. Damn, he didn't know which was worse.

"I don't have a *league*, Ryan," she replied softly. "And Ted is family."

"Trust me on this, darlin', the kid here is not looking at you like you're family. He's looking at you like—"

"Fuck you!" Ted snapped and guided Paige away from him toward the door.

"Exactly," Ryan muttered as he watched them leave. Bad move. Very bad move. He paced around the room and pulled at his beard. He'd look like a total idiot if he showed up at the diner now, but he couldn't bear the thought of Ted making a pass at her. Whatever brought Paige to Perfect, he'd seen the vulnerability. What red-blooded male wouldn't move in on that? "Not good. Not good at all."

"What's not good?" Noah stepped off the freight elevator and looked around. "Where did Ted and Paige go?"

"They went to Jenny's diner for lunch. You hungry?" If he showed up with Noah, he could pass it off as being the boss's idea. He wouldn't come across as such a schmuck. Noah studied him like he was some kind of new species of one-celled pond life he'd discovered under a microscope. Several seconds passed.

Noah smirked. "Sure, let's go eat. How about the truck stop outside of town? They have great burgers."

"I was thinking the diner might be nice."

"Of course you were." Noah barked a laugh, shook his head, and headed for the door. "You're in for it, buddy."

Don't I know it.

❦ ❦ ❦

Paige seethed. She hadn't been able to keep her eyes off Ryan Malloy all morning, and that ticked her off. She'd developed some kind of obsessive fascination with the hairy guy. Was it because his smart mouth didn't match up with the vulnerability she glimpsed in his gorgeous blue eyes? Maybe. Most likely, the attraction stemmed from the fact that she'd never met anyone like him before in her entire life. Not up close, anyway. That had to be it. Seeing him naked sure didn't help matters much. He certainly was well proportioned. Broad shoulders, narrow hips, his lean, muscled torso...the dark-blond chest hair leading her gaze farther south to his...*Stop it!*

She shook her head, disgusted with herself. No matter where she'd managed to hide out in the building, all she'd wanted to do was head straight for him. Had she learned nothing from her most recent disaster?

Stay away. Get your act together, and focus on your career.

Plus, he'd behaved like such a prick. Again. He'd been so sweet with Lucinda and Sweet Pea. He'd even been fun to talk to while they worked together. Normal one minute, primo-jerk the next, and intensely attractive in between—to her, anyway—which should have been a big clue to stay clear. "I wonder what he looks like under all that hair?" she murmured.

"What's that, Paige?" Ted asked.

"Um...nothing." Heat rose to her cheeks. "How's school coming along?"

"It's tough. Between work and school, I don't have much time for anything else." He flashed her a wry grin. "It's temporary, though. If I want to keep half ownership in the business, I have to finish."

"My brother is brilliant, and he wants the best for you. I hope you know that." She hooked her arm through his and turned her

- 3 6 -

face up to the sun's warmth. It had been chilly and overcast when she'd left home. Here, spring had already begun, and the temperature was a balmy seventy.

"Yeah. I know." He nudged her with his shoulder. "What about you? How's the new job?"

"Eh, I'm not real happy there. I'm trying to come up with a new plan." She looked away. Telling lies and half-truths all morning made her stomach hurt. She bit her lip and tried to come up with a way to turn the conversation in another direction. "What's with your newest employee?"

Ted let out a heavy sigh. "Ryan served under your brother in Iraq. I guess he was in the same Humvee as Noah when they got hit." His jaw tightened. "Noah has this new mission. He wants to save all the veterans he can, and I'm afraid all of them are going to end up working for L&L."

She frowned at him. "You see that as a bad thing?"

"Not in principle, no. It's a worthy cause. I'm just not happy about how he excluded me from the hiring process. I didn't have any input. I didn't even get to meet Ryan before he was hired, and I'm supposed to be a full partner." He glanced at her. "There are limits, or there should be. You saw how Ryan behaved. Noah says I have to put up with it until he's got the guy on the mend."

"Noah thinks it's his job to fix Ryan?"

Ted nodded. "He feels responsible for what happened in Iraq, so he also sees it as his job to make it right. He has this funny notion about Perfect holding some kind of healing magic for veterans."

Paige smiled. "I think he got that from your aunt, and anyway, Noah has always been like that. He's always been the one to step in to fix things for others." She shrugged. "You gotta admit, though. Despite the crazy, Ryan seems to have skills that lend themselves well to L&L."

"Yeah. Enough about him. Here we are." Ted opened the door to the diner and ushered her in.

Delicious smells, warmth, and welcome enveloped her the moment she was through the door.

"Oh my goodness! Will you look at who just walked through our door, Harlen?" Jenny headed straight for them, menus tucked under her arm.

Harlen smiled her way from behind the cash register. Paige couldn't help but notice how content the two of them looked. Jenny's hair had grown back to its usual length, with a lot more silver and a lot less blonde. Right now, it was busy trying to escape from the clip she wore at the crown of her head to hold it up. Lord, it was good to see her so healthy and happy. Jenny was one of the lucky ones. She'd survived breast cancer.

"It's wonderful to see you, Paige." Jenny threw an arm around her and gave her a squeeze.

Paige had the urge to put her head down on Jenny's shoulder and confess all of her troubles. Instead, she returned the hug and blinked away the sting in her eyes. "It's good to see you too."

"Come on. Have a seat. Do you two want a booth?" Jenny led them through the filled tables and the curious locals staring Paige's way.

"Sure, a booth would be good."

Ted placed his hand at the small of her back. She was startled by the touch, and Ryan's words echoed in her head. No, Ted was just being a gentleman, that's all. She slid into the side of the booth facing the door, and Ted sat across from her.

"What's the special today, Aunt Jenny?"

"You're in luck. Lasagna with a Caesar salad and garlic toast." She laid menus in front of them and fixed her speculative stare on Paige. "What brings you to Perfect?"

Paige studied the menu. "I needed a niece-and-nephew fix. I haven't seen them since Toby's baptism." She risked a glance upward. Jenny wasn't buying it—that much she could tell.

"Things happen for a reason." Jenny patted Paige's shoulder. "You're right where you're supposed to be. You have something to accomplish in Perfect."

She and Ted both watched her walk away.

Ted shook his head. "My aunt is a little bit freaky sometimes."

"No kidding." The front door opened, and her heart tumbled over itself. Ryan and Noah snaked their way toward them. Ryan got there first and scooted in beside her. Noah frowned and took the seat next to Ted. She knew her brother preferred to sit facing the door, preferably with his back against a wall. Did Ryan have to do the same?

"What're y'all having?" Ryan stretched his arm out across the back of their seat and threw a smug look Ted's way.

"Behave," she gritted out. Ryan's brilliant blues fixed on her, and heat spiraled right down to the tips of her polished toenails. This close, she could smell the laundry soap he used, mixed with his own unique masculine scent. Why the hell did he smell like temptation? She tried to move away.

He followed, leaned in, and whispered, "I'll behave if you will, darlin'."

Noah shook his head and chuckled low in his throat.

"You couldn't pick somewhere else to eat?" Ted muttered.

"And leave you alone with my girl?" Ryan raised an eyebrow. "I don't think so, kid."

"Your girl?" Paige sputtered. "I'm not—"

"Well, if it isn't Mr. Johnny Appleseed." Jenny placed four plastic glasses of ice water down in the middle of the Formica table, along with four straws.

"I see Lucinda got to you too." Ryan grinned. "How're you doing today, Mrs. Maurer?"

"I'm doing fine, and quit with the formality. Call me Jenny."

"Yes, ma'am."

She watched Jenny's glance touch on Ryan's arm across the back of the booth. His hand dangled dangerously close to touching her shoulder. Paige sighed audibly. "It's not what you think, Jenny."

"Why, sure it is." Ryan dropped his arm around her shoulders and tucked her up next to his side. "She's already seen me naked."

"It's true. I did. By accident, not by choice." She handed her menu over. "I'll have the special, and you'd better bring Ryan a double order of the same. There's nothing to the boy but skin and bone." Paige shoved at him. "Let me out. I have to use the restroom."

Ryan moved out of her way, a triumphant look on his face. "Hurry back, sweetheart."

"Oh, I will," she murmured and made her escape to the rear of the diner. Once behind the closed door, she let out a growl of frustration. He wanted to goad her into reacting—that much was clear. But why? She turned on the faucets and washed her hands. He had no idea how competitive she was. She wasn't about to let him get the best of her.

The door to the small two-stall restroom opened, and Paige's eyes widened. Had Jenny followed her? "Hey, did I mention how great you look?"

"Thanks. I feel good, and I couldn't be happier." Jenny smoothed her apron. "Don't let Ryan fool you, honey."

"Fool me?" She frowned.

"That young man is in a world of hurt."

"I get that. Noah was too, remember?"

"I sure do, but Noah dealt with it differently. He wanted desperately to connect with people again. Ryan is trying real hard to drive you away. He tries to drive everyone away."

Paige shook her head. "We don't even know each other, and I'm only going to be here for a couple of weeks. Why work so hard to annoy *me*?"

"You don't know?" Jenny chuckled. "Give it time, and it'll come to you. He's a good man. Try to see through all the bluster and the bull."

"If you say so." Paige reached for a paper towel. "I'd better get back out there before he has time to think up some new form of torture."

"That's the spirit." Jenny patted Paige's cheeks. "Don't let him push you away. None of us are going to let him do that anymore."

She watched Jenny leave, blew out a huff of air, and squared her shoulders. Yep. She could give as good as she got, and Ryan Malloy was about to have his ass handed to him on a diner plate—a freaking blue plate special.

CHAPTER THREE

Ryan slid out of the booth to let Paige back in, bracing himself for a look of loathing or another hissed expletive. It would hurt, but the brief pain was necessary. It never came. Instead, she scooted back into her place with a sexy sideways glance that stopped his poor heart.

"If your 'she saw me naked' remark was meant to embarrass me, Malloy, you gotta do better than that. You don't have anything I haven't seen before, and nothing stood out." She grinned. "Oh, wait. *Something* stood out."

Damn. Stunned again. Not good. Try harder. "Nothing but skin and bone, you said. I guess I'd better put on a few pounds." He rubbed his stomach and winked at her. "Don't want the little woman unhappy with the goods."

"Oh, I never said I was unhappy with…'the goods.'" Paige let her gaze roam all over him, meeting his eyes with a smoldering challenge in hers.

His faced burned. He tried to reply, but his brain refused to connect with his mouth. Did she mean she *liked* what she saw? Confusion clouded his ability to reason.

"Score one for the spoiled little rich girl." She canted her head and raised an eyebrow. "It's a tie. Give it up. You can't win."

"She's right. You can't." Noah shook his head. "Paige grew up with two older brothers, and we were brutal. You can't faze her."

Ryan blew out a breath and leaned back against the vinyl. He needed to regain his equilibrium, and Ted's fuming glare from across the table didn't help. He checked out, let his mind go. Unfortunately, all he could think about was how good it felt to have Paige's warmth and soft curves tucked up against him. He relived the smoldering once-over she'd just given him. What did it mean? Could this flutter in his chest be the small stirring of some kind of twisted hope? Naw. His jaw clenched, and reality tossed a bucket of ice water in his lap. She was just messing with him to get even.

"What kind of advertising have you done?" Paige asked as salads and a basket of fragrant garlic toast were set before them by a server.

"We haven't really done any advertising." Ted reached for a piece of toast. "Our website and social media are pretty much it. We can afford to do more; it's just that Noah and I are already stretched thin between production and admin stuff."

"While I'm here, can I do some marketing for you?" Paige stuck her fork into her salad. "You should get a few print ads out there. We can start with regional magazines. I'm sure a city Evansville's size has a local upscale spotlight magazine. Let's place a few ads, wait and see if sales rise, and then you can make a decision about whether or not to aim for the better-known national magazines."

"Absolutely." Noah nodded. "You can do the search and copy, and Ryan can put the graphics together. That's one of the reasons we hired him."

Whoa. They'd have to work together. She'd be close. Dangerous. On the other hand, he'd have the opportunity to ferret out her reasons for hiding away in Perfect. Plus, the thought of creating ads appealed to him. "Sure. A few ads would be great." He glanced at Paige and reached for garlic toast at the same time she did. Their hands touched. His pulse went off grid. *Fight it, soldier. She's not for you. Keep it professional.*

She was only going to be here for two weeks, tops. He could keep it together for fourteen days, and Noah would appreciate knowing what was going on with his sister. He caught Noah studying him again. Ryan cleared his throat. "You know, seeing as how Paige is only going to be here for such a short time, why don't I start driving myself into work? You two can have some brother-sister time in the morning."

"Sure." Noah's mouth twitched like he was trying not to smile. "If you think that'll help."

❦ ❦ ❦

Ryan sat on the couch with the sketchbook on his lap. A picture of Sweet Pea took shape beneath his hand. He'd head into Evansville soon for Cray-Pas and colored pencils. Once he added some pigment to the dog's portrait, he'd mat and frame it for Lucinda. Maybe he'd even sign it "Johnny Appleseed." He smiled. Yeah. That's what he'd do. Lucinda would like that.

Johnnie Walker stood on the coffee table, along with his pistol, the letter, and pictures—the ultimate way out, his macabre version of a security blanket. He didn't take a drink. Drawing required a steady hand, and J.W. would mess with his artistic muse. Ryan sighed, put the pencil down, and leaned his head back against the leather to stare at the ceiling.

Exhaustion tugged at his eyelids. Keeping up with Paige and their verbal sparring had taken a toll. Being anywhere in her proximity revved him up, and the effort to stay one step ahead of her razor wit took everything he had. Closing his eyes, he rubbed his face with both hands. A few minutes. A short break, and then he'd finish the sketch.

The distant rumble of thunder and a sudden rise in the wind were their only warnings. When they'd set out for the Antelope Hills, the day had been clear and sunny. The storm came out of nowhere, approaching fast, and Ryan's horse danced with tension beneath him. No big deal. He'd ridden through worse, but Theresa was inexperienced. "Turn around and take the lead. We're heading home, honey. Keep a light rein on the mare."

"All right." Her brow furrowed with worry, and she tensed up, making the mare even more skittish.

"I'm right here, babe. I won't let anything happen to you." Clouds rolled in, and the day took on a greenish cast. The ozone-tinged scent on the wind raised the fine hairs on his neck. The mare neighed and reared, and he caught a glimpse of the panic on Theresa's face. "Whoa. Let me get in front of you, Theresa."

Ryan urged his gelding forward to pass her just as lightning split the air, striking a ponderosa pine to the left of the trail. The tree split with a loud crack, followed by thunder loud enough to shake the ground.

Theresa's horse bolted. "Hold on!" he shouted as he kicked his horse into a gallop.

This was not the kind of trail to take at a run. Too many boulders and exposed roots, too many steep drops into rocky ravines. Keeping Theresa in his sights, he leaned forward and let his gelding eat up the distance between them. He had to catch her. She'd lost the reins and clung to the horse's mane, bending low over its neck. Another lightning bolt hit the ground somewhere ahead of the mare, and she went into a stiff four-legged stop, her haunches almost hitting the ground. Everything went into slow motion. Theresa lost her hold and somersaulted over the horse's head. Ryan watched in horror, helpless to do anything but try to get to her as she hit the boulders headfirst and tumbled over the edge. His heart seized. He leaped off his horse and scrambled down the rocky slope after her.

Ryan's head jerked up. God, he knew where that dream led, and he didn't want to go there. He reached for the whisky and took a long pull. His eyes burned. He and Theresa had been so happy. They'd just finalized their wedding plans and sent the invitations. They'd been excited about their future together and deeply in love. His throat constricted, and his chest ached. He took another drink and then another.

Theresa hadn't wanted to go riding that morning. He'd teased and cajoled her into it. *"You're marrying into a ranching family, darlin'. You're going to have to get used to being in the saddle. My family will expect our help with the spring roundup."* That's what he'd told her. Why the hell hadn't he just let her be?

Letter. Pictures. Gun. Bottle.

Ryan took another pull. He didn't deserve happiness. Hell, he didn't deserve to live. The ghosts came then. Starting with Jackson and followed by the other four soldiers who had made the ultimate sacrifice that day. Bloody, missing body parts, they circled him with their accusatory stares. Why hadn't he fired that round into the insurgent's payload? Why hadn't he let Theresa off the hook? It was all his fault. He lacked judgment. Hell, he didn't make decisions. He made mistakes. Mistakes that cost lives.

Eyeing the .357, Ryan took another drink and another. He drank until the hell he was in turned to a fuzzy haze. He drank

THE DIFFERENCE A DAY MAKES

until the faces of the dead were indiscernible and the bottle was empty. When had this night taken such a nasty turn? He glimpsed the sketch of Sweet Pea lying on the floor. He slipped down the couch onto his side and tucked himself into a fetal position. Grateful for the reprieve, Ryan let J.W. take him away to a place without dreams—to a place without memories.

❦ ❦ ❦

Paige sat in one of L&L's second-floor offices with her laptop opened to an employment site and clicked through the postings. She found a few that fit in with her plans and shot off a round of résumés. Her phone began to play her mother's ringtone. "Crap." She fished her cell out of her back pocket and considered the merits of letting it ring until her mom gave up and left a message. No. Better come up with something fast. "Hey, Mom. What's up?"

"I wondered if you're free for lunch today. I haven't seen or heard from you in almost a week."

"I can't." Paige's stomach flipped. "I'm out of town on business. I'll call as soon as I get home, and we'll do lunch and maybe some shopping."

Noah rounded the corner with a frown on his face, and her heart joined in with the flipping thing her stomach had started. "I gotta go, Mom. I'll call you later."

"Paige—"

She hit End Call—*Oh my God, I just hung up on my mother!*— and faced her brother.

"Out of town on business?" He scowled down at her. "Since when do you lie? Mom and Dad don't know you're here, do they?" He widened his stance, crossed his arms in front of him, and did his commander stare.

Man, she hated that.

"What's going on? What kind of 'business trip' is this?"

"I…I just need some time to figure a few things out," she stammered, closing her laptop so he couldn't see the employment site.

"Call Mom and Dad. At least let them know you're here, or I will."

"No! Don't call them. You took time off to figure out your life. Why can't I do the same without getting the first degree?" She lifted her chin. "I'm an adult, not a child."

"Because we love you, that's why. We're family. You can count on family."

Her throat tightened, and she had to blink back the sting in her eyes. "I know that, but you know how Dad is. I don't measure up."

"That's not true. He—"

"He thinks I'm fluff with my own designer pair of rose-tinted glasses." She blew out an exasperated breath. "I heard him tell you, so you can't act like it's not true."

"Paige—"

"Did Ryan ever show up? I've chosen a few magazines." She rose from her chair. "We need to get started on those ads."

"What's going on? What happened with that guy who 'dented' your heart?"

"I don't want to talk about it. If you don't want me here, just say so, and I'll leave." The tears started in earnest now. She swiped at her cheeks, hating her own lack of control when it came to anything emotional. *Fluff.* Noah wrapped her up in his arms, and she was five years old again, being comforted by her adored big brother. Her hero.

"All right. No more inquisition. You can stay here forever, as far as I'm concerned. You know that, right?"

She nodded against his shoulder and sniffed. "That's good to know."

"I think you're brilliant. So do Mom and Dad."

If you only knew..."Promise me you *won't* call them." She backed out of the hug and wiped the tears from her cheeks.

"On one condition." Noah ran his hand over the back of his skull. "Tell me what's going on."

"I will...eventually. Not now."

"You're not pregnant, are you?"

Now that really did bring her back from the brink. She choked out a laugh, grabbed her laptop, and passed him, heading for the hallway. "Let's get to work."

"Paige...You're not pregnant, are you?"

"No." She shook her head. "It's nothing like that. Let it go for now." They rode the freight elevator down to the first floor in silence. She could almost hear the hamster wheel squeak away in her brother's head as he tried to work it all out. Once she got over the shame and had a few interviews lined up, then she'd tell him the whole mortifying story of how she'd been played like a second grader's recorder.

Ted glanced at them over his shoulder as they left the lift. "You do realize Ryan hasn't made it in to work on time since the day you two stopped carpooling, right?"

True. Her first day had been Monday, and it was Thursday already. Ryan had come in late three days in a row, looking haggard. He hadn't had time to talk about the ads she wanted to do, and he'd worked late to make up for the missed time. Something ate at the guy, and it broke her heart to see him looking so troubled.

"I know." Noah sat on the stool in front of his workspace and started tracing a pattern onto a piece of wood. "I'll talk to him."

Ted shook his head and turned her way. "You interested in seeing a movie or something tomorrow night?"

"I can't. I promised Ceejay I'd babysit so she and my brother can have a date night," she replied. "That reminds me, Noah, I won't be in tomorrow. I also promised I'd watch Toby so Ceejay can run errands and get her hair done without dragging the little guy with her."

"Not a problem. Thanks for helping out." Noah smiled at her, then turned back to his task.

"How about I pick up a couple of pizzas and bring a few movies over?" Ted came to stand beside her. "One for the kids and one we can watch after they go to bed."

"That would be wonderful." She grinned. "Does Toby eat pizza yet?"

"Heck, yeah. He'll eat anything but peas." Noah grunted in amusement. "He hates peas."

"So do you, as I recall. Like father, like son." She laughed, relieved that the mood had lightened. Ryan walked through the door then, and all her attention shifted. His eyes were bloodshot, and he looked like he hadn't slept in…three days.

He glared back at the three faces turned to him. Paige's heart skipped a beat. Clearly the demons tormenting him were winning. She wanted to throw her arms around him and hold him tight until the light came back into his eyes.

"Let's go upstairs for a minute." Noah headed for the elevator and hit the up button.

"Sure." Ryan jammed his hands into the front pockets of his jeans and followed.

Paige watched them go. Her brother was a stickler for self-discipline and punctuality. Ryan was about to get an ear beating. She sighed. There was nothing she could do about it.

Turning to the small space she'd made for herself next to Ryan's workstation, she picked up the magazines she'd purchased at the grocery store. *Evansville Living* and *Evansville City View* were the perfect publications to test their ad campaign. Hopefully, the ads would bring customers to their showroom. If they discounted the samples, they'd make a sweet little profit. She opened her laptop, closed the employment search, and brought up the copy she'd been working on for their campaign. A list of possible hashtags she'd created came up.

What was Noah saying to Ryan right now? She couldn't imagine what kind of hell kept the cowboy up at night. Half an hour later, the two men exited the elevator. Both wore solemn expressions, and neither was talking. Ryan took his place without a word and booted up his computer.

"Are you all right?" she whispered.

He glanced at her out of the corner of his eyes. "Define *all right.*"

"Do you want to talk about it?"

"I just did. What do you think we were doing upstairs?" he snapped as he brought up a photo of one of their upstairs bedrooms decked out like a nursery. "Let's get to work. You got some idea what kind of typeface you want to use?"

"Jerk."

"I'm not familiar with that particular typeface." He raised an eyebrow. "Are you name-calling again, Spoiled Little Rich Girl?"

"I might be, Hick in a Stetson." She raised an eyebrow and made a show of looking over the shag carpeting he wore on his face. "Or should I say Sasquatch in a Cowboy Hat?" His attempt to squelch the grin that fought to break free fascinated her. Her heart warmed. "Make that Yeti in a Stetson."

"You know what this is, don't you, darlin'?"

Ryan turned those gorgeous eyes her way like they were lethal weapons aimed straight for her heart. She almost slipped right off her stool. "No. Why don't you tell me what *this* is?"

"Foreplay."

She gasped and fought the urge to pick up one of the magazines to fan her face. "Let's start with Book Antiqua and see how it looks." She swiveled her laptop his way. "I've come up with a list of possible log lines. Take a look while I go get a soda. Do you want anything?"

"Make that Chickenshit Spoiled Little Rich Girl."

"You wish, Malloy. Be afraid. Be very afraid." She adjusted her posture and strode away, purposefully swaying her hips a little more. Gratified, she took in the sound of his chuckle. The first she'd heard. She wanted more.

❦ ❦ ❦

Paige snatched a piece of the red pepper she was chopping for their salad and popped it into her mouth. "I love how you two remodeled this kitchen, Ceejay."

Her sister-in-law glanced around her with an expression of satisfaction, her gaze settling on Toby, who banged his sippy cup on the tray of his high chair. "Thanks. I love it too." She went back to chopping onions. "Are you going to tell me what's up? It's driving Noah crazy."

"I know." She shrugged while her heart raced. *Fired. Sleeping with the worm who sabotaged me.* Not really something she wanted to admit. "I just…I'm not ready."

"I love having you here." Ceejay moved closer and bumped her with a shoulder. "You know that, right? You can stay as long as you need to."

"Thanks. I love being here." Paige nudged back. "You have no idea how great it is to see Noah so happy, and…" Tears stung her eyes. Sheesh, her emotional pendulum was swinging out of control these days. Losing her job had yanked the rug of self-confidence right out from under her. She'd lost the steam propelling her toward her ultimate goal, and that loss had left her shaky inside. "I love Lucinda and Toby so much. You and Noah are such great parents."

"We try." Ceejay glanced at her. "Do you want a family?"

"I do. I really do." Where had that come from? When had she come to such a momentous decision? She wanted to take over the family empire. "Someday." She peered out the new patio doors Noah had put in where the kitchen's back door used to be. Her brother stood by the grill with an iced tea in his hand. "I think the grill is almost ready. We'd better make those burger patties."

"I'll make them. I want *you* to go to the carriage house and tell Ryan he's joining us for dinner."

Paige frowned. "Can't you just call him on his cell?"

"He doesn't have one—or a landline either."

"What?" She shook her head. "No phone at all? I can't even imagine."

"I know, huh? Noah says it's another way for Ryan to isolate."

"Sad." The image of Ryan's rare smile flashed into her mind, along with the way she'd managed to coax that smile out of him. Her heart ached. She wanted to pull him from the isolation he worked so hard to create for himself. It was almost as if he didn't believe he deserved to be happy.

Ceejay sighed. "Yeah, it is. Go get him, and don't take no for an answer. Jenny and Harlen will be here in about fifteen minutes, and the Offermeyers are staying too, since they're bringing

Lucinda home. Tell Ryan if he doesn't come up to the big house for dinner, we're going to have our gathering in his living room."

"All right. I'll do my best." Paige rinsed her hands, dried them on a kitchen towel, and took off her apron, draping it over a kitchen chair. "Wish me luck."

Ceejay gave her a thumbs-up, and Paige slid the patio door open. Sweet Pea sat by the grill, a hopeful expression on his big wrinkled face. She patted him on the head and grinned at her brother. "Ceejay sent me to fetch Ryan."

"If he gives you any trouble, tell him I'll come drag him out by the hair of his chinny-chin-chin."

"Read to the kids much?" She crossed the backyard and around the corner to the carriage house door. She knocked and stepped back. Nothing. She rapped louder. "Ryan, answer the door."

"What?" The door swung open. He glared down at her.

He wore nothing but a pair of cutoff sweatpants, and her eyes were immediately drawn to his bare chest. Not an ounce of fat on the guy, and the sparse, golden chest hair led her on a path straight down to the scar visible above the elastic waistband on his right hip. She stuffed her hands into her back pockets to keep from reaching out to trace that scar to wherever it might lead. "I'm supposed to bring you to the big house for grilled burgers."

"Not interested." He started to shut the door.

She jammed the door open with her foot. "Come anyway."

"No."

"Yes."

He huffed out a breath. "It's a one-syllable word, darlin'. Not too hard to understand if you try real hard. *No.*"

She could smell alcohol on his breath from where she stood. Not good. "This too has only one syllable. *Yes.*" She glared back.

"I'm to inform you that if you don't come to dinner, Ceejay is bringing the whole clan into your living room to eat here." She raised an eyebrow. "If that doesn't sway you, Noah says if you give me any trouble, he's going to come down here and drag you out by your beard."

He threw his head back and let out a growling sound. "What is it with you people? I just want to be left alone."

"No, you don't. Not really."

"What do you know about it?" His head snapped down. His brow furrowed, and his expression turned inward. "What do you know about anything?"

"It doesn't matter what you think I know or don't know. You're going to go put on a shirt and a real pair of pants, and then you're coming to share a meal with us." She flashed him her best haughty look. "And tomorrow you're going to get yourself a cell phone."

She could see she'd gotten to him. He fought hard, but the flicker of a smile broke free.

"Is that so, little girl?"

"It is. I'm going to help you pick it out." She gestured toward the interior of his apartment. "Go. Get dressed. I'll be right here waiting." She took her foot away from the door, expecting him to close it. Jenny was right. Ryan Malloy was in a world of pain. Isolating. Drinking alone. She swallowed the lump in her throat. Some instinct she didn't even know she had kicked in. She knew if Ryan didn't turn a corner soon, he'd be lost for good.

"I can't." His face, what she could see of it, had gone pale, and sweat covered his forehead. "Tell them I already ate."

"Ryan—"

"Please, Paige." His tone was desperate, and his jaw muscle twitched. "Not tonight. I promise to let you help me pick out a cell phone real soon, only…I…I just can't be around a bunch of people right now."

He shut the door, and she stared at it for several seconds, wondering what to do. Her mind flew back to when Noah first came home from the VA hospital. She'd seen her brother get shaky like that. It had been more than two years, though, and Noah had come so far. Why hadn't Ryan? She wanted to pound on his door until he let her in. Not just into his apartment, but into his head, and maybe even his heart.

Whoa! No, no, no. She had a promising career ahead of her. She had goals. Ryan brought out her nurturing instinct the same way an injured stray would. That was all.

Sure. Keep telling yourself that.

One thing for certain, she had to tell Noah. She made her way back to the patio, where he was dropping burgers and brats on the grill. "Ryan isn't doing too well. He won't come."

"Hmmm. Here, you take over, and I'll go talk to him."

"He's been drinking, Noah. He broke out into a sweat and got all shaky at the thought of being around people."

"Damn."

"Right. Damn." Something about Ryan got to her, made her want to drag him kicking and screaming back to the world of the living. "How come you've gotten so much better, and he hasn't?" She had to swallow the unexpected constriction in her throat.

"It's the isolation. You can't get better in a vacuum." Noah's brow lowered. "Let's let him be tonight, and I'll talk to him tomorrow."

❦ ❦ ❦

"Toby really does make a mess, doesn't he?" Paige picked up his cup off the kitchen floor for the fifth time and set it back on his high chair. He threw a banana-smooshed Cheerio at her, and it stuck in her hair. "Hey, little man." She sent him a mock frown, eliciting a giggle.

"He sure does." Ceejay wiped down the counter and grinned. "That's my boy." At his mom's words, Toby started to squirm.

"Mama, Mama, down." He slapped both hands into the mess he'd made on the tray.

"I guess he's done with breakfast. I'm going to let in Sweet Pea to pick up the rest of the cereal from the floor." Ceejay headed for her son with a washcloth in hand. She wiped him off, and then the tray. "Lucinda's school bus drops her off at three twenty. Would you mind meeting her at the end of the driveway? I know she can manage to walk by herself, but I worry."

"I don't mind at all. Me and the squirt here will have a nice little walk together." She tousled Toby's downy-soft hair. "Where are you and Noah heading this afternoon?"

A dreamy expression filled her sister-in-law's face, and a twinge of jealousy tugged at Paige, taking her by surprise. *What the hell?* What was going on with her, anyway? She was nothing but happy for Noah and Ceejay.

"We're having dinner where we had our first real date. We'll be at the Red Geranium, and we also reserved a room at the New Harmony Inn. Don't worry, though, we'll be home before the kids wake up tomorrow morning."

"Don't rush. Stay and have breakfast." Paige reached down and lifted Toby onto her lap. "We'll be fine. Won't we, Toby?" She clapped his chubby hands together and kissed his cheek. "Ted is bringing pizza and movies over tonight."

Ceejay's brow rose. "You know he has a crush on you, right?"

"He does not. He's more like a kid brother."

"Not to him. Ted doesn't look at you like a sister, believe me."

Paige's cell vibrated in her back pocket. She put Toby down to toddle around the kitchen and grabbed her phone. Noah's number showed on the screen. "Hey, what's up?"

"Ryan is a no-show again. Can you go wake him up and tell him to get his butt to work?"

She bit her lip. How much had Ryan drunk last night?

"Paige?" Noah said.

"Yeah, yeah. I'll get right on it." She stood, stuffing her phone back in her pocket, and headed for her purse, resting on the counter. "Can you stick around for a little while longer, Ceejay?" She fished the carriage house key out of her bag. "I have to go deal with a Ryan situation."

"Sure. I don't have to leave for another hour and a half." She lifted Toby to her hip. "Send Sweet Pea in for cleanup on your way out."

Paige nodded and let the dog in as she slipped out the back. Her heart was in her throat by the time she reached Ryan's door. Was he passed out, or had he overslept? She knocked, suspecting he wouldn't answer. He didn't. Knocking harder the second time, she waited. Nothing.

Sucking in a breath for courage, she put the key in the door and opened it as quietly as possible. The window blinds were closed, but she could see Ryan's inert form on the couch. She crossed to a window and opened the blinds. Morning light flooded the room. Turning slowly, she took it all in.

He lay on his side with an empty whisky bottle clutched to his bare chest. He didn't stir. The coffee table drew her attention. A folded piece of stationery, two pictures, and a gun had been laid out in a military-precision-straight row. She crept closer and looked down at the items. One of the pictures she'd seen before. Noah had the same one of Task Force Iron, the heavy-combat platoon under her brother's command. It had been taken right after their first deployment to Iraq.

She looked at the next picture, that of a very pretty young woman with wavy brown hair and dark-brown eyes. The photo had been laminated. Obvious signs of frequent handling curled the corners. Who was she? Someone who meant a lot to Ryan, that's who. Another one of those annoying pangs of jealousy gave her a pinch.

Paige reached for the folded paper, opened it, and started reading. She gasped and covered her mouth to stifle the cry already on its way out of her mouth. Hot tears of helplessness and rage filled her eyes. *Damn him.*

Folding up the letter, she returned it to the table and took a few steps back. She pulled her phone out of her back pocket, hit the camera icon, took careful aim so that everything would be clear, and snapped the picture. She sent the image to her brother and texted: *Ryan is suicidal. Come. Home. Now.*

She didn't know what to do with herself. Should she wake him? Leave? Stay? No. She should stay until her brother arrived. Best not to leave Ryan alone. She moved into the kitchen and started going through his cabinets until she found coffee. She fussed with the coffee machine and got a pot started. He'd be hungover. Coffee would be good.

Her insides twisted with turmoil as empathy warred with anger. Ryan was lucky he was still out, otherwise he'd be getting an earful right now. She wanted to smack him upside the head and hold him in her arms all at the same time, and she didn't know how to handle either feeling.

"What are you doing here?" Ryan rasped from his place on the couch. The whisky bottle thunked to the floor.

"I'm making coffee. What does it look like I'm doing?" She couldn't face him, couldn't face the haunted look in his eyes now that she knew what it meant. "Noah is on his way. You're late for work. Again."

"You coulda just woke me up, you know. You didn't have to call your brother."

"Oh, yeah, I did." She kept her back to him while the battle between her heart and head waged on. Pissed. Mostly, she was just pissed.

"Nobody asked you to come into my place."

His surly tone grated on her last nerve. She whipped around and stomped over to him. "Actually, your employer asked me to check on you. You remember him? The man who placed his faith in you? The man who gave you a job in the hopes that you'd make something of yourself?"

He averted his gaze, but she didn't miss the rapid bob of his Adam's apple or the brightness in his eyes. All her anger dissipated, and the vacuum left in its wake filled with heartbreak. What kind of pain did you have to be in to contemplate ending your own life?

Thank God she heard footsteps outside, because she had no idea what to do next. Noah walked into the room and surveyed everything, including the empty whisky bottle. He picked up the suicide letter, skimmed it, and faced Ryan with a grim expression.

Paige grabbed the gun from the coffee table and headed for the door. "I'll leave you two alone to talk."

"Hey, where do you think you're going with my gun?"

Without another word, Paige kept right on walking—all the way down the sloped lawn to the Ohio River. Standing still as stone on the bank, she watched the spring-swollen muddy water flow by while visions of Noah in the VA burn unit flashed through her mind.

The second- and third-degree burns blistering along her brother's left side, along with his gauze-wrapped stump, caused him so much agony. For months, he wouldn't talk to any of them unless he was lashing out in explosive anger. Her invincible brother had always been her hero. His withdrawal and uncharacteristic hostility had frightened her. Had he ever considered ending it all?

She stared at the gun in her hand, then brought her arm back and flung the revolver as far as she could, gratified to see she'd managed to get it all the way to the middle of the river. It landed with a plop and a splash and sank into the murky depths.

She'd only known Ryan for a handful of days, but she'd glimpsed the suffering in his eyes and heard the pain in his voice. He isolated and drank himself into a stupor every night. He saw ending his life as the only way out of the pain and despair he suffered, and that tore her apart.

Paige remained fixed to the spot, watching the river as her tears formed their own currents down her cheeks. How petty and selfish could she be? She'd lost a job. Big deal. Her situation hardly registered when compared to what Noah and Ryan faced every day of their lives. No more pity-party for her. For as long as she remained in Perfect, she'd do her best to see that Ryan didn't face his demons alone.

CHAPTER FOUR

RYAN'S FORMER LIEUTENANT RUBBED THE back of his skull
with the palm of his hand, which meant he was thinking things
through before he spoke. *Shit.* Ryan had seen him do the very
same thing countless times in Iraq, usually when he had a lecture
coming to him.

"I'm not an alcoholic." He swallowed hard. "I never drink
during the day, only at night. It's the only way I can get any rest."

Noah turned his commander stare on him. "How's that
working out for you?"

"It's not." Defeated, Ryan rested his elbows on his knees and
buried his face in his hands as his eyes filled. *Fuck. I've turned
into a blubbering idiot.* Wasn't it bad enough that Paige had seen
him passed out with an empty whisky bottle clutched to his
chest? Did he have to make it worse by crying in front of Noah?

Noah's weight shifted the cushions of the couch as he sat
down. "There's more to this than Iraq. Am I right?"

Ryan nodded, not trusting his voice.

"Do you want to tell me about it?"

Hell no. If Theresa's name passed through his lips, he'd break
down completely. He shook his head.

"Self-medicating only exacerbates our problems, Ryan. You know that."

Another nod was all he could manage. Holding it together took everything he had.

"Here's what's going to happen." Noah's voice was dead calm and his tone low. "I don't want my wife or my children to *ever* see someone they know and *care* about carried out of this apartment in a body bag. *I* don't want to see that. Which means you have some decisions to make."

Ryan forced himself to sit up. "I'm not going to off myself. Sometimes the pain gets to be too much, and I—"

"You're going to make an appointment to see a therapist at the Marion VA center in Evansville," Noah commanded. "That's not all. I get together with a group of veterans every Tuesday night. You want to keep this job, the drinking stops *now*. You're going to start coming with me to group, and you're going to see a therapist on a regular basis."

Noah placed his hand on Ryan's shoulder and gave it a squeeze. "I know about the pain and being haunted, believe me. I understand what you're going through, but I can't have this"—he gestured to the suicide letter and the empty whisky bottle on the floor—"anywhere near my family. I didn't bring you here just to lose you again." Noah's voice came out a hoarse rasp.

Ryan nodded, robbed of speech yet again. Paige was right. Noah had given him a chance to improve his life, and he'd almost squandered what he had. Worse, he'd broken Noah's trust—further proof that everything he touched turned to shit. "I'm sorry, man. I know I've let you down."

"No, you haven't. Not yet. You have the weekend to think things over. I expect your decision by Monday morning."

Ryan blew out a shaky breath. The decision was already made. No way did he want to lose the little scrap of sanity working with Noah provided for eight hours each day. It was the nights and weekends that twisted him. "All right."

"I'm going to tell you what my wife told me a few months after I landed here. To heal, you have to find your passion. You need something in your life that takes you out of yourself, out of your PTSD, and fills you up with something better."

"I don't know what that is." Tears filled Ryan's eyes again, and hopelessness opened its ugly maw to swallow him whole. "I've been lost for so damned long…I'm afraid I won't…that I can't…"

Noah's arms came around his shoulders. He gave him a fierce hug and let him go. "You will, and you can. You're not alone, bro. Now, get ready for work."

Ryan scrubbed at his face with both hands. "Paige isn't going to be there today, is she?" God, could he sound any more pathetic?

"No, she's not." Noah grunted. "You have enough on your plate without adding Paige to the mix. You need to focus on getting your own shit together right now. Let it go."

"Right." *Sucktacular.* Noah had seen right through him. Time to steer the subject in another direction. "There's something I've been wondering." He glanced at Noah. "Why did you call that second time?"

Noah's brow furrowed. "What do you mean?"

"The night you called me with the job offer. The phone rang. I didn't answer, and then it rang again a few minutes later. What made you decide to call back that second time?"

"I didn't. I only made the one call."

Ryan's skin prickled the way it did when his ghosts visited, leaving goose bumps in its wake. "Probably my folks."

"Huh. That's another thing. When's the last time you called your mom?"

"Damn, Noah." He scrubbed his face again.

"Had enough, eh?" Noah slapped Ryan's back and rose from the couch. "Call your folks. I'm sure they'd appreciate knowing where you are and that you're alive."

"Sure." *No way.* Ryan watched Noah cross the room to the door.

"I'll drive you to work from now on. Come up to the big house when you're ready." Noah walked outside and came right back in. "Paige is down by the river. I don't like the idea of my little sister with *your* .357 in her hands. Your gun. Your problem. You hear me?"

"Yes, sir. I'll take care of it." Ryan hurried to his bedroom, dropped his cutoff sweats, and pulled on jeans and a T-shirt while steeling himself for whatever flack he'd get from Paige. Once he was out the door, he caught sight of her. She had her back to him, and her arms were wrapped around her midsection as if she were in a world of hurt. Fragile. He'd done that. His poor heart sank to the hollow bottom of his gut.

Both her hands were visible, and neither one held his gun. At least she wouldn't shoot him. He came up beside her, jamming his hands into his pockets to keep from dragging her into his arms. "What did you do with my gun?"

She pointed to the middle of the river and made a jerky, breathy sound.

Was that a hiccup? Ryan turned to check her out. "Are you crying?"

"Of course I'm crying, you idiot." She took a swing, connecting with his biceps. "No more guns. No more suicide notes. No more suicidal thoughts. Or I'll shoot you myself." Another fist connected with his shoulder. "Do you hear me, Ryan? Never. Ever. Again."

"You don't understand." His chest twisted into a tight mess, and his damn eyes filled again.

"You're right. I don't. How could you *possibly* see suicide as an acceptable option?" She sniffed and swiped at her eyes. "I can't imagine the kind of pain you're in, but I have news for you. Suicide leaves everyone around you with a load of shit they don't deserve."

"Hey, now—"

"Are your parents still living?" She turned to face him, her expression full of anguish. "Can you imagine for a second what it would be like to lose a child that way?" She turned back to stare at the Ohio. "A good friend of mine from high school lost her father to suicide. I understand plenty."

"No, you don't." Her words salted the open wounds in his soul. "You might think you do, but you don't." Anger and frustration pulsed through him. Who did she think she was to talk to him like that? Then she did something so unexpected and amazing that all the anger left him in a whoosh—along with all the air in his lungs. She snaked her arms around his waist and held him, laying her cheek against his shoulder.

"You survived, Ryan," she whispered. "That's a gift. Instead of falling to your knees and thanking the powers that be, you want to put a bullet through your head?" She leaned her head back to look at him, and her eyes plumbed his with a depth that drew him under for the count.

"It's you who doesn't understand, cowboy. You're too close to the pain. Don't you see? You've lost all perspective and have no objectivity."

The subtle musky scent of her perfume wafted up around him, mixed with her own unique smell. He could get drunk on that alone. *Oh, Lord. I'm lost.* He tangled his fingers in her silken hair, tipped up her face, and let his mouth collide with hers like a heat-seeking missile. Wrapping his arms around her, he hung on for dear life. Miracle of miracles, she kissed him back.

His chest expanded until it couldn't contain any more of the mind-bending sensations spinning through him, making him dizzy. Hope. How long had it been since he'd opened up enough to get close to anyone, especially a woman? Fear and panic drove that fragile flicker away. Once Paige truly saw him for the wreck he was, she'd surely run the other way.

Desire stole his breath, and all thought momentarily left his head—until fear and panic kicked his ass again. *Shit.* Hope, fear, desire, panic, desire...hope. Warring emotions chased around inside him, until her tongue slid along his. Then his heart hammered away at the panic and the fear until the only thing left was the soft, warm miracle of having Paige in his arms. He struggled to keep his legs under him. Long before he was ready, she ended his brief foray into heaven and stepped out of his hold.

Scratching at her chin and cheeks, she blinked up at him. "That was like kissing my uncle's sheepdog."

Despite Noah's warning, he couldn't walk away, not from Paige. He raked a trembling hand through his hair. "Damn if you aren't the most confounding woman I've ever met."

"No doubt." A grin tugged at her luscious lips.

He wanted more. He wanted to get drunk on her taste, on the feel of her warmth against him. She'd give ol' J.W. a run for his money—that's for damn sure. Maybe having Paige in his arms would keep his nightmares at bay.

"What happened to Theresa?"

"Dammit, Paige!" His brow shot up. "You *read* my letter?"

"Yes, I did, and if I had it all to do over, I'd read it again." Her chin came up a defiant notch. "You mentioned she died, but you didn't say how. What happened?"

"Trust me"—he stared out at the river and growled low in his throat—"you don't want to know."

"Don't tell me what I want or don't want. I asked, and I think it would be good for you to talk about it."

"What, are you my shrink now?" All the good feelings he'd gleaned from their kiss disappeared. What right did she have to poke around in his shit? Wait. He wanted to poke around in hers, right? He glanced at her. "Quid pro quo."

"Huh?"

"I'll tell you everything if you do the same."

"What are you talking about?" She frowned. "I don't have anything to tell."

"Sure you don't." He tried his best to imitate Noah's commander stare. "What brought you to Perfect, little girl? You're hiding something, and I want to know what it is."

"Crap." Her face fell, and her shoulders slumped.

Ryan wanted to kiss the distress right out of her. Instead, he held his ground, feeling a little better now that he was off the hot seat.

"All right." She glanced at him through her lashes. "It's a deal. I'll show you mine if you show me yours."

"You've already seen *mine*, darlin'." He winked, and a glimmer of a smile curved her sexy lips. He liked that he had that effect on her.

"Not here, though." Paige glanced back toward the big house. "This stays between you and me. Agreed?"

"Agreed." What the hell could she possibly have to hide? "I've been meaning to take a trip into Evansville for some art supplies. How about coming with me? Let's go tomorrow after Noah and

Ceejay get home. We can grab some lunch and do some snooping around. I also have to stop by the VA center to make a couple of appointments. It won't take long."

"Now, see, if you had a phone, you could *call* and make those appointments." She gave him a pointed look. "We'll pick one out tomorrow."

He groaned. "If you insist." Her answering smile set off another chain reaction of hope, lust, and panic. Seeing a therapist sounded better and better every minute. He had no idea how to deal with everything this little spitfire stirred up inside him. Swallowing hard, he stiffened his spine against the onslaught. "I'll pick you up around eleven."

"I'll be ready."

"Vintage .357s like the one you chucked into the river don't come cheap. You owe me. You'll be the one buying my phone, little girl."

"Don't count on that, *little boy*." She turned away and started walking. "Go get ready for work. I'll see you tomorrow."

His gaze fixed on her curvaceous form as she sashayed toward the big house. Was she swaying those hips a bit more for his benefit? A grin broke free. *Hoh.* When was the last time he'd smiled just because? *Damn.* He had a date.

🐏 🐏 🐏

Toby was down for his nap. Finally. Who knew taking care of a fifteen-month-old would be so exhausting? Paige plopped onto the living room couch next to the baby monitor. She opened her laptop and brought up the job search site while her mind went back to the morning's drama. Ryan's kiss had shaken her world— not that she'd let him see it.

She couldn't help comparing. Anthony's kisses had never affected her the way Ryan's did. His touch, the way he held her so close, like he wanted their bodies to meld, sent orgasmic currents of heat sizzling through her, along with a yearning so deep she almost started tearing up again just thinking about it. Dang. She'd lost her breath—and a little bit of her heart.

Oh, man. Her heart.

Had she really agreed to spend the day with him, as in a date? Not a good idea. Maybe she could play it like it was nothing more than two friends hanging out. She needed to remain focused on her goals. Ryan Malloy didn't fit into her schemes, not to mention the fact that the man didn't just have baggage. He had his own designer set of luggage when it came to emotional issues, and she was not prepared to deal with them on any level other than as a friend helping out a friend.

Plus, she'd only be here for another week or so. If she could pretend that he didn't tug at every single tender part of her the way he did, everything would be fine. No reason she couldn't be here for him for another week. Then she could head home to Philly, go on interviews, and get her life back on track.

An opening for a John Deere account executive for the Pennsylvania, Maryland, and Delaware region caught her eye. Definitely a male-dominated industry. She read it through, tweaked her cover letter to match what they were looking for, and shot them a response. Moving on, she found a few other possibilities and sent three more résumés. How many did that make now? Eight. She had eight résumés out there. Surely she'd hear back from a few.

It might take weeks before anyone got back to her, though. They'd take résumés for a while; then HR would review the applicants. First interviews. Second interviews. Background checks.

She hadn't even listed Ramsey & Weil in her job history. What if something about her firing turned up in a background check? How would she deal with it? She cringed as the familiar burn of humiliation churned through her.

By the time she was done with her job search for the day, it was after three, and Toby hadn't made a peep. Taking the baby monitor from its jack, she rose from the couch and headed outside to meet Lucinda's bus.

The school bus pulled up just as she got to the highway. Lucinda hopped out, gripping a large piece of white construction paper.

"What do you have there?" Paige held out her hand.

"A picture of Johnny Appleseed." Lucinda gave her the picture.

As they walked back to the house, Paige studied the stick figure with its tangled yellow hair and equally wild beard. The resemblance to Ryan brought a smile to her face. A few apple trees made up the background, with fat, red apples scattered across the ground. "Wow, you really did a great job of capturing Johnny's likeness. Let's put this on the refrigerator."

"You know what, Auntie Paige?"

She smiled down at her niece, and a rush of love for the adorable little girl filled her. "What, honey?"

"If you marry Johnny Appleseed, you could stay with us forever."

Her heart tripped—partly from the fact that Lucinda wanted her to stay and partly from the images getting into bed with Ryan Malloy sent streaking through her imagination. She tucked the drawing under her arm and shifted the baby monitor so she could reach for Lucinda. "You want me to stay forever?"

Her niece clasped the offered hand and nodded. "You could live in the big house with us, and your husband can stay in the carriage house."

Paige chuckled. "Don't you think Johnny Appleseed might want to live with his wife in the same place?"

"I guess." Lucinda shrugged, as if the question didn't merit a great deal of consideration.

"Ted is bringing pizza and movies in a couple of hours. Do you want a snack to tide you over?"

"Mommy always gives me a 'nola bar or graham crackers and fruit." She looked up at her aunt with a hopeful expression. "Can I have ice cream instead?"

"I think we'd better stick with your routine." Toby's babbling burst from the monitor. "Let's go get your brother, and you can both have a snack while you tell me all about your day."

"Toby!" Lucinda hurried up the stairs to the front door. "Don't let him get hold of my picture." She turned to Paige as she opened the front door. "He'll tear it up. He's just a baby, and he doesn't know any better. That's what Daddy says."

"Your dad is a smart man."

"I know." Lucinda's head bobbed in agreement. "I have the best daddy in the world, and you know what, Auntie Paige?"

"No, what?" She set the monitor and picture down on the credenza next to the stairs.

"He picked *me* to be his daughter. My bi-logical daddy died, and my *real* daddy 'dopted me."

"I do know. Did you know that your biological dad was my half brother, and my mom is your biological grandmother? That makes me your aunt, and I don't even have to adopt you." They'd reached Toby's door by the time she and Lucinda had gone over the ties that bound them as a family. She opened the door to find Toby standing up against the railing of his crib. All his stuffed animals now littered the floor. He gave her a toothy grin and bounced up and down.

"Down. Down," he squealed.

"That's for sure, squirt." She picked up all the toys on her way to the crib and tossed them back in before lifting him. "Oooph. You're soaking and stinky, little man."

He patted her face and put his head on her shoulder. "Mamamamamama."

"I know, buddy. She'll be home tomorrow." She laid him down on the Langford & Lovejoy changing table to clean him up.

"Auntie Paige, if you marry Johnny Appleseed, he'll be my uncle."

"You certainly are relentless."

"What's *relentless*?" Lucinda's expression turned serious.

"You don't give up. That's the Langford part coming through."

"Oh." Another little girl shrug. "If you marry Johnny Appleseed, and he turns into my uncle, I could bring him to school for show-and-tell."

"Aha. The ulterior motive is revealed." She laughed. "I'll think about it." The memory of Ryan's kiss sent a thrill of anticipation traipsing through her. Right or wrong, she couldn't wait to spend the day with him tomorrow.

By the time she'd fed the two children their snack, played with them on the living room floor, bathed them, and wrestled them both into their jammies, she was exhausted. With Toby perched on her hip, the three of them made their way downstairs, with Sweet Pea taking up the rear, just as the front door opened.

"Pizza time," Ted announced as he walked in, holding two cardboard boxes with a pile of DVDs stacked on top.

"Pizza, pizza!" Lucinda jumped up and down. "What kind did you bring?"

"One cheese and one with everything on it." Ted handed her a few of the DVDs. "Here, Luce. Pick out a movie for you and Toby."

"Toby won't care. He's too little." She looked at each one carefully. "*Tangled*—that's the one I want to watch."

"*Tangled* it is." Ted smiled at Paige and nodded toward the boxes of pizza. "Do you want to eat these in front of the TV or in the kitchen?"

She snorted. "Have you ever seen Toby eat?"

"Good point. Kitchen it is."

She followed him into the kitchen and put a squirming Toby into his high chair. "I should've waited until after he ate to bathe him." She put a large bib around his neck and snapped it into place, giving the toddler a stern look. "No messes, little man. Understand?" He slapped the tray with both hands and bounced in his chair. She laughed. "One tiny piece at a time, then."

Ted put plates on the table and opened the boxes. The delicious, cheesy smell made her mouth water. "Lucinda, would you please get me a fork and a knife so I can cut this up for Toby?"

"I got it." Ted fetched silverware and napkins. "Where's his sippy cup? I'll get their milk."

"In the dishwasher. It's clean." She sent him a grateful look. "They can both have chocolate milk tonight."

Lucinda's eyes widened. "Did Mommy say we can?"

"She did." Paige tousled her niece's chestnut curls. "We're having a party."

"Why?"

"Don't look a gift horse in the mouth, Luce." Ted put a glass of chocolate milk in front of her, pulled a piece of cheese pizza from the box, and set it on her plate.

"I'm getting a gift horse?" Her face lit up. "I'm not ten yet. Mommy says I gotta be ten first."

"Uh, no. It's just an expression." Ted pulled another piece of cheese pizza from the box and placed it on the plate next to Paige. "That's for Toby. Do you want cheese or deluxe?"

"I want a piece of both. Thanks. You're really good at this kid stuff, Ted. Most guys would've sat down and helped themselves, leaving me to take care of everything."

"I'm not 'most guys.' When I have a family, I plan to be an equal partner in the child-rearing and housekeeping duties. Most women today have jobs. No reason why the work at home shouldn't be shared."

The intensity in his eyes as he looked at her made her vaguely uncomfortable. The way he'd placed his hand at the small of her back the other day came back to her, and Ceejay's words rang in her ears. Great. The last thing she wanted was for there to be any awkwardness between them. "Sit down and eat. We have movies to watch."

She turned her attention to cutting Toby's pizza into bite-size pieces. Should she say something? No. She was probably imagining things.

Dinner went by quickly, with Lucinda and Toby chattering away between mouthfuls, and she relaxed. Ted emptied the dishwasher and loaded it back up with their plates and glasses while she wiped the tomato sauce and cheese off Toby and got him out of the high chair.

"Who's ready for *Tangled*?" Ted rubbed his hands together and winked at Lucinda.

"I am." Lucinda snatched the DVDs from the counter and took off for the family room, which had once been a front parlor. Ceejay and Noah had turned it into a cozy space with a large

LCD TV and a sectional couch that formed a *U* around an over-size ottoman. A brick fireplace took up one wall, and the mantel held a ton of happy-faced family pictures.

Paige took some of Toby's toys out of the wooden box they kept in the room and set them on the rug next to the couch. Once his feet hit the floor, he toddled over to his toy box and started tossing the contents all over the room. She sighed. "You're high maintenance, Toby."

Ted laughed. "I have lots of nieces and nephews. He's pretty typical for a boy." He grabbed the remote, loaded the DVD, and hit play. "He'll wear out soon."

"I only hope I last as long as he does." She sighed and sank into the cushy sectional. "My respect for Ceejay and Noah has grown by leaps and bounds after today. I don't know how they do it."

Ted grinned. "They plan to have four."

"Auntie Paige, you know what?" Lucinda climbed up to settle in beside her.

"No—what, squirt?" Paige hugged her close.

"I'm always going to be the *oldest* sister."

"That you are." Paige caught Ted's look of amusement and returned it. The movie started, and she settled in to watch. Toby played happily in the middle of the mess he'd created, while Lucinda held a couple of Barbie dolls and watched the movie. Occasionally, she yawned, and soon the dolls were set aside and she leaned against her. Toby came over and placed his chubby hands on Paige's knees.

"Up, up." He rubbed an eye with a fist and yawned.

"Come here, you." Ted picked him up. Toby stuck two fingers in his mouth and laid his head on Ted's shoulder.

"You're a natural." Paige glanced at Toby as his eyes closed.

"I've done a lot of babysitting. I have older siblings who are married with children, not to mention all the cousins." Ted shrugged a shoulder. "I like kids. I want a few of my own someday."

"You're a rarity. Most guys your age are out partying and whooping it up. Having a family is the last thing a twenty-one-year-old guy thinks about." She shook her head.

"I'm not so young I don't know what I want." He shot her a heated stare.

Gah! Did she have no sense at all? Talking about family and kids with him was far too intimate. Sitting here with the children, watching a movie like they were a family? Huge mistake. She was going to have to set him straight—and soon.

"He's out." Ted put his arm around Toby and rose from the couch. "I'll take him upstairs and put him down."

"You want me to do it? He'll need changing first."

"Nope. I got it."

Paige played with Lucinda's curls and wondered how she could keep her friendship with Ted from dissolving into hurt feelings.

"Auntie Paige." Lucinda sighed.

"What, honey?"

"You gotta marry Johnny Appleseed."

She grinned and gazed down at her niece. "Why is that?"

Lucinda tucked her legs up on the couch and laid her head on Paige's shoulder. "'Cause he needs you."

"You've been talking to Jenny, haven't you?"

"No." She shook her head. "I heard Mommy and Daddy talking. Daddy says Ryan is sewer-sidle. What's that mean?"

"Hmmm. It means he's hurting inside." A lump rose to her throat, and she had to blink hard to keep the tears back. "You called him Ryan."

BARBARA LONGLEY

"Uh-huh. That's his *other* name. Daddy says he's going to make sure Ryan gets help." She snuggled closer. "You could help him feel better."

Paige glanced down at her niece. "What makes you think so?"

"I just know. Aunt Jenny says I'm like her. She knows things too."

If only it were that easy. "Come on, time for bed."

"Will you carry me piggyback style? Daddy always carries me that way."

"Sure. Hop on." Paige leaned forward, and Lucinda climbed onto her back.

"I miss Mommy and Daddy."

"They'll be home tomorrow." She started up the stairs. "We had fun tonight, didn't we?"

"Yep." Lucinda wrapped her arms tighter around her neck. "I love you."

"I love you too, squirt." Paige laid her on the bed. "Scoot up so I can get these blankets out from under you." She tucked her in and leaned down to give her a kiss on the forehead. "Sleep tight."

Lucinda nodded slightly as her eyes closed.

By the time she got back downstairs, Ted was already on the sectional with the DVDs in his hand.

He held them up. "What do you want to watch?"

Sinking down on the couch, she let out a long breath. "To tell you the truth, I'm beat. Taking care of little people is hard work. I might have to call it a night and take a rain check on the movie."

He slid his arm around her shoulders and drew her close. "How about I tuck you into bed?"

Adrenaline streaked through her veins, and she stiffened. She opened her mouth to reply, and he leaned in and planted his lips on hers. *Crap!* Placing her hands on his chest, she pushed him away. "What are you doing?"

"I'm trying to get something going here." He leaned in again. "You gotta know I'm attracted to you."

"Stop." Again, she pushed him back. "I don't have those kinds of feelings for you."

"Not yet."

"Not ever. You're like a younger brother to me."

"We'd be great together." He took her hands in his and shot her an earnest look. "Give me a chance to change your mind."

She shook her head and tugged her hands free. "I don't want things to become uncomfortable between us, and they will if we don't stop this now."

"All I'm asking for is a chance to change your mind." Ted's gaze bored into her. "This doesn't have anything to do with Ryan, does it? Tell me you're not attracted to that basket case."

"I don't owe you any explanation other than the one I've already given. I care for you. You're family. Let's leave it at that."

Shooting up from the couch, he gathered the DVDs and stared down at her, his expression wounded. "I'll let it go for now, but I intend to change your mind."

"Don't." She averted her gaze. *Damn.* This was exactly what she didn't want. Maybe it would be best for everyone if she headed back to Philly sooner rather than later. "We're family, and I hope we're friends." She glanced at him. "Let's not mess that up."

"Think about it, Paige. Don't say no to something that could be amazing just because we're shirttail relatives." He leaned down and kissed her forehead. "Give me a chance to change your mind. That's all I'm asking." He straightened. "Just a chance."

He headed for the front door without looking back. Groaning in frustration, she leaned her head back and closed her eyes. Not good. His infatuation with her would cause tension at Langford & Lovejoy, and more tension was something none of them needed.

CHAPTER FIVE

RYAN STARED AT HIS REFLECTION in the bathroom mirror and scratched his fingers through his beard. *Like kissing my uncle's sheepdog.* He grinned. No matter what, Paige couldn't deny kissing him back. With tongue. He wanted another shot, one where she didn't pull back so quickly. Eyeing the scissors and razor, and then the sink, he made up his mind and put the plug in the drain.

Excitement pulsed through him at the thought of spending the day with her. Thinking about it had helped him get through the night without J.W. Sure, he'd still had nightmares when he dozed off, but they were interspersed with erotic dreams of Paige naked, her limbs tangled with his, their mouths and bodies fused.

All the blood left his head and rushed to his groin. *Shit.* He'd better concentrate, or he'd slit his throat by accident. *Wouldn't that be ironic?* Forcing his thoughts away from naked Paige, he reached for the scissors and trimmed his beard, tossing the hair into the trash bin. He lathered, shaved, rinsed off, and studied the results.

Ah, yes. There they were—the burn scars circling his throat like phantom fingers. How would Paige react when she saw them? Would she be repulsed? His eyes riveted on the physical reminders of the hell he'd lived through, and the distant echo of that long-ago explosion reverberated through him. In an instant, he was flying through the desert heat with his uniform in flames. The smell of his own burning flesh came back to him in a rush— along with the crunch and snap of his bones shattering when he hit the ground. Remembered pain racked his body, and the cries and moans of his squad bounced around the inside of his skull. Jackson, with his face frozen in shock, stared at him through lifeless eyes.

Ryan braced himself and fought against the sensory assault dragging him back to that day. He gripped the edge of the porcelain sink and gulped air into his lungs. *Paige.* He had a date. Maybe even another chance at a kiss. *Focus.* He concentrated on new memories—the snooty way she'd looked down her nose at him that first night and the way she wrapped him up in her arms while they stood by the river. Latching on to those images, Ryan followed them like a trail of breadcrumbs leading the way out of hell. Sweat beaded his forehead, and he shook like he had the DTs.

Forcing himself to move, he placed one foot in front of the other until he was in the shower and turning on the water by rote. Hot water pounded over his head, and he closed his eyes, imagining Paige scolding him out of his flashback. His heartbeat gradually slowed, along with his breathing. The shakes washed down the drain with each exhale until he stood solid again.

A half-strangled laugh burst from him as he reached for the shampoo. What would Paige think if she knew her nagging ways had brought him out of flashback hell? Best to keep it to himself, or she might just get it into her head to boss him around 24/7.

Dried, shaved, and brushed, he stood in nothing but his boxers, contemplating his limited wardrobe. Might be time to do some shopping. Online. No way did he want to subject himself to a crowded mall. Even thinking about mall throngs made him shudder. Shaking off that thought, he grabbed his best pair of jeans from the heap and dug through the pile of clean clothes for a decent shirt. Garments in hand, he headed to the closet for the small ironing board and iron.

He ought to straighten up the place a bit. He glanced at the kitchen clock. Tomorrow. He only had half an hour before heading up to the big house. Another thrill raced along his nerves as he ironed the button-down shirt.

Noah had made it pretty clear Ryan should leave his sister alone until he got his shit together. Yeah. Not going to happen. Even though he knew he was setting himself up for more pain, staying away was not an option. She was his polar opposite, the positive to his negative charge. How could he fight a force of nature like that?

He dressed and moved to the living room to sit down on the couch. Flipping his sketchbook open, he studied the portrait he'd done the night she'd plastered her sweet curves all over him. Should he give her the portrait? The likeness was spot-on. Beautiful mixed with a tablespoon of snooty. Yep. She should have it.

Ryan rolled the sketch into a cylinder, grabbed his Stetson, and headed out the door. He climbed the veranda steps and knocked. Paige swung open the door, took one look at him, and gasped.

He deflated. "What? Is it the scars?"

"Huh?" Her eyes roamed over his face, stopping on his mouth and then roaming again, only to come back to his mouth. "You have scars?"

Heat swept through him. Her pupils were dilated, and it wasn't the burns she was looking at. "Yeah, here." He put his hand up to his bare neck. It felt odd to be without his camou-flage. Naked. Oh, man. That set off a slew of other thoughts of nakedness.

Her gaze touched on the spot he indicated, then slid over his face again. "To tell the truth, I didn't even notice."

He cleared his throat. "I brought you something." He handed her the sketch, and his eyes fixed on her face as she unrolled it. Another gasp escaped her. She studied the image and tipped her face up to his. He couldn't help basking in the warmth he glimpsed there. "It's from the night you burst into my apartment."

"This is how you see me?" Her voice came out a little husky.

"It's how I saw you that particular night. Do you like it?" He took his hat off so he'd have something to do with his hands.

"I love it. You made me look beautiful, Ryan. A tad…haughty, but in a good way."

She did that throaty chuckle thing, and the sound skimmed over him like her skin on his. His mouth went dry. More than anything, he wanted that skin-on-skin feeling for real.

"Stay here for a second." She grinned. "We have another resi-dent artist whose work you have to see."

She disappeared into the house, and he tried to tame his raging libido. He stepped over the threshold to wait. Sweet Pea ambled over to him for a scratch. "Hey, boy. Where is everybody?"

Paige came toward him, holding out a large piece of white construction paper. "They're all upstairs having a family reunion. I swear, the way the kids are carrying on, you'd think Ceejay and Noah had been gone for a month."

He took the picture and studied the stick figure. "Your work?" he teased.

"Ha, very funny. It's Lucinda's. She wants to bring you to school for show-and-tell, by the way."

He laughed. "She's going to be upset when she sees I've shaved."

"True, but I'm not." She reached out and ran her palm over his cheek. "I've been dying to see what you looked like under all that shag carpeting."

Her touch sent his heart rate off the charts again. *Damn.* Could he survive a whole day with her? "Hope you're not disappointed."

"Not by a long shot." Her voice came out smooth and thick, like red clover honey. She took the Johnny Appleseed artwork from him. "Let me put this back on the fridge, and we'll go."

Had he heard right? She liked the way he looked? He stood a little straighter and put his hat back on as she approached. She wore jeans, a snug pink T-shirt, and a denim jacket. Sexy. No matter what she wore, she made it all look sexy. She swept past him, and he caught a whiff of her scent, taking it deep into his lungs. Her keys in hand, she aimed for her car. He overtook her in a few strides. Putting his hands on her shoulders, he steered them toward his truck.

Paige dug in her heels. "I thought we'd take my car today."

"Why is that?"

"Yours looks like a roadside breakdown waiting to happen." She frowned. "That's why."

"My truck runs fine. I take good care of the engine. You don't have to worry."

"Yeah, but—"

"But what?" He scowled. "You expect me to fold myself into that Matchbox toy you call a car?" He nodded toward her Mini.

"You'll fit."

"It's all about appearances, right? My ol' truck has a little rust and a few dents, so you don't want to be caught dead in it.

Ain't that right, Spoiled Little Rich Girl?" He folded his arms and glowered at her. How did she do it? One minute he was following her with his tongue hanging out and his tail wagging. The next he wanted to give her a good swat on her sweet backside to dislodge the broomstick she rode. "Stuck-up much?"

"Maybe." She glared back with her fists on her hips. "Stubborn much?" She raised a single upper-class eyebrow at him.

He wanted to stomp and holler to get his way. Instead, he hauled her into his arms and planted his mouth on the stubborn straight line of hers. What started in frustration quickly transformed into pure-D lust. Tense at first, she caved and melted into him. Her lips opened under his, and he took advantage, deepening the kiss. Her palms skimmed over his jaw to his cheeks, coming up to knock the hat off his head so she could tangle her fingers into his hair.

He broke the contact and rasped, "We're going in my truck."

"Fine." She tugged on his hair until his mouth came back to hers and kissed the smug right out of him.

"Whoa, darlin'." The last thing he wanted to do was stop, but they were in Noah's driveway, and if they didn't slow down, he'd have her up against his pickup with her legs wrapped around his waist in no time. Better yet, he'd set her on the tailgate so he could stand between her thighs after he peeled those sexy jeans off, or…*Shit.* He held her at arm's length and almost dragged her back in when he caught a glimpse of the heat simmering in those lovely green eyes.

He'd put that sexed-up expression on her face, and that did things to him, like rearrange all his major internal organs. Especially his heart. He leaned over to pick up his hat off the ground and tried to adjust the crotch of his jeans to ease the tightness. "Let's get going while the going is good."

"Don't expect that tactic to work every time, cowboy."

"Why not?" He tucked a strand of her hair behind her ear and grinned, then groaned at the sight of Ted's Mustang pulling up the drive. The kid parked his classic next to Ryan's Chevy— his rusted-out, dented old Chevy.

"Hey." Ted spared him a cursory nod and turned to Paige. "I stopped by to see if you'd be interested in going to New Harmony today. There's a huge craft fair going on. Are you free?"

"No. She's not *free*." Ryan's jaw clenched, and his gut twisted. "We already have plans, pup."

Ted let out a huff of frustration and scowled. "You gotta be kidding me, Paige. You can't be going out with—"

"That's enough," Paige snapped. "We had this conversation last night, and I believe I made myself clear." She opened the door to the truck and climbed in.

"Yeah, and I made myself clear too. Like you said, we're family." Ted glared at Ryan and stuck out his chest. "No reason why we can't hang out together."

"Not gonna happen today, *Ted*." *Or ever.* Ryan's hands balled into fists, and adrenaline put him on battle-ready status. He sauntered closer, hoping the kid would get the message and back down.

"Jeez. All that testosterone must be *such* a burden." Paige slammed the door and cranked the window down. "Go ahead. Take your dicks out and compare them. I'll wait." Crossing her arms, she stared out toward the orchard and away from them. "I'm not going to watch, though. Size doesn't matter."

His tension dissipated, and he fought the urge to laugh. Noah was right; nothing fazed her. Ryan unbuckled his belt with a flourish, biting the inside of his cheek when he heard her utter a few choice expletives under her breath. He raised his brow and stared at Ted. "Let's see what you got, *kid*."

"Asshole."

"Yeah? I have one of them too. Wanna see?" Ryan unbuttoned his jeans and caught Paige peeking at him out of the corner of her eye.

Ted shook his head, climbed into his convertible, and peeled out in a spray of gravel. Fastening himself back up, Ryan worked his way around the hood of his truck and slid into the driver's seat. Paige sat stiff-necked beside him with an air of haughty superiority. Dang, she did that well.

Half the time he was with her, he didn't know if he was coming or going, and he liked that. She gave him something to think about other than the usual shit hammering away at his sanity. "Are you going to be mad at me all day?"

"Why do you bait Ted the way you do?"

He shrugged and started the truck. Had she not heard the implied put-down he'd just received? Was he supposed to take Ted's insults lying down? *I don't think so.*

"Really. I want to know what it is about him that brings out the worst in you."

"You think *that* was the worst?" He glanced her. "Not even close," he murmured. She stared at him with that one eyebrow still raised. Ryan kept his eyes on the gravel driveway and turned his truck onto the highway toward Evansville. Noah had nothing on his little sister when it came to commander stare-downs. The silent stare rattled his nerves, and he blew out an exasperated breath in surrender.

"Don't you think I'm aware every single day that Ted doesn't want me at L&L? His resentment toward me is palpable." He snorted. "The weird thing is, I have a lot of respect for the kid. He's got an outstanding work ethic, does a fantastic job, and despite the fact that he annoys the shit out of me, I like it when the three of us are in the same space and working together. Being at L&L calms me. It's…" He shook his head and concentrated on the road.

"My brother didn't include him in the hiring process. Ted is supposed to be a full partner. Plus, he's the primary business administrator. He's frustrated, that's all. It's not you he resents."

"Really? 'Cause it sure feels like that vibe is aimed my way." Again sounding like an eight-year-old—a whiny eight-year-old. He glanced at her again to gauge her reaction. She was still staring. "Would it make you happy if I made more of an effort to get along?"

The smile she graced him with stole his breath, and when she slid a little closer to him on the seat, he remembered why it was so important they take his truck. Mini Coopers had bucket seats. "So I gather you and Ted were together last night." Petty, but he couldn't help himself. He was jealous, plain and simple. "I thought you were babysitting for Ceejay and Noah." Damn, if that smile, with all of its warmth, didn't disappear from her face. *It's official. I'm an idiot.*

"That's not really your business."

"He made a move on you." His grip tightened on the steering wheel. "I got that much from the conversation."

"Still not your business."

Based on the interaction he'd witnessed, she'd turned Ted down, so he let it go. "What do you want to do first—eat or talk?"

Her brow furrowed. "We can't do both at the same time?"

"Nope. I'm not spilling my guts in some restaurant full of unfamiliars."

"Oh." Her expression turned pensive. "We could get takeout and find a place where we can talk while we eat."

"There's a park on the Ohio River by the levee." He warmed to the idea. "I think I have an old blanket in the tool chest in back. We can have a picnic." Steering the truck onto the exit toward Evansville, he processed the fact that he was happy. Paige did that for him, even when she bullied him into being a better man. Too bad she'd only be around for another week. *Damn.* He was in trouble, because it was going to sting like a bitch when she left.

🐏　🐏　🐏

Paige hadn't been able to take her eyes off Ryan since she opened the door for him. Lord, he was one good-looking cowboy. His eyes had been devastating enough; the rest of the package did her in. When he smiled, one side of his mouth curved down slightly, while the other quirked up. The overall effect was entirely too sexy and kissable to resist. Plus, he had that double-dimple thing going for him. One set bracketed that adorable crooked mouth, and the other indented his upper cheeks. Even his long hair turned her on. He wore it neatly brushed and tied back today. Along with the Stetson, jeans, and boots, it made him look like he'd walked straight off the set of an old western movie. Hot. She was having a difficult time keeping her hands to herself. Hadn't she sworn to be only a friend?

Hmmm. Maybe friends with benefits? No. Not a good idea. She wouldn't be able to keep her heart out of it, and it wouldn't be fair to him. She turned to watch the passing scenery. It took about two minutes before she couldn't resist the pull he exerted over her and turned back to stare some more.

"You have something on your mind, darlin'?"

She managed to tear her gaze from him. "I have lots of things on my mind. Why?"

"You keep looking at me like that, and I'm going to have to pull over somewhere and kiss you again."

"Kissing is your one-size-fits-all solution to everything now? Maybe it's time to shop for a new bag of tricks." She made the mistake of looking back just in time to catch one of his dimpled, lopsided grins. Her heart ratcheted up a notch, and her mouth went dry.

Her phone started chirping her mother's ringtone. *Crap.* She didn't want to lie today. It was too nice out, and all she wanted to do was enjoy the day. She fished her cell out of her purse and hit Ignore. Maybe she'd get lucky and her mom would leave a message instead of calling back.

Ryan sent her a sideways look. "Who don't you want to talk to, Paige?"

"That was my mom." She squirmed under the intensity of his blue-eyed scrutiny. "I thought we were going to get our lunch before we launched into my petty problems."

Ryan shrugged a shoulder. "I can wait."

Good. She turned to face the approaching city, and a billboard caught her attention. "Hey, look at that." She pointed. "The World's Toughest Rodeo is going to be in Evansville next weekend." She grinned at Ryan. "I've never been. You grew up on a ranch, right? Did you go to lots of rodeos?"

"You're looking at a junior saddle bronc champion three years running." He tipped his hat at her. "My uncle and cousins will probably be there. They raise rodeo bulls. In fact, six out of the past ten years, the Malloys have been named Stock Contractor of the Year."

"Cool. Let's get tickets. I'd love to see a rodeo, and you can visit with your uncle and cousins."

Ryan glanced at the billboard they were about to pass. His expression turned inscrutable. "Aren't you leaving next weekend?"

She averted her face so he couldn't see how the reminder affected her. What did she have to go home to? Facing her parents and friends with no job? "I can leave on Sunday. That leaves Friday or Saturday for the rodeo."

"I haven't seen any of my family since I left the VA hospital," he murmured. "I don't know if it's such a good idea right now."

"What? Oh, Ryan." Thoughts of his suicide letter brought a lump to her throat. How long had he been estranged from his family? "Don't you think they'd appreciate knowing where you are, and—"

"You don't understand," he snapped.

"Help me to understand, then." She put her hand on his shoulder, reveling in the hard muscle under her palm. He didn't answer, and she took her hand away and surveyed the approaching city as they entered the outskirts of Evansville. "There's a deli in that strip mall to the right. Let's stop and pick up some food."

His jaw muscle twitched and his expression kept its closed-for-business look as he turned into the lot and parked. He reached into his back pocket for his wallet and took out some cash. "Would you mind doing this part? Get me whatever you're having. I'm not picky." He handed her some cash, and his Adam's apple moved up and down. He'd gone pale, and a fine sheen of perspiration covered his forehead.

"Are you OK?" Paige ran her hand over his shoulder again. He covered it with his and squeezed.

"I will be."

He glanced at her, and she caught the panic in his eyes.

"Go on, now. I'm hungry."

She didn't want to leave him until whatever he was going through passed. "Ryan—"

"I'll be fine," he gritted out.

"Sure you will." She could apply some of that one-size-fits-all strategy too. She scooted over, cupped his face with both hands, and kissed him. The sudden intake of his breath and the instinctive pull back only firmed her determination. She ran her tongue over the tight seam of his mouth until he groaned and opened for her. He took over in a big hurry. Wrapping his arms around her, he drew her close. Relief and a whole lot of heat sluiced through her.

She broke the kiss to nuzzle along his neck to his ear. He smelled so damn good. She inhaled, with her face planted in the sweet spot just beneath his ear. Too bad that scent couldn't be bottled. She'd take a whiff a few times a day at least. "Better?"

The low chuckle coming from him caused a butterfly riot in her middle—and lower.

"Yeah, I guess you could say I'm *better*." He stroked her hair. "I could get addicted to your kisses, Paige."

That last part came out almost a whisper, his tone hesitant, vulnerable. Her heart wrapped around his words and took them in deep. Blinking hard, she forced herself to back out of his arms. She couldn't fall for Ryan Malloy. She had plans, and staying in Perfect was not one of them. "Food." She slid over and opened the door. "I'll be right back."

It was still too early for the lunch crowd; there weren't any other customers in the deli. Which was a good thing, because she didn't want to interact with anyone. She placed her order and used the wait time to get herself back under control.

Paige crossed the lot and climbed back into the truck with the bags and bottles. She found Ryan staring at another shop and followed his gaze to…the Quilter's Depot? A colorful quilt in a starburst pattern hung in the window. "What are you looking at?"

He nodded toward the display. "Would you mind if I went into that shop for a minute?"

She glanced at him in surprise. "You want to take up quilting?"

"I just want to check something out."

"Sure." She set their lunch stuff on the seat. Curious, she reached for the door handle. "Let's go."

The shop had an old-fashioned metal bell that tinkled when they walked in. More quilts hung from dowels along the walls, and bolts of fabric formed aisles on either side, arranged according to color. Quilting frames of various sizes, thread, needles, and batting took up the rear, along with a large display of books. Paige followed Ryan as he checked out each quilt. An older woman with silver hair and a tape measure dangling around her neck approached them.

"May I help you?" She smiled a warm welcome.

Ryan's gaze didn't leave the array of quilts. "Are these for sale?"

"They are. All of them are handmade and locally produced by the Amish."

"Are there templates or some kind of pattern book for something like that?" He pointed to one of the quilts.

"That particular pattern is called Drunkard's Path, and yes, we have several books containing templates for that design and many others."

"How much is the Drunkard's Path quilt?"

"Ryan, what are you thinking?" His sudden intensity mystified her. He practically vibrated with focused attention on whatever it was that had caught his attention.

"I'm thinking I might take up quilting." He grinned at her and reached for her hand.

Her breath tangled in her chest on its way out at the teasing sparkle in his eyes. "Really?" She cleared her throat, embarrassed by her breathless tone.

The salesclerk turned a tag attached to the quilt. "This one is four hundred and fifty. Would you like to look at some of the pattern books?"

"I would, and I'll take the quilt."

Dazed, Paige let Ryan lead her to the rear of the store and stood a few paces behind him while he and the older woman went through a number of the pattern books and packages of plastic templates. What was this sudden fascination all about? She followed him to the cash register with his armload of stuff and waited while he and the salesclerk took his new, very expensive bedspread down from its place, folded it up, and added it to the pile of templates and books stacked on the counter. He pulled a card from his wallet and handed it over.

A smile lit his face, and excitement shone from his eyes as he handed Paige the sack holding his new books. He thanked the storekeeper, snatched up his wrapped quilt, and headed for the door.

She hurried to keep up. "What's with the sudden interest in quilting?"

He opened his truck door and tucked the quilt behind the seats, then reached for the plastic bag she held. "I have an idea."

"Are you going to share it?" He was still smiling, and she loved seeing him this way.

"Sure, when I've had some time to work it through." He put his hands on her waist and brushed a quick kiss across her forehead. "I'm starving. Let's head to the park."

Still curious, she climbed in and tried to figure out what his idea might be. He navigated through the city like he knew the area. "How do you know your way around so well?"

"I studied Google maps on my computer the other day." He shrugged. "After lunch, we have to head to Waterford Avenue. That's where the VA outpatient clinic is located. I need to make a couple of appointments."

"Noah's idea or yours?"

"It's a stipulation to my remaining employed." He shot her a wry look. "But it's time."

He quickly averted his gaze, and she reached out to cover his hand where it rested on the gearshift. She didn't say anything, just twined her fingers with his, hoping he understood how glad she was to know that he'd be getting the help and support he needed.

Ten minutes later, they pulled into a metered parking spot next to an expanse of green bordering the Ohio River. Picnic tables dotted the park, along with large oak and maple trees heavy with bursting leaf buds. Ryan went to the back of his truck for the blanket, and she gathered their lunch and climbed out. "Have you been here before?"

He nodded. "I did a little exploring a few weeks ago. Come on, darlin'. I know the perfect spot."

She followed him to a huge old oak. He spread the blanket and then took the bottles of water from her. Dropping their bagged lunches on the blanket, Paige lowered herself and settled against the trunk. The fresh spring air filled her lungs, and the sun warmed her skin. Her stomach growled, and she reached for one of the white paper bags. "I got one turkey with Swiss cheese and one ham-and-cheddar sandwich. I figured we could share them both." She started pulling out food. "We also have chips, fresh fruit, and coleslaw."

Ryan scooted up to lean on the trunk beside her, and their shoulders, hips, and thighs touched. Heat flooded her cheeks.

THE DIFFERENCE A DAY MAKES

She fussed with the bags to avoid looking at him and handed him a packet with plastic utensils and a napkin. "Dig in."

He took a bite out of his half of the ham sandwich and nudged her with his elbow. "You first," he said around his mouthful.

Gazing out at the surrounding park, she wondered how to tell her story without sounding like a pathetic fool.

"I won't judge, sweetheart. I promise. Cowboy's honor."

"Speaking of cowboys, I really want to go to that rodeo. If you won't go with me, I'll find someone who will."

"Like Ted?" He stiffened beside her.

She gave him a noncommittal shrug and picked at her fruit salad. *Not nice.* Using Ted as a delay tactic or to manipulate Ryan was beneath her. She swung her gaze to his. "I was thinking more along the lines of Ceejay and Lucinda. A girls' day out."

He relaxed. "I'll take you, but I don't want to go hunting down my relatives."

"All right. I won't force the issue."

"Start talking, little girl. We have a deal."

Her appetite disappeared, and her stomach knotted. "Why do I have to go first?"

"Because you read my letter without permission. You snooped. You start."

"Fine," she huffed. "I worked at a manufacturing company for large construction equipment." She launched into her tale of woe. "Anthony Rutger, this coworker of mine, offered to take one of the bids I'd worked on to the courier waiting in the lobby. I was on the phone with a client at the time." She blew out a breath as memories of that day came back to her. "He'd also offered to drop a couple of my bids into the outgoing mailbox a few times. I trusted him." She shrugged. "Turns out he set me up. He never gave the envelope to the courier and delayed putting my bids in the mail. Because of my naïveté, we lost a big account, and I had a few complaints against me for lateness. I got fired from my very first real job."

Unwilling to meet his eyes, she stared toward the river. "I am currently unemployed, as in completely without an income." She waited for him to say something. When he didn't, she turned to find him deep in thought. "Say something."

"There's more to this story, right?"

"Does there have to be more?" She picked at the sandwich in her lap.

"Paige…"

Several tense seconds ticked by. The intensity of his perusal brought heat rushing to her face. "Oh, all right. Anthony and I were dating. I should've known something was up when he insisted we keep our relationship a secret. I…I'm such a fool. I even thought we had a future together," she mumbled as mortification burned a hole through her.

"You loved this Anthony fellow?"

"No." She fussed with her water bottle. "I thought I did, but afterward, I didn't feel heartbroken, only angry."

"Do you want me to head up to Philly and rearrange his face for you?"

The intensity of his brilliant blue gaze kicked her pulse into overdrive. He meant it. Ryan's anger on her behalf warmed her, and all the bunched muscles in her neck and shoulders relaxed. "No, but thank you for that." The sudden sting of tears made her blink, and he reached for her hand.

"You didn't deserve what happened, Paige. The only thing you're guilty of is trusting the wrong man. That's not your bad—it's his." He gave her hand a squeeze. "If it's any comfort, everyone gets fired at least once in their lifetime. Hell, it's kind of a rite of passage."

She chuffed out a teary chortle and swiped at her eyes. "Not Harvard graduates. Not Langfords." She sniffed. "I…I can't tell my parents until I'm back on my feet."

"Why is that?"

How could she tell him she didn't measure up in her father's eyes? She didn't want Ryan to see her that way. "They spent a lot on my education, and I don't want to disappoint them. Once I have a new job, then I'll tell them." Or at least she'd tell them part of it. All they had to know was that she'd left Ramsey & Weil for something better. Not a complete lie. Ryan scrutinized her again. She fidgeted with the plastic utensil packet.

"OK, now, see, some of this doesn't make any sense to me at all."

"Like?" She peered at him through her soggy lashes.

"Like why you feel you have to hide this from your family, for one thing. From what I know about Noah, your family would be nothing but supportive. Plus, I'm having a hard time visualizing you working for a company that produces large construction equipment." He tipped his head down to meet her gaze. "Why construction? I see you more as…"

"As what?" She stiffened. "Fluff? Are you saying you don't think I'm capable of succeeding in that kind of industry? Because—"

"Hoh, boy. I hit a nerve." He drew back, and his eyes widened. "I believe you could be a success at anything you set your mind to, darlin'. I'm just trying to understand what motivates you."

"I'm not fluff." Or at least, she didn't want to be. "And I'm not a spoiled little rich girl either." She jutted out her chin in challenge. Ryan chuckled, and that mouth of his melted her insides into…marshmallow fluff. *Dammit.*

"Hell no, you aren't." He put his arm around her shoulders and gave her a hug. "Who made you feel that way?"

Her heart put up a fuss, and her palms grew damp. Did she want to bare it all? No, but hadn't she barged into his apartment to find him passed out and clutching an empty whisky bottle? Not to mention that letter she'd read without permission. She owed him the same degree of revelation if she meant to be his friend. "All right, here's the thing." She sucked in a calming breath. "Has Noah told you much about the family business?"

"L&L?" Confusion clouded his expression.

"No." She bit her lower lip and wondered how to explain her own inadequacy. "Langford Plumbing Supplies. My family owns a plumbing supply empire that began generations ago." She glanced at him to see how he took that bit.

"Go on."

"Dad wanted Noah to take over at some point, but my brother had his own plans. Noah made it clear he had no interest in the plumbing industry or in taking over." She straightened. "I, on the other hand, want to take over the family business, and my dad won't even consider me for the job. He won't consider me for any job within the company." The discussion churned up the disappointment she always carried with her, souring her stomach.

She fisted her hands in her lap. "I went to Harvard to get my degree in business administration and marketing with the idea that an Ivy League MBA would convince Dad I'm worthy of his trust." Her chest tightened, and all the rejection she'd suffered, knowing she didn't measure up in her father's eyes, overwhelmed her. "It didn't. I overheard him talking to Noah. My own father is the one who said I'm mostly fluff—naive fluff, to be exact—and didn't I just go and prove him right?"

Ryan drew her closer. "Maybe I should rearrange *his* face."

A twisted laugh broke free. "You asked why large construction. I figured if I can make it in a place like that, he'd have to take me more seriously. I mean to prove to him that I'm up to taking over the family business."

"Hmm," he murmured and absently stroked her shoulder.

"What's that supposed to mean?" She glanced at him.

"It means I'm thinking. Which is no easy feat with such a gorgeous, warm, non-fluffy woman sitting beside me." He waggled his eyebrows at her.

"Gorgeous and non-fluffy?" She giggled, loving the way he'd lifted her out of her funk so deftly.

"Let me ask you something." He peered down at her. "Do you have a passion for toilets, fixtures, drainpipes, and faucets? Is that what occupies your mind every waking minute?"

"No." She shrugged. "I don't know a thing about plumbing fixtures, nor do I care to. It's the *business*, Ryan. Don't you see? I do know business and marketing. What difference does it make what it is that I'm marketing, so long as I'm good at it?"

"Huh." He nodded and went pensive again.

"What?"

"I don't know. It seems to me your whole fixation with running the family business has more to do with proving something to your old man than it does with the actual company you claim you want to run."

"Yeah?" She blinked. "So?"

"Well..." He hesitated, took his arm from around her shoulders, and turned one of his inscrutable looks her way.

"Spit it out, Malloy. Whatever you're thinking, I want to hear it."

"You don't have anything to prove to anyone but yourself, darlin'. Did it ever occur to you that you might be a whole lot happier if you found something to do that really excites you?" He nudged her. "It sure doesn't sound like you're all that enamored of plumbing supplies. There'd be no stopping you if what you market is also something you love with a passion."

"You don't understand," she snapped.

"Huh. Don't I? Seems to me I'm not the only one who's a little too close to be objective."

She opened her mouth to retort, only to close it again. Proving herself to her father *was* her passion. She wanted that moment of triumph more than anything. "Let's finish up here and go buy that phone you need so badly." She grabbed her turkey sandwich and took a big bite, chewing what tasted like cardboard in her mouth. "Seeing as how I have no income, you get why I'm not going to buy it for you."

"But you're still going to insist that I have one, right?"

"I am. You *will* have a phone before we leave Evansville today."

He chuckled low in his throat. "You, Paige Langford, are a force of nature. Glorious, indomitable, and obstinate. You're a whole lot of things, darlin', but fluffy isn't one of them."

Her eyes widened. "You think I'm glorious?"

"Hell yes, and it breaks my heart you're going to take all that glory away from Perfect when you leave."

Her breath caught. He was only teasing, yet leaving him behind was going to hurt her for real. *Crap.* She reached into one of the bags and pulled out two huge chocolate chip cookies. "Here." She handed him one. "Surprise."

His face lit up like a little boy's, and she glimpsed what he must've been like before his life had imploded. "I have family here, Ryan. I'll be around."

"Not the same at all," he murmured and turned away.

Her throat tightened, and her eyes stung. Did he have any idea how he affected her? "Don't forget you promised to bare your soul as well. Quid pro quo and all that."

Sighing, he nodded. "Cookie first." He took a big bite, leaned his head back against the broad tree trunk, and lowered his hat over his face.

"Oh, no, you don't. You're not going to nap." She took his hat, placed it on the blanket, and elbowed him in the ribs.

"It was worth a shot." He grinned at her with all of his dimples tugging at her heartstrings.

"Out with it, cowboy."

"Damn, you're a pushy woman." His eyes closed, and his face tightened. Several seconds ticked by before he finally spoke. "I had just finished my master's, and—"

"You have a master's degree, and you enlisted in the army?" Her brother also had his degree before he'd enlisted, but it was because he wanted a military career. Having a degree meant the difference between commissioned or noncommissioned officer status, and for Noah, it made sense. "Did you want a military career?"

"Hell no. Don't interrupt, or I won't get through this."

"Sorry."

"My master's is in fine arts—hardly a degree that would get me anywhere in the army." He ran his thumb back and forth over the back of her hand. "I was engaged to be married. I'd just accepted a job in Dallas at a small advertising firm, and Theresa and I were in Oklahoma to visit my folks. We were finalizing the plans for our wedding." His head dropped to his chest, and the muscles in his jaw danced under his skin.

Now that he'd shaved, every emotion he experienced showed clearly on his expressive face, leaving him exposed and vulnerable. He'd been hiding all that agony from the world, and her chest ached for him. "Go on."

"I wanted to take her horseback riding through the Antelope Hills near our ranch. It's a wilderness area bordering the Canadian River, and it's really spectacular. She didn't want to go."

His hand gripped hers so tightly it hurt, but she didn't let go. Instead, she gripped back and waited while he gathered himself.

"I insisted," he gritted out through clenched teeth. "I pushed her into doing something she didn't want to do." His chest heaved, and his Adam's apple bobbed with each hard swallow. "A storm came up out of nowhere while we were riding. Lightning spooked her horse, and it bolted. I went after her, and another lightning strike hit the ground ahead of us. Theresa was thrown." His entire body grew rigid beside her. A strangled sob broke free, and he snatched his hand from hers to scrub at his face. "She broke her neck and split her skull on impact. My fault—it was all my fault she died."

"Oh, Ryan, I'm so sorry." She ran her hand over his back, stung when he jerked away from her touch.

"Yeah, me too." He shot to his feet and started pacing.

"It wasn't your fault."

"Wasn't it?"

"You didn't use force. You persuaded her to go riding. Theresa was an adult. She could've said no and stuck with it. You didn't cause the storm or make the lightning strike, and you didn't make that horse take off the way it did. It was a tragic accident. Accidents aren't anybody's fault. They just are."

"You about ready to go?" Ryan snatched up the trash from their lunch. His eyes were bright and his voice hoarse.

"Sure." *Be his friend. Don't let him face his demons alone.*

There were things she wanted to say, but couldn't—not without driving him further away, and that wouldn't help. She understood him a little better now. He wanted to punish himself for something entirely out of his control, and if she did nothing else before she left, she meant to convince him he was wrong.

CHAPTER SIX

❧

RYAN HATED HAVING PAIGE SEE him for the emotional wreck he'd become. He couldn't be near her, and the hurt in her eyes when he pulled away stabbed at his conscience. It couldn't be helped. Every ounce of his will turned to the task of keeping himself in the present.

He paced around the perimeter of their picnic spot, his chest heaving and his head pounding as he waged war against the flashback threatening to take him over the edge. Theresa's broken and bloody body flashed through his mind, chased by the gruesome image of Jackson in pieces across the desert. He forced himself to keep his eyes open, focusing on the park and the scenery surrounding them.

"Are you OK?" Paige shook out their picnic blanket and folded it into a neat square.

A nod was all he could manage, and he concentrated on her actions. If she'd seen the way he kept that old rag stuffed in his tool chest, she wouldn't have bothered folding the thing. Her efforts almost made him smile, and that helped more than anything. Gulping air into his lungs, he shoved his memories as far back into his consciousness as possible. *Stay in the present. Pull yourself together.*

"Do you mind if I ask you a question, Ryan?"

"Go ahead." Maybe talking would help.

"What made you decide to enlist?"

"After the accident, I had a lot of anger. Enlisting in the army gave me an outlet. Plus, I wanted to do my duty." His chest eased a bit, and his pulse slowed. He might just make it through this without a complete breakdown. He took another breath, forcing himself back to the here and now.

She stopped fussing with the blanket to study him. "How's the anger issue now?"

"I guess you could say it's been replaced with a whole lot of other shit." He crushed their trash into a compact ball. "Let's head for the VA center; then we can find the Ford Center for those rodeo tickets. I'll hit the art supply store on our way out of town."

"Phone." Paige tucked the blanket under her arm, slung her purse strap over her shoulder, and came to stand beside him with her face a study in dogged determination. "Don't forget the phone."

"No, ma'am. I wouldn't dare." A real grin broke free, and his insides finally settled. Once again, she'd helped him find his way back from hell. Reaching for her hand, he led her toward his truck. If only he could keep himself from checking out all the rooftops in town for insurgents, he might get through the rest of the afternoon like a normal human being. *Sure. Keep dreaming, cowboy.*

The rest of the afternoon flew by, and he managed to get everything on his list done. He stowed most of his purchases in the tool chest, made his first appointment with the therapist, and now Paige sat beside him with his new smartphone on her lap. She plugged in the car charger and connected it to the phone as he pulled into traffic for the trip home. "What are you up to, darlin'?"

"I'm programming a few telephone numbers into your address book." Her thumbs tapped away on the tiny keyboard.

"Yours?"

"Mine, Noah's, and Ceejay's." One side of her mouth quirked up. "And Ted's."

He feigned dismay at the mention of Ted's name, while warmth flooded his chest. She wanted him to have her number. That had to mean she didn't find being with him entirely distasteful, right? "Will you put my number in your contacts?" She shot him one of her *You're an idiot* looks, and he raised an eyebrow. "What's that supposed to mean?"

"It means I already put you in my contacts while the guy at the store set up your account." Paige placed his phone beside her on the seat and opened his glove compartment. She brought out the rodeo tickets and held them up in front of her. "Saddle bronc riding champion, eh? So, what does that involve?"

"Riders have to stay on a bucking horse for eight seconds, and they get a score based on their skill, form, and the horse. You have to keep one arm in the air and synchronize your spurring action with the horse's motions, stuff like that." Warmth flooded through him at the look of anticipation on her face as she studied the tickets. Friday couldn't come fast enough. "The bull riding is the biggest draw."

Paige's expression turned puzzled. "Why is that?"

He shrugged. "It's the most dangerous rodeo sport there is. Bulls are two thousand pounds of whoop-ass. A horse will throw you and run off. All they want is to get away. But a bull's instinct is to gore and trample you to death once you've been thrown."

"Oh." She bit her lip. "Did you ever ride bulls?"

"Sure. I did it all when I was younger." How different things had been back then. His life had been filled with family, laughter, and a sense of security and optimism. He'd had Theresa by his side. *Theresa.* He kept his gaze on the road, and his grip on the wheel tightened. Paige had helped him break the downward spiral he'd been in after spilling his guts, and the load he carried on his shoulders had lightened a bit. "I haven't...Other than family, I've never shared what happened to Theresa with anyone. Thanks for listening. I'm glad we did this today."

Plus, Paige had confided in him—not her brother, her sister-in-law, or Ted. She'd trusted him enough to share her secret, and he sat a little straighter because of that confidence. At least he knew what had brought her to Perfect. He wanted to have a few words with the guy who'd set her up. Words involving his fists.

"Same here. If you ever want to talk about her or about what happened, I hope you know you can come to me."

"I'll keep that in mind." *Not going to happen.* Talking about it today had been hard enough. "Even though we spent most of the day running errands, I had a nice time." He glanced at her for a reaction, pleased by the dreamy smile she turned his way.

"Me too. I'm looking forward to the rodeo."

"And after that, you're leaving." Why did saying the words make his insides go hollow and achy? He'd only known her for a week, not to mention the fact that he was in no shape to get serious about pursuing her. He wanted to, though. Man, he wanted her in the worst way.

"I have a condo in Philadelphia. I need to find a job and get back to my life." Paige studied the passing scenery. "I can't hide out at my brother's forever."

"Course not." *Stay. Look for a job in Evansville, or hire on with Langford & Lovejoy.* The words got stuck somewhere between his heart and his head. He had no right to ask anything of her, but that didn't make the longing go away.

A companionable silence settled between them, and Paige fiddled with his radio until she found something to her taste. He liked hearing her hum along to the music, and having her near kept him centered and in the present. What would it be like to have a regular life, one where he allowed himself to get close enough to love again? Did he have it in him to open up like that anymore?

For the rest of the ride home, he pretended Paige belonged to him. Memories of Theresa threatened to steal the fantasy away, but he pushed them back and indulged in a few moments of make-believe happiness. What was the harm? Paige wouldn't be in Perfect long enough for the fantasy to turn to shit. He pulled into the Langfords' driveway and brought his truck up next to Noah's.

"I'll help bring your stuff to the carriage house." Paige unplugged his phone and tucked it back into its box.

"Thanks." *Hoh, boy.* They'd be alone in his apartment, and maybe he could maneuver her into more kissing. He grabbed the box with his phone, climbed out, and gathered his purchases from the back.

Paige carried his new quilt, and he took the sack of books from behind his seat. He led the way to his door. "Let's see how that quilt looks on my bed."

"Sure." She hung back as he unlocked the dead bolt and swung it open. "You do know no one else in this entire town locks their doors, right?" Flashing him a wry look, she walked past him inside.

"I know." How could he explain? He needed to lock up, just like he needed to have a weapon nearby. She'd tossed his .357 into the river, but he still had his knives, and they were always within easy reach when he went to bed—if he went to bed at all. It had taken a lot of effort not to perform his usual rooftop surveillance in Evansville today, but he didn't want her to see that piece of crazy. She would've made him talk about it, and he'd done all the talking he could handle for one day. Paige took the phone from him, bringing him back to the present.

They laid his purchases in a heap on the coffee table, and Paige plugged his new cell into an outlet next to the recliner. Unwrapping the quilt on the way down the short hall, he admired the bold combination of colors. The jewel tones and pattern appealed to him. Shaking it out, he let it settle over the bed. It had to be for a queen-size mattress, because the spread hung over the sides almost to the floor. "Come tell me what you think," he called.

"Hmm." She came to stand beside him. "It's impressive. I love the colors, but they kind of overwhelm this little room."

"Yeah." Ideas for a larger room with a bed he designed crowded into his brain. "It'll do for now." She sighed softly beside him, drawing all of his attention. Here they were in his bedroom next to his bed. All the erotic dreams he'd had about her came back in a rush. His heart took off at a gallop, and his mouth went dry. "I think I could use a little of that one size-fits-all remedy about now."

"Do you think it's wise for us to keep doing that?" She worked her lower lip between her teeth. "I'm only staying for a little while, and—"

"We're adults, and I'm only asking for a kiss. What guy wouldn't want to kiss you after a date?"

"Were we on a date?" Her head canted to the side as she thought it over. "Couldn't we be friends who just hang out together?" She glanced at him through her lashes.

He caught the breathlessness in her tone and the quick rise and fall of her chest. No doubt about it. He got to her like she got to him. His gaze fixed on that chest, and he wondered if her nipples were rose colored or peaches and cream. He could practically feel the soft, warm weight of them in his hands. How would her skin taste? Sweet.

"A friendly kiss, then." Ryan slid his arm around her waist and drew her close. Placing a finger under her chin, he tilted up her face, gratified to see her eyes already had that dreamy, sexy look he loved so much. The moment his lips touched hers, an explosion of sensual heat scorched through him. Her arms came around him, and she kissed him back with an urgency that made him weak in the knees. Oh, yeah. He got to her.

Good thing they were right next to a bed. Running his fingers through her hair, he cradled her head and plundered her sweet mouth, losing himself in the soft press of her curves. She let out a moan, and he lost all control. Ryan scooped her up into his arms without breaking the kiss, lowered her onto his mattress, and stretched out beside her.

"I don't know if this is such a good idea," she murmured against his mouth as she kicked off her shoes.

"Oh, it is, sweetheart." He trailed kisses down her throat to her collarbone, eliciting a gasp that turned him inside out. "It's a real good idea. One of the best I've ever had." Throbbing with need, Ryan tucked her under him. Skin. He wanted to feel her skin. "You don't need this jacket on in here, do you?" He peeled it off, his heart soaring when she helped.

"You smell so damn good." Desperate to touch her, he tugged at her tucked-in T-shirt until the hem broke free from her jeans. *Oh, God.* Running his palm over the bit of exposed skin at her midriff, his entire focus narrowed to the feel of her velvety warmth, the smoothness of her belly against his callused palm. He ached to have her naked beneath him, every inch of him pressed against every inch of her. *Paige.* He had to have more.

She nuzzled his neck, sending a current of need straight to his groin, turning him rock hard. Her hands slipped under his shirt, and the skin-on-skin contact robbed him of any of the reasons why they should stop. She ran her hands over his back—and froze.

"What?" He pulled away to peer at the expression of shock on her face. *Oh, fuck.* He rolled off her and covered his eyes with his arm so he didn't have to see the revulsion that would surely follow. "My scars."

"I wasn't expecting—"

"Yep. I get it." He shot off the bed and kept his back to her so she couldn't see the raging hard-on she'd caused.

"They don't bother me, Ryan. I was just surprised, and—"

"No need to explain." He scrubbed his face with both hands. What had he been thinking? No way did he have a ghost of a chance with a woman like her. *Fantasy squelched. Thank you very much, reality.* "We should call it a day."

"Don't do that. Don't shut me out."

"OK. Look, I'm tired. I suggest you head on up to the big house now."

She got up, tucked her shirt back in, and snatched her jacket off the bed. "I hate when you do that."

He didn't respond. Shame and self-loathing had him by the balls, and he wanted her gone while he melted down—for the third time today.

"Let me know when you grow up." She shoved her feet into her shoes and stomped out of his apartment with her spine stiff.

"Don't hold your breath," Ryan muttered. He'd screwed up, overreacted, and pushed her away. *Shit.* Probably for the best. He had no business laying his hands on her perfect body.

He needed a drink. Hell, he needed several drinks—bad. And that scared him. Too much had been dredged up today, tearing his guts out and exposing the ugliness inside. Paige brought all the things missing in his life into a sharper-edged focus, slicing and dicing his soul into painful, bloody bits and pieces.

He'd had his shot at happily-ever-after with Theresa, and he'd blown it all to hell. He couldn't survive another loss like that, yet he couldn't get free of the hold Paige had on him either. *I'm doomed.*

He needed to get his mind off this disaster trail, or he'd soon be heading for the nearest liquor store. Jamming his hands into his pockets, he stared at the bags on his coffee table. *Art. Design.* Hadn't he gotten all fired up today when he saw the starburst quilt hanging in that window? Ideas had poured into his consciousness almost too fast to count.

He strode back to his bedroom and stood at the foot of the bed, studying the new quilt and trying not to notice the mussed-up spots where he and Paige had lain together mere moments ago. The concave and convex pieces creating a crooked path across the fabric intrigued him, along with the contrasting darkness of the hunter green mixed with the raspberry red against the gold background. How could he incorporate a similar pattern using wood as the medium instead of cloth? He needed to get his ideas down on paper, and he needed to get his mind off Paige.

He made his way to the living room and gathered his materials, finally settling himself on the couch. Good thing he'd thought to include slide rulers and ellipses templates in his purchases. Everything had to be scale.

He flipped through one of the quilt books, looking at the many patterns while assessing the possibilities. Inlay would be a challenge, since he had no idea how to make quilting patterns translate to wood. His woodworking skills were pretty basic, but Noah would have the knowhow, or at least he'd be able to point him in the right direction.

He started with a coffee table in a Log Cabin quilt pattern. The design involved a square center surrounded by narrow rectangles that grew longer with each placement—simple and perfect for learning the inlay process. Next, he designed a dining room table with a starburst center. Ryan lost himself in designing the prototypes, adding dimensions and notes on the side, along with wood types and stain ideas.

After what seemed like a few minutes, he stretched and glanced at the clock on his kitchen wall. *Damn.* Almost midnight. He'd worked without stopping for a good six hours.

Still buzzing with ideas, he got ready for bed. First thing in the morning, he'd find Noah and talk to him about the plans he'd come up with.

Ryan stopped in his tracks. He hadn't caught a glimpse of his ghosts all night, and that had him fighting the impulse to call Paige. After being such a jerk, he owed her an apology, but calling her at midnight wouldn't help his cause. Hell, he'd get down on his knees if necessary and beg for forgiveness. Paige topped his list when it came to wanting to talk to someone. Hadn't he spilled his deepest and darkest secret to her today? He'd never told another living soul what he'd told her. That had to mean something.

Yep. It means you're heading for a whole lot of heartache, and you're just stupid enough to let it happen—'cause you're that fool.

Tomorrow he'd apologize, and then he'd tell her about his night without ghosts. Maybe he'd show her the sketches. Ryan slid into bed and pulled the new quilt over his shoulders. More ideas flooded his brain. He wanted to make a bed with the spool pattern on the headboard, or maybe he could come up with a new design all his own. Thoughts of the bed he wanted to create led to dreams of who he wanted next to him in that bed. Their bed. His and Paige's.

Certifiable. Good thing he already had an appointment set up with the shrink.

❧ ❧ ❧

Paige yawned and reached for the coffeepot. She hadn't slept a wink last night. Ryan's reaction to her shock at finding his back covered with scars had played through her mind over and over, keeping her tossing and turning. *Damn.* Why hadn't she considered how sensitive he'd be to any hesitation on her part? Had she learned nothing about him yesterday, like how hard he tried to shield himself from the world?

At some point today, she had to find Ryan and apologize for reacting the way she had over the scarring on his back. Somehow, she'd make him understand it had nothing to do with repulsion and everything to do with the heartache she'd experienced just thinking about the pain he'd suffered.

Filling the glass carafe with water, she let her mind drift to memories of Ryan's kisses, his lopsided smile, those heart-stopping dimples. Sensitive, creative, gorgeous...wounded. Her heart fluttered. Despite the wounded part, she wanted him. A lot. Paige shook her head and groaned at her own foolishness while she started the coffee brewing. Tightening the belt of the old flannel robe she'd stolen from Noah, she stared out the kitchen window and listened to the birds coaxing the sun to rise.

"You're up awfully early." Ceejay stepped out of the back stairway with Toby in her arms.

"Yeah. I had trouble sleeping, so I gave up." Paige ran her hand over Toby's warm back. "You're up early too."

Ceejay dropped a kiss on her son's head. "He's an early bird, which means I'm always up at this time."

"Bird," Toby chirped and pointed out the window. "Peep, peep." Paige chuckled. "He's so dang cute."

"He knows it too." Ceejay placed him in his high chair and moved to a cabinet to get a box of Cheerios. "I have a shift at the hospital tonight, and I promised Noah some quality kid-free time today before he's on daddy duty. Are you up to an outing with me and the kids?"

"Absolutely. What do you want to do?"

"There's a huge arts and crafts fair going on in New Harmony this weekend. They also have a little carnival area and petting zoo. I thought we could go check it out."

"Ted mentioned it." She blew out a breath. "You were right, by the way. He made a pass at me the night you and Noah were away."

"Oh, no." Ceejay flashed her a sympathetic look. "Do you want me to talk to him?"

"That's OK." She shook her head. "It's something I need to deal with. He showed up just as Ryan and I were leaving for Evansville yesterday. Those two don't get along at all."

"And you're in the middle." Ceejay put a handful of cereal and sliced banana on Toby's tray. "You spent the day with Ryan?"

Her sister-in-law kept her eyes on her son, but Paige picked up on the subtle probe for more information. "We're friends. I helped him pick out a phone, and we ran errands. It wasn't a date."

"Oh." Ceejay nodded. "Good."

"Why is that good?" Paige's pulse surged with the need to defend him. "Don't you think he's date-worthy?"

Ceejay's eyes widened. "He's definitely date-worthy, or he will be once he's dealt with some of his issues. But do you really want to start something with him while he's in such a precarious place? What will that do to him when you leave?"

What would it to do to him? What about me? I'm already in way over my head. She needed to stop kissing him. No more lying down on the bed with him either. She didn't mean to lead him on; it's just that she had no resistance when it came to Ryan Malloy. "I'm not trying to start anything. I'm only trying to be his friend." She grabbed the cream from the fridge, filled a couple of mugs with coffee, and handed one to Ceejay, placing the cream within easy reach. "I'm not exactly in a place to start anything with anyone either."

"Noah told me you had your heart broken by some guy in Philly."

"Not really. I made the mistake of dating a coworker, and it didn't work out, that's all." She'd shared her story with Ryan, and he'd shared his with her. If nothing else, at least they'd keep each other's secrets safe. She held on to that little bit of intimacy and pressed the warm mug between her palms.

"I'm sorry." Ceejay came around the counter and hugged her shoulders. "Do you want to talk about it?"

"Nope." Paige hugged her back and sighed. "I need to go home. I'll be out of your hair by next weekend."

Ceejay straightened. "You're not in anybody's hair. Stay as long as you want. If you're not happy with your job, you could always look for something around here. I love having you close." She grinned, and her eyes filled with mischief. "Having you here means I get to slip away for a night alone with my husband now and then."

"I don't know if staying is such a good idea." Ryan's boyish grin flashed into her head, along with the way she'd melted under him. With those damn dimples, his delectable scent, and all that heat and hardness, despite her best intentions, she couldn't hold out for long. And like Ceejay said, now was not the time to start something with him.

Ceejay flashed her a knowing look. "Maybe not."

Paige let out a long breath and stared out the patio doors. "Is it that obvious?"

"To me, it is. Only because Noah and I have been where the two of you are right now. I don't know what to tell you. I don't want to see either of you get hurt, and at the same time, I don't want to see either of you fight something that might be really great." She studied the coffee in her mug. "It's none of my business."

"Does Noah know?"

"I don't think he gets that it's a two-way street, but he definitely knows Ryan is struggling with his attraction to you."

"Great." Ceejay and her brother's situation had been completely different. "I don't know what to do. I can't ignore the suicide letter and the gun he had laid out on that table." She blinked back the sudden sting in her eyes. "On the other hand, when I'm with him, even though it's obvious he's in a lot of pain, I also see glimpses of the man he could be."

"Hmm." Ceejay peered at her over the rim of her mug. "Do you really think he's suicidal?"

"Don't you?"

Ceejay shrugged. "He's alive."

"And?" What did Ceejay see that she didn't?

"He and Noah have been back from Iraq for three years. Three. Years. Noah told me Ryan blames himself for what happened in Iraq. He believes that if he'd aimed his machine gun into the payload of the insurgent's truck a lot sooner, the IEDs would've detonated in the desert, and no one would've been hurt. That's some pretty serious guilt to carry around, especially considering his best friend died that day. If Ryan were truly suicidal, wouldn't he be six feet under by now?" Ceejay shot her a questioning look. "I think maybe he needs to know there *is* an out, but how suicidal could he be if he's still here after all this time? His actions might be more about punishing himself than they are about ending his life."

"I didn't know he'd lost his best friend. He didn't tell me that part."

Ceejay's expression sharpened. "What part did he tell you?"

"I can't share what he told me in confidence, but knowing he lost someone close that day explains a lot." Add another dose of guilt for his fiancée, and it made sense. Paige rested her chin on her fists and stared out the patio doors again. "He made an appointment yesterday while we were in town. He's going to start seeing a therapist at the VA center."

"I'm glad. He has a lot to straighten out in his head. I do believe he's a good man, Paige. Definitely date-worthy."

🐏 🐏 🐏

Ceejay pushed Toby along in his stroller, and Paige held Lucinda's hand as they moved along with the crowd, visiting booths filled with pottery, jewelry, glass, beadwork, and every form of art imaginable.

"Wow. I've never been to anything like this."

"Really?" Ceejay's eyes widened. "I used to have booths in some of the smaller craft fairs held in local malls. Never this one, though. It's way too competitive and expensive to get into."

"Do you still bead?"

"Not since Toby started crawling. I don't really have the time, but I hope to take it up again at some point."

"Wow. Look at that glasswork." Paige pointed to a booth filled with the most colorful blown-glass bowls and vases she'd ever seen. "Can we stop here for a second?"

"Auntie Paige, I want to go to the petting zoo." Lucinda tugged at her hand.

"In a little while, Luce." Paige picked up a business card displayed in front of an impressive bowl with a ruffled edge and swirls of blue, green, and red throughout. A middle-aged man approached. He wore his long salt-and-pepper hair tied back and had a bald spot on top.

"I'd be happy to answer any questions you might have." He came to stand beside her.

"Thanks." She surveyed the shelves holding glass objects of all sizes.

Toby started to fuss.

"Hey," Ceejay nudged her, "see the booth with the children's toys ahead?"

Paige nodded.

"I'll take the kids, and you can meet us there in a few minutes. Will that be enough time?"

"Sure. I'll catch up with you." Paige turned back to the man. "Are you the artist?"

"I am." He smiled. "Do you see anything in particular you like?"

His stuff would be a great addition to L&L's showroom if they ever started producing more than children's furniture. Why

BARBARA LONGLEY

weren't they making dining room sets? What about bedrooms and living rooms? Tomorrow morning, she'd make a point to ask. "I love your work. I'm not buying today, though. I was wondering if you have a retail outlet."

"No, I don't. Mostly, I sell through word of mouth and at fairs like this." The glassblower's eyes held the glint of interest. "Why do you ask?"

"My brother and his business partner have a showroom in Perfect. I think your glassware would do well there." She studied his card. "They're furniture crafters."

"I'm interested." He folded his arms across his chest and widened his stance. "Tell me more."

"I'd have to talk to them about it first. Do you mind if I take a picture?" She grabbed her phone out of her purse.

"Be my guest." He moved out of the way while she snapped a few pictures.

"I'm Paige Langford, by the way. Their business is called Langford & Lovejoy Heritage Furniture."

"You don't say. I've visited their website." His eyes widened. "My daughter and her husband are expecting their first child in August, and she really wants a Langford & Lovejoy nursery. It's a little out of their price range, though."

"It is pricey, but it'll last for generations." Excitement buzzed through her as an idea for a retail venue fomented. "Come to the showroom in Perfect. We sell the prototypes at a nice discount, and I'll personally see to it that you get a good deal."

"Thanks. We'll do that. I'll bring a portfolio along, and we can talk business while we're there."

"Great. Here's their number." Paige turned over another of his business cards and fished for a pen in her purse. "Call before you come, and I'll make sure Ted and Noah are available to talk

- 1 2 2 -

to you." She wrote L&L's number on the blank side, along with her name, and handed it to him.

Surveying the varied arts and crafts represented at the fair, she settled on the booth where Lucinda and Toby played with sock puppets. Those would do well with the cribs, cradles, and children's furniture. After she left the glassblower's booth, she began gathering information from other artists whose products stood out. Noah and Ted should consider opening a retail store similar to Pottery Barn and West Elm, only better. They could start with Evansville, see how it went, and branch out from there. Offering handcrafted furniture and home decor products made entirely in the United States would appeal to today's consumers and fill a niche market. In fact, the more she thought about it, the more excited she became.

She hurried to catch up with Ceejay, and a pang of regret almost brought her to a halt. Someone else would have to help L&L branch out, because once she planted the seed, it would be time to go home.

CHAPTER SEVEN

SUNDAY MORNING, RYAN GRABBED HIS sketchbook and headed out the door, eager to find Noah. Rounding the corner of the veranda, he heard voices. He recognized Noah's, but not the other man's. "Good morning." He nodded to the stranger sitting at the table across from Noah.

"Come on up, Ryan." Noah pushed out a chair with his prosthetic. "This is our neighbor, Denny. You want a glass of sweet tea?"

"Sure." Ryan set the sketchbook on the table and took a seat. "Thanks."

Noah stood up and headed for the door. "I'll be right back."

An awkward silence fell between Ryan and Denny, a man about his age, late twenties or maybe early thirties. He wore a baseball cap over short-cropped brown hair, and his T-shirt read OFFERMEYER'S MEATS across the front. He regarded Ryan with frank curiosity, which had him shifting in his chair and casting around for something to say.

Denny held out his hand. "I'm Denny Offermeyer. My wife and I own the hobby farm a couple of miles down the road."

He shook his hand. "Ryan Malloy."

"Noah mentioned you. He said you grew up on a ranch."

"That's right."

"My wife's mare had twins a couple of years back—a filly and a colt."

"Hmmm." Ryan nodded noncommittally. He didn't care if he never saw another horse for the rest of his life. Theresa's accident had seen to that. Noah reappeared and set a glass of tea in front of him.

"I was just telling Ryan here about our horses." Denny leaned back with a smile. "One of them will belong to Lucinda when she turns ten. It's a toss-up whether she'll choose the filly or the colt."

"She seems to like the colt best." Noah took a swallow of his tea.

Denny nodded. "She and Celeste—that's my daughter—change their minds every week. My wife used to train horses, but with two kids and another on the way, she doesn't have the time to work with them much anymore."

"I see." Talking about horses brought the horror of that awful day with Theresa rushing back. Ryan's heart started to pound, and his palms started to sweat. Desperate to redirect the conversation, he reached for his sketches. "I brought something to show you, Noah. As I've mentioned before, I think we need to expand our product line beyond baby furniture. Here are some ideas I've been working on." He flipped open the book and handed it over.

Noah took it, and his eyes widened. "Wow."

Denny leaned in to have a look. "Those are really something. I think we have a quilt that looks just like that one." He pointed to the Log Cabin pattern.

"That's where I got the idea. Paige and I were at a quilt store yesterday, and—"

Noah's head came up. "You and Paige?"

Shit. He should've kept that part to himself. "Um, yep. She helped me buy a phone."

Noah's jaw tightened, and he nodded slowly. "These are great. Are you going to build the prototypes?"

"If you give me the go-ahead." Ryan fought the urge to tell Noah to mind his own business when it came to him and Paige. Didn't he realize his sister was all grown up? "I have no idea how to do inlay. I was hoping you might help, or at least point me in the right direction on where to look for information."

"Most inlay today is done with a laser cutter." Noah went back to studying the designs, turning to the next page. "Which we don't have."

"Any idea how much a laser cutter might cost?"

Noah chuffed out a laugh and handed him back the sketchbook. "Around ten grand for a good one. We could do the same with a router and jigsaw, though. Probably even better. This is more along the lines of parquet or marquetry than inlay."

"Can you teach me?" He didn't mind the idea of doing it by hand. That would fit in with L&L's commitment to handcrafting each piece.

"Tell you what," Noah said. "Paige suggested we have a staff meeting first thing tomorrow morning. We can talk about it then. I'm not against expanding our product line." He ran his hand over the stubble on his chin. "But a change like this affects all aspects of the business, and I want to run it by Ted first."

Sucktacular. Ryan's gut soured. Ted held more than one grudge against him already. The kid could bring his project to a complete halt. "If Ted says no, how would you feel about letting me do this in the shop on my own time? Or maybe I could use the bay of the carriage house, like you did when you first started out."

Noah's attention sharpened. "It means that much to you?"

"It does." He closed the notebook and stood up to leave. The whole business of needing anyone's approval to create the pieces he'd designed set his teeth on edge. If he had to, he'd find a way to do it on his own. Once he had something to show for his efforts, he'd approach Noah again.

"Stay, Ryan. No need to rush off. You haven't even touched your tea." Noah leaned back in his chair to peer up at him. "The weather is fine, and it's a rare thing when I get to relax with the whole place to myself."

"Where is everybody?" Ryan frowned as he sat back down, noticing the quiet for the first time. "Where's Sweet Pea?"

"Ceejay and Paige took the kids to the craft fair in New Harmony. Sweet Pea is around here somewhere. Probably giving the squirrels and rabbits hell." As if on cue, the dog barked from the direction of the walnut trees in back.

"I've got to be heading out." Denny scooted his chair back and rose from his place. "Gail sent me into town for milk and diapers an hour ago. Steam will start coming out of her ears if I don't get a move on."

"Thanks for stopping by, Denny. Poker night is at your house this month, right?"

"That's right." Denny turned to Ryan. "You want in? We get together once a month."

"Uh..."

"Next time Noah brings Lucinda by, come with him. You can take a look at our horses."

"Sure. I'll do that." Ryan nodded, knowing full well he had no intention of getting anywhere close to the Offermeyers' horses. Taking Paige to the rodeo would be difficult enough. Denny left the porch and climbed into his truck, lifting his hand in a brief wave before turning down the driveway.

"He's Perfect's butcher." Noah took a deep breath and let it out in a loud sigh. "Take a breath of that sweet country air. Man, I love it here." He turned his chair slightly and stretched out his leg and prosthetic. "Have you given any thought to what we talked about the other day?"

Even though Noah stared out over the orchard, Ryan sensed his hypervigilance. "I made an appointment with an army shrink at Marion, and no more drinking, like you said." His throat tightened. "I've made my decision. I want to get better. I want to keep working at Langford & Lovejoy."

"I'm glad." Noah closed his eyes. "And relieved, bro. You had me worried there."

Ryan swallowed. "Yeah, me too."

"You're coming with me to meet the group on Tuesday?"

"That too." Lord, he wasn't looking forward to that part of their deal. He'd been keeping to himself for so long, isolating, fronting, drinking—other veterans would see through all his bullshit. He'd be exposed, and that scared him to death.

"We've all been there, Ryan. There's not a single thing you've done or felt that someone else in the group won't understand and relate to."

"That's what I'm afraid of," Ryan muttered.

Noah shot him a look of amusement. "I'll be there."

"Is that supposed to make me feel better?" Ryan's brow shot up. "Because it doesn't."

"At ease, soldier." Noah's mouth twitched. "You'll live through it."

"If you say so."

"Drink your tea and unbunch those shoulders." Noah laughed. "Don't you love the smell of spring in southern Indiana?"

Just then a breeze kicked up, bringing with it the distinctive stench of the hog farms to the west. "Yep. You just might be more messed up than I am, Noah."

※ ※ ※

Ryan's sketches lay open on the table. Ted, Paige, and Noah bent their heads over them. Ryan's heart jumped into his throat, and he had to run his palms over his jeans a couple of times to hide the telltale moisture. "What do you think?"

"They're great." Ted turned the page back to the first sketches. "Which of these do you plan to start with?"

Surprise sent a shock wave through him. "You like them?"

"Of course I do." Ted's scowl said, *I don't need to like you to like your work.* "We need to build our product line. I've never disagreed with that. My concern is manpower, materials, and costs."

Ryan glanced at Paige. She looked ready to burst. "What are you thinking, Paige?"

"Your timing is perfect, and these designs are amazing." She practically buzzed with excitement. "I went to the craft fair in New Harmony yesterday and gathered a bunch of information from a number of artists. I think L&L is on the verge of something really great with this new product line. Now might be the time to expand your retail venue as well. Start with the showroom right here in Perfect."

She looked at each of them in turn, her expression so animated and lit up Ryan wanted to leap over the table and taste that buzz with a kiss.

"Offer home decor along with your furniture, like Crate & Barrel or Pottery Barn. Bring your customers to you. Make this site their destination. Advertise and market your products as all

American made." She flipped Ryan's sketchbook to the dining room table with the starburst in the center. "In fact, brand this new line Americana, or something similar. Then, once you've built some capital here, open your second retail site in Evansville, and—"

"All great ideas, but who is going to do all of that?" Ted cut in. "Ryan? We all know he's chock full of charisma." He shook his head. "There are only three of us." He glanced at Paige, his mouth a straight line. "You're leaving."

Paige deflated like a bicycle tire, and Ryan's jaw clenched. He'd promised her he'd make more of an effort to get along with the kid, and he would. Even if keeping his mouth shut right now gave him an ulcer.

"What's eating you, Ted?" Noah asked in his even-toned commander voice.

"Nothing's *eating* me." Ted pushed back his chair and stood up. "We have orders we need to crate up by this afternoon. Let's get to work."

"He's upset because—"

"Paige!" Ted's brow rose.

She kept her gaze on Noah. "When Ryan came on board, you didn't involve Ted in the hiring process, even though he's the business end of your partnership. There are some hard feelings being misdirected Ryan's way for something he had no control over."

"Is that true?" Noah shot Ted a look of surprise.

"Partially." Ted's expression filled with bitterness.

"Why didn't you say something?"

"When? By the time I heard about it, he'd already signed on the dotted line and moved into the carriage house."

"That's not all," Paige added.

Ted's face turned red. "Later. I'm going to get to work."

"Not now," Noah said. "Come back and sit down."

Instead of sitting, Ted leaned against the wall and crossed his arms in front of him.

"Ryan is under a lot of stress as it is." Paige never took her eyes from Noah. "Ted's animosity toward him makes everything ten times worse. Ryan reacts the only way he can by baiting and pushing Ted's buttons."

Ryan's mouth quirked up. He should have been pissed. But he wasn't. None of this was her business, but she had his back, and that stirred something inside him that hadn't been stirred for a long time. "I thought your degree was in business. Shoot. I should cancel my appointment at the VA center and hire you to be my shrink."

She rewarded his comment with one of her specialty *You're an idiot* expressions, and he fought the urge to laugh. Lord, she did things to him, made him feel things, like...*happiness?*

"Would you mind giving us some privacy, Paige?" Noah closed the sketchbook, his mouth forming a straight line. "I think the three of us have a few things to work out."

"Good idea." She rose. "I need to go check my e-mail anyway."

Ryan wanted to go with her. She needed to know he thought her ideas for L&L were spot-on. Maybe he'd suggest she stay and be the one to bring those ideas to fruition. The sound of Noah clearing his throat brought him back to the present.

"Sit down, kid." Ryan gestured to a chair. "For the sake of getting along, I'm willing to play by a few rules if you are."

The kid pushed off the wall and stiff-legged himself back to the table, his expression closed.

"I apologize for making you feel that you weren't a part of the decision-making process," Noah began. "We talked about hiring more help, and you agreed to it. I didn't realize...I've never owned a business before. How the hell would I know how these things are done?"

"You could've asked." Ted still leaned away from the table with his arms crossed in front of him. "We should've placed an ad, taken applications, gone through them, and decided together who to interview and hire."

Noah grunted. "In the future, I'll try to go along with that process, but you know how I feel about hiring veterans. There are going to be times when—"

"So we put something in the ad stating veterans preferred. I'm fine with that. I just don't want to be..." Ted averted his gaze, and his jaw muscle twitched.

"The token business partner?" Ryan raised an eyebrow. "I get that. Noah told me L&L was all your idea, and I respect that."

"Exactly." Ted shot a skeptical look his way before turning to Noah. "I didn't get involved only to be a silent partner who keeps the books and signs the checks. I have ideas, and I'm busting my ass to get my business degree. The least you could do is involve me in the decision-making process."

"Done," Noah said. "What are we going to do about the tension between the two of you?"

Time to man up. "If you agree to rein in your hostility, I'll agree to stop pushing your buttons."

"Right," Ted huffed. "We can give *that* a try."

"Listen, Ted. You have no idea what it means to me to be here." Ryan's jaw tightened. "I have a lot of respect for you."

"Sure you do."

"You do great work. I don't know how you manage school while putting in as many hours here as you do. I mean it when I say you have my respect." Ryan fixed him with a hard look. "You gotta admit, though, you haven't exactly been all warm and welcoming. I had nothing to do with Noah's oversight, but you've been taking it out on me all the same. I'm just the hired hand. It's easier to blame me than to take it up with Noah. Isn't that so?"

The kid's face turned red again, and his mouth turned down. Silence filled the office for several tense seconds until he spit out a response. "It is."

"We don't have to like each other to work well together," Ryan said. "I'll treat you with respect if you agree to do the same."

"Agreed," Ted gave him a curt nod.

"Someday maybe we'll get to the liking part." Ryan shrugged. "You never know. For now, I'm good."

"Great. I'm glad that's settled." Noah stood up. "Are we in agreement on expanding our product line?"

Ryan held his breath.

"I think it's about time." Ted pushed back his chair. "Go for it, Ryan."

Ryan's breath came out on a wave of relief, followed by excitement. "I'm going to need help with the prototypes. My woodworking skills aren't on par with yours and Noah's."

"I'll help. So will Noah." Ted started for the door. "Right now, we have to focus on getting our finished pieces ready to go. The trucking company is going to be here at three this afternoon."

"Ted, before we leave, do you want to talk about Paige?"

Ted glared at him. "I thought you said you weren't going to push my buttons."

"I'm not trying to push any buttons." Ryan picked up his sketchbook and started to follow. "I'm trying to clear the air. The truth is, we're both in for the same thin edge of the wedge here. She's—"

"Hell no. I'm not going to talk to you about Paige."

Ted stomped off, leaving Ryan with the full weight of Noah's scrutiny. "Oh, what? Like you didn't know?"

"Explain." Noah handed him the C-stare with a side of scowl.

"I hate when you do that, bro."

"Do what?"

"The commander stare." Ryan lifted an eyebrow. "Are you telling me you didn't know Ted has a thing for your sister?"

"No, I didn't."

"Well, he does, and it chafes his chaps that she and I have been spending time together after she turned him down."

"I see. Ryan—"

"Let's get to work, Boss." He headed toward the elevator, eager to end the conversation before Noah started in on him about why he shouldn't be spending time with his sister. "The morning is wasting away."

Noah grunted again, but at least he let the subject drop.

The minute the door of the lift opened, Ryan's gaze went straight for Paige, and his feet followed. "You OK, darlin'?"

"Of course. Why wouldn't I be?" She kept her attention on her laptop.

"I think your idea about building the retail venue is exactly right."

She straightened and turned to him. "Of course it's exactly right, but Ted brought up a good point. It would take manpower Langford & Lovejoy doesn't have."

"What if you stayed?" He kept his voice low. "I'm sure Noah and Ted would hire you in a tail wag."

She snorted a laugh. "In a tail wag?"

He nodded. At least she hadn't said absolutely not, and he wasn't going to give her the opportunity. He'd planted the idea, and unless he'd completely misread how excited she'd gotten when she'd shared her ideas, the notion would germinate. "Thanks, by the way."

"You're welcome." Confusion clouded her features. "What are you thanking me for?"

"For having my back in that meeting upstairs."

Shy, sweet Paige made an appearance, and a small smile lit her face. Ryan's breath hitched in his throat.

"You're welcome. Maybe someday you can return the favor."

"Absolutely."

❧ ❧ ❧

Paige couldn't believe it was Wednesday already. Two more days until her rodeo date with Ryan. Four days until she headed back to Pennsylvania and the hard reality of her situation. She had to talk to Ted and Noah about the glassblower before she left. If they didn't go for the idea of carrying some of his pieces, she needed to call the artist and relay the message before he showed up with his portfolio.

Glancing around the workspace, she soaked up the sight of the three men working in harmony. Ted was applying another coat of acrylic to a changing table. Noah was at the jigsaw, and Ryan worked on the sign that would soon be hanging above their storefront. The place hummed with productivity. She loved being in the midst of the men while they worked with their hands, loved the down-to-basics craftsmanship of their enterprise.

Her eyes settled on Ryan. He must've felt it, because he lifted his head and winked at her. She couldn't suppress the answering smile that broke free. "Hey, I got confirmation from the Evansville magazines. Your ad will be in the September issue of both."

"Great." Ted nodded.

She slid off her stool and walked closer. "I know you don't want to expand your retail venue, but I talked with a glassblower at the fair in New Harmony. Would you be interested in looking at his portfolio?" She shrugged. "I got excited about his stuff and kind of suggested it'd be a nice addition to your storefront." All three men stopped what they were doing and stared at her. Heat rose to her cheeks. "I know. I overstepped."

"It's all right. We'll take a look." Ted turned back to his task. "We don't get a lot of traffic here, though."

"You might get more once the ads come out. I put a few lines in about the discount on samples."

Noah peered at her through his safety goggles. "If it's a steady enough increase, we'll think about hiring a clerk part-time."

Her heart turned over. Someone else would take over her… *No, not mine.* She had a goal. Of course, it would help if she'd heard from at least one of the places she'd applied to for a job. Paige shook it off. It hadn't even been two weeks yet, and the application deadlines hadn't closed. "Sounds good. I'll call that glassblower and set up an appointment."

By the time she completed her call and came back downstairs, it was quitting time. The three men began their closing routine, turning off the equipment, sweeping the floor, and putting tools and materials away. Paige shut down the computers, grabbed the dirty coffee mugs from around the room, and headed for the sink to wash them. She'd only been here for a little over a week, but they'd already established a seamless routine, as if they'd worked together for years. She'd miss the relaxed atmosphere once she returned to the corporate world, with all the office politics and one-upmanship. Filling the little tub with warm water and dish soap, she wondered where she'd end up.

"Hey," Ted spoke up behind her. "Do you have any plans tonight?"

"Ted, we discussed this." She glanced at him over her shoulder. "I don't want to date you."

"I know." One side of his mouth turned up. "Does that mean we can't be friends? It's ladies' night at the Hoosier Bar and Grill. I thought we could go have a few beers and a burger."

"Definitely, we can be friends, but—"

"You about ready to go, darlin'?" Ryan came around the corner, and even though he spoke to her, his expression and posture held a challenge turned toward Ted.

Ted stomped off without a word. Paige shook her head and sighed. She rinsed the last mug and put it in the rack to dry. "You two didn't work things out upstairs?"

"Sure we did. Everything is copacetic between us."

"Sure it is." She grabbed a paper towel and dried her hands. "What was that all about, then?"

"Don't know what you're talking about. Noah and I are ready to go, and you rode in with us." He wrapped his arm around her shoulders and aimed her toward the back door. "That's all there is to it."

"Ryan—"

"Come on, darlin'. There's a frozen pizza with my name on it waiting in my freezer. I'm hungry." He squeezed her shoulders. "And I'm willing to share. I have cable. We can watch a movie while we eat."

"Gee. Frozen pizza. Who could resist such a gourmet treat?"

"I know, huh? I'll even dress it up a bit." Ryan steered her toward her purse and jacket, picked them up, and thrust them into her hands. "I think I might even have a few cans of generic cola in the fridge."

"Whoa. Generic cola. You really know how to impress a girl."
She couldn't help laughing.

"Don't forget the grocery-store-brand chocolate chip
cookies."

"No!" Paige placed a hand over her heart. "Cookies too?"

Ryan ushered her outside and turned to lock the doors.
"That's right. You in?"

"Gosh. I think I'll wait to see what Ceejay has to offer first,"
she teased. "If it's leftovers at the Langfords', I'm in for dressed-
up frozen pizza."

"Fickle—that's what you are, darlin'. I can't believe you'd
throw me over for a home-cooked meal." He opened Noah's
truck door with a crestfallen expression.

"I like this side of you." Paige patted his cheek before climbing into the backseat.

Ryan settled into the front. "Noah, do you know what your
wife has planned for dinner tonight?"

"Why? Are you angling for an invite?" Noah started the
truck down the alley.

"Naw. Idle curiosity, is all." He winked at her over his
shoulder.

"I have no idea. Ceejay doesn't consult me about the menu."

Ryan twisted around to look at her. "Is that a gamble you're
willing to take?"

"I'll let you know." She relaxed and peered out the window
at the passing scenery for the rest of their short trip home. Her
mind went back to L&L. At some point, they'd have to hire more
help. Maybe she could do some consulting with whoever took
over the marketing end of their growing business.

In no time at all, Noah turned into the gravel driveway and
bounced along the ruts to the house. Paige noticed an unfamiliar

car parked next to Ceejay's minivan. It had a rental car sticker on the back bumper. She turned to the veranda.

"Oh, crap." Her stomach dropped, and her heart seized. Her father sat at the table with Toby on his knee. Ceejay and Lucinda took up another two chairs. "Did you call him, Noah?"

"No." He parked and sent her a sideways glance. "I told you to let him know where you are, though. Did you?"

"I figured I'd be home by Sunday. There was no need."

Ryan opened his door, climbed out, and held the seat forward so she could scramble out. Her mouth had gone completely dry, and she couldn't draw enough breath.

"Do you want me to stick around?" Ryan whispered close to her ear.

"No. It's fine." She tried for a confident smile, certain it was more akin to a grimace. "He *is* my dad."

He gave her hand a squeeze. "All right. You know where I'll be if you need me."

"Thanks." Paige wiped her sweaty palms on her jeans and walked with Noah to the porch. Her dad stood up and handed Toby to Ceejay. He moved to stand by the railing.

"Hey, Dad." Noah preceded her up the steps. "What brings you to Perfect?"

Her father stuck his hands deep into his pockets and widened his stance. "Allie has been worried sick. Your sister hung up on her a few days ago, hasn't returned any of her calls, and gave us no idea where she might be."

"So you came here?" Paige managed to stammer out. Somehow, she got her shaky legs moving up the veranda steps.

"No. First I went to Ramsey & Weil." He scowled at her. "I thought I'd surprise you for lunch and see how you're doing."

"Oh." Paige tried to swallow, but her throat wouldn't work.

"*Oh* is right." He jangled the contents of his pocket. "Imagine my surprise when I found out you no longer work there."

Noah took a seat, and Ceejay herded the children inside. *Damn.* Why hadn't she asked Ryan to stay? She fought the urge to follow Ceejay and the kids. "I—"

"Next, I called Bob Meyer. I thought maybe he might shed some light on why you're no longer at Ramsey & Weil."

"You know Bob Meyer?" she squeaked.

"Of course I do. It's my business to know everyone involved with construction throughout the tristate area." His frown deepened. "How do you think you got the Meyer account to begin with? Bob did me a favor."

"*You're* the reason I got that account?" The world spun, and dots danced in front of her eyes. She reached out for the railing. "I thought…" What could she say? How stupid could she be? She'd believed she'd earned the account on her own, or that it'd had everything to do with her background. Anthony's betrayal came back to her in a rush, making her skin crawl. Had he known her father was the reason she'd landed the Meyer account? He probably believed he should've had it. How he must have resented her.

I didn't deserve the account or the office with the window. Damn.

"Meyer says you let him down. What happened, Paige? I put my reputation on the line to give you that opportunity."

"Dad," Noah interrupted. "You're—"

"It's all right, Noah." Her hands fisted at her sides, and all her distress morphed into anger. Her own father had proved once again he had no confidence in her by arranging her life before she'd even begun to live it. "I got fired, OK? I screwed up my first real job and proved you right. Are you happy now?"

"Happy?" He grunted. "Why would you think this makes me happy? What are you talking about?"

"It doesn't matter." Tears clouded her vision. "I'm unemployed, but I have several applications in, and—"

"Come home, Paige." Her father jangled the keys in his pocket. "I'll let you work at Langford Plumbing Supplies."

All the air left her lungs in a rush. "You'll...You'll *let* me work for you?" Hurt and mortification burned through her. "Wow, Dad. As wonderful as that offer sounds, I think I'll pass." Lifting her chin, Paige walked past Noah and her father into the house and continued straight through to the back patio doors and out again.

Wanting to lick her wounds in private, she made a beeline for the river. She ducked under the hanging branches of the old weeping willow and sank down to the cool, soft ground. Hugging her knees to her chest, she leaned against the trunk just in time for the first sob to break free. *Damn. Damn. Damn.*

Now, more than ever, she needed to prove to her family that she could succeed on her own. She didn't need her dad to throw her crumbs. Tomorrow she'd get back to the job search with a vengeance. Maybe she could find another plumbing supplier willing to hire her. Wouldn't that be sweet? She'd gladly work for her family's competition.

There is no revenge sweeter than success.

CHAPTER EIGHT

RYAN EMERGED FROM AROUND THE corner of the Langfords' porch. He should have felt bad about eavesdropping on Paige's confrontation with her dad. But he didn't. Where Paige was concerned, his protective instincts came out full force. Right now, the urge to go after her tore at him. First, he had a few things to say to Mr. Langford. He strolled around to the stairs, shoved his hands into his front pockets, and stared up at the tough SOB who'd just made his daughter cry. "You set her up with the Meyer account?"

"Who the hell are you?"

"This is Ryan Malloy." Noah nodded toward him. "Ryan, this is my dad, Ed Langford."

"I'm a friend of your daughter's." Ryan walked up the steps and took a seat. "Does the name Anthony Rutger mean anything to you?"

"I've never heard of him." Mr. Langford frowned. "Why do you ask?"

"He's the reason Paige got fired." Relief coursed through Ryan. For a second, he'd wondered if Paige's father had also set her up with the snake who'd caused her downfall. "I can fill you in on what happened at Ramsey & Weil."

"Paige told you, and she didn't tell me?" Noah's eyes widened. "I'm her big brother."

"And she needs you right now." Ryan shot him a pointed look. "Sometimes it's easier to share things with a stranger. Things you can't bring yourself to tell family."

Mr. Langford jangled the contents of his pockets and leaned against the porch railing. "What do you know about this?"

"Paige started dating this Rutger fellow shortly after she started working for Ramsey & Weil. Once he gained her trust, he started sabotaging her."

"How?" Noah's brow lowered.

"He'd offer to drop her stuff off at the mailbox, and instead, he'd hold on to it until he knew it would be late. Things like that. She was on the phone when the same-day courier showed up for the Meyer contract. Rutger offered to take it down to the lobby for her. She trusted him and handed it right over." Ryan looked at Mr. Langford. "He never gave the courier the envelope. Meyer never got the contract. Paige lost the account for Ramsey & Weil and got fired."

"She should've known better," Mr. Langford muttered.

"How? How would she have known not to trust the guy she was dating?" Ryan shook his head. "Listen, that's only part of what's going on here. She's—"

"I don't need *you* to tell *me* about my own daughter." Ed Langford pushed off the railing and widened his stance.

"Dad," Noah chided. "Ryan's only trying to help."

"Don't worry about it." Ryan rose. "Do you mind if I cut through the house?"

"Go ahead." Noah told him. "But Paige is probably with my wife by now."

"Got it." Ryan turned to glare at Ed. "You don't want me to tell you what's going on with her. Fine. I won't. I just hope you figure it out before it's too late."

"What the hell is that supposed to mean?" Ed glared back.

Ryan opened the screen door and walked into the Langfords' house without answering. He found Lucinda sitting on the stairs leading to the second floor. "You eavesdropping, squirt?"

"I don't know. What's 'dropping eaves' mean?"

"Were you listening to the grown-ups talking out there?" He gestured with his thumb toward the screen door.

She nodded.

"Then 'eavesdropping' means you and I have something in common." He touched the end of her nose. "Where's your mom?"

She wrinkled her nose. "She's changing Toby's stinky diaper."

"Is your aunt with her?"

Lucinda shook her head.

"Can you show me where Paige's room is?"

"I can, but she's not in there." The little girl looked up at him with solemn eyes. "Auntie Paige was crying."

"I was afraid of that. Where'd she go?"

She pointed toward the kitchen "Out that way."

"Thanks." Ryan started for the back patio doors.

"Are you going to give her a hug and make her feel better?" Lucinda called after him.

Ryan stopped and turned back. "Do you think I should?"

"Yes." She stood up. "You can make her feel better, and she can make you feel better."

"You're one smart little kid." He smiled.

"You don't look like Johnny Appleseed anymore."

"I know. Are you disappointed?"

"No. Well, maybe a little." She peered at him over the banister. "Better go find my auntie Paige."

"Yes, ma'am." He saluted her and made his way through the kitchen and outside. Glancing toward the river, he didn't see her at first, then caught a glimpse of her blue jeans peeking out from behind the willow. He ducked inside his apartment, grabbed a couple of colas from the fridge and a few paper towels.

He shut his apartment door behind him, glanced toward the big house, and headed for Paige. It broke his heart to see her huddled against the tree with her head on her arms. "Hey." He slid down beside her. "I brought you generic soda."

"Thanks." She made a watery snorting sound, but didn't raise her head. "I'm sure brand-free soda will fix *everything* wrong with my life."

"I also brought paper towels." He placed the sodas on the ground and thrust the paper towels into her hand. "There's nothing wrong with your life. Take it from me, this is a minor glitch in the grand scheme of things." That got her attention.

She raised her head finally and wiped the smeared mascara from her cheeks. "Y-you know what he said? My dad said he'd *let* me work for the family business."

"Yeah, I heard the whole conversation."

"You did?" She blinked. "How?"

"I stuck around in case you needed backup."

"Oh." She nodded slightly and blew her nose into the paper towels.

"Isn't working at Langford Plumbing Supplies what you wanted? What's the problem?"

"He said he'd *let* me work there, not that he wanted me to." She shot him a *Catch up, would you?* look. "Can you imagine what that'd be like? He'd be watching me every minute to make sure I don't mess things up again. How much responsibility do you think he'd give me after what happened at Ramsey & Weil? No. Thanks."

His poor ol' heart tapped out a hopeful rhythm. "Does that mean you've given up on the notion of taking over the family business? Are you thinking about looking for something for you instead of trying to prove—"

"No to both." She sniffed, picked up one of the soda cans, and popped it open. "I'm more determined than ever to prove myself. I want my dad to *beg* me to come work for LPS."

"I hate to be the worm in your apple, darlin', but—"

"Then don't be." She scowled his way while she took a sip. Her lovely green eyes were puffy and red from crying. "Don't be the worm in my apple, or the fly in my soup, or…or…I don't need an argument, Ryan. What I need is a hug." She sniffed. "You said you'd have my back."

Ryan put his arm around her shoulders and pulled her against his side. "I do have your back. More than anything, I want to see you happy." He wrapped his other arm around her and held her tight. She laid her head on his shoulder. Fresh tears fell from her eyes, each one eating away at his heart a little bit more.

For a while, he held her that way, with neither of them saying a word. Wouldn't she be much better off doing something that brought her joy instead of this misery? "You in the mood for frozen pizza?" He gave her another squeeze.

"No." She burrowed in closer. "What I really want is a bacon cheeseburger with extra-crispy fries and a chocolate shake."

"OK." Ryan chuckled. "That sounds good too."

She nodded against him. "Have you ever eaten at the truck stop off the interstate heading toward Kentucky?"

"Nope. Noah has mentioned it, though." He kissed her forehead. "Let's stop at my apartment first so you can wash those tears away. Then I'll take you out for the biggest, juiciest bacon cheeseburger you've ever had." Her arms wrapped around him, and his insides slid into bliss.

"Thank you, Ryan," she whispered. "Thank you for being on my side."

"Always." For the first time in forever, someone needed him. Not just anyone—Paige needed him. Ryan swallowed the lump in his throat while he handed over his heart. Yep. He was a goner, and the recipient of his damaged, broken self had no idea that his world hung on every one of her sighs. "Let's go. I'm starving."

"Me too." She sent him a watery smile. "Nothing like a good cry to make me hungry."

He helped her up, grabbed the sodas, and held her hand all the way to his tiny bathroom. Ryan leaned against the doorframe while she washed away the evidence of her tears. "We're taking my truck."

"Whatever," she mumbled through the washcloth. "I can't afford the gas anyway."

"Is your dad staying the night?"

"I don't know." She grabbed the towel hanging from the rack next to the sink. "You heard the entire conversation. He didn't say."

"Do you want to talk to him before we leave? Your dad meant well when he recommended you to Meyer."

She made another snorting sound in response.

"He's a dad doing what dads do, darlin'. It's his job to look out for you."

"I really don't want to talk about this anymore." She glared at him over the towel. "Didn't I *just* stop crying? Do you really want to get me started again?"

"No. Sorry." He refrained from grinning. He loved how direct and open she was with her feelings and what she wanted. With Theresa, he'd had to poke and prod to get anything out of her. It was always a guessing game with her. His chest constricted, and guilt spiraled through him. Disloyalty—another brick to add to the load of shit he carried around on his shoulders.

"What's wrong?" Paige folded the towel over the rack. "One minute you looked ready to laugh, and the next your expression went in a completely different direction."

"It's nothing." He pushed off from the doorframe, unable to meet her eyes. "Ready?"

"Ryan…"

Confusion over opposing loyalties made his head spin, but he wanted to explain. What he admired about Paige was her openness. Didn't he owe her the same? "I had a moment. It happens. Sometimes something triggers a memory, and all I can do is hang on until something else brings me back to the present."

Paige wrapped her arms around his waist and snuggled up against him. "Iraq?" she whispered.

His arms went around her like they belonged there—casual and intimate, all at once. "No. Theresa."

She searched his face. "I'm sorry, Ryan. Do you want to talk about it?"

He sighed. "Theresa was shy. I always had to coax things out of her, like what she wanted to do or how she felt." He shook his head. "Your openness is refreshing, but thinking that felt…disloyal somehow."

"Noticing the differences between people doesn't make you disloyal." She studied him. "I'm sorry you lost Theresa, but…"

He tensed. "But what?"

"Maybe it's time to let her go," she murmured.

"Humph." His eyes stung. "Let's get going."

Paige took his face between her hands and brought him in for a kiss. His heart slammed into his sternum, and all the blood in his head rushed south. He backed her up against the wall and lost himself in the feel of her warmth and softness. Tangling his fingers in her silky hair, he tilted her face to gain better access to her luscious mouth, plunging his tongue deep to taste her sweetness. She rose on tiptoe, threw her arms around his neck, and pressed herself even closer. Lord, he wanted her, but not like this. Not when she was upset about her dad and feeling vulnerable.

He forced himself to break the kiss and rested his chin on the top of her head. "You do things to me, Paige. You know that, don't you, darlin'?"

"Ditto." Her chest rose and fell as rapidly as his. "That was to get your mind off—"

"It worked." He chuffed out a laugh. "And now I can't walk to my truck." He sucked in a few deep breaths. "You're gonna have to give me a minute." One of her deep, throaty laughs sent a fresh wave of lust crashing over him. "Not helping, Paige."

"What's not helping?" She slid away from him, finger-combed her hair, and looked at him in question.

"That sexy laugh of yours, that's what." His comment elicited another sexy sound from her. A cold shower might help, but even the thought of getting naked while she was anywhere in proximity made his cock twitch and harden even more. He let out a growl of frustration and headed toward his kitchen. "Do you want the rest of your soda?" He snatched both cans from the coffee table.

"Not really."

He dumped the opened can in the sink and put the other back in the fridge. "Bacon cheeseburger, extra-crispy fries, and a chocolate shake, here we come." *Come.* Oh, he'd love to come, deep inside her, while she cried out his name and writhed naked beneath him. Ryan knocked his head against the refrigerator door, only to be subjected to another one of her sexy laughs. Wouldn't matter what came out of her mouth. At this point, everything she said or did lit him up like one of those motion-detector floodlights. He turned to find her right behind him, one side of her mouth quirked up and her green eyes filled with mischief.

"Out." He pointed to the door and followed her swaying hips into the warm spring evening. "Unfair—that's what this is. Entirely unfair."

She laced her fingers with his and slid him a sideways look. "What is?"

"You've seen me naked, and I haven't even caught a glimpse of you." He pulled her in for another kiss.

She sighed against his mouth and draped her arms over his shoulders. "What are you suggesting?"

His breath snagged against his racing heart, while her gaze roamed his face, settling on his mouth like she had when he'd first shaved. When her eyes came back to his, her pupils were dilated, and her lips parted slightly. He gulped. They were on the edge of a precipice here. Somehow, he managed to retain just enough of his fraying wits to recognize how crucial his next words were. He wanted a chance at more than a few weeks with her.

Pressing his forehead against hers, he took the leap. "I'm suggesting that whenever you're ready to remedy the inequity, you let me know. I'm putting you in charge, darlin', because I can't be trusted to think straight when you're near me." Judging by the pleased look suffusing her face, he'd said the right thing. Might as well go for broke. "And one more thing—you don't have to prove a damn thing to me. I already think you're the reason the sun rises and sets each day."

She swallowed a few times, and her eyes grew bright. "Thank you, Ryan. I…That means a lot to me." She bit her bottom lip, and color rose to her cheeks. "We should get going."

He kept her hand in his on the way to his truck and tried to keep a dignified expression on his face while his heart soared. They rounded the corner to find Noah, Ceejay, and their kids assembled next to Ed Langford and his rental car. Paige's grip on his hand tightened.

"Are you leaving already?" she asked her dad.

All eyes turned their way, even baby Toby's. Ceejay, Noah, and Mr. Langford glanced at his hand entwined with Paige's, ping-ponged between them, and finally exchanged glances with each other. *Shit.* Group disapproval.

"I am." Mr. Langford opened the passenger side of the coupe, threw his briefcase onto the seat. "Your mother is expecting me to attend a literacy fund-raiser this evening, and I don't want to disappoint her." He fixed Paige with a fatherly look as he walked toward them. "Call her, Paige."

"I will, Dad." She let go of Ryan's hand and twisted a finger around a lock of her hair. "I'm…I'm sorry I let you down. I should've—"

"Let me down?" Mr. Langford's brow creased, and he drew his daughter in for a bear hug. "You think this is about letting me down? We were worried sick about you. We didn't know where you were or what was going on."

"I got fired," Paige muttered. "Not exactly something you want to write home about. I wanted to work it all out and have a new job before I told anyone." She disentangled herself and turned away. "Ryan and I were just heading out for a burger. Tell Mom I'll call her tomorrow."

"Noah tells me you served under him in Task Force Iron." Mr. Langford turned to Ryan with an inscrutable stare.

"Yes, sir. We were in the same Humvee when we got hit."

"Nice to have met you." Mr. Langford offered him his hand, and they shook briefly. "Are you coming home soon, Paige?"

Paige nodded. Ryan's heart dropped to his boots.

🐏　🐏　🐏

"We're taking two cars to work this morning," Noah told Paige as they walked down the veranda steps. "I have to run to Evansville this afternoon to pick up a load of oak. Do you want to ride with me or Ryan?"

"Depends." She bit her lower lip. "Are you going to lecture me if I ride with you?"

"Probably." He pinned her with a sharp look. "I can't believe you didn't tell me what was going on."

"I'm sorry." Her throat tightened. "I've never been fired before. It's humiliating. I was too ashamed to tell anyone."

Her brother slung his arm around her shoulders. "You're going to come out of this just fine. In the meantime, you're welcome to stay here as long as you want."

She had to swallow a few times before she could respond. "Thanks. I love being here with you, Ceejay, and the kids. I hope you know how much I appreciate it."

"It's mutual."

He gave her another hug and let her go as Ryan came around the house. Her heart skipped at the sight of him, and she couldn't tear away her gaze. He wore his cowboy hat today, a tight pair of faded jeans, and an equally snug T-shirt under a denim jacket. The whole ensemble emphasized his lean, corded frame. He still needed to put on a few pounds. Even so, the man was so damn sexy with that blue-eyed blond, troubled-cowboy thing he had going on. A sigh escaped her, and Noah cast her another intense look. Heat flooded her face. "I'll ride with you, Noah."

"That's good. I want to hear the whole Ramsey & Weil story." Noah nodded a greeting to Ryan. "We're taking two cars today. I have errands this afternoon."

"You coming with me or riding with Noah?"

Ryan aimed his baby blues her way, causing another internal flutter fest in her midsection. "I'm riding with my brother." A momentary flash of disappointment crossed his face, and it tugged at her. "He wants me tell him what happened at Ramsey."

He nodded. "See you there."

She watched his very fine backside as he made his way to his truck. *Get a grip!* She blew out a frustrated breath and followed her brother. As soon as she was buckled in and they were on the road toward town, she began. "I started dating a coworker my first week on the job. That was my first mistake." Retelling the story brought back all the mortification. She'd been so stupid to trust someone else to do what she should've done herself. Never again. Along with proving herself to her dad, she needed another chance to get it right for herself.

"A painful lesson." Noah shook his head in sympathy. "Anthony Rutger is an ass, and I'm sure he'll get what's coming to him in the end."

"Ryan offered to rearrange his face for me." She smiled at the memory.

"Speaking of Ryan…" He glanced at her, then back at the road. "What's going on between you two?"

"We're getting to know each other." She stiffened. "Why do you ask?"

"I'm concerned. He's not in a place where he can handle any kind of hurt or disappointment."

"Wait." She frowned. "You're concerned about him and not me? You think I'm less vulnerable?"

"You don't have PTSD, and you haven't recently considered committing suicide." His jaw twitched. "That I know of, anyway."

"The thought of harming myself has never entered my head." She studied the dashboard, while the mix of guilt and anger dashed around inside her. "Ryan and I are friends. I enjoy his company, and I believe he enjoys mine." Heat rose to her cheeks as she remembered the kisses she and Ryan had shared. Not something she wanted to tell her older brother.

"Friends?"

"That's right."

"For now." Noah slid her another pointed look.

"It's none of your business." She crossed her arms in front of her and scowled. "Ryan and I are both adults."

"I don't want to see *either* of you get hurt, that's all."

"Thank you for your concern," she snapped as they pulled into his parking space in the alley. Not wanting to wait for further comment, she hopped out and headed for the door the second he put his truck in park. Ted and Ryan were bent over the plans for the first piece of the new product line. She walked past them to the small kitchen area to pour herself a cup of coffee. None had been made. Frustrated, she opened the cabinets one after the other, looking for coffee. "We're out of coffee," she called.

"I know," Noah replied behind her. "Here's a couple of twenties. Would you mind going to IGA for a few cans?"

"No, I wouldn't mind." She took the money from his hand and breezed past him into the workspace. "Is there anything else you need besides coffee?"

"Yeah," Ted answered. "Pick up a box of sugar and some creamer."

"Will do." Wow. In and back out the door in less than five minutes. A new avoidance record for her. Her brother's words echoed inside her head with each step down the sidewalk. What right did he have to interfere, and why did he assume anyone would get hurt? Maybe, just maybe, something extraordinary would come of her friendship with Ryan, like…Like what? She had goals and dreams that would take her far from rural Indiana.

She stopped walking for a second. Would Ryan consider coming with her or pursuing a long-distance relationship? *Get. A. Grip.* She got her feet moving again. Just because Ryan wanted to see her naked didn't mean he had any intention of starting something deeper. Did it?

The way he'd left it all up to her sent a surge of tenderness through her. He was so damn sweet it made her heart ache, and the thought of getting naked with him kicked her pulse rate into overdrive. Her brother's words chased the naked Ryan images away. Didn't Noah realize she was every bit as likely to be devastated?

By the time she reached IGA, perspiration dampened her face. The day promised to be still and humid with unseasonable heat. She glanced up at the hazy sky on her way inside the store. The coolness of the air-conditioned interior brought a welcome change. Only the middle of March, and it had to be in the high eighties already. She hadn't brought clothing for this kind of weather. Another good reason to head home on Sunday.

Grabbing a small basket on the way, she went to the coffee aisle and grabbed an expensive bag of a brand-name dark roast along with a can of the cheap stuff the guys usually kept on hand. She needed good coffee this morning, and since she'd been sent on this errand, she made the choice.

By the time she was on her way back, Paige had calmed down. Noah cared about Ryan. The two had been through so much together—how could he not be concerned? And her big brother had always been protective of her. She had to admit she'd been equally concerned about Noah's relationship with Ceejay at first, and look how well that turned out. She had a smile on her face as she entered L&L's workspace through the back door, only to find it empty.

"Where'd everybody go?" Maybe they were busy with something upstairs. She deposited the new supplies in the kitchen and started a pot of the dark roast. Her phone vibrated in her back pocket. She brought it out and read the text: *When you get back, come up to the conference room.* Puzzled, she walked to the freight elevator and headed up to the second floor. Paige entered the room, noting Ryan's smile, Ted's neutral expression, and her brother wearing his serious face.

"What's up?"

"Have a seat. We want to discuss something with you." Noah gestured to the chair next to him.

"Here's your change." She pulled the bills and coins from her pocket and placed it on the table in front of Noah before taking a seat.

"I can't believe you didn't tell us you were unemployed." Ted folded his arms in front of him.

His hurt and disappointed expression knotted her stomach. Her eyes narrowed. "Is this going to be a discussion about all of my shortcomings?" She started to rise. "Because I could really do without that right now."

Ryan glared at Ted before turning to her. "Nope. Ted's done with that. Right, kid?"

"Sorry." Ted's face turned sheepish. "I know you've been through a rough patch."

"We have a proposal we'd like to make." Noah's gaze went around the table and settled on her. "We've discussed your ideas for expanding our brick-and-mortar presence in the market, and if you're interested, we'd like to offer you a position." He grinned. "We even came up with a title. You'd be the VP of marketing for Langford & Lovejoy."

Shock sent a wave of adrenaline coursing through her, and all she could do was blink.

"It doesn't pay much." Noah shrugged. "Room and board and some spending money are about all we can manage until things take off on your end. We can also offer a twenty percent commission on any of the sample pieces you sell."

"What do you think?" Ryan's face lit up with pleased expectation.

Had he engineered the whole thing? Paige frowned. "I need to talk to my brother for a minute." Ted and Ryan both remained seated with their eyes riveted on her. She raised her brow and stared back. "Alone."

"Oh." Ted nodded and rose. "Sure."

Ryan's eyes clouded, and his mouth tightened. He didn't say a word as he followed Ted out the door. She waited until they'd left before turning to Noah.

"Listen, Paige. Before you say anything, just listen." He covered one of her hands with his. "I know about your ambition to take over Langford Plumbing Supplies. I even understand what drives you toward that goal, but—"

"Whose idea was it to offer me this position?" If Ryan had come up with it, that worried her. No matter what was between them, she didn't want to have more crumbs thrown her way, especially not by him. She needed his respect, and she needed to earn her way through her own abilities. Did no one understand?

"Mine. I think you're brilliant. Ted and Ryan agree with me. Dad's out of his mind not to snatch you up, and I'm happy to take advantage of his stupidity."

She relaxed, and warmth flooded through her. She and Noah had always understood each other, and she knew he wouldn't have made the offer if he didn't really want to. "I have a counterproposal."

He leaned back in his chair, eyeing her speculatively. "Let's hear it."

"I'll take the job with the understanding that it's temporary. I'll put my heart and soul into growing the store. When and if I manage to find another job, I'll help you hire someone well qualified to take my place. I'll provide consulting on a continual basis free of charge." She prayed he'd understand. "I have...goals I need to achieve for my own peace of mind."

Noah covered her hands again. "I get it. I really do. Just so you know, I'm hoping you'll love it here so much that you'll want to stay. Keep an open mind."

"I love you, Noah." She grinned.

"Ditto, Paige." He squeezed her hands and rose. "Let's go tell the guys."

"I'm going to have to head to Philly for my stuff. It gets hot here much earlier than it does in Pennsylvania. I need to see Mom. Which reminds me, I promised to call home today."

"Let's go tell the guys first, and then you can call Mom. If you need to take a few days off, that's fine." He opened the door for her. "Ted will have some paperwork for you to fill out."

"I like my new title." Happiness bubbled up. Even though the job was temporary, VP of anything sounded great on a résumé. Ideas about how to arrange the showroom streamed through her mind. Now she could contact the artists she'd talked to at the craft fair. "Do I have a budget?"

"Talk to Ted. I'm sure we can scrape something together."

She couldn't keep the smile off her face on the way back down to the first floor. "I bought expensive coffee."

"Yeah?"

"As VP of marketing, I just gotta say the crap you guys get has got to go."

Noah laughed as the elevator doors opened onto the workspace. He ushered her into the room and announced, "Meet our new vice president of marketing."

Her eyes drew a bead straight to Ryan. Their gazes locked. Her heart stumbled, and a pang shot through her. He looked so damned pleased, and her brother's warning hit home. If she weren't careful, she could destroy him, and if she let him, he could break her heart as well. She couldn't let that happen. The first opportunity she got, she had to explain her counteroffer.

This was only temporary.

Paige walked to the storefront and moved behind the counter. Perching on the stool, she pulled her cell phone out of her pocket and hit her mom's number. She was not looking forward to this conversation. Maybe her mom wouldn't answer, and she could leave a message. *Coward.* Her mom picked up after the fourth ring. *Drat.*

"Hi, Mom." Guilt gnawed at the edges of her heart.

"Paige…"

"I know. I know. I should've called you back right away." She bit her lower lip. "I'm sorry."

"Called back? What I want to know is, why didn't you come to us right away after you were let go from Ramsey & Weil? Your father and I have been worried sick." She paused. "You told me you were out of town on business. Since when do you feel you have to lie to me?"

"I…I did do some business. Putting together print ads for L&L counts."

"Paige…"

"All right. The truth is, I was too embarrassed." Saying the words out loud, she realized how foolish she'd been.

"Don't you think your father and I have had a few setbacks along the way? Everybody gets knocked around a little at the beginning of their careers. It's to be expected. You pick yourself up, shake off the dust, and move on. Hiding things like this from us is beneath you."

"I'll bet Dad never got fired."

Her mother sucked in a breath, but she didn't comment. "We were worried. We didn't know where you were or what had happened. Don't do that again."

"I won't. I promise." Her eyes misted. "I'm sorry I caused you to worry."

"You're forgiven. Are you coming home soon? You have no reason to hide anymore, and your father and I will help you through this rough spot."

"No. I'm going to work for Noah and Ted until I find something else. I'll have to make a trip home soon, though. How about next weekend? I'm running out of things to wear. Are you going to be free?"

"I'll make sure I'm free. If you need anything—"

"I know. I'll call you right away if I do. Thanks, Mom." She eased the tight grip she had on the phone. "I love you." She should've known better than to cause her parents needless worry. They didn't deserve what she'd put them through.

"I love you too, sweetheart. Call me if anything changes. I'm here for you if you need to talk."

"I will. I have to get back to work." They said their good-byes, and she heaved a sigh of relief and put her phone away. She should've made the call days ago.

The rest of the day flew by in a blur. Paige wrangled a small budget from Ted, and she called the vendors from the fair who could supply items to create a charming nursery setting for the showroom. The glass blower agreed to provide a few of his pieces on consignment to start, with the promise that once the Americana product line was up and running, they'd buy wholesale from him. While they talked, he made an appointment to visit the showroom with his family. If she made a sale, she'd get her first commission.

Ted and Ryan came in from hanging the new sign above the shop doors out front. Both were dripping sweat. "It's nasty out there." Ted grabbed a few paper towels from the staff kitchen and wiped his face before walking toward the shelves to put his tool belt away.

Ryan carried the ladder they'd used and propped it up against a wall. "You about ready to head home, Paige?"

"Sure. Let's clean up and get going." She shut down her computer, and they all took up their closing routine like a well-oiled machine. The day had grown darker and more ominous by the hour, and the atmosphere was thick with the promise of violent weather. Ryan placed his hand at the small of her back as they walked toward his truck.

"See you tomorrow, Ted," Ryan called.

Ted nodded. "The sign looks great, by the way, and welcome aboard, Paige."

"Thanks." She waved and climbed into the truck. As soon as they were on the two-lane, she said, "I made a counteroffer to Noah."

"Oh?" Ryan's brow creased. "What was that?"

"It's temporary."

He glanced at her. "What's temporary?"

"My job with L&L. I'll stay until I can get my career back on track; then I'll help with finding my replacement. I'll always be available as a consultant."

His grip on the steering wheel tightened, and his jaw clenched.

"You know what my motivation is and what I hope to accomplish," she reminded him. "Nothing has changed."

"And you know there's no guarantee your father will hand the plumbing empire over to you one way or the other," Ryan snapped. "You could end up spinning your wheels in that direction your entire life—without ever gaining any ground."

"I thought you weren't going to be the worm in my apple," she snapped back.

"I thought you had more common sense." He shot her an incredulous look. "Do you enjoy beating your head against that brick wall, or are you just so hardheaded it has no effect?"

She averted her face. "Ouch."

"Paige," he gritted out, "why do you want to set yourself up for the same misery over and over? Let it go."

"Listen to you." She glared. "Have *you* let go?"

"We aren't talking about me." His eyes flashed with hurt, and he shook his head slowly. "I'm not the healthy one here, and I'll be the first to admit it."

Guilt sent heat rushing to her face. "I'm sorry. I'm being defensive, and you didn't deserve that."

"No apology necessary. It's your life. You have the right to screw it up however you see fit."

"How very sideways of you," she cracked. "Wherever I end up, it doesn't mean we can't continue our friendship."

His grip on the steering wheel went white-knuckle. "Is that what this is?"

She nodded, unable to form words around the constriction in her throat. She'd hurt him, and that sent a sharp pain through her as well. They turned into her brother's driveway, just as the weather siren went off. "Great."

Ryan parked the truck, and they hurried out. Ceejay stood on the side of the porch with Toby in her arms, shouting at her daughter, "Lucinda, come inside right now!"

Paige followed the direction of Ceejay's stare. Lucinda was near the walnut copse, with her back to her mother. "What's she doing?"

"She's looking for our stupid dog. Sweet Pea hates the siren and storms. He's hiding." Ceejay called her daughter again.

"We'll get Lucinda and Sweet Pea." Ryan started toward the trees, just as the branches began to whip around with the rising wind. "Take Toby to the cellar. We'll be right there."

Ryan's stride ate up the ground, and Paige had to run to catch up. "Lucinda, let's go," she urged.

"I gotta find Sweet Pea," she pleaded. "He's 'fraid of storms."

"I'll get the dog." Ryan put his hands on Lucinda's shoulders and tried to get her moving. "You go in with your aunt."

"Sweet Pea," Lucinda cried, refusing to move from the spot.

The wind that had kicked up mere seconds ago disappeared. A greenish cast and stillness settled over them, and a chill ran up her spine. "Now, Lucinda. Sweet Pea will be all right.

Animals have instincts about the weather. He'll know to hole up somewhere."

"Who told you that?" Ryan's expression turned skeptical while he searched the tall grass growing by the edge of the trees.

Paige grabbed her niece's hand and started pulling her toward the house. "Come on, Ryan," Paige called. "This storm is going to hit any second."

"You go on. I'll be right in."

She hoisted Lucinda into her arms. "Leave the dog. Let's go."

He must've sensed something in her tone, because he stopped searching and turned to her. "I'll be fine. Take Lucinda to the cellar, and as soon as I have the dog, I'll follow."

"No. Come inside with me now. You are *not* putting your life on the line for a dog." Her heart hammered against her ribs, and Lucinda's tears dampened her T-shirt. "Please." She couldn't disguise her rising panic. "Please," she repeated.

He took off his cowboy hat and raked his fingers through his hair. "All right. I'm right behind you."

"Sweet Pea!" Lucinda squirmed to get out of her arms.

Paige held her niece tight and ran for the front door. "Hush. Sweet Pea will be fine." They got to the front door, and Ryan reached around her to open it. The moment she was inside, the wind started howling again, and marble-size hail pummeled the house and ground. The sirens kept up their wail, and everything went as dark as night. Paige rushed to the cellar door off the kitchen and hurried down into the musty dampness with her niece held securely in her arms. It wasn't until they were in the small windowless root cellar that she realized Ryan was not behind her. "Shit."

Lucinda gasped and pulled back to peer at her. "You said a bad word."

"I couldn't help it."

Toby sat in the midst of his toys in a portable playpen. The oil lamps Ceejay had lit cast a dim yellow glow over the old wicker furniture set up around the space so they could sit out any storm in relative comfort.

"Ryan is still out there," Paige muttered. "He's looking for the dog." She put Lucinda down and walked to the bottom of the stairs.

Ceejay's cell phone rang, and her sister-in-law answered.

Paige knew it was her brother checking to see that they were all safe. Straining to hear Ryan's footsteps on the floor above, she silently fell apart. Panic, anger, and fear swirled through her until she couldn't breathe. She imagined the worst. He'd be hit with lightning or a falling tree. Maybe he'd be swept up into the funnel of a tornado. *Oh, God. Please don't let anything happen to him.*

"Ryan will be fine." Ceejay put her hand on Paige's shoulder. "He's within sight of the house. It's not like he's stranded out in a field somewhere."

Paige nodded. A boom of thunder exploded, shaking the house. Hail hitting the outside walls pinged in her ears, and the wind took on the cadence of a freight train. Still, she strained to hear the reassuring thump of Ryan's footsteps above. She held her breath, and her eyes never left the door at the top of the stairs. She didn't want anything to happen to him. She didn't want to lose him for any reason. Not now. Not ever. *Crap.*

The door at the top of the steps flew open, and Ryan appeared at the top, carrying the soaking mutt draped over his shoulders. He picked his way carefully down each step until he reached the bottom. "Get the door for me," he told her as he squatted to free the dog.

Relief swamped her, followed by rage. Paige raced up the steps, slammed the door shut, and ran back down, ready to kill him. "Don't ever do that again," she growled with her hands fisted by her sides.

"Don't ever do what again?" He swiped at the rainwater dripping from his face.

"You said you were right behind me, and then you disappeared. I can't believe you'd risk your life that way for a dog," she gritted out. "Do you have any idea how worried I was?" Her voice broke, and she had to turn away.

"You had no reason to worry." Ryan drew her into his arms and held her. "I'm fine, darlin'. I was never in any danger."

"You ran out into a storm, Ryan—into hail, lightning, and possibly a tornado! Who does that for an animal?" she cried.

"Look." He nodded toward what he wanted her to see.

She followed his gaze to Lucinda and Sweet Pea. Her niece had her face buried in the wet dog's fur and her arms wrapped tight around his thick neck. Toby patted the mutt's head through the slats of his playpen. Sweet Pea's tail thumped against the floor.

"I didn't put my life at risk for the dog. I did it for them." He leaned back to peer into her face. "Besides, I was close to the house. Oklahoma is smack-dab in the middle of tornado alley. Don't you think I know how to handle that kind of danger?"

"You're right. I'm sorry." She wrapped her arms around his waist and laid her cheek against his chest, soothed by the steady rhythm of his heartbeat. Surrounded by his strong arms and enveloped in his scent, she felt her own racing heart slow and the tension gripping her leach away. Oh, man. She'd already given him her heart. Without even realizing, she'd done it—she'd fallen for Ryan Malloy.

Friendship my ass.

CHAPTER NINE

RYAN CONTEMPLATED HIS REFLECTION IN the mirror while he shaved for his date with Paige. Was it his imagination, or did he look healthier, more human? Naw. Looks could be deceiving, and he no longer had a face covered in fur, that's all. Besides, if the way his stomach tied into knots at the thought of running into his uncle or cousins tonight was any indication, he hadn't gotten any closer to healthy in the past week.

His first appointment with the army shrink was coming up next Thursday, and that got him thinking. He'd been through the obligatory therapy sessions after the suicide bombing in Iraq, and he knew how it worked. A shrink would draw him into open-ended questions to imply that avoiding his family was not in his best interest. They didn't come right out and say those kinds of things. Nope. Head doctors loved to lead conversations around in circles until you eventually came to the conclusions they wanted you to come to in the first place. Shrinks were good at that kind of thing. In this case, maybe they were right.

If his uncle and any of his cousins were in Evansville for the rodeo—and more than likely, they were—he'd be an ass not to at least stop by and say hello. Maybe he'd even screw up the courage to call his parents next week. His folks would appreciate knowing where he was and what he was doing. Hadn't Noah as much as ordered him to call his mom?

The thought of reconnecting with his family, facing them after all this time, sent a tremor of dread sluicing through him. He tensed for the onslaught of memories sure to follow. They didn't come. Instead, a gut-wrenching longing to see his brothers, sister, and parents brought a hollow ache to his chest. Blowing out a slow breath, he snatched the clean shirt from the hook behind the bathroom door and put it on.

He needed to ground himself in the green of Paige's eyes and hear her voice. He needed to have her beside him with her hand securely gripped in his. Shaking off the melancholy thoughts of family, he grabbed his cowboy hat from its peg on the wall and headed for the big house. He took the veranda steps two at a time and knocked on the front door.

Lucinda opened it and leaned her head back to stare into his face. Sweet Pea stood beside her with his tongue out and saliva hanging in slobbery strands from his huge jowls. "Hey there, Lucinda, is your aunt Paige ready to go?" He leaned down and scratched the dog behind his ears. "How's ol' tubba-ugly today?"

"You saved Sweet Pea." The little girl looked far too serious for her age.

"He would've made it through all right on his own, Luce. I'm just glad everything turned out the way it did." The storm had raged by them. Hail had flattened some of the smaller bushes out front, and a few tree branches had come down, but that's all the damage they'd suffered.

Lucinda threw her arms around his knees and gave him a fierce hug. His heart dissolved into a puddle at the bottom of his stomach. He held her by the shoulders and squatted down to eye level. "Hey, now, it's all right." He opened his arms, and she came in for a good, long hug. Sweet Pea moved in and gave his face a couple of grateful licks. "Yuck, I've been slimed."

Lucinda giggled, and Ryan patted her back. "You OK now, sweetheart?"

She nodded against him, and his chest swelled. He heard movement from the stairs and looked up. Paige and Ceejay stood on the second-floor landing. Lucinda backed out of his arms, and he rose. "She wanted to thank me for rescuing Sweet Pea from the storm. Do you mind if I head for the kitchen sink to rinse Sweet Pea's gratitude off my face? He thanked me too."

"Yeah, we saw." Ceejay laughed. "Go ahead."

Ryan winked at Paige and hurried to rinse off the drool covering his cheek. By the time he returned, Paige waited alone for him by the door. His pulse raced at the sight of her. She wore snug jeans that accentuated her curvy hips, while the tank top she wore under her cotton blouse gave him a teasing glimpse of cleavage that sent his blood rushing.

Her sleeves were rolled up, and her shirt was unbuttoned, with the tails tied at her waist. As if that weren't enough, she wore her sexy black boots. He studied them, imagining her wearing nothing but the boots and a provocative smile.

"I don't own cowboy boots." She held one foot out and turned it from side to side. "I hope these will do."

He swallowed. "They'll do just fine." His voice came out a little hoarse, and he cleared his throat. "Let's go."

One side of her mouth quirked up. "Are we taking my car today?"

"Not a chance." He sent her a mock glower. "It would be against the cowboy code of ethics to show up at a rodeo without my truck." Her laughter washed through him, leaving a wave of lust in its wake. He placed his hand at the small of her back, inhaled the soft musky scent of the cologne she used, and ushered her out the door. Lord, he wanted her in the worst way. Why the hell hadn't he chosen to wear a looser-fitting pair of jeans?

Once they were at his truck, he turned her by the shoulders and smoothed the hair back from her forehead. "You look good enough to eat." He planted a soft kiss on her lips, opened the door, and helped her into the seat. Hurrying around the hood to the driver's side, he wondered how he could coax her into his bed sooner rather than later. He'd placed the whole matter into her hands, but that didn't mean he couldn't help her along with the decision.

In a burst of wishful optimism, he'd picked up a box of condoms that afternoon. Not that he expected anything to happen tonight, but once she'd agreed to stay at L&L, making love with her was no longer a matter of *if* but *when*. He buckled his seat belt and started the Chevy down the driveway. "I've been thinking…"

"That must've hurt," she teased and shot him a wicked grin.

"Very funny." He glanced sidelong her way. "If you wouldn't mind, I thought we'd head to the back of the arena to see if my uncle and cousins are in town tonight."

"I'd love it." Her hand shot out to settle on his forearm. "What changed your mind?"

"I've made a commitment to get better. Hiding from my family hasn't…It's not helping me any, and it isn't fair to them." His gut clenched, and he blew out a breath. "None of what happened is their fault."

"None of what happened is *your* fault either, Ryan. Not the suicide bombing or Theresa's accident."

Her hand smoothed back and forth over his bare skin, and his insides tumbled. Such a simple gesture, and yet her comfort had a profound effect. He nodded, reached for her hand, and brought it to his lips, pressing a kiss on her knuckles. "You're going to have to hold my hand through the whole ordeal, though." He slid her a hangdog look, angling for a little sympathy. "I hope that's all right with you."

She chuckled in that sexy way of hers. "Done."

"Of course, if I knew I had a reward coming at the end of the evening, that would really help matters." He waggled his eyebrows, eliciting another throaty laugh from her. Lord, he could listen to that sound all night long.

"Good try, cowboy."

"I don't know where your mind is taking you, darlin', but all I was hoping for is a kiss good night." He flashed her his best hurt-puppy eyes. "A couple of kisses, maybe, like two…or ten."

"Sure you were." She snorted and rolled her eyes. "Keep hoping."

He grinned and changed the subject. "How'd the phone call go with your mom?"

"It went fine. She forgave me." Paige shifted in her seat to face him. "I'm going to spend some time with her next weekend. I'm heading home to pick up more of my stuff. I don't have any warm-weather clothing here."

"Do you need any help? If you want, I can come along." His pulse raced. One, he wanted to spend an entire weekend alone with her, far, far away from Noah, and two, maybe they could pay Anthony Rutger a little visit.

"That would be nice." Her lips curved up into a half smile. "I could use the help packing and carrying."

"I have a lot of room in my truck to haul stuff, if you want to bring any furniture or larger things."

She made a clicking sound against her teeth. "Do you think this old truck will make a trip that long without a breakdown?"

"I made it here from Texas with no problem." He glanced at the odometer, which registered 260,000 miles and some change. Maybe it was time to look into buying a new vehicle. It wasn't like he didn't have the money. All he'd done since Theresa's accident was tuck what he earned into the bank, including his military pay. Other than rent, food, and booze, he'd lacked the enthusiasm to buy anything new for himself.

He glanced at the woman sitting beside him. Was that changing because of Paige or because he was finally ready to return to the land of the living? Maybe it had something to do with the new job. Working with Noah and Ted and creating things with his hands settled him. He'd experienced moments of contentment and satisfaction, and that gave him hope.

Soon they were driving through the outskirts of Evansville toward the arena. "The actual rodeo won't start until seven thirty, but there are exhibition shows prior to the main events, and the stadium halls will be filled with vendors. We can go see my uncle and then check out the booths."

"Booths?" Paige's brow furrowed. "What kind of vendors?"

He chuckled. "Everything a cowboy or cowgirl might want to buy will be there. Boots, clothes, hats, art, tack, belts, jewelry, purses—you name it, you'll find it, even furniture. Lots of guest ranches and real estate agents set up tables to advertise too."

"Oh." Her eyes widened. "Too bad I'm currently underfunded. I could do some real damage tonight."

"I'd like to buy you a hat, if you'll let me." He smirked. "You're going to want one once we're inside."

"What does being inside have to do with anything?" She turned a puzzled look his way.

"You'll be the only one there *not* wearing a cowboy hat." He squeezed her hand. "I'm thinking a nice straw for the summer.

THE DIFFERENCE A DAY MAKES

Something with a tooled leather band or maybe silver-and-turquoise conches." Ryan joined the line of traffic heading to the parking ramp next to the sports center. The closer they got, the more pedestrians in western wear filled the sidewalks, milling around in bunches. *Unfamiliars.*

His nerves rebelled, and adrenaline hit his bloodstream. His heart pounded, and his mouth went dry. *You can do this.* He'd been to hundreds of rodeos in his lifetime. He knew what to expect, and it wasn't insurgents or improvised explosive devices. This was home, not some desert in the middle of Iraq. No matter how many times he said it, sweat still beaded his forehead, and a chill wearing combat boots marched down his spine. "I wasn't kidding about the hand-holding, Paige."

The sudden intake of her breath confirmed his worst fears. He looked like hell, sweaty and pasty white.

"What's wrong?" Her eyes filled with concern.

"It's all the people, the crowds." He sucked in a deep breath and let it out slowly. "Paranoia is part of the deal." They were in the ramp and searching for a parking spot. He did the deep breathing thing a few more times, fighting to remain in the present. He found a spot large enough for his truck and pulled in. Shutting off the engine, he unbuckled his seat belt, leaned back, and closed his eyes tight.

"We don't have to do this, Ryan." She undid her seat belt and scooched closer. "We can have dinner somewhere quiet and head home."

"Sure we can." He grunted, disgusted by his own weakness. Opening one eye a crack, he peered at her. "The thing is, I *want* to go in. I *want* to share this with you." He sat up and placed both hands on the wheel. "Every man, woman, and child in this country ought to experience a rodeo at least once before they call themselves Americans. It should be a prerequisite for citizenship."

"Really."

She laughed, and he soaked up the sound, taking it deep inside his shattered soul. It wasn't just the crowds that set him off. The loss of who he'd once been got to him more than anything. Rodeos, his family's ranch, the easy, carefree way he used to approach life—all gone, and he might not ever get any of it back. Knowing his uncle would likely be here made it all sharper, brought what he'd left behind into focus in excruciating detail. The reminder was too damned painful to face.

"Give me a minute." He eased the aching clamp of his jaw. "I know you probably think all that business about me needing you to hold my hand through this was bullshit, but—"

She reached for his hand and brought it to her lap, holding on with both of hers. "I've got your back, Ryan. I won't let you go." As if to prove her point, she tightened her grip.

"Ow!" he teased. "You don't need to go breaking any bones there, darlin'." Something inside him shifted and fell into place. He swallowed the constriction in his throat and managed a grin.

"Sorry." She eased up on the pressure.

"You have quite the grip for a girl." He turned and pulled her close. "I like that about you."

Her expression softened, and her gaze roamed over his face. Shy, sweet Paige came out to play, and his heart stuttered and missed a beat. "One-size-fits-all remedy might help."

She nodded, and her breath hitched. Ryan leaned in for a kiss. She opened for him, and he took her mouth. She was like his own personal IED. Touching her detonated an explosion of need deep inside him, sending his world rocking on its axis. He slid his tongue in to circle hers and started a reconnaissance mission of exploration over her lush body. Running his hands up her slender, curved waist, he inched his way up to the swell of her breasts. He slid his thumbs over her nipples. She arched into him, and he went gun-barrel hard, nearly coming at the sound of her responsive moan.

"I want you, Paige. You have no idea how badly I want you," he whispered into her ear and kissed his way down to her collarbone. Her chest rose and fell in a rapid rhythm, and her nipples pebbled at his touch.

"If we keep this up, we aren't going to make it to the rodeo." She pulled him to her for another scorching kiss.

A group of adolescent boys walking by hooted and hollered as they passed. One of them shouted, "Ride her, cowboy!"

Ryan pulled back, aching and breathless. "Right. Time to get going before we give the locals a real show." He ran his knuckles down her cheek. "Damn, woman, but you make it hard for a man to think straight, much less walk."

"I'll take that as a compliment." Reaching into her handbag, she pulled out a brush and ran it through her hair. "Come here."

Bossy Paige appeared, and laughter rumbled through his chest. "You are *not* going to brush my hair."

"Fine. I won't."

"Fine, 'cause I wasn't going to let you anyway." He reached into his pocket for one of those elastic hair things, ran his fingers through his hair, and pulled it back. "I'm thinking about getting it cut off." He picked up his Stetson off the floor, dusted it off, and put it back on.

She straightened her blouse, retied the ends, and slung her purse over her shoulder. "Noah goes to a barber in Perfect who does a really nice job."

Just like that, everything went back to ordinary everyday life. Normal. Ryan shook his head and barked out a laugh.

"What now?" Paige raised an eyebrow as they climbed out of his truck.

"A minute ago I was melting down." He circled around the truck to her side, laced his fingers through hers, and started them toward the elevator. "I held you in my arms for a couple of minutes, and everything shifted back to ordinary everyday stuff."

"Let me get this straight." She stopped walking and faced him. "You're saying I make you feel *ordinary*?" She frowned. "Wow. You really have that whole sweet-talking thing down pat." She shot him the *You're an idiot* look and started walking again. "You smooth-talking devil, you," she said in a flat tone. "Be still my heart."

He laughed, and once he caught a glimpse of her disgruntled expression, he couldn't stop.

Paige took her hand back and crossed her arms in front of her. "What's so frickin' funny?"

His sides ached, and so did the muscles in his cheeks. He couldn't remember the last time he'd laughed this hard. "Hoh, darlin', you have no idea..." *No idea how crazy I am over you or what you do to me.* "No idea at all how good ordinary feels to a guy like me."

"Yeah?" Her mouth still formed a straight line, and her eyes flashed green sparks.

"There's not a single ordinary thing about you, believe me." He put his hands on her shoulders and leaned down to stare into her eyes. "That's not what I meant."

"What did you mean, then?"

"You're magic. Somehow, you manage to drag me back from hell with your kisses and your touch." He drew her stiff body in for a hug. "You'll never know how grateful I am for the ordinary you give me, Paige." His voice was hoarse with the strong emotions whirling through him. *You mean the world to me.* He couldn't say that. Too needy. Hell, he was needy when it came to her. Needy, achy, hopeful, and scared shitless, all at once. "It means the world to me."

"All right." She relaxed against him. "That's better."

He laced his fingers with hers again. "Let's find my uncle and then a hat." Once they were out on the street, his gaze automatically went to the rooftops. Hyperalert, he surveyed his surroundings—shadowed doorways, the civilians walking along with them, then back to the places where a sniper might hide.

"Ryan"—Paige nudged him with her shoulder—"what are you looking for up there?"

"Hmmm?" *Busted. Time to front.* "Just checking out the architecture." To make it more legit, he took a gander at the huge multistoried glass front of the main entrance to the steel-and-concrete stadium. "The rigs and animals will be in back." They stopped at a traffic light. "We should cross here and head that way." He pointed.

"Noah used to do that too."

"Do what?" The light changed, and they split from the herd heading for the entrance.

"My brother said he used to check the rooftops for insurgents when he first came home from Iraq. He also scanned the shadows for men holding cell phones or other electronic devices that could be used to detonate an IED."

"You got me." He slid her wry grin. "He doesn't do those things anymore?"

"Nope. He used to swerve his truck away from suspicious piles of trash where an IED might be hidden too." She shook her head. "He went through therapy for a while and got into a group.

When he started talking to other veterans, he found out they all did stuff like that, and he felt better, calmer. They check in with each other all the time, and that really helps."

"I guess I can't pull anything over on you, Dr. Langford." His jaw tightened. She knew the worst about him. Hell, she'd been the one who discovered him passed out and hugging an empty whisky bottle to his chest like a lover. She'd read his suicide letter, seen the pictures and his gun. Yet here she was, walking beside him with her hand in his. Was it pity on her part?

Could they shift from where they were right now, or would she always see him as a suicidal, paranoid wreck? Lord, he hoped he could turn things around. He wanted her to see him as whole, capable of setting his own course. More than anything, he wanted her to see him as a man she'd be proud to be with.

Sure enough, he was headed for a train wreck, because he knew what Paige wanted, and it wasn't the quiet life in Perfect, Indiana, with a head case like him. A fool could hope, though, and he truly was that fool.

The rear parking lot came into view. Large livestock trailers, semis, RVs, pickups, and portable metal railings forming chutes and corrals took up the entire acreage. He searched the rigs for the familiar signage. "They're here." He gestured toward the dark-green semi cab with MALLOY RODEO RANCH painted on the door and a gold shamrock underneath. Hitched behind the cab, their camper trailer and livestock trailer made the whole getup look like a train. He saw no sign of movement near the rig. "They must be inside."

His heart pounded out a mixture of anticipation and nervousness as they approached the double doors, which were thrown wide open. Rodeo riders stood around the entrance, talking shit, catching up with friends who, like them, followed the circuit cross-country in the hopes of big money.

It all came back to him in a rush. The pre-event jitters, preparing his gear, the camaraderie, and the eight-second adrenaline high of the ride. Man against beast. He missed it, even though he'd never considered ranching or competing in the rodeo as a viable lifestyle. He'd always wanted to do something artistic, creative. Drawing a saddle bronc held far more appeal than suffering multiple bone fractures being thrown from one.

A police officer stood casually but watchfully by the large double doors. "Hey," Ryan greeted the man with the badge, showing him their tickets. "I was wondering if I could get word back to Shawn Malloy to let him know his nephew Ryan is here to see him."

"Runt!" A voice thundered from the dimness inside. "Is that you, you son of a bitch?"

His cousin emerged and shoved his shoulder. Ryan grinned so hard it hurt. "Hey, Austin. It's been a while."

"That it has. How've you been?" Austin clasped Ryan's hand for a few seconds. His gaze settled on Paige.

"This is Paige Langford. Paige, this is my cousin, Austin Malloy. He's the ugly one of the batch."

"Evening, Paige." His cousin touched the brim of his cowboy hat and dipped his head. "What's a good-lookin' woman like you doing with a scrawny runt like him?"

Paige blew out an exasperated breath and looked between him and his cousin. "Is the cockiness a cowboy thing or a Malloy thing?"

Ryan found himself laughing again. Austin joined in, and something akin to happiness bubbled up inside Ryan. "It's an Austin thing. I'm never cocky."

Paige reached out her hand to shake Austin's. "It's nice to meet you."

Austin held on to her for too long, shooting Ryan a challenging look. "Come on back, you two. My dad is going to shit his pants when he sees you, Ryan."

"Aren't you a married man?" Ryan extricated Paige's hand from his cousin's. Austin hadn't changed much. He was five years older and about four inches taller than Ryan, with a workingman's body, callused hands, and muscled shoulders and chest. He had a few more laugh lines around his standard-issue Malloy baby blues. Lines also bracketed his mouth, his smile standard-issue Malloy as well—lopsided as all get-out.

"Sure am. We have two boys of our own now." Austin winked at Paige. "Just 'cause a man's on a diet doesn't mean he can't read the menu."

"That is so old." Paige laughed, her eyes twinkling. "Not to mention lame. Now I can't wait to meet this uncle of yours." She ran her hand up and down Ryan's biceps.

Was it a possessive gesture—or protective? Either way, it sent his blood racing along the horndog trail. "Lead the way, Austin." Ryan put his arm around Paige's waist, and they entered the bowels of the Ford Center. Ryan kept an eye on Paige as they walked by the makeshift corrals penning in the broncos, riding horses, steers, and calves for the evening's events. She took in everything, wrinkling her nose at the animal smells.

He couldn't help noticing the cowboys and ranchers doing double takes as they passed, their appreciative stares resting on the spectacular woman walking beside him. Pride filled him, and he stood a little straighter. "You're making quite an impression, darlin'," he whispered into her ear.

"Hmmm?" Her brow rose in question.

"Don't you know how gorgeous you are?" He squeezed her close. "You're turning every head in the place. Even the cowgirls are looking our way. They're jealous."

"Ha. It's a Malloy thing." She chuckled in that throaty way of hers. "Just as I thought, you're all full of—"

"Ryan Patrick Malloy!" his uncle boomed. "What the hell are you doing here?"

❦   ❦   ❦

Paige had to let go of Ryan's hand or have her shoulder dislocated when his uncle pulled him in for a bear hug. Seeing him laugh as he returned the hug with equal enthusiasm, anyone would think this was nothing more than a happy family reunion. She knew better. As finely attuned as she was to Ryan, she also caught the frequent swallows, the brightness in his eyes, and the crushing grip he kept on her hand. He hadn't been kidding—all of this must be terribly difficult for him.

"Uncle Shawn, this is Paige Langford." Ryan averted his face for a second and passed a hand over his eyes. "Paige, darlin', this is my uncle Shawn. He's my dad's twin."

"Glad to meet you, Paige." Shawn turned all of his attention to her. "Are you the reason my nephew's in Indiana?" He took her hand and held it in both of his. At least six feet tall, with graying blond hair and bright blue eyes, Shawn had the same crooked smile as Ryan and Austin. A slight paunch hung over his belt, and he smelled like Old Spice and livestock. Oddly enough, not an unpleasant combination.

"Umm, no. He works for my brother."

"Yeah?" He let her go, his attention returning to Ryan. "Last I heard, you were living in Dallas and still working the factory job."

"I moved here a couple of months ago." Ryan took off his hat and studied the makeshift pen holding his uncle's bulls. "I'm working for Langford & Lovejoy Heritage Furniture. It's owned by my former lieutenant." He glanced at his uncle, and an unmistakable flash of pride lit his eyes. "I'm designing a new product line for the company."

"It's incredible," Paige chimed in. "He's creating a number of pieces based on American quilt patterns. Ryan and I have also been working on an advertising campaign set to launch this coming September."

"You don't say." His uncle's glance bounced between them with a speculative glint.

"Before I ran into the runt, I was on my way to snag a couple of pizzas from across the street," Austin said. "Now that y'all are here, stick around and share a meal with me and my dad."

Ryan raised his eyebrows in question, and she nodded.

"That would be great." Ryan grinned. "It'll give us time to catch up."

"Come on over here. I have a table and folding chairs set up by the bulls." Shawn nodded toward the corral containing about a half dozen huge, intimidating bulls with very sharp, long horns. Following her gaze, he flashed a grin. "They won't cause you any harm as long as you don't try to ride them," he said with a wink.

"My uncle's bulls are really rank." Ryan reached for her hand again.

"Yeah, that's what you told me earlier, but I don't know what it means."

"It's her first rodeo," Ryan explained to his uncle. "Rank means they consistently score high points for the ride they give."

"My bulls have put more than a few cowboys in the hospital," Shawn boasted. "That red one there"—he pointed to one of the beasts—"is called Sidewinder, and the tan one against the far side is Diablo. That's Spanish for 'the devil.'" He beamed. "Bull riders love to pull our bulls in the draw. They're the rankest anywhere."

"Putting cowboys in the hospital is a good thing?" she asked. Both men nodded and smirked. "Great." She pulled out one of the folding chairs next to a card table and took a seat. A cribbage board, two mugs containing the dregs of old coffee, and a deck of cards sat in the middle of the plastic cover. Shawn took the seat across from her, and Ryan sat to her left.

"Do your folks know you're living in Indiana now?" Shawn leaned back, stretched out his long legs, and crossed them at the ankles, fixing Ryan with a sharp look. "Seems to me they'd have sent us word if they knew."

"Uh, no. I plan to call them real soon."

Pulling his phone from the leather holster attached to his belt, Shawn eyed Ryan. "Why don't we give them a ring right now?"

"Maybe later." Ryan tensed beside her, his jaw muscle working away.

"You're killing your parents. You know that, right?" Shawn crossed his arms over his chest. "What did they ever do to piss you off so bad you felt you had to cut your own family out of your life the way you have?"

Ryan shot up from his chair, grabbed her hand, and pulled her up beside him. "It was great seeing you, Uncle Shawn. Austin too. We gotta go."

Crap! "Whoa. Everybody take a breath." Paige tugged back before Ryan could bolt. "Mr. Malloy, I know this is none of my business, but Ryan has been through a lot. Cut him some slack. He'll call his family when he's ready, and no sooner."

Shawn's eyes widened, and his brow rose. He opened his mouth to reply, but she wasn't done. "We just got here, Ryan. Please sit back down. Your uncle means well. It's clear you come from a loving family, and there's no doubt in my mind your silence has put them all through hell."

"Well, I'll be damned." Shawn threw his head back and laughed. "I like this girl of yours, son. You'd better hold on to her, or I might have to introduce her to our youngest." The Malloy lopsided grin made him look years younger. "Kit's a lot better looking than my nephew here." He jerked his thumb toward Ryan. "And taller. You'd like him."

"I'll keep that in mind." She held her breath, letting it out slowly when Ryan finally sat back down. "I'm going to get a soda. Do either of you want anything?"

"I'd love something to drink." Ryan reached for his wallet, pulled out a ten, and handed it to her. "Do you want me to come with you?"

"No. I can find my way." She slid the bill into her front pocket and glanced between them. "You two catch up."

"Wait a second." Shawn moved to a footlocker sitting against a stack of hay bales behind them. He lifted the lid and pulled out a lanyard attached to a plastic name-tag holder identical to the ones he and Austin wore. The Malloy logo was printed at the top, with their participation and permit numbers in black beneath. "My other son was going to come, but his wife is going to have a baby any day, and he decided to stay close to home. This'll get you past security, and if you get lost, any cowboy with a number pinned to his back can help you find your way."

"Thanks." She leaned over and kissed Ryan on the cheek, and left the two to work out their issues. Once she was through the door leading to the front part of the Ford Center, she found herself swallowed up by the crowd of people moving slowly past numerous booths carrying a myriad of cowboy gear. Ryan was right. Everyone wore cowboy boots, western belt buckles, and hats. She didn't fit in.

A map of the stadium took up a large space of concrete wall between restrooms. She located the closest food vendor, took note of her surroundings, and headed down the hall, stopping now and then to try on a cowboy hat or to look at hand-tooled leather purses. Maybe next year...

Right. By next year, if everything went according to plan, she'd be back in Pennsylvania or another city, working her way up some corporate ladder. Did the rodeo come to Philadelphia? More important, would Ryan still be a part of her life? A dull ache carved out a place in her chest. It would be asking too much to expect him to carry on a long-distance relationship. He was finally starting therapy and trying to come out of his self-imposed isolation. It wouldn't be fair to make any demands on him just because she had ambitions.

By the time Paige returned, the three Malloys were sitting at the table together, laughing and talking. Three pizza boxes rested in the middle. Paper plates and napkins had been set at each place. Austin saw her first and stood up to pull out a chair for her.

"Did you walk all the way to Illinois for those soft drinks?" Shawn teased. "We were about to send a posse out after you, girl."

"I have a cell phone. Ryan could've texted me when the pizza arrived." Paige shrugged, placed Ryan's soda in front of him, and took her place at the table. "I did some shopping." She glanced at Ryan. "I found the hat I want."

"That's great," Ryan said, opening the pizza boxes. The cheesy, garlicky aroma wafted up. "Better take all you want of this pizza, Paige."

"That's right." Austin nodded. "Ladies first, and don't be shy."
"We mean it." Shawn cocked an eyebrow. "Don't be shy."

She helped herself to a piece of the combination pizza, placing it on her plate.

"Is that all you're planning on eating?" Austin's brow rose.

"I don't know. Maybe I'll have another slice in a while." The three Malloys shook their heads and chuckled.

Ryan placed another combo piece on her plate, along with a slice of the pepperoni. "Will this be enough?"

"Sure." Puzzled, she glanced around the table.

"Great." Austin rubbed his hands together. "Let's put the feed bag on, boys."

Paige watched in amazement as the three devoured the meal like they might never have another.

"You gonna eat those?" Austin eyed her plate.

"Yes." She pulled her plate a little closer and picked up a slice, taking a big bite.

Ryan laughed. "Now you get why they wanted you to take yours first? You should see what happens at our family get-togethers. The little ones are served first, then the women, because they know once the Malloy men get started, they aren't going to leave anything behind."

"Ranching is hard work." Shawn cracked a sheepish grin. "We work up an appetite. Bring her home for the Fourth of July shindig." He wiped his mouth with a paper napkin. "Let her see for herself what kind of family she's getting involved with." He winked.

Heat rose to her cheeks, and she couldn't help noticing the color creeping up Ryan's neck at the same time. Who knew where they'd be four months from now? Her heart raced, and she couldn't catch her breath.

"Maybe I'll do that," Ryan murmured, his glance darting her way. "We'll see." He wiped his mouth and hands and smashed the empty cardboard boxes together. "I promised Paige a cowboy hat, and I'd better deliver." He rose. "Do you want to bring your plate with us?"

"Nope. One slice is plenty." Paige placed her pizza on a napkin and stood to go. "You two can have the rest." She smiled at Austin and Shawn.

"Generous *and* pretty." Austin grabbed one of the remaining slices. "She's a keeper, runt."

"We look forward to seeing you again, Paige." Shawn rose, came around the table to shake her hand again. "Put the Malloy's Fourth of July gathering on your calendar. We'd love to have you. There's plenty of room."

She nodded, her cheeks growing hot again. "It was really nice to meet you both."

"Come here, Ryan," Shawn commanded, his voice breaking as he hugged him again and slapped his back. "Don't you be a stranger."

"I won't." Ryan hugged him back. "Thanks, Uncle Shawn. It was really good to see you and Austin. Say hello to everyone for me, and tell them I'm OK."

"Tell them yourself. Wait." Austin pulled out his cell phone. "Do you have a number where you can be reached?"

Ryan recited his number and put theirs into his contact list. He and Paige said their good-byes again and left to find their seats.

"I'm glad we stopped by to say hello, Ryan."

"Me too." He heaved a huge sigh.

"How long has it been since you've seen or talked with your family?"

"You gonna start in on me now?" His mouth tightened.

"No." She squeezed his hand and let the subject go. By the time they bought her hat and found their seats, the pageantry of the grand entrance had begun. Galloping horses carrying cowgirls and cowboys wearing glittery chaps and carrying flags streamed into the arena. A group of marines marching in dress uniform followed. The announcer gave a speech about how none of them would be free to enjoy tonight's rodeo if it weren't for the sacrifices made by all the men and women serving in the armed forces. Then he called for all the veterans in the audience to stand.

Paige surveyed the crowd, noticing all of the veterans who rose to the thunderous applause. They came in all sizes, shapes, and ages. Ryan stood beside her, his posture military straight and his chin held high. Pride in the man beside her tightened her throat, and the back of her eyes stung.

She'd witnessed so many facets to him in such a short time—the way he liked to tease, his interactions with his uncle and cousin, how he melted down and fought his way back, his creativity…Her mind went back to the storm, and Sweet Pea's rescue for Lucinda and Toby. She'd never met a man like Ryan before, and deep in her gut, she knew she never would again.

The whole time he stood, Ryan never let go of her hand, and she wasn't about to let go of his.

CHAPTER TEN

BY THE TIME THEY LEFT the rodeo and were on the highway heading home, it was already ten thirty. Ryan glanced at Paige. She was fiddling with the band on her new cowboy hat, her face soft with a pleased half smile he wanted to touch. "Did you have a good time, darlin'?"

"I did." Her smile grew. "Will there be more rodeos around here this summer?"

"Sure. They're all over, and you'd love outdoor rodeos. Are you interested in going to a few more?"

Shy Paige gave a little nod. "Thank you for the hat. I love it."

"You're welcome. It looks really good on you." He pictured her naked, wearing nothing but the hat he'd bought her. Adding her sexy black leather boots to his fantasy brought a smile to his face. *I gotta buy her a pair of cowboy boots. That's it. Paige naked except for the hat and a pair of cowboy boots...Idiot. She's not your personal doll to dress and undress.* He reined in his thoughts and shifted in his seat to ease the growing pressure in his lap. "What did you think of Shawn and Austin?"

"They were great, and it was fun watching their bulls in action after meeting them." She reached out and stroked his shoulder. "I know seeing you meant a lot to them. I'm glad you decided to visit, after all."

"Me too." Should he kiss her good night in his truck, outside his truck, or by the Langfords' front door? What would she say if he invited her to the carriage house for coffee? No, too late for coffee. Generic soda? *Damn.* He shook his head. How out of practice could a man be?

"Why are you shaking your head?" Her eyes lit with amusement.

"Just givin' myself hell."

Paige laughed. "You do that a lot."

He shot her a wry look. "I guess I do."

"Are you going to tell me what you were giving yourself hell about?"

Again with the shoulder rub. He gulped. "Nope."

Her low, throaty chuckle shifted his pulse into four-wheel drive. Had she guessed where his thoughts had taken him? More likely, she'd caught a glimpse of the physical evidence. Maybe he should cover his lap with his hat like he had the night she'd broken into his apartment. That had him picturing the way she'd plastered herself against his naked body. He sucked in a breath and shook his head again. *Naked, naked, naked.* Lord, he ached to get his hands on her. *Think about something else, cowboy. Naked is not going to happen tonight.*

"Why do I get the feeling there's a whole conversation going on inside your head without me?" Paige ran her hand down his biceps.

A rueful grunt of laughter escaped. "Probably 'cause there is." The Langfords' driveway came into view, and anticipation stampeded through him. Even though he knew better than to make a move on her tonight, his body saw things differently. "When do you want to head to Philadelphia?"

"I'm hoping we can take half of Friday off and leave around lunchtime. Maybe we can start work early that morning so we don't miss as many hours."

"Sounds like a plan." Ryan parked his pickup in its usual spot and shut off the engine. He tossed his hat behind his seat. Didn't want it to get in the way when he kissed her. Hopping out, he hurried around to Paige's side to help her down. "I'll walk you to the door," he murmured. *Lame.*

She snorted. "Because we live in such a dangerous neighborhood?"

The occasional hoot of an owl and the quiet whoosh of the river meandering by were the only noises to be heard. "That's right." He raised an eyebrow. "You never know when some marauding raccoon might attack."

She smiled. "I really did have a lot of fun tonight, Ryan. Thanks to you, I'm now an official rodeo fan."

"I had a great time too." They reached the door, and his heart hammered away against his ribs. He ran his hands down her arms, taking both her hands in his. "I'll look online for more rodeos and let you know."

"Great."

The porch light cast her face in shadow as she glanced at him through her lashes. He leaned in for a kiss, and she met him halfway. Sweet and brief, the kiss ended. "Good night, Paige."

Her palm came up to touch his cheek. "Good night, Ryan."

She went inside, and he remained standing on Noah's front porch, reliving the night in his mind. Grinning, he recalled the way she'd stepped in and taken over when things got tense between him and his uncle. She had his back, but she didn't let him pull any bull either. Paige was good for him, and something deep inside reached for that goodness with everything he had, knowing full well he'd probably come away empty-handed and brokenhearted. Still, he couldn't help himself. "Reach away, cowboy."

Shoving his hands into his front pockets, he headed for his apartment and the cold shower awaiting him. No doubt Austin or Shawn would pass his number on to his folks. He'd better call them before they called him. His gut twisted with trepidation. And remorse. Always present, the guilt lay across his shoulders like a yoke. Maybe it would be best to wait until he started working with the therapist before making that call.

Ryan unlocked his door, flipped on the lights, and locked up again. He tossed his keys on the coffee table as he walked by on his way to the bathroom. The evening had taken a lot out of him, and exhaustion weighted his eyelids. He'd forgo the cold shower and live with the discomfort for the time being. Sleep took precedence, and besides, a case of blue balls never killed anyone that he knew of.

The fluorescent light in his bathroom buzzed to life a few seconds after he pulled the chain. He reached for his toothbrush, loaded it up with minty freshness, brushed, and rinsed. Stripping on the way, he headed straight for his bed, pulled the covers back, and fell in face-first and spread-eagle. Thoughts of naked Paige played havoc with his body as sleep pulled him under.

❧   ❧   ❧

Ryan flew through the air, along with the flaming debris from the detonated IEDs. He landed hard, and the pain of his bones shattering wrenched a scream from somewhere so deep he didn't know the place existed. The stench of burning flesh brought bile up to scald his throat. He rolled to put out the flames eating up his back and almost passed out from the searing pain pulsing along his nerve endings. Every beat of his heart sent another throb of torture through him until he craved nothing more than to leave his broken, burning body behind.

He wanted his mom—wanted to see his family one more time before he died and knew he wouldn't get the chance. He was going to die here in this desert, alone and far from home. Tears flowed from the corners of his eyes, etching a macabre path through the soot and dirt encrusting his face.

Theresa would be waiting for him on the other side. He'd join her soon, and that brought him comfort, but did nothing to ease the unbearable pain.

Horrific groans and screams assaulted his ears, and the acrid stench and thick black smoke choked him. Ryan opened his eyes to survey the damage. Turning his head, he let out a hoarse shout. Paige lay broken and bloody in the dirt mere feet from him. Her empty, lifeless eyes stared right at him.

No! No, this isn't right. Not Paige...

"NO!" Ryan woke with a start, gasping for air and covered in a cold sweat. Shaking from head to foot, he sat up and buried his face in his hands. His ghosts marched in formation behind his closed eyes, taunting him with their lifeless stares, reminding him that he didn't deserve happiness. He didn't deserve Paige. They hurled silent accusations and took turns shredding his soul.

He shot up and paced around the room, sucking air in huge gulps. He needed a drink. Hell, he needed an entire fifth. Right now, he missed his old friend Johnnie Walker on a cellular level. Scrubbing his face with both hands, he contemplated his choices. Bars were still open. *Shit. Not good. Not good at all.*

Panic arced along his nerves. He glanced at the clock on his end table again, noticing his cell phone. Noah would understand. He could call him, and it would be all right. He knew Noah would talk him through this rough spot.

Ryan strode around the bed and grabbed his phone from the table. Scrolling through his contacts, he found Noah's number. The phone rang and rang, finally taking him to voice mail. He ended the call.

Eyeing the jeans he'd dropped on the floor, he calculated how long it would take to get to the bar on the west side of Perfect. He had around two hours till closing time. More than enough time for a couple of shots. Just enough to take the edge off and help him sleep. He took a step toward his discarded clothing. Guilt and shame burned its way up to his face. Was he so weak he couldn't even make it two weeks without a drink?

He sat on the wire edge of a crisis, and one wrong move would cut him deep. Left with only one thing to do, he pushed number one on his speed dial and plastered the phone to his ear. With each unanswered ring, he bargained: If she didn't answer, he'd head for the bar. If she did, he'd—

"Ryan?" Paige's sleepy voice filled his ear. She yawned into her phone.

The bones in his body turned to rubber, and his muscles went slack with relief. "Yeah. Yeah, it's me. What are you doing?" *Stupid thing to say.* He smacked his palm against his forehead as she made an incredulous snorting noise. Imagining she wore her *You're an idiot* face, he smiled stupidly into the darkness.

"Well…"

A long silent pause followed.

"I *was* sleeping. It's after midnight." She yawned again. "What's wrong?"

"I'm having some trouble here. Talk to me." He shut his eyes tight and leaned his head back. One messed-up wreck, that's what he was.

"Is it the booze?"

"No...Yes. It's complicated." He swallowed hard. "It's the ghosts, not the alcohol. The drinking has always been about the ghosts and the nightmares, Paige. Whisky shuts it all out...so I can sleep."

Another long silence stretched between them. She didn't understand. How could she? Only someone who'd been through what he had, seen the things he'd seen, would get it. "Look, I'm sorry I woke you. Go back to sleep." He started to take the phone away from his ear so he could end this mistake before things went from bad to worse.

"Wait."

His heart raced, and he brought the phone back. "Yeah?"

"What can I do to help?"

"Talk to me." His legs wouldn't hold him anymore. He sank to the edge of his bed and flopped back, pinching the inside corners of his eyes. "I don't care what we talk about. As long as I hear your voice, it'll help."

"Hold on. I'll be there in a minute."

"Wait." He sat up fast. "You don't have to..." *Shit.* She'd already ended the call. Paige was on her way. Not what he'd intended at all—another meltdown witnessed by the woman of his dreams. *Great.*

Ryan turned on his bedroom lamp, snatched up the clothing littered all over his bedroom floor, and tossed the heap into the closet. He opened his dresser drawer and dug through his stuff for a pair of cutoff sweats, slipping into them just as her knock sounded on his door. Grabbing a T-shirt, he tugged it on as he hurried down the hall.

He opened the door and took her in, from her sleep-tousled hair to her slippered feet. She wore a tattered old flannel thing with a distinctively masculine print. "Nice robe. Sexy." He smirked, while the sight of her filled him with achy tenderness.

"I know, huh?" She tightened the frayed belt. "I took it out of Ceejay's rag bag. It used to belong to my brother."

Ryan opened the door wider to let her in. "You didn't need to get out of bed. We could've talked on the phone."

"Do you want me to leave?" Lifting her chin, she laid whatever happened next at his feet.

"Hell no."

"Good. Come with me." She took him by the hand and led him toward his bedroom. *Hoh, boy.* "What do you have in mind, darlin'?"

She chuffed out another snort. "Not what you're thinking, *darlin'*. I'm going to give you a back massage, and you're going to introduce me to your ghosts. I'm not the one who needs to talk. You are. I'll stay until you talk yourself out and fall asleep."

"It's generally *after* I fall asleep that the trouble starts."

"Then I'll stay a while longer to make sure your ghosts don't come back tonight."

Even all business and bossy Paige turned him on. "My own personal superhero, guarding me from my demons."

"Something like that." She chuckled. "Take off that T-shirt, and lie down on your stomach."

He froze. Heat suffused his face. He hadn't bared his scars to anyone other than doctors and nurses. The way she'd reacted the first time she touched them came back in a hot mess of mortification. "I'll leave the shirt on, if it's all the same to you." His voice sounded terse, even to him.

"No, you won't. This is part of the deal, cowboy." Paige stepped closer, jutting out her chin. "I know what you're thinking, and you're wrong." She tugged at the hem of the cotton shirt.

He stopped her, his heart thundering and his mouth dry as desert wind. "No."

"Ryan," she cajoled. "Do you remember the day you bought the quilt?" Her hands snuck past his and slid up his bare chest.

A slice of pleasure penetrated his defenses and fogged his brain. "There's nothing wrong with my memory, Paige. I have PTSD, not traumatic brain injury." His response elicited a low chuckle, weakening his resolve a smidge more.

"I didn't stop touching you that day because I found your scars repulsive. I stopped because…"

Where his heart thundered a second ago, now it came to a complete standstill. He held his breath, his attention riveted on the tenderness filling her eyes. "Because why?"

"I couldn't bear the thought of the pain those burns caused you. I…" Her voice broke. "I couldn't stand the thought of you being hurt." She tugged at the hem of his shirt again, and he let her take it from him.

"Your scars don't bother me the way you think they do." She kissed the center of his chest and ran her hands over his shoulders and down the tight, twisted skin on his back. Her touch went straight through him, all the way to his battered soul.

"Are we clear on that?" She searched his face.

All he could manage was a mute nod.

"Good. Lie facedown on the bed."

Yes, ma'am. Facedown was a good idea, because his dick had no qualms about letting her know how he felt about her. "You're bossy." He lay down on his stomach, propping his chin on his fists.

"So?"

Laughter vibrated through him. "So I like it." The bed creaked and the mattress dipped as she perched on the edge, nudging him with her hip.

"Scoot over."

He did as he was told, making room for her to sit beside him. Her warm hands settled on the knotted muscles where his neck met his shoulders—scars and all. Digging in with her fingers and thumbs, she kneaded, poked, and prodded until the knots untied.

"You might relax more if you put your arms down by your sides," she suggested, moving along his spine, using her knuckles to loosen him up.

Again, he did as he was told. Finding her bare knee, he draped his arm over it and hugged it closer to his side. A long sigh slid out as the tension melted away bit by bit.

"Tell me about your ghosts," she whispered.

He groaned and shook his head.

She stopped massaging.

"Not fair," he muttered.

"I'm not trying to be fair." She brushed the hair from his face and teased him with a kiss. "If you want me to continue, you have to give me something in return."

"The more I tell, the more you'll do?" The lustful optimist in him soared...

"We'll see."

...and crashed. "You're a cold, hard woman," he teased.

"Ha!" She resumed her ministrations. "We both know who's hard right now, and it's not me." Leaning down, she kissed his back and ran her hands along his sides.

He grunted. "All right. Paige, meet my best friend Lance Corporal Benjamin Jackson, soldier, husband, and father." His throat tightened. "He drove the Humvee your brother and I were in the day we got hit, and he's the one who first spotted the civilian truck heading straight for us. Ben had a wife and a kid to get home to. He…He didn't make it. I did."

"You must've been a better friend to him than he was to you."

"What are you talking about?" He jerked out of her reach. "Jackson was a great guy, and one of the best friends I've ever had."

She followed him across the bed and pushed him back down. "Good friends don't punish each other, Ryan. Do you believe he's spiteful enough to haunt you? Do you really think a great guy like Ben Jackson would blame his best friend for what the enemy did to him?"

"You don't understand."

"Fine." She massaged his shoulders. "Explain it to me."

"Noah ordered me to fire a round into the dirt to warn those Iraqis off. I could've aimed my machine gun into the payload of that truck while it was still out in the desert. If I had—"

"So let me get this straight. You plan to second-guess yourself for the rest of your life? You're going to shoulder the blame and punish yourself for a split-second decision that wasn't even yours to make?"

"Yes," he snapped.

"I see. All hail the what-if game." She dug the heels of her palms into the tight spots below his shoulder blades. "Introduce me to another ghost."

"Besides Jackson, four other soldiers died that day. They like to make their presence known."

"Were the four of them close to you?"

"No. We were in the same platoon, but none of them were in my squad. I didn't know any of them personally."

"And these soldiers you hardly knew, and who hardly knew you, are somewhere right now thinking, 'If only that schmuck had aimed for the payload…'" She huffed out a breath. "Really, Ryan? I'm sure these spirits have better things to do with their time than to blame you for what happened that day. Maybe they're somewhere right now wondering why the hell you won't let them go in peace. Did you ever think of that?"

"No. I never did." He couldn't help the flicker of a grin that broke out. What she said was so ridiculous. "They aren't *real* ghosts, Paige. They're memories and nightmares concocted by my fractured psyche."

"I know. That's exactly my point." She pinched him. "You've concocted the whole scenario so that you can punish yourself forever for something completely out of your control."

"Ouch." He flipped over onto his back, wrestled her down beside him on the mattress, and covered her legs with one of his. "After all this torture, I should at least be allowed to cop a feel."

She burst out laughing. "Feeling better?"

"I will in a minute." He kissed her, running his tongue along the side of hers while he untied the ugly robe. "Let's get rid of this old thing."

"Let's not." She caught his hands. "We have one more concoction to address." Biting her lower lip, she glanced at him. "Theresa."

"I already told you about her." He rolled onto his back and covered his eyes with his forearm. "What more is there to say?"

"From everything you've told me, I'm guessing Theresa was a wonderful person with a big heart. How do you think she'd feel if she knew you blamed yourself for her accident?"

He made a growling sound from behind his hands. "You aren't going to cut me any slack tonight, are you?"

"Nope." Paige pried his arm from his face, brushing her lips across his closed eyes once she'd accomplished the task. "If your roles were reversed, would you want Theresa carrying around all that guilt weighing you down? Would you want her life to remain stuck in the past while any chance at a great future passed her by?"

"No, of course not. I'd want her to be happy." His chest tightened, and his eyes stung.

"Let me be sure I have this right. You'd want her to move on, love again, and find happiness, but you don't believe she'd want the same for you? Is that how it is?" Paige stroked his forehead and stared into his soul. "She loved you, Ryan. I can't believe Theresa would want you to continue holding on to all this emotional baggage."

His breath caught, and her words hit the bull's-eye in the deadened center of his heart. Blinking against the tears in his eyes, Ryan's jaw tightened. Breaking down in front of Paige was such a bitch. She must see him as a complete wuss.

She slid her mouth across his and nipped at his bottom lip. "You still want to see me naked?"

His eyes widened. "Hell yes." *Lust. Instant tears-be-gone remedy.* "But not if you're offering because you feel sorry for me or out of—"

"I don't pity you, Ryan. Your stubborn refusal to give up the load you insist on dragging around like a cinder block and chain mostly just ticks me off."

"Of course." He chuckled. "I should've known better."

"That's right. You should've." She untied her robe and shucked it, revealing an old faded Harvard T-shirt and a pair of matching boxers.

"Wow, Paige. Sexy robe and even *sexier* pajamas."

Her throaty chuckle filled him. She pulled off her shirt, revealing her perfect, lush breasts with their dusky-rose nipples, exactly as he'd imagined. *Oh, Lord.* He reached out to test their warm, soft weight against his palms, running his thumbs over those perfect nipples until they peaked for him. "You are one beautiful woman. I hope you know that."

She sighed, arching into him. "Do you have protection, cowboy? Because after watching all those bronc and bull riders tonight, I could really go for a good, long ride myself."

"Are you saying this is going to happen because of the rodeo? Shoot. We're going to find a new rodeo every week from here on in." God, he loved the way she could be shy one minute and bold as brass the next. He loved her intelligence, wit, the way she looked—everything about her. Ryan sat up, holding her around the waist as he rose. He reached for the bedside table and pulled the brand-spanking-new box of condoms from the drawer. "It just so happens, I do have protection."

❦   ❦   ❦

"Good." Ryan believed she wanted him out of pity? If he only knew. This ranked up there as one of the most selfish acts she'd ever committed. She'd wanted him since the night she'd fallen against his naked hardness. Selfish and risky, yet she couldn't help herself. He filled her with such longing. He needed her, and if she were to be honest, she needed him too.

While he fumbled with the box of condoms, she indulged. Feasting her eyes at the sight of his corded torso, she followed the line of dark-blond hair down to his navel. The cutoff sweats he wore tented in front. It was all she could do to keep from licking her chops like some kind of sex-crazed animal. *Admit it. You are a sex-crazed animal. For Ryan, anyway.*

She wasn't in the habit of initiating sex. In her limited experience, the guys she'd dated never tired of trying to bump up against her. Not one of them had ever given her the chance to take the lead. Ryan had placed the decision in her hands, empowering her like nothing else could, and she swelled with that power now, savoring each moment.

Paige leaned in and ran her tongue over one of his nipples, continuing to do the same to the other. The sudden intake of his breath sent a rush of slick heat flooding her center.

He tore the wrapper and set the condom on the table. "I want to see you, Paige. I want to lay you out and eat you up with my eyes." Lifting her to her knees, he tugged down her boxers and panties. "Lord, have mercy, my hands are trembling. Help me out here."

She giggled and flopped over to pull her clothes off the rest of the way and tossed them to the floor. "Your turn."

"Yes, ma'am." Ryan lifted his hips and yanked his shorts off, sending them to the floor with hers. "You don't have to ask me twice." His erection sprang free, bobbed and twitched against his flat belly.

"Would you mind if I..." She swallowed hard, and heat engulfed her entire body.

"What, Paige? Whatever you want, just tell me." He lay back, watching her with hooded lids, his blue eyes a few shades darker.

"I want to do the looking and touching first." Fascinated, she watched the artery in his neck pulse in time to the achy throbbing in her sex. She couldn't tear her eyes away from all of his magnificent nakedness and reached for him, running her hand along his shaft, absorbing his heat through her palm. The throb between her legs grew stronger, and she couldn't draw enough breath.

His hips thrust into her touch. "I don't know how long that's gonna work, but I'll do my best. The touching part is...so... damned...good."

Paige loved the strained hoarseness of his voice, how turned on he was for her. Smiling, she came up to kneel beside him, looking her fill and raking her fingernails lightly up his muscled thighs. She caressed his testicles, smiling when they tightened against her hands. Continuing on, she stroked his cock, belly, and ribs. Rolling his nipples between her thumbs and fingers, her heart raced as he shivered and jerked with each new exploration.

"The touching part *is* good," she agreed. The scar on his hip drew her, and she leaned close to kiss the curved, twisted path. His belly quivered, so she had to kiss and lick that too. Working her way up, she tasted each indentation of his ribs, finally laving a nipple with her tongue. She blew on it, pleased when it puckered into an even tighter nub. "I love how you taste and feel."

Draping herself over him, she aligned her thighs, belly, and chest with his and lost herself in his brilliant blue eyes. She tangled her fingers into his hair and kissed him, thrusting in her tongue to dance with his. He bucked beneath her, and the low, purring rumble he emitted reverberated through her. Kissing her way along his jaw to his ear, she ran her tongue over the velvety lobe, then nipped, smiling when he sucked in a breath.

"That's it. Can't take anymore," he rasped and flipped their positions. "My turn."

Paige surrendered control, relaxing her muscles and opening herself to his heated stare.

"Oh, yeah." He spread her knees apart, and his breath caught. "You are one sexy goddess, woman. You take my breath away."

His eyes roamed all over her, and she swore she could feel the heat of his gaze on her bare skin. He stroked and petted, starting with her collarbone, sliding down to her breasts. His callused palms created a delicious friction, tightening her into a ball of need.

"I love the girls here. Just look at how those twin peaks stand up at attention for me."

He leaned over, took a nipple into his mouth while palming the other. She almost came off the bed as a high-amped jolt shot straight through her. "That feels so good," she groaned.

"Yeah?" His eyes captured hers. "How about this?" He went back to flicking her erect nipple with his tongue and ran his hand down to the junction of her thighs. Inserting his finger into her cleft, he used some of the slickness to lubricate the pulsing bundle of nerve endings of her clit. Barely touching, he began tracing circles around it, sending her into frantic, writhing desperation. The pressure built and built. Paige lifted her hips, seeking more contact, harder touch. He obliged, moving his finger in tighter, harder motions.

Ryan made that purring rumble again, and his pelvis nudged against her thigh. She shuddered with her release, coming against his hand. A record for her, that took, what, ten whole seconds? She wanted more. She sighed, put her arms around his neck, and drew him in for a kiss. He continued to stroke and tease, and she did the same, caressing every inch of him.

Pulling back, he snatched the condom from the table. "Time to get serious." He slipped it on and came back to her. Settling himself between her thighs, he propped himself up on his elbows and stared into her eyes with such intensity she could hardly bear it.

"I want to look at you while we make love. I want to see every sensation and reaction play across that pretty face until you come apart in my arms."

She nodded, unable to speak. He guided himself into her in a slow thrust until he filled her, withdrawing almost immediately. The second thrust hit a spot that sent waves of pleasure crashing over her. She closed her eyes and moaned.

"Open those gorgeous green eyes, sweetheart. I want that connection with you while we make love."

She lifted her hips to meet his next thrust. "Can't be much more *connected* than this." Another wave of pleasure crested, and she forced her eyes open for him. "Ohhh. Connect a little faster, Ryan."

"Demanding." He chuckled deep in his throat, cupped her face between his hands, and kissed her. His tongue thrust in and out of her mouth as he picked up the pace. So, so good, everything in her world narrowed down to the building pressure. She tried to keep her eyes open for him, but it was impossible. Reaching for his fine butt, she pulled him in harder and faster, crying out with her release, then floating with the aftershocks. Ryan threw his head back and groaned long and slow as he followed her into the clouds.

He rolled off to lie beside her. Gathering her close, he whispered, "Stay." He nuzzled the sensitive spot just below her ear. "Sleep with me tonight."

Paige tangled her legs with his and ran her hand up and down his arm. "All right."

"I'll be right back. Don't go anywhere."

He got up and headed for the bathroom, giving her a view of his backside. Her throat closed up at the sight of the scars marring his back. Strong emotions welled, bringing tears to her eyes. Ryan deserved to be happy, and Perfect was the right place for him to be. Working with Noah, going to therapy, and meeting with other veterans was the best thing for him, and she wanted the best for him.

She bit her lip, worry and guilt flushing away all the pleasure she'd just experienced. What now? What about what she needed? Giving up on her goals and ambition would make her even more of a failure—not only in her father's eyes, but in her own. Not to mention she'd be a quitter, which was not acceptable. There had to be a way to work it all out. There had to be.

Ryan returned, slid into bed next to her, and reached for the drawer holding the condoms. He pulled out another one and placed it on the surface of the table. "Just in case." He winked.

She shook her head and laughed. "Even cowboys gotta sleep."

He scooted down, pulled the blankets up around them, and snuggled up against her. "Cowgirls do too." Sighing, he settled himself, wrapped his arm around her waist, and closed his eyes. "Good night, darlin'."

"Good night, Ryan. If the ghosts come around, wake me up so I can fight them off."

The rumble of his laughter sent a thrill through her.

"That's my girl," he whispered into her ear, brushing a kiss across her shoulder. "Superwoman Paige Langford."

His girl. She liked the sound of that way too much. Lying awake beside him, she listened to Ryan's deep, rhythmic breathing. Once she was sure his ghosts were done for the night, she allowed herself to fall asleep as well, all the while trying to come up with some kind of solution ensuring that both of them would come out of this affair with no new scars.

❦ ❦ ❦

Paige awoke to find herself enveloped in Ryan's arms and in his irresistible scent. He had a leg wedged between hers, and one of his hands cupped her breast. Shivers ran down her spine as he nibbled the back of her neck, while his erection nudged against her bottom. She grinned. "Well, gee, good morning to you too." She twisted around to face him, brushing the hair out of his face. Mischief lit his eyes, and his dimples set off all kinds of fireworks in her chest.

"Morning, darlin'." He kissed her. "Mmmm. You taste good."

"You're crazy. I have morning breath." She pushed at his chest. "Let me up. I have to go."

"No, you don't. It's Saturday. There's no reason to rush off."

"I meant I have to *go*. I need to use your bathroom."

"Oh, right." Ryan rolled over and tucked his arms under his head. "Go on, then. I'll just stay here and enjoy the view." He winked.

She rolled her eyes. "You are such a guy."

"So?"

"So I like it." She laughed and crawled over the bed, arching her back and throwing him a seductive smile over her bare shoulder when she got to the end.

"Oh, baby, hurry back," he rumbled. "We've got some serious business to take care of on the workbench here." Ryan patted the mattress.

She sashayed to the tiny bathroom, aware of his eyes on her ass the whole time. Once she'd closed the door, she took care of her needs, washed, and used a finger full of his toothpaste to freshen her breath. Still smiling, she returned to him, thrilling at the way he tracked her every move with blue-eyed intensity. She sighed and stretched out next to him. "So, what was that about this being a workbench?"

"I've got plans for you, darlin'." He rolled her onto her back and kissed her.

Tangling her hands in his hair, she pulled him closer. Where last night's lovemaking had an urgency to it, this morning's kisses were long and lazy. They took their time exploring and tasting each other. Ryan's tenderness, the reverent expression he wore, and the slow heat he forged within her touched a place in her heart she hadn't known existed. She ached with the primitive, instinctual need to bind her heart with his. Her breath caught, and tears stung her eyes. *Why not? What's stopping you?*

Ambition. The driving force in her life to take over a plumbing empire, that's what.

"I want you, woman." He reached for the condom on the bedside table and put it on. "You're really something special, and anyone who doesn't see that is blind."

Had he read her mind? She frowned.

"What's wrong? Aren't I doing this right?" He nudged her knees apart and entered her.

"Ohhh," she said on a sigh. "You do everything exactly right." She lifted her hips to meet his, losing herself in the sensations, then crying out his name with her release and catching him in her arms when he shuddered with his.

He propped his weight on his elbows and moved a little inside her. Resting his forehead on hers, he murmured, "I like what we've got going on here."

"'Course you do." She chuckled. "Like we already established— you're a guy, and what we have going on here involves sex."

He kissed her briefly and peered into her face. "It's not just the sex. I know L&L isn't where you want to be, but have you considered looking for a job in Evansville?"

Her heart raced. "The search engine I use brings up jobs nationwide, Ryan. There's nothing in Evansville that meets my criteria."

"Can't you change your *criteria* a little bit? I know you want to prove you can make it in a man's world, but hell, if that's all it takes, L&L definitely qualifies. Noah, Ted, and I *are* an all-male staff."

"Noah is my brother. L&L doesn't count." A weight settled on her chest that had nothing to do with the man turning her bones to mush. "I know how important it is for you to be where you are right now." She stared into his eyes. "I wouldn't ask you to change your plans for me. Don't ask me to give up my dreams or change for you. We'll only end up hurting each other."

"You don't know that." He rolled away from her and sat on the edge of the bed. "All the psychoanalysis you did on my behalf last night entitles me to do the same." He glanced at her over his shoulder. "Your brilliant plan is to live your life trying to prove something to somebody else." His mouth tightened. "You're wasting your time, Paige. Why not use all that ambition and talent building something for yourself? Stop worrying about what your daddy thinks, and start doing what's right for you."

"I *am* doing what's right for me. Don't you get it?" Her throat and chest constricted, making it difficult to breathe. "Langford Plumbing Supplies has been in my family for generations. Noah didn't want it. I do."

"Why?"

"Why what?" She scooted out of bed and gathered her clothing from the floor.

"Why do you want Langford Plumbing Supplies?"

"Didn't I just say why? It's a multigenerational family business."

"That's not good enough. It'll still be the family business whether you head it up or not."

"I gotta go." She slipped her pajamas back on and jammed her arms into the robe.

"What're you afraid of?"

"*Afraid*?" She froze. "Why would you say such a thing?"

"You're running away from this discussion, that's why. You're running away from me."

"No, I'm not."

"You know what I think?" He plowed his hands through his hair and scowled at her. "I think starting something from nothing scares you, and maybe that fear is what your dad sees when he thinks about handing over the family business. You've been spoiled your whole life, and doing without while you build a future on nothing but a dream is a risk you don't want to take."

"That's bullshit." She glared back. His words stung. She located her slippers and avoided looking at him. Langford Plumbing Supplies was a family business, and she was family. Fear didn't enter into it. The fact that her own father didn't factor her into the equation when it came to LPS hurt her deeply, but that hurt had strengthened her will and determination to prove herself. That's all there was to it. "You suck at psychoanalysis, and you don't know me at all."

"If that were so, what I said wouldn't bother you. You'd laugh it off." He scowled at her from under his lowered brow. "Look at you, Spoiled Little Rich Girl. Your hackles are up and your hands are fisted. Before you dismiss what I say out of hand, why don't you put it into that salad bowl you call a brain and toss it around for a while first?"

"Ass." Her heart thundered so loud the ringing echoed in her ears. She stormed out of his apartment and kept storming all the way to the back door of the big house. Sliding it open, she stepped inside. Ceejay was pouring herself a cup of coffee, and Toby played with Sweet Pea on the floor. *Damn.*

"Oh, yeah." Ceejay took another mug down from the hooks under the cabinet and poured another cup. She arched an eyebrow and smirked. "I've made *that* walk early in the morning a time or two." She handed Paige the coffee, came around the counter, and took a seat at the table.

"It's not what you think," Paige muttered, pouring cream into the much-needed brew.

"Of course not." Ceejay laughed. "It never is. So, how was it?"

Paige splayed her hands out on the table, leaned over, and knocked her forehead against the wood. "Too good. Way too good." She shot her sister-in-law a desperate look. "Ryan had a crisis last night. He called and asked if I'd talk him through it." She bit her lip. "He didn't invite me to come over. He only wanted to talk, and I could've done that over the phone."

Ceejay's eyes took on a knowing look. "You went to the carriage house anyway."

"I did."

"And ended up spending the night."

"Guilty." Paige blew out a breath. "I made him tell me about his demons, gave him a back rub to help him relax, and…One thing led to another."

"Do you regret it?" Ceejay asked and took a sip of her coffee.

"No…Well, maybe a little. Sleeping with him complicates things." She shrugged. "We argued this morning, and I stomped off."

"What about?"

"He said I have a salad bowl for a brain." The indignation still burned.

Ceejay made sympathetic noises. "Did you know your brother once compared me to a scab he couldn't stop picking?"

"Men are idiots." Paige snorted. "Ryan and I just want different things, and—"

Heavy footsteps came from the top of the back stairs, accompanied by Lucinda's lighter steps and chatter.

Paige's pulse shot up. "Do me a favor. *Don't* tell my brother about last night."

Ceejay smirked again. "He's going to find out. You can't hide stuff like this from people who care about you. Believe me, I've tried."

Noah walked into the kitchen and frowned at her. Paige slid her sister-in-law a look of desperation, hoping she'd understand what she was asking. Ceejay gave her an almost imperceptible nod, and Paige sagged with relief.

"So that's what happened to my favorite robe. I've been looking all over for that." Noah pointed at Paige. "Give it back."

"Ceejay let me take it out of the rag bag. I'm keeping it."

"Hey, way to throw me under the bus!" Ceejay cried.

"Ha. It's yours for now. It's got to go into the laundry at some point." Noah poured himself a mug of coffee and leaned against the counter, fixing her with an inscrutable stare. "I heard you get up and leave around midnight, but I didn't hear you come back." His mouth formed a straight line. "Oddly enough, this morning I noticed I'd missed a call from Ryan at about the same time."

Ceejay laughed. "I told you so."

Heat beat a hasty path up to her cheeks. *Crap.* "Yeah, Ryan had a crisis last night and needed someone to talk him through it."

Noah's eyes narrowed. "So, you and he...*talked* all night."

"That's right." Paige shot up from her place. "I'm going to go shower."

Didn't things just keep going from bad to worse for her? Dealing with her brother's disapproval was the cherry on top of her upside-down cake, and hiding out in Perfect belonged in the *You're a dumbass* column of her life.

CHAPTER ELEVEN

EDGY AND TENSE, RYAN KEPT his eyes on the surface of the table during their Monday-morning staff meeting. Even though he was hyperaware of her sitting across the table, he couldn't bring himself to look at Paige. After the way she'd stomped off Saturday morning, what would he see in her eyes? Did she regret sleeping with him? An ache banded his chest at the thought. He had no clue what to expect, and not knowing left him more off-kilter and confused than usual.

"Here's what I need for next week's sample sale." Paige placed a list in the middle of the table. "Would one of you gather pieces of the types of wood we use with the different stains we offer? I'd like to keep them in the showroom. There might be customers who decide to go the custom route if they don't find what they want on the floor."

"Sure. I can do that," Ted volunteered. "I'll mount them on a piece of plywood, and we can hang it on a wall so it's permanent."

"Thanks. That would be great."

Noah picked up the list and scanned it. "We're offering a discount on custom orders during the sale?"

"Yep, it's twenty percent off custom and thirty-five percent off the floor samples," Paige answered. "We have ads in a few Sunday newspapers, including Evansville's, and I've posted the information on our website and social media. I want everything to be ready by Thursday. I'm heading to Pennsylvania on Friday to get some of my stuff."

"You need help?" Ted sat up straighter, looking like a puppy about to get a juicy bone. "I'd be happy to drive to Philly with you."

A red-hot poker stirred up the anger always sloshing around in Ryan's gut. The thought of Ted alone with Paige made him want to strike out at the kid. Biting his tongue, he glanced at Paige and caught her staring at him. The second their eyes connected, she turned away. His heart lurched, and a lump formed in his throat, blocking his airway.

Had he pushed her too hard or come across as too desperate? Maybe she didn't want to have anything to do with him anymore. After all, she'd made it clear her plans weren't going to change because they'd slept together. Where did it leave them?

"Thanks, Ted, but Ryan already offered." Paige turned to her brother. "We plan to start work early Friday morning so we can leave around lunchtime. Is that all right with you?"

A powerful rush of relief surged through Ryan. He released the breath he'd been holding and eased the grip he had on the arms of his chair. She hadn't kicked him to the curb—not yet, anyway. Noah's mouth turned down at the corners, and he ran his hand over the back of his skull. *Damn.* Ryan knew that gesture well. Noah wasn't happy.

"Just be sure you're back by Sunday night." Noah shot him the commander stare across the table. "Be careful."

"Of course." What did he mean by that? Careful as in, *Don't even think about sleeping with my sister?* How would he react if he knew they'd already done the deed? "Are we through here?" Ryan asked. "I'd like to get the coffee table finished today. Hopefully, we can put it on the website this week and include it in the sample sale."

"We're done, as far as I'm concerned," Ted grumbled as he stood up. "I have a changing table to build."

"No, we aren't. We need to talk about the new line. The prototype is not going to be a part of this sale." Paige's gaze touched his for a second. "I want to wait until we have the entire Americana line, and there has to be more than a coffee table in one pattern. Who wants a coffee table without matching end tables, an entertainment center, or at least shelves?"

"She's right." Ted sat back down. "It doesn't have to be quite as complicated as the coffee table. Maybe a fraction of the quilt pattern on a drawer, cabinet door, or a panel here and there. We should spend some time today coming up with companion pieces."

"Great idea," Paige agreed. "Do the dining room pieces next, and use a different pattern." She stood up and started gathering her things. "Now we're done."

Hanging back, Ryan waited until the other two men had left the office. "Are we good?" he asked Paige.

"Of course. Why wouldn't we be?"

"I pushed too hard, said some things—"

"You're entitled to your opinion." Her chin came up. "No matter how far off the mark that opinion might be."

He wanted to laugh, but knew better. "Good enough."

"I've got to get the showroom into some kind of order and price the blankets and toys." She started moving toward the door. "The glassblower and his daughter are going to be here soon."

"I have an errand to run after work. You want to come along and maybe grab a bite to eat after?"

"Not tonight. I'm watching the kids while Noah and Ceejay play poker," she answered without looking at him.

Paige headed for the front stairs, and he let her go. Today's forecast: prickly, with a chance of cold shoulder. He could deal with that. Ryan grinned. At least she was talking to him, and he had the weekend to look forward to.

The day flew by, and it was quitting time before he knew it. Ryan stepped back to give the coffee table another inspection. Satisfied, he cleaned up his workspace. Tomorrow he'd apply the first coat of acrylic, and by Wednesday afternoon, his prototype would be ready.

The marquetry method worked well. Through trial and error, he and Ted had worked out a plan and pieced together the quilt pattern like a jigsaw puzzle. The walnut contrasted nicely with the ash, and they'd both agreed not to add any stain. The natural colors and grains enhanced the overall effect. He'd worked on the specs and pattern as they went along, and now anyone in production would be able to replicate the piece.

"Hey, have you and Noah ever considered selling our patterns or putting together do-it- yourself kits? There's a market for stuff people can build themselves."

"I'd rather keep the designs in-house." Ted cleaned his brush in the utility sink. "We've applied for patents for each design. Every piece we produce is an original, from the first cut to the finished product. That's what sets our company apart."

"You're right." Pride in what they did welled in his chest. "It was a stupid idea."

"No, it wasn't." Ted glanced at him over his shoulder. "Keep the ideas coming, man. We need them, even if they don't all fit.

At some point, we might consider creating simpler pieces to use for kits. You never know."

"How old are you?" Ryan teased. "I swear, sometimes you sound like you've been around way longer than you have."

"Old enough." Ted dried the brush and put it away, wiped down his area, and headed for the door. "See you tomorrow."

"Take it easy." Poor guy. Ted still had it bad for Paige, and being in the same boat, he could sympathize. He had to hand it to the kid. They'd managed to maintain a respectful standoff, and he'd even enjoyed working with him on the coffee table. Maybe, someday in the distant future, they'd be friends.

"You ready to go?" Noah asked as he emerged from the showroom. Paige followed.

Ryan grabbed his thermal coffee cup and shut down his computer. "Yep. How's the storefront coming along?"

"You'll have to take a look tomorrow." Noah grinned. "You won't believe the transformation. It's starting to look like one of those fancy-schmancy upscale yuppie stores."

Paige laughed. "I'll take that as a compliment." She glanced at him. "I earned my first commission today. I sold a complete nursery suite to the glassblower's daughter and her husband."

"Good for you." No cold shoulder now. Warmth spread from his heart outward, and he placed his hand at the small of her back as they left. She didn't pull away.

"You should've seen how excited they were." Paige beamed. "They loaded it up and took it away so quickly I think they were worried we'd change our minds about the discount."

"You gave them forty percent off. That's cutting the profit margin a little too close." Noah hit the unlock button on his keychain. "They had good reason to worry."

"Word of mouth, Noah. They got a great deal on heirloom-quality furniture, and believe me, they'll spread the news about our sample sale to everyone they know. Pregnant women have a tendency to hang out with a lot of other pregnant women." Paige climbed into the backseat. "That reminds me. Once we build up a surplus again, I'll place an ad in a parenting magazine." She buckled her seat belt. "They left a bunch of really nice glasswork behind. Our sale is going to be great. You'll see."

How was it that a brilliant woman like Paige didn't recognize how excited and happy working at Langford & Lovejoy Heritage Furniture made her? Ryan shook his head. Hell-bent on extinguishing the spark that lit her up like a Fourth of July sparkler, she gave stubborn a whole new meaning.

"You're shaking your head again, Ryan." Paige placed her hand on his shoulder. "Are the voices in your head telling you to do things you don't want to do?" she teased.

Noah barked out a laugh and started the truck down the alley. Heat crept up Ryan's neck, and he kept a tight rein on his tongue.

❧   ❧   ❧

Ryan pulled into the Chevy dealership and parked his truck. Late Monday afternoons should be slow, so hopefully there wouldn't be too many other customers around. He already knew what he wanted—another truck like the one he had, only with an extended cab and a few extras. Scanning his perimeter and then the rooftops, he got out and headed for the showroom. He hated the way salespeople hovered over a prospective sale, hated the games they played, and the closer he came to the front door, the edgier he got.

Soldier up. Gritting his teeth and bracing himself, Ryan swung open the glass door and stepped inside.

"Can I help you?" A middle-aged man approached, wearing false friendliness like a uniform.

"I'm looking for a new truck to replace my old one." Ryan gestured to his pickup parked close to the door. "I want a midsize pickup with an extended cab and a nice sound system."

"Two-wheel or four-wheel drive?" The man's eyes took on an avaricious glint.

"Two-wheel is fine, and four on the floor. I don't want an automatic."

"I'm sure we can find exactly what you're looking for on the lot. The name's Frank." He held out his hand.

"Ryan Malloy." He shook Frank's hand briefly. "Lead the way." They walked through the lot until they came to a row of midsize trucks fitting his specifications. A shiny black Colorado caught his eye, and he walked closer to read the details pasted on the side. Peering into the interior, he checked out the tan leather seats. Paige would like this one. The only holdback was that it had four-wheel drive. Not a deal breaker, and as long as he kept it in two-wheel drive, the mileage should be better. "I'll take this one."

Frank's eyes widened. "You don't want to take a demo out for a test drive?"

"Nope. It's the same model I've been driving for years, only newer. I don't have any patience for this sort of thing, so let's get this done as quickly as possible."

Frank's wide-eyed expression turned to a frown, and he pulled the slip from the plastic envelope taped to the window and copied the VIN number on the corner. "You sure you don't want to look around for a while?"

"I'm sure." Ryan stuck his hands into his front pockets and followed Frank to his cubicle.

"What kind of loan are you looking at?" Frank brought his computer screen to life. "Do you want a thirty-six-, forty-eight-, or sixty-month term?"

"I'm paying cash." Ryan scanned every warm body in the place. A family with two rambunctious boys and an infant were looking at the crossovers on the floor. The baby wailed, and the boys chased each other around the SUV, squealing and shouting. He forced his attention back to the transaction at hand. He took out his wallet and handed Frank his driver's license, debit card, and proof of insurance. "What kind of deal can you give me?"

"I'll have to go check with my manager." Frank started to rise. "I'll be right back."

A ball of tension started in Ryan's gut and spread to his chest. The sound of the squalling baby and screeching kids scraped against his nerves like fingernails on a chalkboard. "Listen, Frank." Ryan took a deep breath and leaned forward. "I'm a veteran, and I don't deal well with bullshit. If you want this sale, don't play any of the usual car-sales games with me."

"My daughter is deployed right now. She's air force—stationed in Afghanistan at the Kandahar Airfield." Frank plopped back down, and the false face slipped away to reveal the haggard lines of a worried father. "No games." His eyes slid to the burn scars on Ryan's neck and quickly turned back to his computer. His fingers flew over the keyboard for a few seconds before he turned the screen to Ryan. "Here's the best I can do."

Good ol' Frank had managed to take a good chunk off the sticker price for him. "Done. Can you take the old truck off my hands? All the paperwork is in the glove compartment."

"We can, but you won't get much for it in trade."

"I don't care about that." Ryan rose and wiped his palm on the front of his jeans before offering his hand to Frank. "Thanks for understanding. How long do you need to get everything ready?"

"Give me an hour." Frank stood and shook his hand. "I'll run this through and make a copy of your license and proof of insurance. Wait here a minute." He picked up the pile of plastic Ryan had set on the desk.

Staring out the floor-to-ceiling window, Ryan tried to tune out the raucous family. He spied a barbershop a block down. Summers in Indiana were hot and humid, and his thick hair had to go. Another item to check off his to-do list. Haircut first, then he'd find a restaurant with a corner booth where he could have dinner and hide out.

How would Paige react to his new pickup? She'd look good riding shotgun. That image led to thoughts of making love to her on the brand-new leather backseat. Were they too old to contort?

"You're going to love that new truck. It has a really nice ride." Frank interrupted his fantasy. "Here you go." He handed him back his stuff.

"I know I will." Ryan put everything back into his wallet. "I'll be back in an hour."

※ ※ ※

True to his promise, Frank had everything ready to go by the time he returned. His shiny new truck was parked by the front doors with the temporary license slip stuck to the rear window. A mixture of excitement and buyer's remorse churned through him. He'd just taken a huge chunk out of his savings for something that would lose value the minute he put it in gear. But hell, it would last him for the next ten years, and he was way overdue.

Ryan straightened his shoulders, walked in, and did all the signing and glad-handing he could stomach. Then he climbed into his new Colorado, found some tunes on the radio, and headed home. Frank was right—the new truck rode like a dream, and the leather seats cozied up to his backside like it had been custom-made for his ass. Tomorrow morning, he'd offer to drive the carpool.

Pulling into the Langfords' driveway, Ryan tamped down the urge to find Paige and show off his shiny new toy right away. How would she look in his cab? He imagined her spread out on the backseat, naked, her creamy skin and tawny-blonde hair next to the cashmere-colored leather...Oh, Lord. Had he chosen the truck to match the girl?

Speaking of the girl, there she was on the porch, with Toby in her arms and Lucinda beside her, talking to Noah and Ceejay. His heart and stomach did their leapfrog routine at the sight of her, and anticipation lit him up as he parked. She'd love the truck. He just knew she would. No more worries about his vehicle breaking down. He was the man, providing a safe ride for his woman.

Noah and Ceejay came down the stairs as Ryan climbed out. Unable to contain the urge to strut, he sauntered around the hood and nodded to Noah. "You two on your way to play poker?"

"We are." Noah walked over to take a look at his new Chevy. "Nice ride. This must've set you back some."

"Ohhh, leather seats," Ceejay gushed as she peeked in at the interior. "I like it, Ryan."

From the corner of his eye, he watched Paige approach. He liked the way she looked with a child in her arms. Sweet, soft, and utterly feminine. His chest tightened with the longing for a family of his own. A longing he hadn't felt in years. He waited for the appreciation he had coming.

She eyed his truck, and then her gaze swung to him. "You cut your hair."

"My hair? I just dropped a bundle on this new truck, and all *you* noticed is the haircut?" Ryan ran his hand over his face and growled low in his throat.

Noah laughed and took his wife by the hand. "We'll be home by eleven, Paige." He sent Ryan a look of sympathy. "Are we taking your new pickup to work tomorrow?"

"It hardly matters, does it?" Ryan muttered. "It's Paige's turn to drive. Let's see how many clowns we can stuff into *her* teacup vehicle."

"Hey." Paige scowled. "My car has a BMW engine." She gave him her back and headed back up the steps of the porch.

"Well, lah-dee-fucking-dah." He kicked a pebble.

"Malloy," Paige called from the front door.

His head came up. "Yeah?"

"I love the new truck."

"I knew you would," he called back, but she'd already disappeared. Grinning like a fool, he walked back to his apartment, unaware of the ground beneath his feet.

❦   ❦   ❦

Paige sat on a stool behind the shop counter, the new desktop computer open to L&L's retail software. A few more items to code and price, and then the window dressing, and things would be close to ready.

As she surveyed the showroom, a deep satisfaction filled her. Each matching suite had been set up like a nursery, complete with handmade quilts draped over the railings and plush stuffed toys filling the corners. One wall had been lined with shelving to display the glass vases and bowls. At some point, they would have more to display, but for now, everything looked pretty darned good.

Lamps. The place needed nursery-appropriate lamps, and she'd look for some for the next sale. She hummed as she worked, smiling at the memory of Ryan driving in with his new pickup. He looked so damn sexy standing next to that shiny black truck with his new haircut. It was all she could to do to keep from dragging him to the leather seat in the back to break it in properly. *Hmmm.* She'd never done it in a vehicle, and they *were* going to go on a road trip…

Her phone vibrated in her back pocket. Probably her mom asking for the fifth time when she'd be arriving. She pulled it out and checked the caller ID. An adrenaline surge hit her bloodstream at the John Deere name and number displayed on the screen. "Hello?"

"Ms. Langford, this is Janice Pederson. I'm calling about your recent application to John Deere for the account executive position. Are you still interested?"

"Yes, I certainly am." Paige's hands shook.

"I see on your cover letter that you live in Philadelphia. Can we set up an interview for sometime next week?"

"My permanent address is in Philadelphia, but I'm currently working in southern Indiana as a marketing consultant. I have to be here next week for an event we have planned. Can we set up the interview for the following week?"

"Do you have Skype?"

"I do, yes."

"Would you be willing to do a Skype interview next week? We can be flexible about time."

"That would work if we can set it up for first thing in the morning your time."

"All right. How about Wednesday morning, nine a.m. eastern standard time?"

Paige wrote the appointment down on a scrap of paper on the counter. "Perfect." Her mind raced. She could get to work a little early and set up her laptop on the second floor, where the Wi-Fi signal was the strongest.

"After the first interview, we'll narrow the pool of candidates and set up second interviews. If you make it through the first cut, we'll fly you to our headquarters here in Pennsylvania," Janice informed her. "Let me give you our Skype information, and I'll need yours."

Janice rattled off their account address, and Paige wrote it all down and gave the HR rep her information in return. "Thank you, Janice. I'm looking forward to the interview on Wednesday." They said their good-byes and ended the call. Paige jumped up from the stool. Excitement buzzed through her, and she wanted to share her good news. *Ryan.* She wanted to tell Ryan.

Her stomach dropped. Why bother? She knew exactly what he'd say. "Are you passionate about tractors, Paige?" she muttered under her breath.

No, but that didn't mean she couldn't learn to appreciate them, and it didn't mean she wouldn't be stellar at the job. "It's just sales. What difference does it make *what* you sell as long as you're good at what you do?" He didn't understand. Telling Ryan was out for now. She'd bring it up while they were driving to Philly.

Paige plopped back down on the stool, put her elbows on the counter, and rested her chin on her fists. Who *could* she tell? Noah and Ted wouldn't exactly welcome the news. She reached out a finger and spun her cell phone like a top. "I'm pathetic." She bit her lower lip, stopped the spinning phone, hit speed dial, and brought it to her ear.

"Paige?" her mother answered after the third ring.

"Hi, Mom." She sighed. "Are you busy?"

"No. What's wrong?"

"Nothing. I called to share good news."

"Huh, you don't sound very happy about your good news. What's up?"

Mothers were too damned intuitive. "I have an interview with John Deere next week. They have an opening for their Pennsylvania, Maryland, and Delaware region." She waited several seconds for the expected squeal of delight from the other end. It didn't come. "If I get the job, I'd be moving home. Isn't that good news?"

"Noah told us he made you VP of marketing for L&L. Aren't you happy working for your brother?"

"Sure I am, but it's not what I want to do forever." Paige swallowed the disappointment. "I told Noah that when I accepted the job. He knows it's temporary."

"Your father and I didn't know it was temporary. We think it's the perfect job for you, and Noah is beyond thrilled to have you there to help them grow their business."

Right. Foist me off on my big brother, and LPS is no longer a bone of contention. No wonder they both thought this job was so wonderful for her. "The perfect job?" She wanted to throw her hands up in the air. "Don't I get to decide what's right for me?"

"Of course you do, honey. Why are you being so defensive?"

"I'm not being defensive, Mom." Paige rolled her eyes at the whopper she'd just told. "I thought you'd be excited for me, and clearly you aren't, that's all."

"Don't be ridiculous. Of course I'm excited for you. This just came as a bit of a surprise. I'd love to have you here in Philly."

She paused. "Let me take you to lunch on Saturday. We can talk more then."

"I'll have a friend with me."

"Invite her too. My treat."

"It's a—"

"Oh, I have another call coming in. I have to take this, Paige. I'll see you on Saturday."

"All right, see you then. Bye."

Her mother ended the call, and Paige set her cell back on the counter. Wasn't anybody on her side? She started twirling the phone again, propping her chin on one fist.

"Where do you want this?" Ted walked into her domain with a large piece of plywood painted dark brown with fancy gold lettering and columns for each type of wood: oak, maple, ash, and black walnut. Under each heading were several blocks with the different finishes available.

"Over on that wall." She pointed to the space on the opposite side of the door leading to the back. "You can see where I left space." She blew out the last self-pitying breath allotted to her for the day and got up to help him mount the display.

"What's eating you?" Ted leaned the board against the wall and sent her a sharp glance.

"I'm feeling sorry for myself. Not very attractive, I know."

He looked around the store, coming back to her. "Trouble with Ryan?"

"No. The trouble is with me." Should she tell him? Surely Noah had mentioned her temporary status. "I got some good news today and have no one to share it with."

"You can share it with me." Ted pulled a tape measure and pencil out of his tool belt and marked the wall. "We're still friends, aren't we?"

"Yeah, but it affects L&L. Or it might, anyway."

"Noah already told me you don't plan to stick around forever, Paige. Go ahead and share your good news. I'd love to hear it."

His mouth tightened, and she couldn't tell whether it was because he was concentrating on his task or if he didn't really mean what he'd said. Either way, she wanted to be forthright with everyone at L&L. "I have an interview with John Deere next week. They're looking for an account executive."

He handed her a bunch of hardware to hold while he drilled. "So, you and Ryan aren't all that serious?"

"That's what you come away with?" She blinked. "Not, 'Oh, you might be leaving us soon,' but..." She gasped. "You didn't want to hire me in the first place, did you?"

"No." He shrugged. "Not really."

"Why not?" She straightened. "Don't you think I can make this place grow like gangbusters?"

"I'm sure you can." He kept working. "You know how I feel about you. Do you imagine it's easy for me to watch you and Ryan all day long?"

"What do you mean? He and I hardly talk during the day."

"You don't have to talk." He snorted. "The pheromones and hot looks are bad enough."

She crossed her arms in front of her. "I do not—"

"Yep. I'm surrounded by idiots."

"How did I jump from sending hot looks to being an idiot?"

"You and Ryan—"

"Need help back here?" Ryan strode around the edge of the wall, his posture all tense and his glance bouncing between the two of them.

Ted shook his head and muttered, "Idiots." The corners of his mouth turned down, and his jaw muscle twitched.

"That's it." She did throw her hands in the air this time. "I'm going to lunch." Men and their stupid testosterone. Reaching for her purse on the way, she stomped toward the front door.

"It's only ten a.m.," Ryan called after her.

"Brunch, then. I'm going to brunch." She swung the door wide and marched out with no idea where she wanted to go. Slamming the door behind her, she looked down the street. The Perfect Diner caught her eye. She wasn't hungry. Mostly, she needed a place to cool down, and it would be nice to see Jenny. Life just wasn't going the way it was supposed to go, and that pissed her off.

She opened the door to the diner and stepped in. The scent of waffles, maple syrup, bacon, sausage, and coffee wrapped her up and drew her in. Several tables were full of farmer types chowing down on their hearty breakfasts or lingering over coffee and conversation. Paige took a stool at the counter and hung her purse over the backrest.

"Morning, Paige." Jenny put a glass of water and a menu down in front of her. "How are you doing? I heard you're L&L's new VP of marketing." The corners of her eyes crinkled with warmth. "We're all thrilled about that."

The sudden sting of tears took Paige by surprise. Her throat closed, and she tried to swallow the tightness. She snatched a couple of napkins from the metal dispenser and brought them to her face. Unable to speak, she fought to get herself under control.

"Oh, my." Jenny hurried to the end of the counter, where her assistant manager was wiping down the ketchup bottles. "Carlie, honey, you're in charge. Paige and I are going to take a little walk." Jenny came back to her, snatched a few more napkins, and took her arm. "Come on, now. It's a lovely day. You and I are going to go have a little talk."

Paige rose obediently and followed Jenny through the back of the diner to the door leading out into the alley.

"Let's head for the park and sit a while." Jenny put her arm around Paige's shoulders and steered her to the intersection. "Take a deep breath, and then tell me what all those tears are about."

She wiped her eyes and blew her nose. "I don't even know where to start."

"Start with what brought you here in the first place."

"I...I got fired." The floodgates burst, and the whole story poured out. She bared her soul, and by the time she got to the part where Ted admitted he didn't want her working at L&L, they'd reached the park.

Jenny led her to a bench and sat her down. "You surely are going through some growing pains."

"I know." She sighed.

Jenny chuckled. "You don't like your job at L&L?"

"No, I love it, but that's not the point. I have dreams and goals, and nobody understands what they mean to me. Or they don't care."

"Huh. When you say 'nobody,' who all does that include?"

Heat flooded her face, because when it came down to it, she knew her family understood. They just didn't agree with her career track. The one person she wanted on her side, the one whose stubborn refusal to cheer her on...*Crap*. She couldn't tell Jenny that, so she said nothing at all. Biting her lower lip, Paige studied the ancient playground in the center of the park.

"I've noticed Ryan is making some pretty drastic changes lately."

Her heart raced. "Yeah. He's going to group with my brother tonight, and he's starting therapy at the VA center this week."

She glanced at Jenny out of the corner of her eye. "Did Ceejay tell you what happened? How I found him with the suicide letter and gun?"

"She did." Jenny patted her arm again. "I'm so glad that all came out into the open. Your coming here has been a real turning point for him. You're having quite an impact."

"I don't think I had a lot to do with it, other than telling Noah what was going on."

"Don't you?" Jenny stared off into the park. "He's shaving now, and I noticed he finally cut off that mop of hair."

"He bought a new truck too." Paige smiled, remembering how he strutted around the shiny black pickup. "It's really nice."

"So, is Ryan on your list?"

"What list?" Confusion fogged her brain.

"Your list of important people who don't understand you."

"Oh." She swallowed. "That list."

"What is your heart telling you, honey?" Jenny nudged her.

"It's telling me that if I set goals and don't see them through, that makes me a failure. I'd be a quitter." Her hands tightened into fists on her lap. "I *have* to prove to my parents I'm capable of taking over the family business. I want to be the one to run Langford Plumbing Supplies after my dad retires."

"And Ryan doesn't agree?"

"No, he doesn't." She frowned. "He says I'm wasting my time trying to prove anything to anyone other than myself and that I ought to focus on finding something I'm passionate about." She turned to Jenny. "He said my brain is like a salad bowl. What does that even mean?"

"It means he spoke while in the grip of some pretty powerful emotions where you're concerned. Does his opinion matter to you?"

She opened her mouth to reply and shut it again. Confusion and an achy kind of wanting swirled around inside her. "I don't know."

"Fair enough. When you got that call from John Deere, did it make you happy?"

"Yes. I was really excited and wanted to tell—" She clamped her mouth shut.

"Ryan? You might want to give that some thought." Jenny raised an eyebrow and sent her a pointed look. "Were you excited because you at least have an interview, or were you excited at the prospect of working for a tractor-producing company?"

She thought about it. "After all the crap I went through at Ramsey & Weil, being selected for an interview is definitely uplifting. I would've reacted the same way no matter what company wanted to interview me for a job."

"But you didn't tell Ryan, even though he was the first person who came to your mind."

"No, I didn't, because I know exactly what he'll say."

"Is there some truth to what he says? Have you thought about why you react the way you do when he challenges you?"

"Sure I have." She bit her lip. "It's because he's wrong, and he refuses to see it."

"Is that right? Things are often much more clear when we're on the outside looking in." Jenny chuckled. "Noah is stubborn too. It must be a Langford trait. Sometimes we become so focused on what we think we want that we're blind to the gifts life lays at our feet. Allow yourself some room to grow and evolve, Paige. You're too young to be rigid. Things change. Dreams change." She rose from the bench and stretched. "I have to get back to work."

Was she stubborn? Rigid? "Thanks for listening." Paige remained seated. "I think I'll stay here for a little while longer."

"You do that." Jenny smiled. "Let go of what's in your head, honey. Once you realize your heart is the only compass you need to worry about, you'll never go wrong."

Paige frowned. Hadn't she been listening to her heart? Isn't that where her determination and resolve stemmed from? She blew out a slow, shaky breath. Wrung out and empty from the emotional purge, she was in no state to think about it now.

CHAPTER TWELVE

RYAN WIPED HIS SWEATY PALMS on his jeans for the third time. His heart pounded so loud he swore he heard the echo off the walls as he headed down the corridor of the Marion VA center toward the mental health unit—toward hell. His pits were soaked, and the stain had spread under the arms of his shirt. What a mess. Was it too late to hightail it out of there, find a bar, and hide himself in the bottom of a bottle?

Paige's image sprang into his head. Yep. Far too late to bail. The yearning for something better outranked the bunker he'd built around his heart and soul. He longed to be free of the ghosts, nightmares, and anxiety plaguing him.

Meeting up with Noah's group of veterans Tuesday evening hadn't been so bad. They met in the back room of the VFW, ate dinner, drank coffee, checked in with each other, and mostly just hung out. He hadn't said much, and no one pushed. Maybe Dr. Bernard wouldn't push either, and he could ease into things at his own pace. He gulped in a breath and walked up to the check-in counter. "I'm Ryan Malloy. I have an appointment with Dr. Bernard."

An older woman with silver hair and a bored expression handed him a clipboard with a pen attached to a thin chain. "Fill this out. I'll need to make a copy of your VA insurance card and driver's license."

"Yes, ma'am." He removed the requested items from his wallet and handed them to her. She walked away to make a copy, and he slid to the end of the counter to fill out the medical history forms. In true military style, the questionnaire went on and on, with plenty of repetition thrown in for good measure. The last box to be checked finally came into view, and he returned the clipboard to the assistant behind the counter.

She took the forms from him and handed back his cards. "Have a seat. Dr. Bernard is with someone right now. He'll come get you when he's ready."

"Great." He surveyed the reception area and chose a corner chair, away from the others waiting to be seen. Picking up a hunting magazine from the stack on the end table, he flipped through the pages and thought about the past couple of years.

Letter. Pictures. Gun. Bottle.

If Noah had waited one more day to make that call...*Shit.*

"Ryan Malloy?"

A powerful surge of adrenaline hit his bloodstream, and a whole new drenching sweat broke out. "Yes, sir." He shot up out of his chair.

"I'm Dr. Bernard." A tall, balding man with piercing gray eyes and a lean, fit body gestured toward the hall. "Come on back to my office, Mr. Malloy. Let's talk."

"Sure." He followed the doctor down the narrow hall and into his office. "Call me Ryan, sir." He noticed the doctor walked with a slight limp. The edge of his slacks rose up, giving him a glimpse of a prosthetic inside his shoe. Had he lost his leg in active combat? Ryan's tension eased a fraction.

He cased the room. Several pictures on one wall formed a circle around the doctor's credentials. Military units, marines. Ryan moved closer. Yep. He found a younger version of Dr. Bernard in every picture.

"The Gulf War and Afghanistan." The doctor sat in a leather chair and indicated the chair opposite to his. "Have a seat."

Ryan moved away from the pictures and sat as ordered. A fat file with his name on the tab caught his eye. Bernard picked it up, spread it open on his lap, and put on a pair of reading glasses. The requisite forms he'd filled out a week ago for his caseworker lay on top of the pile. He braced himself.

"You can call me Doc, by the way. Everyone does." He continued to scan the contents of the file, giving nothing away in his expression. "Nightmares, flashbacks, anxiety, self-medicating, and suicidal. Hmm. It says here you've been playing a solo version of Russian roulette for the past two years." Dr. Bernard glanced at him. "Tell me about that."

Swallowing hard a few times first, Ryan forced himself to begin. "I had this vintage .357 revolver. I'd get home from work, lay everything out on my coffee table, spin the cylinder with one bullet, and start drinking." Sucking in a huge breath, he blew it out slowly. "I got it into my mouth several times, but I only managed to pull the trigger once. Most of the time, I passed out drunk."

Doc's eyes widened for a fraction of a second. "It's a good thing you hit an empty chamber."

"I didn't. I hit the chamber with the bullet."

Doc shot him a questioning look.

"I was aiming at my couch that night. I killed it dead." Ryan studied the ceiling and tried to blink the burn away. "I didn't really want to die, Doc. I was just desperate to get away from the pain of not knowing how to go on living."

Dr. Bernard nodded and cleared his throat. "Two twelve-month deployments in three years"—Bernard flipped through his file—"as an artillery specialist in a heavy combat unit."

"Yeah, Uncle Sam was experiencing a severe shortage of boots on the ground."

"Your last deployment, you were injured in a suicide bombing? I see you've already been adjudicated for PTSD." He raised his gaze. "You went through therapy then. Tell me about that."

"I fronted—did what I had to do to get through." Ryan scrubbed his hands over his face. "I wasn't...interested. The doctor assigned to me had never been deployed...never engaged with hostiles. What did he know about what I was going through?"

"What's changed?"

He shifted in the chair. *Everything.* "The night I shot my couch, I got a call from my former lieutenant, Noah Langford. He offered me a great job, and I moved here a few months ago. One morning, his sister found me passed out next to my suicide letter, a couple of pictures, and my gun." He chuffed out a breath. "She tossed that .357 into the Ohio River and read me the riot act. She ordered me to cease and desist, or else she'd shoot me herself." The memory brought the flicker of a smile to his face.

"Noah said if I want to keep my job, I have to work on my issues." He swiped his hand over his face. "I don't want to lose what I have here. For the first time in forever, I have a reason to get up in the morning. For the first time, I *want* to work on getting better, and I'll do whatever it takes."

"Here's the deal. You can't front with me, Ryan. Nothing will take if you do."

"I know."

"It's not going to be easy. The nightmares and flashbacks will get worse before they get better. You might want to talk to your primary physician about meds to help you manage your symptoms."

"Let me think about that, Doc." Ryan rested his elbows on his knees and buried his face in his hands. "I kind of went off the deep end with my good buddy Johnnie Walker Red. I don't know if I want to start taking anything right now."

"All right. Let's see how you feel in a few weeks."

No fronting. If this was going to work, he had to be honest and bare all. "I've got something to say, sir. I want to tell you about something that happened before I enlisted." Tightness banded his chest, and his hands formed fists in his lap. "Is that allowed? It's not military related."

"Of course." Doc closed the file and placed it on the small table between their chairs, replacing it with a legal pad and a pen. "What we do here is about you—the whole you, not just the part pertaining to your military service."

Once he could manage it, he took a fortifying breath and launched into the horror that had been the beginning of his end. "I was engaged before I enlisted." He related the entire tale, leaving nothing out, including the way he'd forced Theresa to go riding that day. "She died in my arms, and it's my fault." Swiping at his eyes, he forged on. "After her death, I enlisted because I wanted to blow shit up and shoot off a gun until I couldn't shoot anymore." In his heart, he'd always carried the niggling fear that his desire to fire at an enemy made him a bad person. Bad people didn't deserve good things.

"Rage is a normal part of grief." Dr. Bernard reached into his pocket and pulled out a quarter. He handed it to Ryan. "Do me a favor."

Confused, he stared at the quarter in his hand. Did the doc want him to go feed a parking meter somewhere? "Sure."

"Behind my desk over there, you'll find one of those plastic watercooler jugs. I want you to drop this quarter into it for me."

Ryan moved to the area behind the desk and found the container shoved into a corner. The thing was almost half-full of quarters. It would add up to some serious money once the jug was full. He added the quarter and went back to his chair, totally baffled.

"That's my fishing trip fund. Every time another soldier comes into my office and blames himself or herself for something completely out of their control, the jar gets another quarter." Doc peered at him over the rims of his reading glasses.

Ryan blinked. "There are a hell of a lot of quarters in there."

"The visual has quite an impact, doesn't it?" Doc smiled. "Think about that the next time your mind goes into shame and blame mode." He leaned back in his chair. "Tell me about the woman who threw your gun into the river."

Ryan's entire body relaxed. "Paige. Her name is Paige, and she's as tough as nails and soft as dandelion fluff, all at the same time. She's brilliant. It took her all of ten minutes to figure me out, but when it comes to figuring herself out? She's clueless." One side of his mouth quirked up. "She's a spoiled little rich girl with a heart of gold. Paige is a gorgeous package of contradictions, and I'm crazy about her."

"Is she a major factor in your decision to seek help?"

What was the doc getting at? "I guess. Is it important?"

"I want to be clear about what motivates you."

"You mean, if things don't work out with Paige, am I going to slip back into the abyss?"

"It's not about what I think. This is about you, Ryan. What are your thoughts?"

"Paige has already made it clear she plans to go on to bigger and better things, Doc. Is she one of the reasons I'm here? Yeah, but not in the way you think." He looked him in the eye, firm in his resolve. "I need to be here, and I want to get better. When she leaves, I'm not going to survive the loss if I'm not already working through some of my shit and building a support network." His throat constricted, and his eyes misted again.

"Losing her is a foregone conclusion in your mind?"

"Pretty much, yeah." What did he have to offer to a woman like her? A new truck? *Shit.* He wasn't any good for anybody, not even to himself, if he didn't start building a ladder out of the hell he lived in—one rung at a time. "No fronting. No bullshit. You have my word."

"Good. I'd like to see you every week for now. Do Thursday afternoons work for you? If they do, we can set up a schedule for the next six weeks."

"Let's do that. Thursdays work for me. My boss has given me permission to leave early for this." The doc wrote something down on yet another form and handed it to him. Ryan couldn't help it. A few hot tears slipped out, and he sagged with relief. He'd taken the first step.

"I'd like to get you into a group. We'll talk more about that next week." Dr. Bernard took off his reading glasses and rose. "Ryan, I've been where you are, and I promise, things will get better."

"I hope so, Doc." He pushed himself out of the chair and walked toward the door.

"Stop by the front desk to set up those appointments."

"Yes, sir. I will." His insides had turned to a washrag that had been wrung out one too many times. His legs barely supported his weight, and he had to lean against the counter while he handed over the sheet of paper the doc had given him to set up the six-week schedule.

Only five in the afternoon, and all he wanted to do was go home and go to bed. First, he had to pack for the trip to Philly. Thinking about his weekend with Paige went a long way toward perking up his energy level. They were going to stay in her condo. The two of them. Alone. "I'll bet she has a really nice bed."

"I beg your pardon?" The silver-haired receptionist stopped entering his appointment dates into the calendar and stared wide-eyed his way.

"Uh...Sorry, ma'am. I was just thinking out loud. Are we about done here?"

❧   ❧   ❧

"Will you get the cooler on the porch?" Paige tossed her overnight bag and backpack into Ryan's backseat next to his stuff and set two thermos bottles between the front seats. "Noah has to go into Evansville this morning. He'll be in later, but he said we can head out whenever we want. I packed food for the entire trip. If we leave at ten instead of lunchtime, we can be at my condo by eleven tonight." She pulled out a wad of folded papers from her purse. "I have a Google map for you. I'll navigate."

Ryan took the wad of papers from her hand and tossed them into the truck. "Whoa, there, Ms. Bossy Pants. Take a breath."

She didn't know what to do with herself or how to act. They hadn't spent any time alone with each other since the night she'd helped him through his crisis. Her nerves hopped all over the place at the thought of spending the entire weekend with him. "Fine. I'll get the cooler." She turned on her heel and started for the veranda.

Ryan caught her by the shoulders and brought her around, his eyes glinting with humor. He drew her in and kissed her. "Relax, sweetheart. It's just me." Guiding her to his truck, he helped her in. "I'll get the cooler."

His new haircut made him look more mature and devastatingly handsome. The absence of all that hair emphasized his adorable dimples, crooked smile, and brilliant blue eyes. Throw in the Stetson, his cowboy boots, faded jeans, and the snug T-shirt clinging to his lean frame, and the backseat of his sexy new truck was starting to look like a place she wanted to visit. Soon. Yes, indeed. She'd turned into a sex-crazed animal, and it was all his fault.

He hefted the plastic cooler into the back and climbed into the driver's seat. The engine hummed to life, and he started down the drive. "So you like my truck, huh?" He glanced at her as he shifted into second gear. "You don't have to worry about breakdowns anymore."

Had he bought it just to put her mind at ease? Her heart turned over, exposing another tender spot he'd managed to touch. "I love the truck. It looks really good on you, but you have to admit you've been dissing my car ever since I got here. I couldn't very well gush all over your pickup with my Mini parked nearby. It would've been disloyal. By the way, my car is an excellent ride."

"The truck looks good on me?" He shot her a lopsided, little boy grin.

"Like the Stetson." She smiled back. "You wear them both well, cowboy."

"That's good. I'm glad you think so."

His blue eyes filled with heat, and her insides warmed all the way through. Only Ryan affected her this way. A single look from him, and out-of-control lust spiraled through her. "I love the leather interior." She darted a glance at him and ran her hand over the side of his seat so she almost touched him. "Especially in the back." He made a deep purring sound, and a shiver of pleasure traipsed down her spine.

"I'm so glad you like it, darlin'. I have plans for that backseat, and I'm going to need your help."

Gah! Her brain turned to mush, and she had to fight the urge to turn his air-conditioning on. "Oh, yeah?" *Oh. Yeah. Geez, is that the best you can do?* Under the circumstances, yes. Those two words were all she could manage.

They pulled into his parking spot.

"I'm all for leaving at ten, if not earlier." He winked.

Oh, man. She really loved when he did that.

"Ted and I are working on specs for an entertainment center I've designed to go along with the coffee table. It shouldn't take too long to finish. What do you have left to do before the sample sale next week?"

"Everything is set. I'm going to update the website and social media this morning and then research a few more outlets for future ads." She climbed out of the truck. "Come get me when you're ready."

His eyes smoldered into hers. "I'm ready right now, Paige."

Lord, so am I. He caught her looking at the fly of his jeans, and she stumbled on the uneven pavement leading to the door. "Stop it."

"Stop what, sweetheart?"

"Stop looking like you do, and stop being so damned"—her gaze drifted to the bulge in his jeans again—"ready." She straightened her posture and headed into the building. Thoughts of what they could do in the backseat danced through her mind. The two of them naked and sweaty, with her on top…Ryan's laughter made her knees go weak.

Ted stood at his workstation with a partially assembled crib before him and wood glue in his hand. He raised his head when they entered, looked between them, and shook his head. "Morning, Ted." Ryan gestured toward the crib. "Are you going to have time to work on the specs before we leave?"

"Probably not. This crib, an armoire, and a changing table all have to be shipped on Monday, along with a couple of orders Noah is working on." He bent back to his task. "Once we have everything crated, we can spend the rest of Monday working on the new projects." Ted spared her a glance. "There's a check on the counter in the front. It's your first paycheck, including the commission for the stuff you sold."

A thrill bubbled up. "My very first commission check from L&L," she crowed. "I'll have some spending money for the weekend."

"Good." Ryan cocked an eyebrow. "You can help with gas."

"And…There it goes." She shrugged. "Are you sure you don't want to take my Mini? It costs under thirty dollars to fill her up."

"Hmmm. Not much of a backseat, though, is there?" He shot her a hot look.

"There is that." She sighed. "The truck it is, and I'll kiss my spending money good-bye."

"Jeez, you two." Ted grumbled. "Take it somewhere else. I'm trying to get some work done here."

Her face flamed, and she squelched the laugh that wanted to burst out. "Right. Let's get to work." One more sneak peek at Ryan, and she headed to the kitchen area to make a fresh pot of coffee. She wanted the good stuff this morning. After all, her first official paycheck was cause for celebration. She hummed one of her favorite songs while she got the coffee going.

"I like the sound of that, darlin'."

Ryan's voice startled her, and she looked at him over her shoulder. "What are you talking about?"

"You were humming." He reached around her for a mug. "It does my heart good to see you happy."

"Maybe I'll hum all the way to Pennsylvania," she teased. "By the time we hit Ohio, it'll drive you nuts."

"Oh, I'll make sure you hum, darlin'." He put his arm around her waist and pulled her against his chest. "You can count on that, and you already drive me nuts."

"I'm still here," Ted called from the back. "And I still don't want to listen to that shit."

"Sorry." Paige laughed and left Ryan waiting for the coffeepot to fill. Deep satisfaction filled her as she entered the storefront. Splashes of color drew the eye to each nursery suite. The unmistakable hallmark of excellence branded each piece of handcrafted furniture. L&L really was an amazing enterprise. Pride in what the three men were building here in this small town swelled in her chest.

The challenge would be managing growth while maintaining their commitment to artisanship. It could be done, but it would take finesse and the right person. A twinge of regret stole her breath. Someone else would have that pleasure.

Shrugging off the twinge, she booted up her computer and went to their website to check for orders and perform updates. No doubt about it, Ryan's new line would expand their market exponentially. How would they handle the increase in orders with just the three of them? She had some ideas, and if she did somehow manage to get the John Deere job, she'd share them with the guys before she left.

Hopping off her stool, Paige went to the printer to pick up the new orders and brought them to the in-basket nailed to the wall in production. She arranged them by date so that the first order placed would be the first order filled. "New orders," she announced.

"Great. Thanks." Ted straightened. "You two can go. I know you're both chomping at the bit."

Ryan shut off his computer, put his drafting tools and sketch pad away, and stood by the back doors. "You don't have to twist my arm."

"I'll go shut the front down." Paige hurried to the storefront, stopping to fill a cup with the good coffee first. One more look around, and she shut off her desktop, grabbed her purse, and walked toward the back door. She'd never been quite this excited about a long drive before.

At some point, she had to tell Ryan about her upcoming interview with John Deere, but not right now. Not while everything felt so right between them. "Road trip." She grinned as she climbed into his truck and set her coffee in the holder. "Are you going to let me drive some of the way?"

"Do you know how to operate a stick shift?" Ryan backed out of his space and drove down the alley.

"No, but it can't be too hard."

He grunted. "When we get back, I'll teach you on a back road. Once I'm confident you can handle it, I'll let you drive my truck." He shot her a grin. "I'll do the driving for now."

"Fair enough." She picked up the Google map. "I'll navigate."

"When it gets close to lunchtime, keep your eye out for signs pointing to a state or regional park." He pulled onto the highway and shifted into fourth, the muscles in his forearm rippling with his movements. "We can have a picnic—and check out that backseat."

Images of their tangled, naked bodies writhing together in his backseat sent scorching heat through her. Time to steer the conversation in another direction, at least until they were safely parked. "How did your first session go with Dr. Bernard?"

"It was difficult, but good. He's a veteran of hard combat himself—a marine. That helps."

Paige studied him, reaching out and running her hand over his shoulder. "You sure have gone through some changes lately. Remember the night I burst into your apartment?"

"How could I forget?" He waggled his eyebrows. "You couldn't keep your eyes off me."

"It's not every night a girl smacks into a naked man like that." She laughed. "I didn't know what to think. You looked like a wild homeless guy with a gun, and look at you now. Clean-shaven, a great haircut, and you're making a huge difference at L&L." Her breath caught. "Seeing you so happy does my heart good too, Ryan."

He reached for her hand, and his Adam's apple bobbed. She twined her fingers with his and held on. "I've got a ways to go, Paige. A long ways to go."

"It's funny, isn't it?"

"What is?"

"The difference a day can make in a person's life." She continued to study the changes she saw in him. "If Noah hadn't made that call, you'd still be in Texas with your wild hair and beard, drinking and playing a game of chance with your life. If I hadn't handed Anthony the Meyer's bid that day, I wouldn't have been fired. We wouldn't have met when we did."

"Speaking of Anthony, would you like to pay him a visit on this trip?" He glanced at her out of the corner of his eye, his mouth set in a straight line. "I'd like to have a few words with the creep."

"No. I'm equally to blame for what happened." Paige shook her head. "What goes around comes around. Eventually, he'll run into someone who will play him the way he played me." She blew out a breath. "Besides, I understand why he did what he did. I got *his* office with the window, and I was handed the Meyer account—because of my dad, not because I earned it. Anthony resented me."

"All right. If that's the way you feel, I'll let it go. But, Paige, Anthony was just one guy. Can you imagine the resentment you'd face at Langford Plumbing Supplies? Is it possible your dad won't hand it over because he wants to protect you?"

"Of course it's possible," she snapped. "In fact, I'm sure you're right. That's why I need to toughen up at some other company first."

"That's what you want?" He scrutinized her for a few seconds. "You want to 'toughen up,' become hard, cynical, and distrustful, for the sake of LPS?"

"Yes." She moved her hand away from his and fiddled with their driving directions. "Do we have to talk about this?"

"Nope." He put both hands on the wheel. "We don't. I hope you know I just want you to be happy."

"Same here." Her attention shifted to the road ahead of them. "Our exit is coming up. We want Interstate 70 east."

For the next couple of hours, she napped, listened to music, and daydreamed. The ride of silence had gone on for far too long, and she ached for the easy, relaxed way they'd interacted before. "It's getting close to noon. I'm hungry." *Hungry for you.* Starving for the closeness they'd shared earlier.

"I could eat. Start looking for a park."

"We should've brought an atlas." She searched the highway for signs pointing to a park.

"There's an atlas under your seat." Ryan reached over and popped the glove compartment open. "I stashed a few maps in here too. I bought one for each state we're driving through. You won't find what we're looking for in the atlas."

"You thought of everything." She accepted the map he handed her. "Where are we? I haven't been paying any attention."

"We're on I-70, just inside Ohio."

Paige opened the map and started searching. "You're going to have to get off the interstate at Highway 503 and head south. There's a regional park on the Twin River." She peered out the windshield. "We didn't pass it already, did we?"

"I don't recall seeing 503. We just crossed the border."

"It's about fifteen miles from the state line."

"Paige…" His tone was hesitant, unsure.

"I know. I'm sorry. I get defensive when it comes to the whole LPS thing. Can't we just forget about that for the weekend?" She bit her lower lip. "We were having such a great time until the subject came up."

The smile he turned her way melted her heart. "I was going to say the same thing."

"Good. It's a deal." She glanced at him. "Besides, we have that backseat to check out, and I know exactly how we're going to do it."

He laughed and reached for her hand. "Been givin' it a lot of thought, have you?"

"Maybe a little." She grinned. "Like, since you brought the truck home."

"Sweet. There's the sign for 503."

They almost missed the park. Tree branches obscured the small wooden sign. Ryan turned on the gravel road. The park consisted of a handful of picnic tables, a concrete outhouse-style restroom with a padlock on the doors and sign that said it would open on Memorial Day, a few trash cans, and an old swing set.

A small river rushed by, and the leaf buds on the trees were just beginning to open in the early-April warmth. She and Ryan were the only two there, although, if the beer cans littering the ground around the trash cans were any indication, this was the place to be if you were a teenager looking for a party.

He pulled the truck between a couple of pine trees and shut off the engine. "What'd you bring to feed me, woman? I'm hungry."

"I brought smoked-turkey-and-swiss-cheese sandwiches, fresh sliced pears, and chips. Gotta have fruit or a vegetable with every meal, Auntie Paige," she said, impersonating her niece's refrain.

Ryan laughed. "Noah and Ceejay sure do have a couple of great kids." He got out and headed for the tailgate.

"I know, huh? They're lucky."

"You'd be a great mom, Paige." His brilliant blues snared her with an intense look. "Do you want a family someday?"

"I do." She busied herself with the cooler while her pulse raced. "I didn't realize just how much until this extended stay with my brother's family. They have something so special, and I'm glad for Noah." She risked a glance at him, and the tenderness she glimpsed in his eyes stole her breath. "How about you?"

"Hmmm." He hopped up to sit on the tailgate, unscrewed the cap of a bottle of water, and handed it to her. "A family of my own is something I've always wanted. After Theresa's death, I figured I'd lost my one and only chance." He turned to stare into the woods and murmured, "Lately...Lately, I've begun to hope again."

Her insides shifted, and a fierce longing settled in between her racing heart and fluttering stomach. Paige pushed off from the truck and came to stand between Ryan's knees. "Let's forget about lunch for now." She snaked her arms around his waist, snuggled into him, and laid her cheek against his chest. His heart pounded against her ear. "You want to know what I've worked out for that backseat?" She lifted her head and drank him in with her eyes.

He tossed his sandwich back into the cooler and slid off the truck. Taking her face between his palms, he kissed her so deeply she melted into him like butter on a hot potato.

"Tell me, darlin'." He nibbled his way down her neck while unbuttoning her shirt. "What do you want?"

"I was thinking we'd fold the passenger seat down, and…Oh, that feels good." Somehow, he'd managed to unfasten her bra, and his magic fingers sent tiny shock waves of pleasure through her. "Me on top, straddling…"

"Yeah? Go on. You have my attention." He lifted her, and she wrapped her legs around him as he moved them toward the cab."

"Naked." She tugged at his denim jacket. "You and me naked and touching."

"Touching is good." He set her down just long enough to open the door, flip the front seat down, and move it forward as far as it would go.

Paige took advantage of their separation, unbuckling her belt and pulling off her shirt. "Where's the condom?" Her voice came out a breathless rasp.

"In my back pocket."

She snatched it out. "I like a man who thinks ahead."

"Are you going to spend all our time talking?" He tossed his jacket in the driver's seat and stripped out of his clothing.

Laughing, she kicked off her shoes and did her own strip-down. "A minute ago, you were asking me to talk. Now you want me to stop?"

"Yeah. We're done talking."

They faced each other, naked as the day they were born. She studied every inch of his war-torn body and swallowed hard. Already hot and slick for him, and they'd barely even begun. "Ground's cold, cowboy. In the truck now so I can have my way with you."

"Yes, ma'am," he gritted out, climbed into the backseat, and shoved their baggage down on the floor behind the driver's seat. She started in after him. He caught her around the waist and pulled her onto his lap. "What was that you said about being on top?"

"I want to straddle you."

"Let's do a little exploring first." He leaned her back, supporting her with an arm, and took a nipple into his mouth, circling it with his tongue.

Electric heat streaked through her, and she opened her thighs, aching for his touch.

"Oh, yeah." He chuckled low in his throat. "That's my girl."

His hand slid over her, settling between her legs. He touched her in all the right places with just the right amount of pressure. Lost. She was lost to the world and completely centered on his magic touch. "Oh, you...You do that so well." Her knees came together, and her hips rose against him to increase the sensation. Oh, God. Her toes were actually curling. That had never happened before.

"You're so beautiful, Paige—absolutely gorgeous when you're hot, wanting me, and all laid out in my arms like this." He raised her up to plunge his tongue into her mouth, their chests pressed together while he brought her to climax with his wonderful, wonderful fingers.

While she drifted back to earth, he lifted her and draped her over his lap. While he kissed her, he ran his hands all over her superheated body. His skin against hers wasn't nearly close enough. She wrapped her arms around his neck and tried to get closer, sliding herself over his shaft until the pressure began a delicious swell again.

Breathless, she pulled back. "I...I dropped the condom somewhere." Searching the floor and the seat, she didn't see it anywhere. "Let me find it." She slid off of him and knelt on the floor. Pushing his legs apart, she ran her hands along his inner thighs and stroked his scrotum, working her way up his erection. He sucked in a breath and went taut.

"Not here." Running her hands behind him while pressing herself against his groin, she continued to search. "Got it." She placed the packet in his hand. "I have a little exploring to do too."

"Do tell." He ran his fingers through her hair, watching her with molten eyes that sent heat pooling in her sex.

"Yeah, like here." She swirled her tongue around the head and cupped him.

"I like that," he croaked out.

"Do you? How about this?" She took him into her mouth and sucked, sliding her hands over his torso and chest.

"Ahhhhh, you're going to be the death of me." Ryan threw his head back and thrust his hips against her. He ripped the wrapper off the condom. "I need to be inside you. Now."

She let him go, looked up into his sexed-up face, and licked her lips.

"Shoot. I'm going to come just lookin' at you." He rolled the condom on and drew her into his arms.

His kiss was fierce, his hold on her tight enough to bring on a rush of emotion so strong her eyes stung. She positioned herself so that she straddled his lap, and guided him home while his tongue continued to make love to her mouth. Lowering herself, she absorbed his shudders and groans. She moved over him, finding a rhythm he answered. Throwing her arms around his neck, she rode her cowboy until he shouted her name and jerked helplessly against her as he came. A few more good thrusts, and she followed.

She collapsed against him and tried to catch her breath, while he ran his hands up and down her back and held her.

He purred into her ear, "I'm never going to look at this back-seat the same way again."

Smiling, she closed her eyes and loved him with all her heart. "Me either."

CHAPTER THIRTEEN

RYAN CRADLED PAIGE AGAINST HIS chest as she nuzzled his neck and tangled herself in his heart. Taking a breath, he brought her scent deep into his lungs. "Paige..." *Are we a couple? Do you love me like I love you? Can we find a place to be—somewhere between what you want and what I need?* He couldn't say the words. She was his for today, and that was way more than he deserved.

"Hmmm?"

"My hip is starting to bother me, babe. The one that was shattered in Iraq." Not the words he yearned to whisper, but they'd have to do. She sighed into his ear, sending shivers cascading down his spine.

"OK." She climbed off of him. "I suppose we should eat and get going."

"Bring our lunch to the cab. We'll eat on the fly."

"Sounds like a plan." She worked her way out of his truck and bent over to grab their clothes off the ground.

Lord, she had a fine backside. Closing his eyes, he shook his head to free himself from the haze of lust clouding his brain. He wanted her again, but they had a long stretch of road ahead of them, and he had a bed to look forward to at the end of the trail—with her in it.

The sound of her laughter brought him back. He opened his eyes to find her studying him as she pulled on her panties. He had a front-row seat for that show. Sweet.

"You do that a lot." She grinned and handed him his briefs and jeans.

"Do what a lot?"

"You were shaking your head again, no doubt carrying on a conversation with yourself. I'd pay money to see what goes on inside that brain of yours."

"I was talking myself out of dragging you into the backseat again." He set his clothes on the seat and slipped his feet into his shoes. "I'll be right back."

"Nice butt, Malloy," she called after him. He shook his head again, and her giggles followed him into the brush. By the time he returned, she had their lunch stuff in the cab and everything ready to go. Ryan scanned the small park as he pulled his clothes back on. They'd made a memory here today, one he'd never forget. "I should buy a camera."

"You have one on your phone."

"Oh, yeah. I forgot about that." He slipped his phone out of his pocket and scrolled for the camera icon. "Smile pretty for me, darlin'." Raising the screen until he framed Paige leaning against his truck, he took the shot. "How do I save this?"

She walked over and showed him, and he captured her to get a shot of the two of them. They bent their heads together to check it out.

"Not bad." Paige took the phone from him and set it up so their image became the background picture. "Let's go. We need to hit a gas station soon."

Pleased that she wanted the picture of them as a couple to be his camera's wallpaper, he took another look at their surroundings and shot a picture of the park before sliding the phone into his pocket. "You can go in the woods, you know."

"Not going to happen."

"I guess backpacking and camping in a tent are out of the question?"

"Not even on the radar." She climbed back into her spot. "Hiking in the wilderness would be great, but there'd have to be a nice bed in a cabin or a lodge afterward."

"Spoiled little rich girl."

"Hick in a cowboy hat."

Deep contentment filled him as he got back into the truck and headed for the road. "I don't suppose you'll want to have another *picnic* at suppertime." He winked at her and accepted the half sandwich she handed him. She laid a couple of paper towels in his lap.

"We'll see." She turned on the radio and settled into her lunch.

Ryan drove and ate. "Good sandwich." He took another bite.

"Thanks." She held the opened end of a bag toward him. "I bought the smoked turkey at Offermeyer's in town. Chips?"

He couldn't keep the smile off his face. How many years had it been since he'd felt this relaxed and happy, this normal? Too many. He grabbed a handful of potato chips and set them on the paper towels Paige had so thoughtfully placed on his lap.

She poured him a cup of steaming coffee from one of the thermos containers and handed it to him. He melted inside, loving the way she took care of him. A new truck, a great job, and a beautiful woman by his side. It couldn't last, but he'd take hold of it with both hands while he could.

❧ ❧ ❧

Ryan's eyes burned with fatigue, and he needed to get out and move around by the time he started seeing exit signs for Philadelphia. Paige snored softly beside him, with her seat reclined as far back as it would go. He reached over to nudge her. "Paige."

She stretched and brought her seat up. "Where are we?"

"On the outskirts of Philly. I need you to direct me." He smirked. "By the way, you snore."

"No, I don't." Peering out of the windshield, she yawned and stretched again. She glanced at the clock on his dashboard and sighed. "We would've made a lot better time if we hadn't stopped for so many picnics."

"True." He chuckled. "But they were well worth the delay."

"No argument here." Finger-combing her hair, she glanced around at their surroundings. "Not this exit, but the next, you'll want to get off and head east."

A few miles and a bunch of turns later, Ryan pulled into a parking space under her building. He climbed out and grabbed their bags from the floor behind his seat. It was well past one in the morning, and he was dead tired. "Lead the way, darlin'. I'm about to drop."

"Me too." Paige slung her purse over her shoulder and grabbed her backpack. She led him to a heavy metal door. Opening it for him, she moved aside so he could enter. "My mom is taking us to lunch tomorrow."

His brow rose, and his heart tapped with anxiety. "Is your dad joining us?"

"I don't know. She didn't say." Down a short hallway, they came to an elevator. "You'll like my mom, Ryan. Everybody does." The double doors slid open as soon as she pushed the up button, and they stepped in.

He was too tired to worry about tomorrow. "Right now, all I want to do is fall into bed."

"Ditto."

The elevator opened again, and he followed her down a well-lit hall and waited while she unlocked her door. Once they were inside, she flipped a light switch and led him to the bedroom. He dropped the bags on the floor and started to undress. "I'll take care of this stuff tomorrow."

"Fine by me." She pulled the covers down on the queen-size mattress and tossed the shams to the floor. "This is my side." She got undressed and put on a T-shirt. "I'm not even going to brush my teeth."

Ryan slid into bed beside her and gathered her close. "Me either. Night, Paige."

"Good night, Ryan. If the ghosts bother you, give me a nudge."

Smiling, he let sleep take him, confident that his superhero would keep the demons at bay.

❧ ❧ ❧

The sound of drawers opening and closing and Paige talking softly into her cell phone woke him. Ryan cracked an eyelid and peered at her. Already dressed with her hair still damp from her shower, she piled clothing on the corner of the bed. Her phone was wedged between her shoulder and ear.

A rush of longing shot through him. Not sexual, although he couldn't ignore the physical reactions seeing her produced. This was something deeper, elemental. Permanent. He waited until she ended the call. "Good morning."

She smiled his way. "Good morning. I made coffee."

"What time is it?" Throwing off the blankets, he swung his legs over the edge of the bed and sat up.

"It's after ten. We're meeting my parents for lunch at eleven thirty, so you'd better get up and shower. I'm almost finished putting together what I want to bring back to Perfect."

Dang. Parents. As in Mr. as well as Mrs. Langford. He looked around the master bedroom. "Where's the bathroom?"

"Middle of the hall on your left."

Ryan snatched his duffel off the floor and headed for the shower. Shaved, bathed, and brushed, he got dressed in the bathroom and stuffed everything back in his bag. Drawn by the pleasant sound of Paige's humming, he headed back to the bedroom to find her. "You're doing it again, sweetheart." He dropped his bag on the floor next to his boots.

Shy Paige smiled his way. "I guess I am."

He drew her in for a kiss, marveling at the sweet way she molded her curves against him. Did they have time to make love before they had to leave for lunch? Probably not. "You want coffee? I'll go get some for you."

"That's OK. I'll join you. I'm done here for now." She nipped at his lower lip and turned to leave.

He watched her sweet little butt as she left. He'd better find something else to look at, or they'd be late for sure. Surveying her condo, he noticed that a second bedroom faced hers across the hall. The kitchen and living room consisted of one large blended space, with the end of the carpet and the beginning of ceramic tile forming the delineation. An L-shaped sectional with an oversize ottoman and an entertainment center took up most of the living room.

Paige stood in the dining area holding a mug of coffee and staring out a set of sliding glass doors leading to a balcony.

"You have a nice little place here." He helped himself to coffee and joined her. "With a great view."

She turned to him with a wistful expression. "This condo originally belonged to my half brother. He died a few years ago. Now it belongs to my mom. I rent it from her."

"I'm sorry about your brother. I remember hearing about his passing while Noah and I were in the VA hospital."

"Thanks. Matt is the reason Noah headed to Indiana in the first place. I'm so glad things worked out for Noah the way they did." She checked her watch. "We'd better get moving. I'm going to go make the bed and grab my purse."

Left on his own, Ryan stared out the glass doors at the skyline and sipped his coffee. Paige had been born and raised in this city. Did she miss it? She probably had a posse of friends she'd grown up with here, unless they'd scattered across the country in pursuit of the American dream. For the most part, his family and childhood friends had all stuck pretty close to home. His brothers were helping his folks run the ranch, last he'd heard, and his sister and her family lived nearby in town.

Thinking of home reminded him of his recent visit with his uncle and cousin. They'd invited Paige to join them on the Fourth of July. He hadn't brought it up again, because he wasn't sure he was ready to make the trip home. His mind steered away from thinking about Paige being long gone by then.

"Let's go, cowboy." Paige handed him his denim jacket.

"Yes, ma'am." Draping his jacket over his arm, he took her coffee cup from her and moved to the sink to empty and rinse both their mugs. "Where are we going?" He followed her into the hallway and waited while she locked up.

"Dalessandro's Steaks." She reached for his hand. "You're going to love it. I highly recommend the pepper cheesesteak or the cheesesteak hoagie."

They climbed into his truck, and he started out of the spot. "You're on duty, copilot. Where to?"

She directed him through several neighborhoods, and a half hour later, she pointed. "There it is at the intersection ahead. The parking lot is on the other side."

Ryan pulled into a small parking lot next to an unassuming three-story brick building with a sign hanging off the side over the sidewalk that read DALESSANDRO'S STEAKS & HOAGIES. He parked, climbed out, and scanned the surrounding rooftops.

"The food is so good here you won't believe it, but you wouldn't know it was anything special judging by the building." Paige joined him. "It's super casual. They serve their sandwiches on paper plates, and the fries…Wait till you try their fries." She gestured toward a silver BMW SUV with "LPS 2" on the license plate. "My parents are already here."

Ryan had to smile at her enthusiasm. Taking her hand again, he let her lead him inside. The place was crowded, noisy, and stuffy, and he fought the urge to back himself up against a wall. His pulse surged, and he went into fight-or-flight mode. It took several seconds for his vision to adjust to the dim interior. "I need the chair against the wall," he whispered in her ear.

She studied his face, her eyes filled with concern. "Are you going to be all right? Can you handle the crowd in here?"

"I'll be fine." He swiped his forehead with his shirtsleeve.

"Come on. I see my folks." She waved their way. "They have a table in the corner." Paige took his hand and led him through the packed restaurant. "Dad, would you mind moving? Ryan has PTSD like Noah, and he needs to sit by the wall."

"Should we maybe announce that to the entire restaurant?" He scowled at Paige. *Breathe in. Breathe out. Breathe in. Breathe out.*

"Sorry." She squeezed his hand. "Mom, this is Ryan Malloy. Ryan, this is my mom, Allison." Paige shifted out of the way so he could move to the corner seat. "You've already met my dad."

Mrs. Langford's eyes widened. "When you said you had a friend with you, Paige, I thought—"

Mr. Langford grunted. "Told you, Allie." He shifted into the place to the left of his wife and sent Ryan a sharp look. "I wondered if you might be the *friend*, Malloy."

"It's nice to meet you, Mrs. Langford." *Wonderful.* A crowded restaurant and a father's disdain. He clenched his jaw and focused on his breathing.

"Please call me Allison. If you'd like, we can get our food to go and eat at our house." Mrs. Langford's expression matched her daughter's look of concern. "It is awfully noisy and close in here. I know how Noah would react."

"No, this is fine. Paige has been bragging the place up all morning." He slid into the chair in the corner and surveyed the crowd. His heart started the slow descent from battle-ready to lunch-ready. "No need to change the venue on my account, and it does smell mighty good in here."

"Where are you from, Ryan?" Ed fixed him with an inscrutable gaze.

"Oklahoma, sir. My folks own a ranch near the Texas border on the Canadian River. In fact, most of my relatives are ranchers."

He raised an eyebrow. "But not you."

"Not me. I have an MFA from the University of Texas College of Visual Arts and Design."

"Noah says you're designing an entire new line of furniture for L&L." Allison smiled at him. "He mentioned something about quilts?"

He nodded. "Paige and I were in Evansville one day, and we went into this quilt store in a little strip mall where we stopped to get our lunch. I was so impressed with the patterns and colors that it got me thinking about ways to incorporate them into wood." His heart rate slowed to normal, and his muscles relaxed. "I drew up some plans, and now we're working on the prototypes."

"He's a genius at design, and his drawings are incredible," Paige added. "You'll have to come see what he's done."

"It is about time I visited my grandbabies again." Allison's smile held genuine warmth. "I'd love to see the new line."

A server came by and placed menus and napkin-wrapped silverware in the center of their table and asked if they wanted ice water or anything to drink right away. Paige ordered a fountain soft drink, and Ryan asked for the same.

"So, Paige"—Allison unwrapped her silverware and placed the napkin in her lap—"when is your big interview with John Deere?"

Ryan's heart went right back to pounding, and he turned to her. "You have an interview with John Deere?"

She nodded, but wouldn't look at him. "It's this coming Wednesday."

When had this happened, and why hadn't she told him? The conversation buzzed on, while anger churned and roiled through him. His reaction was unreasonable. She'd made it clear from the start L&L was temporary, but the hurt and betrayal clogging his throat didn't see things rationally. "When were you going to tell *me*?"

Paige kept her eyes on the menu, but he caught the rapid pulse at her throat.

"I was going to tell you on the drive here, but we agreed not to talk about the subject." She glanced at him. "It's no big deal, a first interview via Skype. More than likely, I'll have a lot of those before I land a second interview."

"No. You'll get the job." His jaw clenched, and his head throbbed.

"Noah made you VP of marketing for L&L. Do you plan to get things started there and bail on your brother without a backward glance? That's irresponsible, Paige. You're going to leave him with loose ends he won't be able to tie up." Ed put his elbows on the table and scowled at his daughter. "That's not how Langfords conduct business."

"Langford & Lovejoy was doing fine before I got there, and they'll continue to prosper once I leave." She slumped in her chair. "Come on, Dad. I'm Noah's baby sister. I was unemployed when I landed on his doorstep. What else could he do but hire me?" Her mouth turned down at the corners. "You did the same thing once you found out I'd been fired. You said you'd *let* me work at Langford Plumbing Supplies, remember? I'm a charity case."

"Is that what you think?" Ed's brow creased even more.

"That's not true." Ryan's words came out at the same time as Ed's.

"Isn't it?" She shot him a look, her eyes full of hurt. "If Noah truly wanted me to work for him, why didn't he make an offer when I finished school? He didn't." Her glare shifted to her father. "And neither did you."

"Paige, honey," Allison's tone soothed, "Noah didn't offer you a job because he didn't believe you'd be interested in working for their tiny start-up company. It's not like you've kept your ambitions a secret."

"Right. He didn't offer, and neither did my own father." She shoved back her chair. "If you'll excuse me, I need to use the restroom."

Anger stepped aside to let panic have a go at him. Ryan's poor heart took the beating. He and Paige had never spoken about their future, and he'd known from the start he was in for another tectonic shift. He just didn't think it would come so soon. "Do you know what drives your daughter, Mr. Langford?"

"Of course I know, and it's not going to happen. LPS is not the place for Paige."

"She's going to spend the rest of her life turning herself inside out just to prove to you that she's worthy." He was about to lose her, and there was nothing he could do about it.

"What is my daughter to you?" Ed leaned back in his chair and scrutinized him.

Allison's eyes went wide. "Edward!"

"What, Allie? It's a reasonable question." He turned back to Ryan. "What are you to her?"

"With all due respect, sir, there's no telling with Paige, and it's none of your business where I'm concerned." Ryan focused on the path Paige had taken when she left, watching for her return. Pressure banded his chest, and sweat beaded his forehead. "She's coming back, isn't she?"

CHAPTER FOURTEEN

PAIGE STARED OUT HER BALCONY doors at the Philadelphia skyline. The past two weeks had gone by in a blur of activity. L&L's very first sample sale had been a huge success, and the storefront had emptied out. Her first interview with John Deere had led to the second, and the flush of her recent triumphs had buoyed her confidence enough to face the one sore spot in her life.

Since their trip to Philly, Ryan had withdrawn. He remained polite, sweet, even friendly—in a distant, impersonal way. His abandonment sliced off another piece of her heart every day, and as soon as she got back to Perfect, she planned to confront him. There was no reason why they couldn't find a way to continue what they'd started.

Her phone vibrated in her back pocket, and she brought it up to answer. "Hey, Mom."

"I'm here, Paige. Meet me out front."

"I'll be right down." She stuffed her phone back into her pocket and grabbed her overnight bag. Locking the door, she wondered if she'd be back for good in a few weeks. She made her way to the first floor and outside, where her mother's SUV waited. Paige tossed her overnight bag into the back and climbed into the front passenger seat. "Thanks for the ride."

"I'm always glad to spend time with my girl." Her mom smiled and patted her hand. "How did your second interview go with John Deere this morning?"

"Really well." She grinned back.

"How's Noah taking all of this?" Her mom veered onto the exit leading to the Philadelphia International Airport.

"He hasn't said much. I'll continue to consult for L&L if they want me to, and I'll help them choose the right candidate to replace me."

"Hmm. I don't imagine they will replace you, honey. I suspect they'll go back to the way things were and muddle along as best they can." She glanced at Paige. "It takes all three of them just to keep up with production, and they can't afford to pay someone what you're worth. It would take a very special person willing to start at the bottom and grow with the company."

A twinge of guilt trampled Paige's triumphant high down a notch. She turned to stare out the window at the passing cityscape. "I'm going to create a document outlining a five-year plan for L&L. Hopefully, they'll see the benefit of sticking to it." What if they hired someone fresh out of school? Maybe a young woman. What if this new woman and Ryan hit it off? *He'll forget all about me.* Jealousy stomped the rest of her brief flash of triumph down to the ground.

"What about Ryan? Obviously, he cares a great deal about you, Paige. How do you feel about him?"

Her stomach flipped. Did motherhood come with the ability to read minds? "Everything is up in the air with Ryan. I thought we were going somewhere. Now I don't know." They turned onto the ramp leading to the airport check-in area and merged into the tangle of traffic inching along and dropping people off. An opening appeared in the never-ending stream of cars. "Here is good, Mom."

"Call us and let us know when you hear from John Deere. We love you, Paige."

"I love you too. If I get the job with John Deere, I'll be back in Philly by the first of May." Why didn't that thought make her as happy as it should have? Her mom pulled over to the curb, and Paige hurried out and grabbed her bag from the back.

"Give our love to Noah, Ceejay, and the kids, and tell them we're looking forward to our visit in July."

"I will." She waved and started for the ticketing area. The human resources woman at John Deere said she'd hear one way or the other by Friday. Today was Monday. She had five days to obsess about it. Going through the security check took much less time than she'd expected, and she had time to kill before boarding. She visited some of the shops and chose a couple of inexpensive toys for Lucinda and Toby. One of the benefits of her extended stay in Perfect had been getting closer to her niece and nephew— Ceejay too. She'd miss them. Settling into an uncomfortable plastic seat, she flipped through a magazine and waited to board.

After an uneventful flight, her plane taxied to a stop. Paige hit speed dial on her cell the minute everything shut down. "I'm here," she told Ceejay.

"We're halfway to Evansville. We'll meet you outside the baggage claim area."

"Great. See you soon." Paige checked her watch. Almost three, and it would be four by the time they returned to Perfect. Ryan had started going to a group on Monday afternoons. She'd watch for his return. They needed to talk.

✿　✿　✿

Her heart lodged in her throat, Paige walked along the path to the carriage house. Memories played through her head of that first night when she'd fallen into him, the first time they'd made love, the picnics they'd had on the way to Philly. How could he just turn it off the way he had? She rapped on his door. "Ryan, open up."

The door swung open, and he frowned at her. "What?"

Pushing past him before he could shut her out, she lifted her chin and faced him. "We need to talk."

"All right. How did your second interview go?"

"It went fine. Why have you shut me out?"

"What choice do I have?" He sat on the edge of his couch and flipped his sketchbook closed, pushing it back on the coffee table. "It's not like I have a whole lot of options here."

She paced. "That's it? I *might* get a new job, so we're through?"

"Look"—his mouth formed a straight, unhappy line—"I told you I liked what we had, and I wanted it to continue. You're the one who's leaving, Paige. Not the other way around." He averted his gaze, and his Adam's apple bobbed. "If you don't get this job, you'll get the next. One way or the other, you're already on your way out of my life."

"I love what we *have*, not *had*, Ryan. There's no reason we can't continue. This is the twenty-first century. We have airplanes and cell phones. What if I came to Perfect a couple of weekends a month, and you could—"

"That won't last, and you know it. You're going to travel for your job. Living out of a suitcase gets old fast. Besides, you'll meet lots of new guys out there. You're going to forget all about me."

Impossible. "What if I asked you to come with me back to Philly? Would you?" Her world came to a standstill while she waited for his reply.

Ryan shot off the couch and crowded her space. "What if I asked you to stay? Would you?" His eyes roamed over her face hungrily. "Doc says I already suffered from PTSD when I enlisted. Too many months of heavy combat, the suicide bombing on top of the trauma of Theresa's death...I'm damaged goods, darlin'." He turned away and plowed a shaking hand through his hair. "I have a lot of work to do, and this is the best place for me to be right now."

Her insides imploded. "Ryan—"

"I just want you to be happy, Paige." He faced her again, his expression anguished. "Will you be happy if you get this job and prove yourself to your daddy? If that's what it takes, if that's what you really want, I'm not going to stand in your way."

"It's not that simple. Yeah, I want my dad to see me as someone he can trust to take over LPS, but it's also about proving something to myself." She wanted to pull her hair out by the roots. He was so stubborn. "I got my last job because of my father, not because of who I am or what I can do. I need to know that I can get a job based upon my own merits. I have to follow through on this, or I'm always going to have doubts."

"I get that, and I'm...I'm not going to try and persuade you to do something you don't want to do." The muscles along his jaw twitched. "The last time I did that, the whole thing ended in disaster. Someone died."

"Oh my God! You're comparing our situation to what happened with Theresa?" She did her own hair pulling. With both hands. "There is nothing about this that is even remotely the same. You're just being obstinate."

"I'm obstinate? What about you?" His voice rose. "I watched you during the sample sale, little girl. You were lit up like a Fourth of July sparkler. The ideas you have for bringing L&L forward are amazing, and you love working there. You love it, but you're too damned stubborn to admit it's the perfect job for you."

He pointed at her, his face a mask of hurt and anger. "You're the one throwing us away because of some wrong-minded notion you have about taking over a company you don't even really want. Your own pride has blinded you to what's right with your life. Instead, you choose to focus on what you imagine is wrong."

"You're so far off." Her hands tightened into fists.

"No, I'm not." He moved away and gave her his back. "Go on, Paige. I said everything I have to say. I wish you well, and I hope you find what you're looking for."

Grief and anger grabbed her by the throat and choked the breath from her lungs. Tears flooded her eyes, and the urge to throw things and slam doors propelled her out of his apartment. "Stupid, stubborn man," she shouted, giving in to the urge and slamming his door so hard the window rattled.

Her gut twisted, and tears streaked down her cheeks. She stomped back to the big house. Too bad she couldn't throw open the sliding patio doors, because she wanted to. She pushed it hard enough to make it bounce back and headed for the back stairs.

"Whoa." Ceejay met her at the top of the second-floor landing. She had Toby in her arms and held Lucinda's hand. "What's wrong? What happened?"

Lucinda's eyes went big and round. "Auntie Paige, why are you crying?"

"No reason." She shot past them and shut herself into her room. She threw herself facedown on the bed. She and Ryan were through. The sooner she got a job and left, the better. She cried until she ran out of tears. Spent, she remained where she was, laid out in one big dejected mess on the mattress.

The door creaked open. "Hey." Ceejay walked in, still holding Toby. "I put a movie on for Luce. Do you want to talk?"

Paige groaned. "My life sucks right now."

"I'm guessing this has something to do with Ryan."

"He just dumped me."

"Oh, Paige." Ceejay sat on her bed and set Toby free to roam. He crawled over and patted her damp cheeks, bringing a watery smile to her face. "He went all distant on me after our trip to Philly, and I decided to confront him this afternoon." She grabbed a few tissues from the box on her nightstand. "He doesn't want to...to..."

"Don't you think his reaction might be more about protecting himself than wanting to end things with you?" Ceejay bit her lip and regarded her, as if wondering how much to say. "He's fragile right now and trying really hard to work on getting better. Your leaving is going to be quite a blow. As far as he's concerned, it's another loss in his life when he's already lost way too much."

"Oh, great. Now, on top of everything else, let's add some guilt to my load of crap."

"Paige, it's because of you that Ryan wants to get better. We all know he's crazy about you."

"Sure." She sighed. "That's why he let me go without a fight."

"He has PTSD. He's using all the fight he has just to maintain. You don't have to go, you know. You do bear some responsibility for the way things are ending between you two. Cut him some slack."

Ceejay's words bit into her, because she couldn't deny their truth. *Guilt sucks.* Paige rolled over and let Toby tumble over her. She hugged him and sat up, taking in his sweet toddler scent. "I've made a huge mess of everything. Ted doesn't want me to stay. He says watching Ryan and me together is too difficult. Ryan's already quit me, and being around him would be too hard for me." She shrugged. "I *have* to get this job, otherwise I'm screwed."

"You're not screwed." Her sister-in-law chuckled. "I can't tell you what to do, but I can tell you I've been where you are. All it takes is a single step to turn things around." She rose and reached for Toby. "I'm going to go fix dinner. Want to help?"

"Sure." Wiping her eyes, she got up. "Being useful is bound to be better than wallowing in self-pity."

❧   ❧   ❧

Paige sat in one of L&L's second-floor offices, the same one she'd hid in while searching for a new job. She ended the call with John Deere and waited for the thrill of triumph to kick in. She'd gotten the job all on her own, based on her qualifications rather than a good-ol'-boy nudge from her father on her behalf. Plus, she'd only been unemployed for about two months—quite a feat in this economy.

The thrill never came. Instead, a dull sense of relief consumed her. Leaving the discomfort and pain of being anywhere in Ryan's proximity sounded like a good plan.

Strange. When Anthony Rutger betrayed her, all she'd felt was anger. With Ryan, *devastated* was the word that came to mind, and *shattered* best described her present state. She'd certainly been on one hell of a bummer as far as her love life was concerned. She let out a heavy sigh.

No more men for a while. She'd throw herself into her job, give the corporate ladder a climb, and see if that didn't turn out better than…Tears filled her eyes and slid down her cheeks so suddenly she had no time to fight them off. *Dammit.* She couldn't go downstairs like this. Swiping at her cheeks, she sat back down and struggled to pull herself together. She should be happy. Shouldn't she?

Today was Thursday. Her work at L&L was done. She could head home this weekend and take a week off to regroup before starting her new job fresh on the first day of a new month. She gave her cheeks a final swipe and headed downstairs to make her announcement. Stepping off the elevator, she looked around the production room, her gaze drawn to Ryan. "I got the job at John Deere. If it's all right with all of you, tomorrow will be my last day."

Ryan kept his attention on his workbench. "Congratulations, Paige. Good for you."

"Never doubted for a minute you'd get the job." Ted flashed her a smile.

Noah nodded at her. "You can leave whenever you want. Thanks for everything you've done here. We're going to miss you."

Ryan glanced at the wall clock. "I gotta head out for my appointment."

"Go ahead," her brother said. "I'll catch you later."

Paige tracked Ryan's every move as he cleaned up his stuff and left without so much as a backward glance her way.

"I'm surrounded by morons," Ted muttered.

"So you've said many times." Noah wiped his hands on a shop cloth and turned to lean on his workbench. "What do you have to wrap up tomorrow, Paige?"

"I wanted to finish the five-year plan I started for L&L."

His brow creased. "Look, I know there's some tension between you and Ryan. Maybe it would be best if—"

"I know. I'm sorry. I'm so sorry about this." She wrung her hands together like one of those heroines in an old-fashioned romance novel. "I don't know what to do to make it better."

"Time. Just give it some time." Noah came over and put his arms around her. "You don't have to come to work tomorrow. Take a day to hang out with Ceejay and the kids before you leave. We're going to miss you, kiddo."

"Thanks." She nodded. "That sounds like a good idea. Do you think Ryan will be all right?" *Will I be all right?* She wasn't so sure.

"He's where he needs to be. He's got his group and Dr. Bernard for support. Ryan's going to be fine."

Ted joined them and patted her back awkwardly. "You did us a whole lot of good in the short time you were with us, Paige. The sample sale rocked, and we have the ads coming out in September."

"I really enjoyed working with the three of you. What you have here is amazing, and it's only going to get better." She stepped back. "I'm going to go gather my stuff, and I'll help you clean up." It was over, and the pain of her own losses carved out the last remaining piece of her heart.

❦ ❦ ❦

Ryan couldn't get to the VA center fast enough. The thin ice of his stability was cracking fast, and he had nowhere safe to stand. His jaw ached, and so did his hands. Loosening his grip on the steering wheel, he flexed one hand, then the other, trying to ease the tension. It wasn't like he hadn't seen this boxcar load of hurt coming down the tracks, heading straight for him. He had, and yet he'd still stood squarely on the rails, a glutton for punishment.

Why would a woman like Paige want to stay with a broken man like him? He blinked back the sting in his eyes and concentrated on bringing his pulse back into the normal range.

Turning into the parking ramp, he tried to pull himself together. He had to learn how to stand on his own two feet. He had to do this for himself, or he'd never be fit for anyone else.

Ryan parked and headed for the mental health wing, trying not to run like hell to get there before a meltdown happened. He approached the check-in desk. "Hey, Mrs. Beck. I have an appointment with the doc."

"Have a seat, Ryan. I'll let him know you're here."

"Thanks." His ass had barely hit the fake leather when Dr. Bernard walked into the waiting room. He shot up again.

"Hey, Ryan," Doc greeted. "Let's talk."

Relief washed through him. Doc always started their sessions the same way. *Let's talk.* Translated roughly to mean, *Let me poke and prod until you break down and regurgitate the shit lurking inside your dark soul.* Ryan always left their sessions purged, and the emptiness came as a welcome reprieve from the pain. Once he was safely inside the doc's office, Ryan slumped into his regular chair. "Paige got the job. She's leaving."

"Ah." Doc reached for his legal pad and pen.

He shot him a glare. "What's that supposed to mean?"

"It means tell me how you feel about her leaving."

"Hurts like hell." His jaw clenched.

"Did you tell her how you feel about her?"

"No." He studied a new tear in his old jeans. "Why bother? I don't want to stand in her way."

"Ryan, a couple of weeks ago we discussed how you've cut your parents out of your life. Do you remember?"

He nodded, and his heart crawled up his throat.

"Let me ask you a question." Doc shifted in his chair. "You don't believe you deserve to be happy. Am I right?"

"I *don't* deserve to be happy." He swallowed hard in an attempt to get his heart back into his chest, where it belonged.

"Hmm. You also believe you're responsible for all the bad stuff that has happened in your life. Would you say that's the case?"

"Yeah." He glanced at Dr. Bernard. "Have a pocketful of quarters with you today, Doc?"

Dr. Bernard smiled. "OK. Here's the real question, and I want you to think about it before you answer. What does taking the blame and feeling worthless do for you? What do you get out of it?"

Ryan opened his mouth to reply and shut it again. What did it do for him, other than make his life a miserable hell? "Punishment. The self-imposed isolation and misery are my penance for being a bad person."

"You aren't a bad person, Ryan. You're a good man who has gone through more than most and lived to tell about it." Doc peered at him over the rims of his reading glasses. "Has it occurred to you that if you truly were a bad person, none of what happened would bother you?"

His eyes burned, and he couldn't speak.

"Were your parents abusive toward you? Did you have a terrible childhood?"

"Hell no!" A flash of anger loosened his tongue. "My parents are wonderful people, and I had a great childhood."

"So, who are you punishing by cutting them off—you or them?"

He shot out of his chair, anxiety and rage boiling over. "Me. I'm the one who deserves to be punished. I ruined everything when I talked Theresa into going riding. She died in my arms, man. Her head was cracked open, and her neck was broken…

she…She died as I held her, and I still wear her blood all over me like I did that day. That kind of shit doesn't wash away."

His stomach knotted into a hot, painful mass. "My best friend died because I failed to protect his back the way I'd sworn. I saw him in pieces on the Iraqi desert, because I let him down. I let everybody down. Five soldiers in my platoon died because I didn't do what I knew I should." He pressed his fists into his eye sockets. "I can't get the pictures out of my mind, Doc. How the hell am I supposed to live with that? How the hell am I supposed to be *happy*?"

Doc reached into his pocket, pulled out a few quarters, and handed them over. "Before the traumas, you allowed yourself to be happy, to be part of a loving family. What would happen if you forgave yourself right now? What would happen if you allowed yourself to believe you're worthy of happiness? What would you do differently?"

Swiping at the tears on his face, he pondered the questions and walked to the jug behind Doc's desk. He dropped them in one by one, focusing on the *plink-plink-plink* they made as they hit all the other quarters. He stared at the contents, once again struck by the sheer mass of coins inside the plastic. He wasn't alone in the self-blame game.

"Can your parents forgive you?"

"I don't think they ever blamed me." Ryan reached for the box of tissues sitting on the desk.

"But you can't forgive yourself."

"It would be so great if I could." He blew out a breath. "All this weight and hurt, the loneliness…and guilt…"

"Ryan, this might come as a shock. Is it possible nobody holds you responsible for the things you've suffered through but you? Especially not the dead?"

THE DIFFERENCE A DAY MAKES

"That's what Paige said too. She said my ghosts have better things to do with their time than to blame me for what the enemy did to them."

"She sounds like a smart woman."

"She is."

"She sounds like maybe she's worth fighting for."

"Yeah, but am I?"

"Why don't you ask her?"

His ears rang, and his mouth went dry. He wasn't sure he had the balls to do that. *What would I do differently if I forgave myself?* "So, the road to happiness is self-forgiveness? Sounds too damned easy."

"Simple, yes. Easy, no." Doc made a chortling sound deep in his throat. "How are you coming along with your journaling?"

Ryan made his way back to the hot seat he occupied each week and sank back down. "Good. I journal every night, just like you said I should."

"This week I want you think about the concept of self-forgiveness. What would that look like and feel like in your life?"

"I will."

"How do you feel about group?"

"I like being a part of the group." Thank God he had his group to lean on. He and the other five veterans had bonded, and he knew he could call on any one of them if things got too rough to handle—like any one of them could call on him. He'd come too far and worked too hard to backslide now, and there was far too much at stake.

"I didn't realize how much I missed the brotherhood of being on a team. My squad in Iraq and I were tight. We all had each other's backs, you know? There wasn't anything we couldn't talk about, and nothing we wouldn't do for each other. When you leave the military, all that's gone. It's like having the rug pulled out from under your feet, and you just don't fit in anywhere anymore."

"I know what you mean. It's important to surround yourself with people who share common ground with you. A lot of the friendships started in group last a lifetime. I hope that's the case with you."

"Yeah, me too." His mouth quirked up. "We all go out for dinner together after our session. Each time, I wonder what civilians must think of us. We all make a mad dash for the chairs against the wall."

Dr. Bernard laughed. "Do what my group does—take turns and promise to watch your buddy's six."

"Oh, yeah. Why didn't we think of that?"

"Don't sweat it, army. It takes a marine to come up with the good stuff."

Ryan snorted. "Says you."

Doc leaned back and scrutinized him. "It's time to think about a visit home, Ryan. No pressure. Just think about it for now."

Ryan's palms started to sweat, and his chest ached in the empty space where his family used to live. "I will."

"You have a lot to think about this week. I'll see you for group on Monday." Dr. Bernard stood. "How are the exercises to cope with the anxiety and rage coming along?"

"Still working on that, Doc. It's going to take some practice."

"They'll work if you let them. Keep at it." He set aside his pad and gave him a sharp look. "Trust me when I tell you this: You're a good man, and you deserve to love and be loved. You deserve happiness as much as any of us do."

He choked up and nodded. *If only.*

Doc smiled at him. "I'll see you next week."

"Yeah. See you." The familiar wrung-out weakness settled into his limbs as he left. What would he do differently if he truly believed he deserved to be happy? He would've wrapped his arms around Paige's knees and begged her to stay, that's what. He wasn't there yet, and anyway, she had her mind made up about leaving.

His heart hammered with fear. What if he had begged, and she'd agreed? Would she get into a car accident, or fall down the stairs, or...*Stop.*

Paige wasn't the kind of woman who could be talked into anything she didn't want to do, and his fear had no basis in fact. He was manufacturing the worst scenarios he could, just like he'd conjured his ghosts.

He gritted his teeth. *I'm not going to do that anymore. It might take some time before I can forgive myself, but I'm not going to invent trouble where there is none.* Straightening his spine, he got into his truck and headed home. *Shit.* He had a rough night ahead of him, with Paige so near and yet entirely unreachable.

❦   ❦   ❦

Ryan sat at his workspace and tried to tally how many hours it had been since Paige had walked out of his life. Should he start with their last argument, or should he begin with the moment she drove away on Saturday morning? Saturday, Sunday, to this Monday morning. That's—

"Hey, sad sack." Ted came into his space and hovered there like bad news. "I don't suppose you told Paige how you feel about her before you let her go."

Ryan shifted on his stool so his back faced Ted.

Ted followed him around so he could glare at him. "Why not? She deserves to know."

"How is this any of your business, kid? You didn't want her here in the first place."

"And yet I miss her already. Despite my awkwardness with the situation, I'm man enough to admit she was good for this company." He continued to scowl at Ryan. "You let her make a decision about her life without having all the facts. That makes you a chickenshit."

Ryan practiced his deep breathing and counted to ten. "It's for the best. Noah didn't want me involved with his baby sister, anyway."

"What the hell are you talking about?" Noah came around the edge of the back staircase. "What gave you that idea? I wouldn't have any problem with the two of you together. In fact, I was hoping—"

"Well, then why did you keep warning me away from her?"

Noah's palm came up to rub the back of his head, and a sheepish expression flitted across his face. "It wasn't because I disapproved, bro. I didn't want to see you hurt. I didn't want to see either of you hurt." He shook his head. "Tell me you didn't let her go because you believed I didn't approve."

"I couldn't stop her," he snapped. "It's what she wanted."

"I'm not so sure." Ted looked at him like he was intellectually impaired. "If I know anything about women, it's that they want to know they're worth a little pleading when it comes to the men they love. You let her down big-time, man." He sent him a pitying look.

"Was I this dense?" Noah's brow rose, and he glanced Ted's way.

"Worse. It took you forever to muster up the courage to do anything about the way you felt about Ceejay. Plus, you drooled every time she got anywhere near you." Ted walked to his workbench. "At least with Ryan, all I had to put up with were the googly eyes and the sexual innuendoes."

"Humph. I've seen him drool."

"Will you two shut the hell up? Do you not realize I'm in pain here?" Had he just admitted that out loud? "There's nothing I can do about it now."

"Isn't there?" Ted stared at him through his safety goggles.

Ryan frowned. "Is there?"

"Moron." Ted scowled. "I'm surrounded by idiots, and it drives me abso-freaking-lutely nuts, because you guys always seem to get the girl. You know where that leaves me?" He shook his head in disgust. "It leaves me all alone. I can't fucking stand it!" he shouted. "You don't deserve her, dumbass, and not because you don't *deserve* her, but because you're a chickenshit, and you let her get away without telling her how you feel. Everybody in Perfect knows you love her. Everybody knows except Paige. Criminy!"

He pulled off his goggles, threw them on the workbench, and headed for the back door. "I'm going to my aunt's to get a decent cup of coffee." He stopped to glare at Ryan. "That's another thing. Paige was the only one here who knew how to make a decent pot of coffee, dammit. This is all your fault, Malloy. Fix. It."

"Well, shit." Ryan stared at the empty space where the kid had put on his show.

"I know, huh?" Noah came to stand beside him. "Ted still has the capacity to surprise me from time to time. Don't underestimate him."

"I won't." Ryan scrubbed at his face with both hands. "What the hell am I supposed to do? Paige accepted the job. She's already gone."

"Uh...What do you have in your back pocket right now?"

"My wallet?"

"What else?"

"My cell phone." The phone Paige had forced him to buy and helped him choose. He swallowed the painful lump rising in his throat. How many times had he pulled it out of his pocket over the weekend to look at the picture of the two of them?

"Right." Noah slapped him on the back and walked to his workstation. "You might want to think about using that phone soon, bro. Don't wait too long."

Stunned, Ryan took it all in and let it spin around inside his head. "I need a minute."

"Take two." Noah shot him a wry look.

Ryan took the back stairs two at a time and walked into the office they'd used for their Monday-morning staff meetings—Paige's idea, and a good one, at that. Did the raking over the coals he'd just received qualify as their staff meeting for the week? Confusion and the persistent stir of hope took his breath. Dizzy with all the thoughts clamoring inside his head, he sat down, leaned back, and closed his eyes.

His last session with Doc shouted out the loudest, and he tried to visualize his life as if he deserved good things. Paige's assertion that Jackson and Theresa wouldn't want him to continue carrying around all the guilt weighing him down pushed forward. What would it feel like to let it all go, forgive himself, and reach out with both hands for what he wanted?

The image of his mom and dad popped into his mind, and regret stole his breath. He'd meant to punish himself and managed to hurt them in the bargain. They didn't deserve what he'd put them through, and the sooner he made it right, the better.

Maybe he wasn't ready to call Paige, but the desperate longing to see his family couldn't wait. He knew what he needed to do. Ryan straightened, pulled his cell phone out of his pocket, and made one of the hardest calls he'd ever made.

"Hello?"

"Hi, Mom. It's Ryan."

"Oh, my boy. How are you? Is everything all right?" Her voice broke.

Ryan smiled through the sting behind his eyes. "Yeah, Mom. I'm fine." *If being heartbroken qualifies as fine.* "I miss all of you something fierce, and I want to come home for a visit. Are y'all going to be around this coming weekend?"

"Yes! Come home, baby. We've missed you something fierce too. Shawn and Austin said they ran into you in Indiana. They said you have a new job, and…When did you move? How did this all come about?"

He laughed and heard her gasp at the sound. "I have lots to tell you and Dad. We'll talk when I get there. I'll be home late Friday night. Leave the porch light on for me. I can't wait to see everybody."

"I will. Oh, it's so good to hear your voice, honey. Wait till I tell your father. He'll be so pleased. We'll see you Saturday morning if we can't manage to wait up Friday night."

"Don't wait up." He grinned so hard his cheeks ached. "I love you. See you this weekend."

"We love you too, Ryan. Drive carefully."

"I will. I gotta get back to work." They said their good-byes, and he laid his phone on the table and stared at it. He knew what he had to do to move forward. He worked it all out in his mind. Tonight he'd run things by his buddies, and maybe they'd have some insight about how to cross the great divide separating him from the woman he loved.

Too weak from emotional upheaval to use the stairs, Ryan rode the freight elevator to the first floor. He walked over to the entertainment center he'd started, put on his safety goggles, and carried a piece of lumber to the table saw.

Noah watched his every step. "Did you call her?"

"Nope." Ryan shot him a MYOB look. "I need a few days off, Boss. I'm going home to see my folks this weekend. I'm leaving on Friday and driving back on Monday."

"That's great, bro. Time off granted—with pay." Noah's eye met his and held.

The compassion and understanding Ryan saw there humbled him. "Thanks."

"Paid!" Ted groused. "Since when do any of us get paid time off?"

"Since right now," Noah answered. "If you have a problem with it, take it up with our CFO."

Ted slammed down his hammer. "I *am* our CFO, and our human resources director, payroll manager, production manager, and janitor. Where the hell is my employee-of-the-month plaque? I'm also the most underappreciated employee here."

Ryan exchanged glances with Noah. He'd never seen Ted this on edge. "Can I buy you lunch today, kid?"

"Yes." Ted straightened. "Thank you. Let's head out to the truck stop for a burger. Aunt Jenny doesn't do burgers like they do."

"Deal. You in, Noah?"

"Are you buying my lunch too?"

"Sure, and for the record"—he turned to face Ted—"I appreciate the hell out of you, kid."

"And yet you continue to call me 'kid.'"

Ryan chuckled. "Sorry. I'll try to remember you're all grown-up."

"Moron," Ted muttered.

Noah cranked some tunes, and the three of them went back to work. Ryan settled in and soaked it all up—the sound of the table saw, Ted tapping two dovetailed edges together, and Noah's off-key humming to the country music. Ryan was full to bursting.

He loved working for Langford & Lovejoy, loved working with Noah and Ted. Now all he had to do was figure out how to convince Paige that she belonged here with him, and his world would be complete. And if he failed to convince her? His mind detoured away from the possibility. He'd find a way. He had to.

CHAPTER FIFTEEN

HAD SHE REALLY BELIEVED DISTANCE would bring relief from this choke hold on her heart? Paige stepped out of the shower and wrapped herself in a towel. She couldn't sleep, couldn't eat, and even breathing had become a chore. And now her clothes were beginning to feel loose. The heartbreak diet—maybe she'd write a book, start a trend, and get rich on her misery.

Monday, she'd begin her new job. Surely things would get better then. She'd have lots to learn and tons to occupy her mind. Four more days to get through, and things would start looking up. Running a brush through her hair, she took a good look at the dark circles under her puffy eyes. "Great."

The persistent, irritating prickle of wrongness that had accompanied her the entire drive home continued to plague her. Still, Langfords didn't go back on their word, and she'd accepted the job. No turning back. Move forward. She went to her bedroom and got dressed, choosing an old pair of jeans and an even older T-shirt. What would she do today? She'd already cleaned her condo from top to bottom, including going through the closets—all in an effort to get her mind off Ryan. It hadn't worked.

Coffee. She'd been living on nothing but. Too bad she didn't smoke. Paige imagined herself turning into one of those skinny old ladies who drank coffee and chain-smoked their days away, their leathery faces etched with all the disappointments they'd suffered during their lives. *Gah! I need to get out and do something.*

Maybe she'd use her credit card and go shopping. This funk certainly qualified as an emergency. Dragging her sorry butt to the kitchen, she decided to at least eat a piece of toast so her stomach wouldn't turn on her. She started a pot of coffee and went to the fridge for bread.

Her cell phone rested on the counter where she'd plugged it in to recharge. The tiny red message alert was on. Maybe one of her friends had called to see if she wanted to get together for lunch. One could hope. She popped two slices of bread into the toaster and picked up her phone.

Ryan! His name and number appeared in the call history. She'd missed his call. Cradling her phone in both hands, she moved to her dining room table and fell into a chair. Her heart pounded so loud she heard the echo in her head. All she could do was stare at the screen through tear-blurred eyes. Her hands shook so badly it took a couple of tries before she could get them to work well enough to get to her voice mail. The wonderful sound of his voice washed over her.

"Hey, darlin', it's me. Listen, I shouldn't have let you go without telling you how I feel. Even if it makes no difference, you have a right to know. So…Here goes. I love you, Paige. I know I'm not much to look at, and I don't have much to offer in the way of… well, shoot, in any way, but I'm yours if you want me. I love you with everything I am and everything I'm ever going to be. You make me want to be a better man, and I…" His voice broke. "I miss you like crazy."

She heard him move around on the other end and pressed the phone closer to her ear, waiting with her breath held.

"Aw, hell. I came back to life the day I met you, Paige. The truth is, I need you. I want you, and I love you."

A long pause followed, and tears dripped down her cheeks in a salty deluge.

"I'm going home to Oklahoma this weekend to visit my folks." His voice dropped to barely a whisper. "I wish you were going with me. Sure could use some of that hand-holding through this. I was hoping maybe we could talk when I get back. Call me—if you want to, that is. If not, I'll respect your decision. But I hope you do. Call me, Paige. I'll be back Monday night." Another long pause. "I love you."

She replayed the message three more times. "Oh, God. What have I done?" Loving Ryan wasn't something she'd get over. Ever. And she'd left him for a stupid job selling machinery. Who did that? How thickheaded could she have been? Everyone had tried to tell her—Ceejay, Jenny, Ryan—and she'd been too pigheaded to listen.

Leaving Perfect moved to number one on her dumbest-things-I've-ever-done list. She grabbed a paper napkin from the holder on the table and blew her nose, snatching another to wipe her eyes, then hit speed dial and pressed the phone back to her ear.

"Hi, Paige," her mother answered in a chipper voice.

"Mom," she said, sobbing. "I think I've made the biggest mistake of my life, and I don't know what to do. I'm so confused." She swiped at her eyes.

Her mother didn't respond for several seconds. "I'm on my way," she finally said and hung up.

Paige moved to the balcony door, wrapped her arms around her middle, and stared out at the Philadelphia skyline. What could she do? Perfect was the right place for Ryan to be, and a long-distance relationship would be a strain on him and less than satisfying for either of them. She'd already accepted the job with John Deere. What kind of reputation would she have if she walked away? Fired from her first job and a no-show for her second? What would her dad think of her if she kept ping-ponging from job to job?

No one in their right mind would put her in charge of anything, much less an enterprise as huge as Langford Plumbing Supplies. After this debacle, she shouldn't be allowed to make any decisions on her own behalf for at least a year. Man, she really knew how to make one mess after another. Too bad she had no clue how to clean them up.

She remained fixed where she was until she heard her mom's key in the door. She swallowed against the tightness in her throat. "I hope I haven't ruined any plans you had for the day."

"Don't be ridiculous." Her mother got two mugs out and filled them with coffee. "Sit down, honey." She placed the coffee on the table and went back for sugar and spoons. Taking a seat, her mom studied her for a long moment. Her forehead creased with worry. "You look like hell."

"Gee, thanks, Mom." Paige reached for another napkin. "I knew I could count on you to make me feel better."

Her mother's mouth turned up briefly. "I'm going to wait until your father gets here to ask you what this is about. I don't want you to have to say it twice."

"You...You called Dad?" Her eyes widened. "Oh, God." She groaned and thunked her head against the table. "Wonderful."

"I have a feeling your mistake has a lot to do with his mistakes. You two are like peas in a pod when it comes to stubbornness, and it's time for a good long talk."

"Ohhhh, I hate my life right now."

"Mistakes are how we learn, sweetheart." Her mother chuckled. "You'll live. You're only twenty-five. You're entitled to take a few wrong turns along the way." She reached across the table and patted Paige's arm. "I'd worry more if you didn't make mistakes or if you never learned to admit to them."

"Really?" She straightened just as her front door opened.

Her dad strolled in, carrying two bags from his favorite deli. "I brought bagels and lox." He set down the sacks in the center of her table and slipped his off suit coat, draping it over a chair.

"My life is coming apart at the seams." Her eyes widened. "Do you think bagels and lox are going to put it back together?"

"I brought cream cheese too." He grinned and helped himself to coffee.

"Oh, well, that makes all the difference." She crossed her arms in front of her.

"Tell us what's going on." Her father took a seat. "Then we'll talk about damage control."

She studied the surface of the table. For so long, all she'd wanted to do was to prove to her father she was tough enough to survive at LPS, and now she was a blubbering mess over a guy. No. Not only the guy. Working with Noah, Ted, and Ryan had been a joy. Life had laid a gift at her feet, and she'd trampled all over it.

"Go on, honey." Her mom reached over and patted her again.

"I...I screwed up...again." She couldn't help the tears springing to her eyes.

"How do you figure you screwed up?" Her dad leaned his elbows on the table.

"Well, the first was getting fired from Ramsey & Weil, and the second was walking away from...from..."

He grunted. "Ryan Malloy?"

Anger flared. "Not just Ryan. I walked away from L&L."

"Malloy said you were going to turn yourself inside out trying to prove yourself to me." He crossed his arms and scowled. "Why do you feel like you have anything to prove to me?"

"Because you won't even consider me as your successor at LPS," she cried. "Why do you think I got my master's in business administration, Dad? Why do you think I look for jobs in construction or...or selling tractors and riding lawn mowers?"

"Tell her, Ed." Her mom shot him a long, expressive look in that silent-communication thing they did.

The uncanny way they carried on a conversation without saying a word always freaked her out a little. Paige straightened in her chair. "What?"

Her dad gave her mom an almost imperceptible nod. "I had no choice when I was your age. My grandfather and father started putting pressure on me to take over the family business almost as soon as I could talk. It was expected. No discussion." He sighed. "It might surprise you to know I never wanted to go into business at all. I wanted to become a doctor."

She blinked. "You did?"

"I did. Instead, the day after I graduated from college with a business degree I didn't want, I went to work at LPS. I was only twenty-two and already locked into a career I never would have chosen."

"I had no idea."

"Listen, princess." He shifted in his chair. "Every single day, I face resentment from employees who believe I've been handed the world on a silver platter because my last name is Langford. No matter what I do, they refuse to see that I've earned my place. My entire adult life I've put in sixty- to seventy-hour workweeks at a job I never wanted and don't enjoy." His jaw tightened. "The resentment gets to you. Then there's the labor force constantly demanding a better standard of living than you can afford to give them—unless you're willing to lay off a lot of the younger workers. The younger guys have families to support, mortgages to pay, while the older guys have kids in college and retirement to think about. You can't win." He shook his head.

"You're talented, Paige, and so creative and enthusiastic. Do you really want those qualities crushed by the weight taking over the family business would put on your shoulders? It's not that I think you couldn't do the job if you set your mind to it, it's that I love you too much to put that on you."

Her perceptions were shifting and altering so quickly she couldn't get a handle on anything. "This hasn't been solely about proving myself to you, Dad. I got fired. I had something to prove to myself. Get right back on that horse and all that."

"We understand." Her mom nodded. "So? You managed to get a job at John Deere selling tractors and lawn mowers. Is this what you want to do with your life? Are you passionate about green and yellow?"

"No." A watery chuckle broke free. "Neither of those are my favorite colors."

Her mom smiled. "You proved you could get a job after being fired from your first one, right?"

"I did."

"You can check that off your list." Her dad shrugged a shoulder. "You did it. Feel good. Now, just because you got the job doesn't mean you have to take the job."

Huh? Her insides twisted. "I don't? But I accepted, and they're expecting me to show up on Monday. Langfords don't go back on their word, and we aren't quitters."

"Maybe it's time we started bending a little." Her dad gave her a pointed look. "Noah has taught me a lot about being flexible. I tried to put the same pressure on him that my dad and grandfather put on me. I almost lost my son, and I'll tell you, princess," he said gruffly, "nothing is more important to me than family."

He leaned back. "There's something else you need to know. I'm retiring as of September first." Her parents exchanged another look, this one disgustingly hot. "Your mother and I are planning our second honeymoon, beginning with the South of France and then Barcelona, Spain. We're leaving after Thanksgiving. Don't expect us home until the snow melts."

Her mom reached for his hand, and he took hold, his thumb sliding back and forth across her knuckles. "We want to spend more time with our grandkids. Your mother and I want to travel, take up a few new hobbies, and never again do anything we don't want to."

"Wow." Stunned, she glanced between them, her heart filled with warmth. After all these years, her mom and dad were still so in love it filled the room with a tangible force. Like gravity. She wanted that. With Ryan. "I'm happy for you both."

"If you're still bound and determined to work for the family business, I'll hire you right now." Her father's gaze fixed on her. "You won't start at the top, and it won't be easy. The decision is yours."

All along, she'd been listening to her head. Maybe it was time to listen to her heart. So much of her energy had gone toward achieving her one and only goal—taking over the helm of LPS. Letting it go should have left her feeling bereft. Instead, the relief almost made her giddy. "No. I'm not any more passionate about toilets and drainpipes than I am about green and yellow combines."

"What about L&L? Didn't you enjoy working there?" her mom asked.

"I did. I loved it." Ryan had it right all along. Working with the guys, connecting with customers and crafters, lit her up. She wanted to be the one to finesse their way into the future, and she'd blown it. "I walked away. What if Noah won't give me another shot?"

"There's only one way to find out." Her dad pulled his cell phone out of his coat pocket and made the call, putting it on speakerphone. "Hey, son. How're things in Perfect?"

"Fine, Dad. How are things with you and Mom?"

"Good. There's somebody here who wants to talk to you. Do you have a minute?"

"Sure."

He took it off speaker and handed Paige his phone. She took it, her hands shaking again. "Noah, I made a huge mistake."

"I know. We all know. We were hoping you'd figure it out soon."

"Can I have my job back?" Her heart skipped a beat when he didn't answer right away.

"If something better comes up, are you going to bail on us again?"

"There isn't anything better." She meant it, and the rightness reverberated through her. "I want to help L&L grow. I'm in for the long haul."

He hesitated again. "What if things don't work out between you and Ryan?"

"You're not going to make this easy, are you?" She closed her eyes. "I'm a professional, and so is Ryan. We'll work it out the same way he and Ted have worked it out."

"All right. Here's the deal. Ted is overextended, and I'm worried about him. I want to shift things around and give you a few more responsibilities. I'm offering you the same crappy pay with a bigger workload, and I'm taking the VP title away until you prove to me that you'll stick around. You also have to join the monthly poker games."

"Deal." She smiled so hard her facial muscles hurt. "Do me a favor. Don't let Ryan know. I want to be the one to tell him."

"Done. When are you coming home?"

Home. Perfect, Indiana, had become home, and she would be working for the family business, after all. "Monday evening."

"I'll let Ceejay and the kids know. Your room will be ready."

"Thank you, Noah."

"See you Monday, sis."

She hung up and beamed at her parents. "This feels right. For the past week, I've been miserable, and now I'm…starving." She reached for the bags and pulled out the containers of lox and cream cheese. "Let's eat." She sprang up from the table and went to the kitchen for plates and silverware.

"Incidentally," her dad said, "I had an interesting conversation with Roger Weil the other day."

"Oh?" Paige turned to face him. "How did that come about?"

"Ryan told me what happened between you and that Rutger fellow. I wanted to alert Weil that he had a snake in the grass."

She frowned. "When did Ryan tell you all that?"

"When I came to Perfect. Anyway, it might interest you to know that Rutger is no longer employed at Ramsey & Weil. Turns out, some security guard named George pieced together what happened and alerted Roger Weil." He grinned. "Anthony Rutger was fired shortly after you left."

"Awww." She grabbed plates and silverware and brought them to the table. "I always did like George." Her appetite returned, and she ate bagels and drank coffee while listening to her parents talk about their travel plans. Once she walked them to her door and hugged them good-bye, Paige floated around the condo and made plans. She'd be using her emergency credit card, after all—for a plane ticket and a rental car. At least she knew Ryan's uncle's name, and that gave her a place to start.

Grabbing her laptop, she sat on her couch and Googled the Malloy's ranch. Several mentions popped up, and she scrolled through them until she found Shawn's name. From there, it was easy. They even had a toll-free number under their contact info. She hurried into the kitchen to grab her phone, a notepad, and a pen. Excitement thrummed along her nerves as she entered the number into her phone.

"Malloy Rodeo Ranch, home of the rankest bulls in Texas," a familiar male voice answered.

"Is this Austin?"

"It is. Who's this?"

"Paige Langford. We met a few weeks ago in Evansville. Do you remember me?"

"Of course I remember you. Let me guess. You've given the runt the toss, and you want me to introduce you to my baby brother."

"No, nothing like that." She laughed. "Ryan is visiting his parents this weekend, and I want to be there for him. I need—"

"Don't mess with me." His tone turned serious. "My cousin is going to be in Oklahoma this weekend? He's coming home?"

"Yes, and I was hoping you'd give me a telephone number to contact his mom."

"Well, I'll be damned. Wait till I tell my folks. More than likely, you'll be seeing all of us this weekend. Do you have a paper and pen?"

"I do." She copied down the number he gave her. "Thanks. Say hello to your dad for me."

"I'll do that. It's not too late to change your mind about my brother. Just say the word."

She laughed again. "We'll see you this weekend."

"All right. Wait a half hour before you call my aunt. I want to give her the heads-up. Otherwise, she might not answer an unknown caller."

"I will. Thanks, Austin."

"Later, Paige."

What if Ryan's parents didn't want her to intrude on their reunion with him? Might as well start packing while she waited the torturous half hour. Either she'd be traveling to Oklahoma or Indiana.

❧   ❧   ❧

Bleary-eyed and exhausted, Ryan yawned so big his jaw made a popping noise. He was on familiar ground. Almost home, and he could hardly wait to see the red Oklahoma clay in the light of day. This back road was as familiar to him as the lines on the palms of his hands. He'd learned to drive here, drag-raced with his brothers, and partied in the surrounding hills when he was a teen. Lowering the window, he took in the familiar scent of sweetgrass and clover.

The fresh air helped him stay awake. Glancing at the clock on his dash, he knew his parents wouldn't be waiting up. Their workday started with the rising sun, and it was almost midnight. His heart lodged in his throat at the sight of the porch light coming into view in the distance. The warm glow guided him home after years of self-imposed exile. Turning onto the long dirt driveway, he glanced at the overhead gate, the same old bright-green shamrock with MALLOY written in bold black letters in the center. Home. Childhood memories flooded through him in a happy kaleidoscope of images. His eyes filled, and his cheeks ached with the broad smile he couldn't contain.

Lord, how he wished Paige was with him. She'd call on Monday night. She had to. And if she didn't? *Don't go there.* He swallowed hard, parked his truck, and retrieved his duffel bag from the backseat, remembering the day he and Paige made love on those leather seats. If she didn't want him anymore, he'd have to sell the damn pickup.

Opening the front door as quietly as he could, he entered the dark house. No reason to wake anyone. He took off his boots and walked through the foyer toward the steps. The soft sound of a feminine snore came from the living room. Ryan froze. He knew that sound.

No, it couldn't be. Exhaustion and missing her were playing tricks on his mind.

He took another step, only to stop in his tracks when he heard it again. He peered into the living room, barely able to make out the outline of someone curled into the corner of the couch. A creaking sound and light on the stairway brought him around. His dad stared down at him from the steps. Ryan's duffel bag dropped from his hand, and his heart wrenched. In a second flat, he found himself wrapped in his dad's bear hug.

"Welcome home," his dad rasped out, slapping his back. "We've missed you."

Ryan hugged him back just as hard. "It's good to be here. I've missed all of you too."

His dad let him go and cleared his throat, keeping his voice low. "We tried to get your girl to go to bed, but she insisted on waiting up for you." He gestured toward the living room. "Paige called your mother on Wednesday, said something about making the biggest mistake of her life, and could she come here for your visit." He chuckled deep in his throat. "She's been singing your praises since she got here this afternoon."

"Paige is here?" Wonder stole his breath.

"Yep. We like her. We like her a lot, son." He squeezed Ryan's shoulder and smiled, his eyes bright with the sheen of tears. "You'd better go wake her. I'm going back to bed. I just wanted to make sure you got home safely. We'll talk tomorrow." He turned back to the stairs. "We put her in the guest room. I guess y'all are old enough to work out sleeping arrangements without our help."

"Has my room changed any?" he called softly.

"Nope." His dad chuckled again and headed back upstairs. "The grandkids like it the way it is."

A pair of twin beds with flannel cowboy-print bedspreads weren't going to do it. He wanted his superhero in his arms tonight. Every night. *Guest room it is.* At least the bed in there could hold them both. He turned on a lamp and stood before the couch, hardly believing what he saw. She lay curled in the corner with a throw over her shoulders. Her hands were tucked under her cheek where she laid her head on the armrest.

This moment, this picture of her, would remain etched into his soul for all time. The center of his world, his love, had come all the way to Oklahoma to be with him, and a joy like nothing he'd ever known filled him to bursting.

Perching on the edge of the couch, he brushed the hair from her face and kissed her eyelids. "Hi, honey. I'm home." The last time he'd uttered those words, he'd been on the verge of pulling the trigger. Noah's call had brought him back from the brink, and Paige had brought him back to life.

She stirred, yawned, and stretched. "Ryan?"

"You snore, babe."

"No, I don't."

He laughed. "Is this one of those arguments we're going to have for the next sixty years?" He held his breath, waiting for her reply.

"I hope so." She threw herself into his arms and snuggled against him. "I love you. I'm so sorry. You were right all along."

"So were you, and that makes us right together." Gathering her close, he absorbed the feel of her in his arms, the way she smelled. "I love you too, but I want to be clear about the direction we're heading before we go any further. I need to know." He rested his forehead against hers. "All I have to offer is a handful of dreams, but I swear I'll work like hell to make those dreams come true. I want to grow old with you. I want to build something from nothing, including a family of our own. Are you willing to place your faith in me, darlin'? Do you want me like I want you?" His heart pounded away in his chest as he placed his future in her hands.

"Yes. Oh, yes. I want that too." Her arms tightened around him. "I have so much to tell you."

"Tomorrow." Could a man melt from an overload of happiness? "Come to bed. We can talk tomorrow," he whispered. "All I want right now is to fall asleep with you in my arms. I drove straight through to get here."

"I've missed you so much." Her eyes roamed all over his face as if she meant to memorize his features.

He kissed her, pouring all of the love and longing he had into the melding of their hearts. "Bed," he murmured against her mouth. Oh, and there it was, that sexy laugh of hers, sliding over him like warm honey. He rose from the couch, bringing her with him, content to the marrow of his bones.

❧ ❧ ❧

Ryan sat in the kitchen at the old scarred wooden table and drank his coffee. His brothers had already taken off to do chores, but his dad had stayed behind to spend time with him. His glance went to his mom and Paige, who worked together to get the breakfast dishes stacked in the dishwasher. The two women chatted away like they'd known each other their whole lives. "Dad, I was wondering if I could borrow an ATV and a truck and trailer today. There's something I have to do."

"All right." His dad's eyes narrowed for a fraction of second, then fixed sharply on him. "Going to the Antelope Hills?"

"Yeah. It's time. I've been seeing a therapist at the VA center in Evansville, and it's helping. I need to go back—"

"What happened with Theresa was never your fault, son."

"I'm trying to come to grips with that." His throat tightened.

"I'm coming with you." Paige slid back into the seat beside him.

"I'd like that." He reached for her hand. "When we get back, I want to help out around here, if you'll let me."

"There's always plenty to do. We'll put you to work." His dad grinned. "Don't you worry."

"I'm going to help your mom get ready for tonight's barbecue," Paige said. "I guess it's going to be a huge gathering."

His mom took her usual place next to his dad and set the coffeepot in the middle. "The whole family is coming. Everyone is so happy to have you home." She reached out and squeezed his arm, her eyes bright. "Tell me about this new job of yours."

"I design and build custom furniture with Paige's brother. He's my former lieutenant and a good friend. I'm finally putting my creativity to work." He launched into a description of his new job, the line he was designing, and the ad campaign.

By the time he was done, his mom had tears in her eyes. "It's…It's so good to see you happy, baby. Promise me that you won't…Don't shut us out anymore."

"I'm sorry. Doc says I was already suffering from PTSD when I enlisted. It's been a long, hard road, but I won't do that again. You have my promise."

His dad slid his arm around his mom's shoulders and pulled her close. The love his parents had for each other came through as clear as day. He wanted that with Paige. First, he had to lay things to rest with Theresa. "You ready to go, darlin'?"

"Keys are hanging on the hooks by the back door. The Ford has the trailer hitch for the ATV trailer," his dad told him. "One more cup of coffee with my best girl here, and then I'm heading out. We'll see you two for lunch?"

"Yeah, I'm sure we'll be back by then." Ryan led Paige to the back door and grabbed the keys. They walked across the yard to the machine shed, and a mixture of dread and anticipation roiled through him.

"Are you sure you want to do this?" Paige ran her hand over his shoulder.

He nodded, slid open the door, and located the ATV. "It's time."

She helped him get the trailer hitched to the truck, and he drove the ATV up the ramp and got it secured. "Grab a couple of helmets. They're over there." He pointed to the shelves against the wall. "I'll gas everything up." Like a lot of ranches, they kept a tank of gas on the premises. He drove the truck close enough to fill the tanks and waited for Paige to climb in.

"Why an ATV and not horses?" she asked once she'd settled in and fastened her seat belt.

"I'm not ready to climb back on a horse, and I sure as hell don't want to see you on one." His jaw clenched. "Not today."

Paige bit her lower lip and turned away. "I can't even imagine how difficult this must be for you."

"It means the world to me to have you here." He started the truck, and they were on their way. "Doc says I deserve to be happy as much as anyone else. He says I need to forgive myself."

She shot him the *You're an idiot* look. "Didn't I say exactly the same thing?"

He smiled. "Yep. You did. Last night, you said you have lots to tell me."

"Noah gave me my job back minus the title. I have more responsibilities, the same crappy pay, and he made me agree to join the monthly poker games." She grinned. "I found out my dad is retiring, which came as a total shock. He offered to hire me if that's what I really wanted." She slid him a sideways look. "I turned it down. I'm relieved. I feel like a huge weight has been lifted from my shoulders, and I'm free to put my heart into helping L&L to grow."

"That's good." He held fast to the calming sound of her voice as she talked on. "Poker?" He frowned. "Noah's making the monthly poker games part of the deal?"

"Yes, and I think he expects you to join too."

"I guess I could do that." The Antelope Hills grew closer. He found a spot off-road to park near the trail where he and Theresa had set out that day. He peered out of the windshield at the cloudless blue sky, his gut twisting. "We're here." He climbed out of the truck and went to unload the four-wheeler. Paige followed.

Once he had the ATV on the ground, he straightened and stared toward the wide path winding through the rugged landscape. An overwhelming sense of foreboding brought sweat to his brow. Paige's arms came around his waist, and she pressed herself into his back. He placed his hands over hers. "I feel like I'm walking to my doom."

"You suffered a horrible trauma here. What you feel is normal under the circumstances."

"Why, thank you, Dr. Langford." He grunted. "The sooner I get this over with, the better."

"Think about Theresa and how things were before that day." She retrieved the helmets from the back and handed him one. "Fill your mind with the happy memories."

He tried—and failed. Instead, his mind conjured the way he'd found her after the accident, her head split and her neck turned into an impossible position. A shudder racked his body, and he sucked in a shaky breath.

"You don't have to do this." Once again, her arms came around him, offering comfort and strength.

"I know." He hugged her to him. "I don't have to, but I want to." He climbed onto the four-wheeler, started the engine, and waited for Paige to settle herself behind him. "Hold on to my waist."

He took it slow, retracing the route he and Theresa had taken that day.

"It's pretty through here," Paige remarked.

"Yeah, it is." Trying to see it through her eyes, he scanned the area. "When I was a kid, I spent a lot of time here with my brothers and sister. Once our chores were done, we'd ride our horses or ATVs through these hills." He grinned as memories swamped him. "We used to play outlaw and posse, stuff like that."

"Sounds like fun."

"Do you ride, darlin'?"

"Sure. I went through a horse phase, and my parents got me lessons. I learned English style, though."

"It's not that different." Someday he'd take her riding. Maybe. Stopping the four-wheeler, he pointed. "There's the ponderosa pine that split." He stared at the charred remains of the dead half of the pine, memories flowing through him. Paige's hands on his shoulders kept him centered. "Not far now."

They continued on, and the forest went quiet, as if the hills themselves were holding their breath, waiting. He rounded the bend, tension banding his chest. The boulders bordering the ravine came into view. The closer they got, the harder it was to breathe. His hands shook as he parked the four-wheeler and took off his helmet. His focus turned inward, he approached the place where his life had come crashing down around him.

Paige was beside him, but he couldn't reach for her to save his life. His eyes riveted on the spot, he searched for evidence of the terrible accident that had changed his life forever. There was none. Theresa was gone forever, her life cut short by tragedy, and the Antelope Hills held no trace of her. The land had let her go, and it was time he did the same. Paige's hand slipped into his.

Ryan closed his eyes and swallowed. "I don't know what I expected. I thought her blood would stain the granite—or at least I'd be able to see something from that day." Instead, he was surrounded with the natural beauty of the area, the ruggedness of the pines growing among the boulders overlooking the river. He caught a glimpse of a hawk riding an air current, heard birdcalls echoing through the woods, and sucked in the pine-scented air. Peaceful. Paige squeezed his hand, and he turned to steady himself. "There's something I have to do."

"Can I help?"

"You already have." He reached into his pocket and pulled out his suicide letter, the photo of Theresa he'd carried everywhere, and a book of matches. Moving to the edge of the ravine, he crouched down and set the letter on fire, watching as it burned to ash. "Theresa, I'll always love you, but it's time to let you go. I need to move on, sweetheart, and I hope you can find it in your heart to forgive me."

Tears filled his eyes as happier memories of their time together played through his mind. He held her photo in front of him, traced the image, and said good-bye. Lifting a stone, he placed the picture underneath and stood up. "Rest in peace."

His phone rang. He pulled it from his back pocket and checked the caller ID: Unavailable. "Hello?" Static filled his ear, and a tingling sensation started at the top of his scalp and moved down, like a hand running over his scalp. A chill snaked down his spine, and he ended the call. The phone started ringing again, with the same Unavailable message showing on the caller ID. Goose bumps rose on his arms, and all the fine hairs at the back of his neck stood straight up. "Weird." He ended the call.

"What is it?" Paige came to stand beside him.

"The night your brother called, I was very close to ending my life. I got two calls that night. I didn't answer the first, and the second came from Noah. I asked him why he called back a second time that night, and he said he only called once." He shook his head. "This is going to sound crazy, but—"

"You believe Theresa was reaching out to you, trying to stop you from taking your life?"

"Crazy, huh?" He stared out over the ravine, a deep peace settling his nerves. "The caller ID just now said Unavailable, and there wasn't anyone there. Twice. I got goose bumps all over when I answered."

Paige slipped her arms around his waist. "She's saying good-bye, letting you go with her blessing."

"More likely a wrong number and a poor signal." He drew her in for a kiss. Though he might say that out loud, in his heart he agreed. Theresa had let him go, and he held his future in his arms. His heart was full, and he was well on the way to becoming whole. "Want to go exploring with the ATV?"

"Not today. Your mom needs help with the party stuff. We can come back tomorrow—with horses. I'm a good rider, Ryan. You don't have to worry about me."

He laughed. "I love the way you tell me exactly what you want and what you think, babe. I love you."

"That stupid grin you're wearing is getting on my last nerve." Ted glared at Ryan as he slid into his chair for their Tuesday-morning staff meeting. He set a mug of coffee on the table in front of him. "Only the good coffee makes it bearable."

"Tough. Get used to it." Ryan shot him an extra-wide dumb-ass grin as Noah took his usual place in the corner. Lord, it was good to be home, even better to have Paige beside him.

"Can we get started?" Bossy Paige handed out sheets of paper with the outline for their five-year plan. "Once the new line launches, we're going to need additional help. What I'm suggesting is that we add a second shift and hire them as finishers. It's not too difficult to train someone to sand, stain, and varnish, is it?"

"No. It's doable." Noah scanned her outline.

"Training a crew of finishers would free you three up to increase production, while still maintaining our commitment to handcrafting each piece. Allow employees to work their way into production with a nice raise if they want to." Her gaze turned to Ted. "Within three years, you're going to have your hands full with administrative duties. Eventually, you'll have to quit production and go full-time admin." She turned to Noah. "You'll be in charge of the crew, training, and production. We're hiring veterans to stay true to our mission, and you're a natural-born leader."

Noah's eyes widened. "Is that how you see me?"

"It's how we all see you, bro." Ryan nodded. "Even if Paige hadn't written it down on that piece of paper, the guys would naturally gravitate to you for direction, *Lieutenant*." A wave of gratitude nearly bowled over Ryan. The man had saved his life, pure and simple.

Paige brought them back to task. "Another incentive for our future employees would be giving them the opportunity to come up with ideas for new products. Offer a bonus for pieces we use. Ryan, you'll head up the new design department, which will include advertising. That reminds me, we ought to enter some pieces in crafters' competitions or juried artisan shows. That would be another way to get exposure."

"We have *departments*?" Ted's eyes widened.

"We do now. Are you OK with going into admin, Ted? Will you miss production?"

"I'm fine with it as long as I can drop back in whenever needed."

"That'll work." She smiled. "I want to have a retail venue in Evansville within five years. Does everyone agree to that?" Her gaze went around the table.

"Sounds great," Noah replied. "Ted?"

"I'm all for it."

Ryan turned to face Noah. "One other thing—Paige and I would like to fix up the apartment on the third floor, bring it up-to-code and up-to-date. The carriage house is too small for the two of us, and we'd like to rent the space here. For cheap."

Noah scowled his way. "You want to shack up with my baby sister?"

"Noah…" Paige's cheeks turned a lovely shade of pink.

"No. I'm going to marry your baby sister, and we can't afford a house yet because we don't make squat working here."

Noah laughed, rose from his chair, and offered Ryan his hand. "That's good, because I didn't really want to beat the shit out of you."

Ryan took his hand in his. "Like you could."

Noah grinned. "Sure. Let's fix the place up. I'll help."

"Congratulations, you two." Ted shot him a shuttered look. "I'm happy for you both."

"You'll be fine, kid." Ryan sat back down. "You do realize what has happened, don't you?"

Noah's brow creased. "What's that?"

"Your sister just took over the family business." Ryan grinned, surveying the two men he'd come to care so much about. But it wasn't only the business. Paige had taken over his heart, and though he had a long way to go before he was back on the right side of normal, he had a future.

Read on for a sneak peek of Barbara Longley's next novel set in Perfect, Indiana.

A Change of Heart

Available October 2013 on Amazon.com

"Cory, baby." Her mother knocked on her door. "Brenda Holt is here to see you."

"Tell her I'm not feeling well." She couldn't face anyone. Not now. She pulled the bedspread over her head.

The door creaked open. "I'm not leavin' this room until you agree to come on out and say hello. Brenda made the effort to visit. Now you're gonna make the effort to haul your butt outta that bed. You hear?"

She knew that tone. When Claire Marcel made up her mind, nothing could sway her. "Fine." She threw off the covers and sat up. "Give me a few minutes."

"Good. We'll be in the livin' room."

The door shut, and Cory dragged herself out of bed to the army-issue duffel bag on the floor. She found an almost clean pair of sweats and pulled them on.

She walked down the hall to the shabby living room. The two sat on the couch, huddled over her mother's scrapbook of the media frenzy surrounding Cory's court case. Her stomach hit the dirt. *Dammit.* How could she show that to anyone? Why would she want to? Bile burned the back of her throat, and she turned around and headed back to her room.

"There you are," her mother called. "I was just telling Brenda how proud I am of you."

"Hey, Cory." Brenda took the scrapbook from her mother's hands and set it aside. "It's been forever since we've seen each other. Let's go for a walk."

"Outside?" Her heart raced, and dread spread like an oil spill in her chest.

"Unless you want to walk up and down the hall here." Brenda's expression filled with sympathy, and something else. Concern? "Let's go to the playground like we used to."

"What's it like out there?" Cory bit her lower lip, assessing the risk.

Brenda raised a single arched eyebrow. "Is that a rhetorical question?"

"No, it's more a weather question." She averted her gaze and swallowed hard. Brenda must have thought she'd gone mental.

"It's like a typical June day in southern Indiana. The sun's out. It's hot, and you're way overdressed."

"I'll be fine."

She slipped her feet into an old pair of flip-flops by the door and walked beside Brenda toward the old rusty playground where they'd spent countless hours as kids.

The slide had taken on a pronounced tilt to the right, and the heavy steel frame of the swing set had more rust than she remembered, but otherwise, nothing had changed.

"Your mom is proud of you. We all are." Brenda glanced at her.

"Can we talk about something else?" Cory's empty stomach churned, and she studied the stunted grass growing around the bare dirt under her feet. "What are you doing these days? Last time we talked, you were in school."

"Sure." Brenda sent her swing into motion. "I graduated from cosmetology college, and I work in a really nice salon in town now. I'm doing OK for myself." She planted her feet to stop the swing. "Did you hear Wesley's home? He retired."

"No, I hadn't heard." Her eyes widened. "We were just little kids when he joined the marines." She shook her head. "Has it been twenty years already?"

"Yeah. We were seven when he left. Which leads me to my next question. What are you going to do now that your case is behind you?"

"It's not *behind me*." Hot, angry tears filled her eyes once again at the ultimate betrayal of her loyalty and trust. "The Veteran's Legal Clinic is working on getting disability benefits for me."

"Is that what you want—disability checks for the rest of your life while you hide out in your mom's mobile home? That doesn't sound like the Corinna Lynn Marcel I've known since we were four."

"That girl is gone."

Brenda reached out and touched her forearm. Cory jerked away.

"Hey, it's just me." Her friend set her hands in her lap. "Wesley is working at a custom furniture company in Perfect. The owner is a veteran."

"Oh." Her mind was only half-engaged. The other half floated from a distance, watching the conversation with disorienting detachment.

"Langford & Lovejoy Heritage Furniture only hires veterans. Wes told me they're looking for someone to take over maintaining their social media."

Cory nodded distractedly, the pervasive sense of detachment spreading. Time to head back to bed.

"He told the owner about you."

"What?" Cory blinked. "Why?"

"Because you have skills. You *were* an IT specialist. You're perfect for the job."

Shit. "I'm not perfect for anything. I can barely get of bed. I don't think—"

"Nope. Stop." Brenda shook her head. "This is what's going to happen. You're going to go take a shower and brush your teeth. Please." She waved a hand in front of her nose. "Shave your legs and pits while you're at it."

"Well, that was brutal."

"You need brutal." Brenda stared a hole through her. "I brought my equipment with me. You have a job interview tomorrow evening, and I'm here to make sure you look your best."

"What? NO!" Her blood turned to ice water, chilling her to the sludge-filled center of her bones.

"Yep. Let's go. Hup, hup." Brenda pulled her up and pointed her toward home. "Right, left, right, left. March. You stink, and your hair is a greasy, stringy mess."

"I like it this way."

"No, you don't." Brenda gave her a gentle nudge. "Ready or not, here comes your new life."

"I'm not ready." Panic sent her heart racing, tightening her chest and robbing her of breath. "I'm not *ready*, dammit."

🐏 🐏 🐏

"I can't believe you did it again!" Ted shouted, raking both hands through his hair. "You swore I would be part of the hiring process. You swore." He glared at Noah.

No one seemed to care that he was the Lovejoy part of Langford & Lovejoy. Even though Ted was a full partner *and* the human resources guy, to boot, Noah continued to make staffing decisions without conferring with him.

"This case was an emergency." Noah widened his stance and crossed his arms in front of his chest. "Besides, I said I'd *try* to follow the hiring procedures, and for the most part, I have. Cory is an exception. Plus, you agreed we need someone to take over the web maintenance, social media, and order processing."

"That's beside the point. Did you post the job? Take applications? How about an interview including me?"

"Hey, kid. What's got your boxers in a bunch?" Ryan strolled into the conference room for their usual Monday-morning meeting. "We could hear you shouting from the first floor."

"Maybe it's the fact that you and everybody else around here still see me as a *kid*. I have a fucking master's in business administration, and *I* sign *your* paycheck."

Paige waddled in behind her husband, rubbing her distended belly. "Watch your language. I don't want the baby to pick that stuff up."

And there it was, the other exclusive club he couldn't gain entrance to—the happily married and reproducing group. Ryan and Paige had just finished building their house on the east side of town and were expecting their first child. Noah and his cousin Ceejay were also expecting. This was number four for them. Ted rolled his eyes. "At thirty weeks, I doubt that pea in the pod is paying attention to what goes on at L&L."

"They do." She laid her folder on the table and settled into her chair. "Babies can hear things."

"Whatever." He took his customary place with his back to the door. "I don't care if this Cory guy is a freaking genius. You had no business hiring him without my say-so," he snapped.

Noah's jaw twitched. "Cory is—"

"I'm sorry. Maybe I should leave," a soft, feminine voice said from behind him.

"Don't listen to him, Cory." Paige leaned back and smiled. "Come in and have a seat."

Huh? Ted whipped around, his eyes widening at the sight of the waif standing uncertainly in the doorway. Feathery layers of dark-brown hair with lighter golden-brown highlights framed her wide-set, luminous brown eyes. She wore jeans and a peasant blouse that failed to hide how thin she was. He brought his gaze back to those doe eyes of hers and fell right in. They held a sadness so profound it would take a deep-sea submersible to get to the source.

Noah shot him a look that said he'd better be nice or else. "Ted, meet Cory Marcel. Cory, this is Ted Lovejoy, my sister Paige, and her husband Ryan. Cory is an IT specialist and a whiz with computers."

Damn. Ted shot up from his chair, almost knocking it over in his haste. It couldn't have been pleasant for her to hear his rant. "Welcome to L&L. It's good to have you aboard." Their eyes met and held. Her brow creased, and she looked away, but not before he caught a glimpse of the alarm clouding her features. *I'm alarming? Great.*

Shifting his attention back to their newest employee, he wondered what it was about her situation that had prompted Noah to disregard their protocol. What would it take to coax a smile out of her? He fantasized about what her smile might look like.

What? No. He didn't need or want to get involved. He had enough problems of his own.

Paige passed a sheet of paper to all of them. "This is the list I made of Cory's responsibilities." She turned to face her and grinned. "I can't tell you how happy I am to have another woman in the building."

"Thank you." Cory skimmed the list. "Where will I be working?"

"You and I will share the office at the end of the hall by the stairs," Paige told her.

"Does the…" Color rose to Cory's cheeks, and her expression closed up tight. "Is there a lock on the door?"

Paige leaned forward and rested her elbows on the table. "You're safe here, Cory. The men who work for us are more likely to be overly protective than anything else. As the only woman on this all-male staff for the past three years, I can personally vouch for every one of our guys."

Mystified by the exchange, Ted frowned. "If that's what you need, I'll put a dead bolt on the door right after we're done here."

"Thank you," she whispered, her eyes meeting his for a fraction of second before she dropped them again to the list. "I'd appreciate that."

What the hell had happened to this woman?

ACKNOWLEDGMENTS

I HAVE TO SAY A special thank you to my friend Tami Hughes, who has been with me on this journey since the beginning. Without her input, insights, and support, I wouldn't be here today. I want to thank Jeffrey and Laurel Otis, who put up with my endless "book talk" and still support and cheer me on. A shout-out to my friend Donna Meier. I love our monthly get-togethers. A special thanks goes to the outstanding Montlake Romance editorial staff and author team. You guys rock. Thank you to my wonderful agent Nalini Akolekar. And last but certainly not least, to all of the men and women who put on that uniform every day and serve our country, thank you.

ABOUT THE AUTHOR

Photo by Glamour Shots, 2011

As a child, Barbara Longley moved frequently, learning early on how to entertain herself with stories. Adulthood didn't tame her peripatetic ways: she has lived on an Appalachian commune, taught on an Indian reservation, and traveled the country from coast to coast. After having children of her own, she decided to try staying put, choosing Minnesota as her home. By day, she puts her master's degree in special education to use teaching elementary school. By night, she explores all things mythical, paranormal, and newsworthy, channeling what she learns into her writing.

Made in the USA
Charleston, SC
22 March 2013